Evil Eye

Veronica Di Grigoli

Veronica Di Grigoli

Published in 2008 by YouWriteOn.com

Copyright © Text Veronica Di Grigoli

First Edition

The author asserts the moral right under the Copyright, Designs and Patents Act 1988 to be identified as the author of this work.

All Rights reserved. No part of this publication may be reproduced, stored in a retrieval system, or transmitted, in any form or by any means without the prior written consent of the author, nor be otherwise circulated in any form of binding or cover other than that in which it is published and without a similar condition being imposed on the subsequent purchaser.

Published by YouWriteOn.com

For my Mother
One of the best mothers in the world

Veronica Di Grigoli

ONE

A House On The Corner Of A Continent

Celeste Hamilton stood on the corner of Europe, looking at Asia. The rippling water of the Bosphorus reflected so many dancing shafts of sunlight into her eyes that she was dazzled, and screwed up her eyes until the speckles faded away.

It struck her that this spot, the district of Bebek in Istanbul, may be the best place in the world to stand on one continent and watch another. Istanbul must be the only city where you can live in Asia and commute to Europe every day. Living in a city torn between two continents and two cultures felt right to Celeste, torn as she was between her duties and yearnings. Yet in Istanbul the two continents push so hard to meet each other that they are only a mile apart and the seawater of the Bosphorus has to fight its way between them, squeezing through the narrow channel left for it in a perpetual tumult of rage. Most days it just washes aggressively between streets of houses and mosques and shops, but sometimes it has become so furious that it has taken revenge on the innocent and thirstily sucked in whole ships full of men, drinking them down into its turbulent depths.

Celeste glanced back at the row of slatted wooden mansions behind her, painted in pastel colours gleaming in the sunlight. She was in Bebek to see a room to let in one of these houses, but it was still far too early for her appointment so she decided to stroll along the seafront to pass the time. Beyond the luxury yachts which thronged the seafront and the weather-beaten fishing boats further out in the water, Celeste picked out the hazy silhouettes of several mosques along the skyline on the opposite shore. She slowly made her way towards a fish stall, where a man with a drooping black moustache bought live fish from a boat moored in the water below and threw them into buckets of water. His partner killed them by beating them over the head with a wooden mallet, gutting and frying them as fast as he could, and sold them on toasted bread, wrapped in paper. Some of the fish twitched and flipped over in the hot oil of the frying pan.

Celeste waited by the stall, watching curiously.

"Why don't you try some?" suggested an old woman beside the fishmonger, probably his mother. Celeste was excited that she had understood the woman's Turkish easily, especially as she lisped through several missing teeth. She wore a headscarf in blue with white flowers, so large it encircled her rounded shoulders as well as her head.

"How much is it?" asked Celeste.

"Come here," said the woman, and took hold of Celeste's hand.

Celeste was surprised how firmly the woman grasped her with her cold, bony fingers, twisted with arthritis. She pulled Celeste's hand open and looked at the palm.

"Foreign girl, I see you've come here to find a lost person," she said slowly.

Celeste laughed.

"Actually, I've come here to teach English."

"They may not be lost yet," she woman interrupted her sharply. "The next year will be the most important year of your life. The heart of a daughter will grow into the heart of a mother."

Celeste glanced at the men running the fish stall hoping to appeal for help. This woman might keep her here for hours talking nonsense.

"That will heal your wound. Your mother's death wounded your heart. It will start healing soon."

Celeste gasped, and tried to pull her hand away, but the woman tightened her grip and stepped closer. How could she have known about Celeste's mother dying? Surely it was just an unnerving coincidence.

Celeste looked at the woman's beak of a nose and a few downy white moustache hairs catching the light. She scrutinised Celeste's palm again and then looked up at her pityingly. She was so close now that Celeste felt her breath on her face as she spoke.

"But I see death peering over your shoulder. He has cast his shadow on you."

The words made Celeste feel a plunging sensation in her chest as if her heart were being pulled out of her, and then a rush of palpitations.

"Think very carefully about any choices you make."

Celeste was about to shout at the woman to get away from her, that she was a horrible old witch, but the woman suddenly put a blue glass drop-shaped amulet in the palm of Celeste's hand. There was a white circle at its centre and a smaller black dot within that, to represent an eye. Celeste already knew what it was; a *nazar boncuğu*, protection against the evil eye.

"You'll need this," the woman said. "Wear it always. Remember, the sum of all your choices make up the person you are. You can go now. I know you want to get away from me."

Celeste turned and half walked, half ran, still holding the amulet in her trembling hand. When she glanced back towards the fish stall, there was no sign of the old woman, so she stopped to sit on a bench and look out at the sea. Celeste had only just arrived in turkey but she noticed these evil eye talismans everywhere, small ones worn as pendants and larger ones hung at entrances to buildings. They were supposed to protect against the wasting illnesses and death which people believed were provoked by the glance of an envious person. She took a few deep breaths and shaded her eyes with her hand to stare out at the fishing boats.

What should Celeste do with this amulet? She briefly considered throwing it into the Bosphorus. She looked at it in the palm of her hand and turned it this way and that. The glass was bluer than the sea and the sky, and it glowed so radiantly in the sunlight that she decided to keep it.

Celeste realised it was time for her appointment so, still feeling her heart palpitating, she crossed the road and hurried back along the pavement. She tried to distract herself by admiring the beautiful houses as she walked along, and striving to peer nosily through their ground floor windows. When she rang the doorbell of number forty-two it sounded like a church organ chiming inside the house. She hoped, with a lump in her throat, that the room here would be all right. Otherwise she would have to give up her teaching job and go home with her tail between her legs. She had exactly enough money for one more night in a hotel and a flight home, and no more.

She looked up at the three-storey mansion. The blue, wood-slatted façade was embellished with intricately carved eaves and gables, hanging down to shade the windows like lacy white pelmets. Standing between a smaller house in rose pink and another villa in creamy yellow, it looked truly beautiful. Celeste realised she was crossing her fingers inside her pocket when the front door was flung open by a short, chubby woman wearing orange lipstick and a shiny, electric-blue blouse. A blaze of gold buttons and jewellery flashed in the early afternoon sunlight as the heady smell of perfume wafted toward Celeste. Celeste glanced at the woman's bobbed hair, jet black but with half an inch of grey roots, and concluded she must be in her fifties.

"Welcome," she announced in heavily accented English. "You are Celeste and I am Leman. Come with me."

Her melodious voice seemed at odds with the crudely dyed hair and garish make up. Despite her towering heels, Celeste stood head and shoulders above her and had to break her stride several times as Leman's hurried little steps led her through the grand entrance hall into the living room. The house smelled of beeswax polish and cigarette smoke with, of course, heavy overtones of musky perfume.

"I saw your advertisement for a room to let on the English school notice board, in the staffroom," Celeste blurted out nervously.

"You have tell me on the phone," responded Leman. "In this house is living my husband Ferhat and my son Levent," she explained as she waved her scarlet fingernails vaguely in the air, perhaps inviting Celeste to gaze around the vast room of which she was clearly so proud. Leman's choice of furnishings featured heavy gilding and velvet drapery. She picked up a silver framed photograph from a console table, and handed it to Celeste.

"This my husband, Ferhat," she said.

Celeste duly studied the picture. Ferhat was a handsome man, but his white hair and ivory skin made his large, black eyes stand out startlingly from his face. They struck Celeste as the eyes of someone who had been worn down, and had given up.

"You pretty young girl," commented Leman, suddenly. "Very blue eyes, but brown hairs unusual for English girls, isn't it? Most English girls got blonde hairs?"

"Well, not really," answered Celeste. "I think brown hair like mine is more usual."

"I see," said Leman, sounding unconvinced. She plucked the photograph of Ferhat from Celeste's hand as if she were a teacher confiscating it. "I am offering low rent for this room I am renting, because I want to improve my English and so does need my son, Levent. He is university student. I want him to get best degree. I don't need money, I need English. So we are all speaking English which is good for you, yes?"

"Yes, no problem," agreed Celeste.

"Now you can sit on this," instructed Leman, indicating a large armchair, "and tell me about you."

"Well, I'm twenty-three years old. I come from London, and I've just finished a degree in the History of Art."

"Oh art, my husband loves art and antiques stuff very much. Look all these things that he buys." Leman indicated several valuable-looking antiques, including Persian carpets made from silk and spectacular Iznik ceramics glazed in coral red, turquoise and royal blue. "You can talk art to him. He will be a lot happy."

"Yes, I noticed you have some lovely pieces," began Celeste.

"Tell me, why you decide working in Turkey?" Leman cut in.

"I took a course in teaching English as a foreign language. At the end of the training they offered a few jobs in Turkey, so I decided to accept one. It was quite spontaneous. A bit random, really."

"You done something shameful at home you running away from?" asked Leman.

"No," said Celeste, too startled to feel indignant.

"Why you leave home?" Leman persisted.

"After Mum died, I stayed at home looking after my little brothers. I did it for two years. It wasn't easy pretending to be a mother." Celeste thought of what the old woman on the seafront had said, and realised she was still clutching the *nazar boncuğu* in her sweaty hand. "I need to live my own life for a while now."

"How many brothers?" asked Leman.

"Three. I love my family, but I needed a change of air," said Celeste. "I'm very keen to learn about Turkish culture, and I've been studying the language for a few months as well."

"Hmm, I see," said Leman.

Leman offered to show Celeste the rest of the house. The piles of newspapers stacked in the corners of the living room and even the hallway and stair-landings jarred oddly with the neatness and grandeur. The more Celeste looked, the more incongruity and discord she noticed. Ferhat had bought a Wedgwood vase on his last business trip to England, but it clashed unnervingly amid the garish gilding on his wife's imitation Louis XV cocktail cabinet.

"I've been to the factory in Stoke, where they make this china," Celeste tried to tell Leman. "It was fascinating."

"You tell to my husband that stuff," responded Leman over her shoulder as she stomped towards the stairs. "Come this way."

Celeste squeezed past a large stack of newspapers on the landing and, when they reached the third floor, Leman showed Celeste the bedroom which was offered to let. It was furnished with just a simple bed and wardrobe, and a large desk below the huge window. The panorama across the cobalt blue sea made Celeste's heart almost skip a beat.

"You like this view?" asked Leman. "That is the sea, you know, it isn't river."

"Yes, I know. And I like this room very much."

"It's get cleaned every day. We got cleaning woman."

"That's good," said Celeste. "I'm very fussy about cleanliness."

"If you like cleanness, you made mistake coming to Turkey!" laughed Leman. "Now you can look the rest of the house."

As they talked on the landing bathed in sunlight, Celeste took the chance to peer nosily through the doorway of Levent's bedroom. One wall was lined with bookshelves, with a few pencil sketches propped up against the books. Despite the vast array of computer equipment and the clothes strewn across the floor, the thing which caught her attention was a large glass bowl full of water beside the bed, with a white chicken's egg floating on the water. The bowl rested on a lace doily as if it were a permanent feature of the room. She must have stared too obviously, as Leman hastily closed the bedroom door.

"My son's room private. You don't go in there," she snapped. "You don't think about his things."

Now she had been told not to think about it, Celeste could not get that egg out of her mind.

Veronica Di Grigoli

"Do you like Turkish coffee?" asked Leman, heading towards the stairs.

Celeste sat at the kitchen table, feeling sweaty as the sun blazed in through the window. The red and white gingham tablecloth was crowded with boxes of herbal tea bags, many of them unopened. Leman put equal amounts of coarsely ground coffee and sugar into a tiny copper jug with a long handle, which she topped up with water and whipped off the hotplate the moment the coffee bubbled up to the brim. She shovelled the boxes of herbal tea aside disdainfully to make space for the coffee cups and a plate of Turkish delight, smothered in drifts of sugar. When she opened the fridge to take out a bottle of mineral water, Celeste noticed a heavy glass jar in the door, full of water and with a narrow strip of paper like a piece of till-roll curled up inside it. As the paper bobbed up and down Celeste made out lines of Arabic writing covering both sides. In a second the door was closed again and Leman was sitting opposite Celeste, urging her to eat a piece of Turkish delight.

"What was that jar with paper in the fridge?" Celeste asked, innocently.

"Oh, that's just for good luck," said Leman. "It's nothing. Nothing at all. Drink coffee before it's cold."

"I see you like herbal tea," Celeste observed, just to make conversation.

"I hate this tea rubbish. This was all left behind by woman living here before us. Me and Levent, we move back here three months ago, before that in our house was living for two years another woman, and she left many rubbish here. She was dirty and untidy. She was *orospu*."

"What does *orospu* mean?" asked Celeste.

"I don't know in English, but she much *orospu*," repeated Leman, looking Celeste intensely in the eye.

"Was she renting the house?"

"Not exactly," answered Leman vaguely, as she picked up one of the boxes of tea.

"Did you say just you and Levent moved back here recently?" asked Celeste. "What about your husband?"

Leman ignored the question. Celeste eyed the tea boxes as a way of avoiding Leman's gaze.

"I want to know what is these things," said Leman. "I have a friend who speak French. Later she is coming and she tell me what is these teas."

"I can tell you if you like," offered Celeste, picking out one of the boxes. "I did a year of French and Italian for my degree. This one's strawberry. This means mint. And this one…"

"My friend speak really French," Leman cut in condescendingly, "better she tell me what they is."

Celeste was so taken aback by Leman's reaction that she did not say a word, but she made a mental note to look up the word *orospu* later.

"You want living here?" asked Leman abruptly. "You moving today if want. We are ready."

Celeste hesitated. This place was far better than the flat where an aged lecher had tried to touch her chest and told her, with unshakeable conviction, that English girls are passionate but never wash. It was nicer beyond comparison with the house where she had been bitten by one of the three resident dogs. Frankly it was a world apart from the various bedsits she had viewed, all so dirty she could not discern the original colour of the walls. Nevertheless this beautiful mansion seemed to be harbouring shameful secrets. Celeste felt apprehensive, yet what alternative did she have? It was this house, or nothing.

"Thank you. I'd like to move in."

"That is good," said Leman, smiling with satisfaction. "You like Lokum? You like Turkish delight? We Turkish people think it is good luck to eat something sweet together, to make a new relationship start sweet."

Celeste popped a cube of Turkish delight into her mouth. The moment she bit down on it, she felt a stabbing pain in a molar in her lower left jaw. She had meant to have her teeth checked before leaving England as she already suspected she may need a new filling. It was an ominous start to the new relationship.

When Celeste returned by taxi later that afternoon, Bebek smelt of salty water and excitement. The pavements were now crowded with people and the yachts' masts swayed every time they lurched on the current as the fishing boats plied by. Every section of Istanbul society seemed to be represented here. Rich young men wearing suits from the office were fishing for sport alongside grubby old women trying to catch something tasty for dinner. Little boys with huge, coal-black eyes laughed and played tag amongst middle-aged women in coloured head scarves and retired old men in flat caps. This would be a perfect place for Celeste to sit and do some sketching in her spare time.

The taxi slowed down beside the fish stall. Celeste noted with relief that there was no sign of the old woman any more. The driver stopped outside Leman's blue and white mansion and lifted Celeste's suitcase out of the boot for her.

"You choose good place for live," he told her. "The Bosphorus here by Bebek it's very beautiful. Do you know, this water is sea, not river."

"Yes, I know," said Celeste.

She went into Leman's blue and white house for the second time, as the sun was casting long shadows across the road. This time she noticed a huge *nazar boncuğu* hanging just inside the front door.

Celeste unpacked immediately. She hung up her clothes in less than a minute since the suitcase was at least one third full of books. The paperback novels her father had collected for her made a small tower on the desk.

"You won't find anything in English out there in the wilds of Turkey. You'll enjoy these," he had said during one of his many wistful, pensive visits to her room with offerings to put in her suitcase.

She put her sketch pads, brushes and paints in one of the desk drawers and hid her vast collection of toiletries in the wardrobe. Then she held her small teddy bear, Bruno, to her face. Her mother had made him when she was three years old, cutting a heart shape of red fabric to insert into the bear's body when it was time to stuff him. Her mother had explained that having a heart meant he could return Celeste's love.

"Mummy, I know your heart's near me," she whispered into the bear's fur before sitting him on the pillow.

Her hands trembled a little as she pulled the bubble wrap away from her silver photo frame, the last thing to come out of her suitcase. On the left it held a picture of her mother, laughing at her father as he snapped her in the garden at home. Celeste stroked the glass gently with a finger, as if trying to feel the warmth of her mother when she was still fresh-faced and healthy and her lovely chestnut hair glimmered in the sunshine. On the right was a photograph of Celeste as a self-conscious, spotty sixteen-year-old, cradling her youngest brother in her arms with a bottle of milk. Her mother had bought this frame because she loved the motto engraved on the base: 'A mother should give her children two things: first roots, and then wings.'

Celeste set the frame at the centre of the desk.

"Please forgive me for leaving Dad and the boys. I did as much as I could, but I couldn't be you. You left so many unfinished jobs, Mummy, four children who still needed your help to grow up. Help me find my wings again."

The pavements below the window were emptier now and the sea was darkening to indigo, but she could still make out the profile of the Kız Kűlesi, The Maiden Tower, out in the Bosphorus. A nearby mosque started the evening call to prayer with the tinny sound of a voice recorded on bad equipment and amplified until the words were indiscernible. The same chant soon blared from the other mosques and, as Celeste realised she was fingering the small gold crucifix around her neck, she felt an excruciating pang of homesickness.

She decided to write a letter to her father and the boys. She scribbled a few lines and drew a quick sketch of the view to include with the letter, but made no mention of the mad old woman who had told her she might die, or the bizarre egg that she could not get out of her mind, or the scroll of Arabic writing bobbing in a jar of water. As she slid the letter into an envelope, she remembered to look up the word '*orospu*' in her pocket dictionary. The definition was 'prostitute, whore.'

As she sat back at her desk and sucked on her aching tooth, Celeste thought about Leman, and wondered just how sweet this new relationship was going to be.

TWO

A Desperate Woman

Celeste sat down at the breakfast table. She ate breakfast with the family almost every morning and, after a few weeks together, she now fitted easily into their routines. Ferhat, dressed in his weekend uniform of immaculate beige chinos and a light blue shirt, switched from speaking Turkish to English when he saw her and greeted her with formal politeness. Leman, in her white mini skirt and a pair of glossy tights, mouthed "good morning" as she crossed her chubby little legs and immediately uncrossed them again, sending a cloud of stifling perfume in all directions.

"Leman is wearing her nautical clothes today," began Ferhat almost apologetically, his soft voice sounding weak and defeated, "perhaps because I have been considering buying a yacht."

Hanging on the back of Leman's chair, Celeste spotted a white jacket to match the white mini skirt, with large gold buttons and row upon row of navy and gold braid trim. The cuffs featured three stripes, the shoulders were embellished with epaulettes and the collar was a mass of appliquéd gold cord. Never one to skimp on details, she also wore her chunky gold bracelet and her anchor-pendant necklace, and her brilliant white shoes, the toes embroidered with a picture of a ship's steering wheel in gold thread with a piece of diamante rope twisted through it.

"You liked these clothes last time I wear them, didn't you?" said Leman. She tried to catch Ferhat's gaze as he continued to butter his toast without raising his eyes. "And I am wearing Poison, that perfume you bought for me," she continued with a forced gaiety in her voice. She checked that her hair was tidy and continued to look at him with a smile, which she managed to hold for an impressively long time before she finally gave up and took a sip of her tea. She had had her roots re-dyed, Celeste noticed, so her hair was now a solid swathe of jet-black, trimmed immaculately. She had also renewed her nail varnish, and this time it was a metallic orange.

"That would be exciting, to buy a yacht," remarked Celeste. "Do you go sailing a lot?"

"To be honest, we have only been sailing a few times with friends," Ferhat explained. "It was just a vague, romantic idea I had briefly."

"But Mum has already put herself in command," interrupted Levent from the doorway in his nearly perfect American accent. His glossy black hair still glistened wet from the shower. "What rank is that jacket, Mum? A Captain, or maybe an Admiral?"

Ferhat laughed spontaneously for the first time that morning and Leman forced a coquettish laugh, flicking her newly rejuvenated hair. As she tried to catch her husband's eye and show him her smile, just for a moment, Celeste pitied her. She was trying so hard. Ferhat glanced at his wife very briefly then turned forlornly to the heap of blister packs on the table beside his plate, and picked one up.

"I'll sort those for you," offered Leman, dragging the tablets towards her. Strangely, for a man so wealthy and successful, Ferhat seemed like someone who had suffered so many disappointments in life he could no longer feel genuine happiness. Oblivious to his wife's efforts to win his attention, Ferhat started talking about his recent business trip to Paris while Leman arranged his tablets in a row for him on the table. One was to reduce his blood pressure, one was for his stomach ulcer, one was an aspirin to thin his blood and the last one, from a brown glass jar, was to lower his cholesterol.

"I visited the Louvre on my free day," said Ferhat. "I was surprised to find that a lot of those early religious painting were done on wood, not on, what do you call it, that fabric for paintings?"

"Canvas," put in Celeste, reaching for more toast and honey. Leman silently placed the four tablets on the side of Ferhat's plate.

"Yes, the Madonna and child by..."

"Darling, did you get that contract you wanted?" interrupted Leman, placing her hand on Ferhat's forearm and leaning closer to him.

"Yes, yes, that was all fine," Ferhat answered dismissively. "Did you give me one of your tablets by mistake? This one is brown, but the one I usually take for my cholesterol is white."

Just for a second, Leman's hand froze over her half buttered slice of bread.

"Pharmacy man, he told me they change type of cholesterol tablet," she said edgily. "It is same medicine inside. It is same. It's same." Leman seemed more relieved each time she repeated the words. "It's same inside."

Ferhat seemed reassured, but Celeste was not. She still felt unnerved each time she opened the fridge and saw that roll of Arabic writing bobbing in the water. And every time she looked at Levent she thought of the egg by his bed, resting morbidly on a crocheted doily.

"Sadly, the Mona Lisa was surrounded by so many Japanese tourists that I couldn't get near," Ferhat sighed, after swallowing the brown tablet, "but I saw several other beautiful works of Da Vinci."

"Very lovely," said Leman. "That is good news about contract. You are very clever businessman. Levent, you must try to be like your father."

Ferhat gave up talking about art and set about finishing his tablets.

"I need to hurry up," Leman continued. "I must arrive the orphanage by nine o'clock."

The fact that Leman worked in an orphanage gave Celeste a jolt every time it was mentioned. Learning that she was head of administration, rather than looking after the children directly, only moderately diminished her incredulity.

"Where's the plum jam?" asked Levent. "You know I always have it for breakfast. Why has Maryam only put out honey?"

Leman glanced at the door and tutted.

"Where *is* that woman?" she grumbled. "Maryam!"

The table fell into silence until the maid appeared, wiping her hands on her flowery skirt, and was asked indignantly why there was no plum jam at the table.

"It's run out," she explained, eyes turned to the floor as she adjusted her headscarf.

"Why didn't you tell me?" demanded Leman. "You know it's Levent's favourite. He always has it. My son needs to eat properly and now he's got to go to university all day without a proper breakfast."

"I thought there was some left," apologised Maryam. Her hands were trembling.

"I finished it last night," lied Celeste. "Sorry."

"Shall I bring the strawberry jam instead?" said Maryam. "There's still a lot of that left."

"I like plum," said Levent, looking disappointed.

"*Oğulum*, my son," said Leman. She reached out across the table and gently pinched Levent's cheek, marvelling in contented wonder at the superb male child she had created. Celeste watched Levent's look of long-suffering irritation as he let his mother fondle his face. He was definitely good looking, with his perfect white teeth, glossy black hair and honest, turquoise eyes; yet he was so used to having other people do everything for him, and striving to make his life easy, that it was obvious just from looking at his soft, slack lips and sleepy eyelids. Maryam waited by the table for a few moments, wondering whether she was allowed to leave or not. When she realised Leman was ignoring her she melted away into the kitchen.

"Have you found a girl to take to the University New Year Ball yet?" asked Leman.

"Oh Mother, it's only October!" he protested.

"Everyone else will have chosen their dates and you'll find nobody, and look stupid. My darling son, I have to arrange everything for you," she sighed.

"And you'd hate that, wouldn't you, Mum?" said Levent. He winked at her. "If I start inviting girls to the ball this early, I'll look desperate. Well anyway, I was going to ask Nilüfer."

Maryam had told Celeste about Nilüfer, a friend of Levent's since they were at playgroup together. Her parents were both doctors and, according to Maryam, she gained the highest mark at the University in every exam she did for her economics degree. Levent regularly borrowed her lecture notes and had Ferhat's secretary photocopy them for him.

"That's a good idea," said Leman, stroking his soft pink cheek with her left hand again and gazing at him proudly. "My son, my darling son."

Levent stabbed his fork at a piece of feta cheese, which instantly crumbled into two pieces. The organ-style doorbell indicated that Ferhat's company chauffeur had arrived to take Levent to the university campus for the day as usual. While Levent waited for Maryam to bring him his rucksack, Ferhat went to potter around in his study. Leman and Celeste stayed at the table, Celeste finishing her tea and Leman sweeping crumbs from the tabletop into her hand and sprinkling them onto her plate. Leman seemed to have forgotten she was in a hurry.

"How is going your work at the school?" she asked.

"Oh, fine, thank you. Some of my classes have some awkward students in them, but most of them are very nice. We have a lot of fun."

"That's good. It's better to teach nice peoples." Leman paused, as if considering how to phrase her next statement. "Celeste, you would like going hairdresser? You very pretty girl but your hairs are much messy."

Celeste ran her hands over her wavy brown hair and wondered how much it would cost. Her hair could probably do with a tidy up, to be honest.

"I can take you my hairdresser, you don't worry about money, I pay it for you," Leman continued, as if reading her mind.

"That's very kind of you, but I really shouldn't accept," protested Celeste.

"I insist," pronounced Leman emphatically. "We go together next week. Who give you this?"

Leman frowned as she pointed at the blue glass *nazar boncuğu* pendant that the old woman had given Celeste on the sea front, the first day she came to Bebek.

"A... a friend," answered Celeste.

"Hmm, I see. Can I look please?"

"All right," said Celeste, wondering why Leman wanted to examine it. Surely she had seen thousands of them. She untied the blue satin ribbon and passed the pendant to Leman, who held it up towards the window to look at it with the light shining through it.

"It is can be bad luck," she pronounced gravely.

"I thought they were good luck," protested Celeste, just as the ribbon fell from Leman's hand and the pendant smashed to smithereens on the parquet floor.

"Oh dear," stated Leman in a calm, measured tone.

"Why did you do that?" said Celeste, aghast. "You've got a huge one yourself. How can they be bad luck?"

"They are good for some but bad for others," insisted Leman. "Anyway, you has blue eyes, you didn't need *nazar*. I think nobody want to do you harm. Probably. I give you new necklace, more precious than that."

Celeste had started to feel more at ease in Leman's house, but now she was thrown into a state of panic. Breaking her necklace was such a vindictive thing to do but, worse than that, Celeste was sure Leman had some sinister reason. A *nazar boncuğu* was loaded with significance.

"Anyway," Leman went on, calmly changing the subject, "you think little children's can learn English? I mean, ages from five to like nine and ten?"

"Definitely," said Celeste. "They seem to learn better than adults."

"Childrens?" asked Leman, glancing down at the glittering pieces of the broken *nazar* on the floor.

"Yes."

Leman slid the blister pack of tablets for her stomach ulcer across the table with one of her orange-varnished fingernails, until it was neatly parked parallel to her packet of cigarettes.

"My children in orphanage about this age," she said. "You think you could teach them?"

"Yes, of course," answered Celeste.

"You would like to come with me today?"

"Why not? I'm not working this morning."

Leman smiled triumphantly and popped a black olive into her mouth.

"They don't need English, they will never go to England in their life, it's sure, but they need adults talking to them. It will be very good for them having attention."

Leman stood up decisively from the table and led Celeste into the living room, where she opened a drawer in the writing desk. She took out a small, velvet-covered box and showed Celeste the necklace inside. It was a silver pendant set with a large white opal. Leman took it from the box, indicated to Celeste to lift her hair up, and fastened the clasp around her neck.

"There," she said, a self-satisfied smile forming on her lips. "You are look much better now. This is the necklace I want you to wear."

THREE

The Orphan's Precious Treasure

Leman drove the car through the hot, chaotic city to the orphanage. She pointed out some of the more famous streets and monuments to Celeste as they drove. As usual Celeste was struck, more than anything, by the advertisements which covered entire tower blocks more than twenty storeys high with photographs of fashionably dressed woman, happy smokers and proud owners of expensive new cars.

"We here now," said Leman, yanking the steering wheel to the right and lurching in through the orphanage's open gates. She pulled up abruptly alongside a grassy area with a swing in the corner. "You very good to do volunteery work in orphanage. It will be very good for children."

As Celeste and Leman walked through the large blue doors, they were greeted by a motley assembly of little boys in various stages of dressing. One was in his pyjamas, one had only one sock on, and one was wearing a pair of trousers far too big for him, with double turn-ups which reached almost to his knees.

"*Hoş geldiniz*, Leman," they chorused. "Welcome, Leman. *Hoş geldiniz, Abla.*"

"*Hoş buldum*," responded Celeste and Leman. "I found pleasure."

"Why are they calling me *Abla*?" asked Celeste in English.

"Big Sister? That's polite way childrens talk to respect a girl older than they," explained Leman.

The boys were of assorted ages ranging from five to twelve or so, but Celeste was shocked when she looked at them carefully. Old men's eyes, which had seen far too much of life, looked at Celeste out of these little boys' faces. They already understood far too much of the world and it showed in their glances. As the boys crowded round Leman she spotted one of them wearing a slipper on one foot and a brand-new white trainer on the other.

"Do they fit you properly?" she asked him, pointing at the foot with the trainer on it.

"Yes, Leman, perfectly."

"Well where's the other one, then? Why've you got a slipper on the other foot?"

"Ibrahim wanted to try wearing trainers too, so I lent him the other one."

"You silly boys! It must be four sizes too big for him at least. Go and get it back off him, before he falls over and breaks his nose."

Then she turned to Celeste and continued in English.

"We get things from charities what collect old clothes for us. Some things people send are good, some shops give us totally new things they didn't sell, but also many things are disgusting and we must throw them. I don't understand why they give such things. I find it upsetting. I was so pleased with getting trainers for this one, because his old shoes had holes in them. He play very good football. Trainers are perfect for him."

While she spoke, a scruffy mongrel walked into the entrance hall and started barking at a parrot, sidling to and fro in its cage hanging from the ceiling.

"*Hoş geldiniz, hoş geldiniz,*" the parrot croaked back.

"The dog drives me crazy when they keep him indoors," said Leman. "He shouts all the time and I can't get any work done."

Leman told some of the boys to take the dog outside, and instructed the rest of the group to take Celeste on a tour of the building.

"He was a homeless dog. He has no parents, just like us," they explained to Celeste. "We called him *Pazar,* Sunday, because that's the day that we found him."

The building was shabby but clean. The walls, white everywhere, showed faint smears where they had been washed with a bucket of soapy water. No doubt they had not been painted in years but had been made to look as respectable as possible.

In one of the corridors, Celeste and her little guides passed a middle-aged man wearing dirty, dark blue dungarees, rattling a cleaner's trolley along the corridor, loaded with buckets of soapy water, cleaning cloths and brooms. His protruding chin bristled with several days' beard growth and greasy locks of hair hung over his grimy collar.

"This is Mr. Demirsar, the caretaker," the boys told Celeste, greeting the man politely. Mr. Demirsar returned Celeste's greeting with a brief nod. He unnerved her by gazing fixedly at the hem of her skirt. As his lips parted, she noticed to her surprise and disgust that one of his upper canine teeth was missing and the corresponding tooth in his lower jaw was almost twice the normal length, filling the space left by its missing partner. The effect was like an inverted vampire's fang. He did not acknowledge the boys, but stared at them askance as they ran along the corridor. After they had passed him, Celeste looked back at him standing in the corridor exactly as he had been when they passed him, still gazing intently after the boys. He made Celeste feel apprehensive and she was relieved to turn the corner and get away from him.

After a quick tour of the garden, dormitories and offices, with particular attention paid to the dog's kennel, the children led Celeste back to Leman's office. Leman suggested that, rather than start teaching English today, maybe she would like to help out by sorting through a new batch of clothes which had just been delivered from a charity, deciding what was wearable and what would have to be thrown out.

"There are some shoes also," Leman added. "See if any are the size of Tekin's feet. He's got broken ones which are too much small, even for his tiny feet. Where is he, anyway?"

The children answered that he had just gone out to the garden with Pazar, teaching the dog new tricks in front of a small audience.

"That child can make magic out of anything," said Leman.

The sock mountain which greeted them as they entered the dining hall covered three child-size plastic topped dining tables pushed together and was spilling onto the floor in every direction. Three boys stood around the daunting heap of socks in every size and colour, each one with a sock in his hand, sombrely and silently searching for its lost partner. Celeste was dumbfounded by their behaviour. Her little brothers would have been fooling around, throwing socks at each other or trying to escape the work; these little boys were as conscientious as adults. She had never seen children like these before.

Celeste randomly plucked a sock from the heap; a woolly green sock large enough to fit an adult man, with two dirty stains on the bottom. She slid her hand inside it and pushed the end in to make a mouth. Now the stains looked like eyes, so she started to tickle one of the boys and made the sock creature ask if anyone had seen his wife. At first the boys seemed baffled, but gradually she managed to make them laugh at the sheer silliness of the game and when, finally, the sock creature borrowed into the sock mountain and came up with a sock hanging from his mouth, he was accompanied by gales of giggles. In an instant the boys copied her and the table was surrounded by other sock men chattering to each other. Celeste felt happier to see that, with a little encouragement, these worried little children could remember how to play.

Whilst playing, they continued to work and, gradually, they filled two black plastic bin liners with matched pairs of socks. Many of them were not proper pairs, but if they were the same size and similar in colour, then that was good enough. They filled another bag with the socks which were too threadbare or disgusting to be worn any more, even by orphans. Then they began to pick through an unpromising pile of old shoes, some with holes worn right through the soles. Their enthusiasm gradually changed to despondency and the boys were bitterly disappointed to tell Celeste that none of them would be the right size for Tekin.

"He's really tiny," they told her. "He's like a toy."

They stood for a moment in dejected silence until a fat woman with a dark shadow of hair on her upper lip came rolling out of the kitchen doors, followed by the smell of tripe soup. Her mouth was almost lost beneath her beak of a nose, and beneath her apron she seemed to be wearing at least three different flowery skirts in different stages of disintegration. Below a couple of inches of bare, hairy legs she wore towelling sport socks, one with green stripes around the top and the other with blue, and a pair of slip-on plastic slippers, both of which had been mended clumsily with brown parcel tape.

"This is our Lovely Cook!" cried the boys, happily. Several of them ran up to her to embrace her legs. "We love her food. She's so clever at cooking."

In thickly accented Turkish, which Celeste found hard to understand, she offered to finish sorting through the shoes. She suggested Celeste could take the boys into the art room to do some drawing or practise their English. Then she handed one of the older boys a paper bag full of broken biscuits.

"These are for the dog. Take them outside to Tekin, so he can use them for training," she instructed.

The mention of Tekin's name produced a thrill among the boys. Everyone at the orphanage seemed to speak of him as if he were a celebrity, and Celeste felt intrigued to meet this tiny child.

"They shouldn't be doing jobs like this all the time," the cook said. As she spoke to Celeste, she fixed her gaze on the opal pendant that Leman had given her. "That's strange. Why are you wearing an opal necklace?" she asked, finally.

"It was a present from Leman," explained Celeste.

"Really? Very interesting. Very interesting indeed."

Leaving Celeste baffled, she bustled back into the kitchen, her plastic shoes slapping against the floor as she walked.

In the art room, Celeste and eight boys sat around a table scattered with crayons and paper, the pages pulled from an old desk diary. Celeste drew a house with trees and big flowers in the garden, watched in grave silence, and gave it to the boy on her left when she had finished.

"It's for you to colour" she explained. He thanked her earnestly and started colouring it in as if he had been set some homework. She asked the others if they would like a picture, and they said that they would, very much, if she had time and did not mind. The next boy along the table asked for a taxi, because he wanted to be a taxi driver when he grew up. There was no yellow crayon, so she suggested it could be a London taxi, as they are black.

"Really? So how can people find them at night?" he asked in amazement.

"Well, there are lights on the top which say 'taxi', and lights at the front. There are lights all over them, in fact," she reassured him.

"Can you add some more lights, please?" he asked, sliding the picture back to her across the table. "I want to be sure of getting plenty of customers."

"What would you like to be when you grow up?" she asked another boy, as she added a neon strip to the top of the car.

"A labourer," he answered, earnestly. About nine years old, he had a hooked nose which was bent sideways as if it had once been broken. Glancing at his unusually large hands, Celeste saw the rough skin of someone used to manual work.

"A labourer, did you say?" asked Celeste, thinking she must have misunderstood. "You mean, carrying things around and building things and stuff? That's what you want?"

"Yes, he used to do that with his Dad," explained another boy. "He knows that job."

"Me too," added another boy.

She asked a few more boys and found future labourers, porters, and builders. She tried to fire their imaginations, but nobody wanted to be an astronaut. Nobody wanted to be a fireman. Nobody wanted to be the owner of a sweet shop. How had this happened to them? Who had stolen their dreams away?

Another boy came to join them and, because there was no empty chair for him, Celeste invited him to sit on her knees. He looked at her as if he had misheard.

"Can I really?" he asked.

"Yes, of course, if you want to," she laughed.

He was speechless at the immense privilege bestowed upon him. When asked what he would like to colour, he requested a picture of Pazar.

"Tekin's teaching him to stand on his back legs and eat biscuits from his hand, now," he explained. "He jumps through the hoop when Tekin tells him, and when Tekin shouts 'What's your name?' he barks twice. He's trying to say Pa-zar."

After colouring his picture for a while, the boy on Celeste's lap suggested maybe someone else should have a turn now, and he carefully got down while the next child waited politely to be pulled up onto her knees. After this boy had enjoyed a cuddle for the same amount of time as the first, he too volunteered to make way for the next boy.

"Otherwise it's not fair," he commented to Celeste.

As they coloured and drew and chatted, the orphans took turns to sit on her lap in an unwritten rota, making sure each one of them had the same share of attention and affection, rationed out in fair and equal portions. After Celeste had pinned the pictures up on the wall Pazar barked from the doorway.

"It's Tekin!" the boys chorused excitedly.

Into the room, leading a triumphal procession, came an absolutely tiny boy mounted on the dog as if it were a prize racehorse. He held a piece of string around the dog's neck and was supported by an older boy beside him to make sure he did not fall off, while a motley group of boys sang and skipped along behind them. Tekin's light brown hair stood up messily and his blue-green eyes sparkled with delight. His scrappy white legs hung down from his shorts, so skinny that his scab-speckled knees were their widest point. He was strikingly different from all the others, not because he was the smallest, not because he was the fairest, but because he was the only one with the look of an innocent child in his eyes. Celeste realised why the other boys worshipped Tekin. He was the only one who really remembered how to be a child.

The boys with Celeste ran over and started patting Pazar. They helped Tekin down from the dog's back.

"How old are you?" Celeste asked Tekin.

"Five and one month," he answered.

"He's the youngest here, and also the smallest," said the older boy, Bűlent, who had supported him on the dog.

"How old are you, *Abla*?" Tekin asked Celeste innocently.

"Ssh!" exclaimed Bűlent. "You aren't allowed to ask grown-ups their age."

"That's all right," laughed Celeste. "I'm twenty-three."

"Are you married?" asked Tekin.

"No," answered Celeste.

"Have you got a boyfriend?" asked Tekin cheekily, provoking a peal of giggles as if he had said something saucy and risqué.

"No. But I used to have a boyfriend. He wasn't very nice to me after my mother died."

"Oh," said Tekin. "You're an orphan too, like us?"

"Yes, I suppose I am," said Celeste.

"Why wasn't your boyfriend nice to you?"

"I cried a lot," she answered. "He didn't like that."

She always had puffy eyes and she was no fun any more, he had said when he dumped her. He had told her she was dragging him down. Though she knew he hardly merited a thought, his callousness made her heart pound in anger when she lay awake at night.

The boy who had coloured the picture of the dog led Tekin to the wall where the pictures were pinned up.

"Look, here is Pazar" he said. "You can have this picture because you love him the most."

Tekin was delighted with the picture. The others wanted to see Pazar's new tricks. They cheered and clapped as he jumped through a hoop, barked to command and stood up on his hind legs to reach a piece of biscuit which Tekin was holding as high as he could above his head.

"Will Pazar go with Tekin when his aunt comes?" asked one of the younger boys.

"What was that?" enquired Celeste. "Did you say Tekin's aunt is coming to take him?"

"Yes, I'm only staying here until she comes from America to get me," piped Tekin, putting on an authoritative air. "Mummy and Daddy died in the earthquake, far away, in our home in Anatolia. The other boys really live here, but I'm just staying for a while. I've been here more than one year. She can't come yet, she lives a long way away and she has to organise it, but she'll come and get me. She knows I'm waiting here. She's the only one left in my family because my grandparents all died in the earthquake, too. There's only me and my aunt left now. She's very beautiful, my aunt." Tekin hugged the dog around its neck with both arms. "She's got long brown hair, like you. She looks just like you."

"How did you end up here in Istanbul after the earthquake?" asked Celeste. Tekin looked to Bűlent to answer.

"They moved us, because there were some places here in this orphanage," explained the older boy. "But we come from Anatolia, from a long way east of here, me and Tekin. After the earthquake, everyone lived in the streets for a long time, or in tents, and there was terrible weather and it rained and the wind blew everything away, but eventually they took us and brought us here."

"How many of you came here after that earthquake?"

"Five of us, from that one. There are often earthquakes over there and the orphanages are full, so they send children away to other places. I knew Tekin before the earthquake so I was glad they sent us to the same place. We lived very close. He was in the newspaper after the earthquake because he was buried for four days and they thought everyone was dead after all that time, but little Tekin was alive. He was only three then. He still had his nappy on for the night."

Tekin was standing so close to Celeste now that he was almost hidden in a fold of her skirt. He seemed to be burying his head inside the fabric as if he wanted to disappear. She picked him up and sat down, resting him on her lap.

Evil Eye

"Do you remember it?" she asked him. Tekin nodded. "How did you live all that time after the earthquake?" Celeste asked gently.

Tekin looked up at her and just shook his head. As she held him tighter, he raised one hand and slid his fingers into her hair, playing with a few curls as he rested his head on her shoulder. She felt flattered by the fact that he seemed to have trusted her immediately. Holding him in her arms reminded her of her youngest brother, when he had still been little enough to want to be cuddled sometimes.

"It was so scary," offered Bűlent. "I was woken up by the sound of my bedroom walls groaning. Then the whole house was moving like a ship on a wavy sea. I could hear my wardrobe banging against the bedroom wall and I wanted to get out of bed to go to my mother, but I couldn't even sit up in bed. It felt as if someone's big strong hands were holding me down. Then suddenly I fell out onto the floor. When I got up, I fell over again immediately, so I had to go on my hands and knees like a baby. All the time I was crying out 'Mummy, Mummy' and the house was shaking and shaking. All my toys from the shelf fell on top of me, and my books fell off my desk and one of them landed on my back. All the things that were on the floor were jumping up in the air, higher than me, as if they were alive. I was so afraid I almost couldn't breathe. When I was in the doorway of my room, the floor went away and I fell. When I woke up I was in a tiny little place and I was so thirsty. It kept shaking again, time after time everything kept shaking, like the first time, and I thought the floor would go away again, but it didn't."

"I started to be hungry and then thirsty. Being thirsty was worse, much worse than being hungry. Then finally some people took me out. I could hear voices and I tried to shout to them, 'I'm here! I'm here! Come and get me!' but my throat was so dry I couldn't speak. But they found me anyway. Afterwards, people didn't stay at home, even the people whose houses didn't fall down. Every family gathered in the gardens and parks. Lots of people were walking around calling names to find their relatives. Most people slept in their cars. Lots of people were trying to find their families, and there were people who took us children, and lots of mothers came to look for us, but my mother...I waited for her..." His voice trailed off and he stared hard at the floor for a moment. "Oh, it was terrible," he declared finally. "I hope nobody has to suffer that experience ever again, not only in Turkey but nowhere on this planet."

"We all looked for our parents, but we couldn't find them," continued another boy. "One boy from this orphanage, his father found him here and he went to his house with him. Now he lives with his Daddy."

"Like me," whispered Tekin into Celeste's hair, "When I go to live with my aunt."

Tekin stayed on Celeste's lap while the other boys finished colouring their pictures. Celeste hugged him close to her body with both arms. It was only as she felt her muscles relax, as if weights were being lifted from them, that she realised how tense she had been for as long as she could remember. Holding Tekin was like drinking a healing elixir. He remained on her lap for more than an hour, and nobody said a thing about taking turns.

Tekin asked her to draw a picture of him with his aunt.

"What does she look like?" she asked Tekin.

"She looks like you," he answered. "Her hair's a little bit shorter, but that's the only difference. Oh, and her eyes are blue but they're more greeny than yours. Can you draw me dancing with her? When she comes to visit, she puts on music and we dance. When I was very little she used to hold me in her arms and dance around the room like that. I remember her playing beautiful music when I was very very little and she twirled me round the room until I felt dizzy. It was so much fun."

Celeste drew the picture and added musical notes in the air to indicate the beautiful music Tekin had mentioned. He asked her to colour it for him as he was afraid of spoiling it by accidentally colouring over the edges, he said. He was so pleased with the finished result that he refused to let her fix it on the notice board in the art room, preferring to take it directly up to his dormitory and place it by his bed.

In Leman's office later that morning, Celeste asked about Tekin and his aunt.

"Is it true he's only staying for a while until his aunt comes to take him away?"

"No, it isn't" said Leman.

"Are you sure?" Celeste persisted. "He was so convinced, and the other boys believed it too."

"It's only true in his head" said Leman, sounding impatient. "Didn't you ever dream you was princess when you was little girl? Didn't you dream about having beautiful dress and palace, when your parents admonished you? And magic life where everything was all how you want? These boys are dreaming same way. They dream family is coming to take them away. But they haven't family. No-one is coming. It's only dream."

"Have relatives of any of the boys in this orphanage ever been found?" asked Celeste, thinking of the other boy who had gone away with his father.

"One time I managed it," said Leman, "only one time." Her soothing and melodious voice contrasting oddly with the frustrated expression on her face. As she spoke, she leaned over and opened the bottom drawer of her desk, crammed full of files and papers.

"Look this," she commanded. "This all my information about boys. I do tracing relations and family names, I testing information; I collect documents from home cities. Sometimes we even done blood tests of people saying they were parents, but wasn't true. I spend all my time to try and find parents for these boys. I spend so much time and it is much depressing."

She pulled her cigarettes from her handbag and lit one hastily, taking a deep drag on it before resting it, smeared with lipstick, on a crystal ashtray.

"Tekin and others boys came from far eastern part of Turkey, near Black Sea. There was earthquake in Anatolia there last year. There is many childrens without mother and father after earthquake. They have better chance to live, and adults die more likely. Children can live longer when buried without food before people digs them up. Also it's less chance they get squashed, they fit in little spaces."

As she spoke, Leman removed a newspaper clipping from the folder on her desk, which she handed to Celeste.

'The last person to be saved alive from the wreckage of buildings' read Celeste, *'was a three-year-old boy called Tekin, removed from the rubble of his home in the early hours of yesterday morning after remaining buried for more than three days. The child was still conscious but severely dehydrated and suffering a broken collarbone and pelvis.*

'The bodies of a man and woman, believed to be the boy's parents, were removed from nearby wreckage by rescue workers minutes later. Now said to be in a stable condition in hospital, the boy is unable to tell doctors his surname and is believed to be in a state of profound trauma.

'"By this late stage, we have very little hope of removing anyone else alive," said rescue worker Ali Gurhan. "Tekin survived a remarkable length of time, partly because of his young age, but our expectations of finding any further survivors at this stage are very limited. We are basically working to recover and identify bodies now."

'The announcement of plans for tent cities were made yesterday as thousands of citizens are camped outside because they fear going home -- or have no home left to go to. They are crowded together in gardens, parks, and even on the central reservations of motorways under makeshift tents or bed sheets draped over sticks...'

As Leman pushed the window open wider, there was a knock on the door. When she invited the visitor in, the door catch clicked open and there stood Tekin.

"Come in," she beckoned, looking delighted to see him. "What is it?"

He said nothing, but looked up at Celeste.

"Did you want to say something to this lady?" Leman asked, indicating Celeste.

Tekin scampered towards Celeste but stopped a few paces away, looking up at her timidly. He was grasping something tightly in his left hand.

"What is it, Tekin? Have you got something to show me?" she invited.

He nodded.

"It's for you to keep." He stepped closer and held his hand up towards her, above his head. His fist was still clenched tight.

What is it?" she asked encouragingly.

As he looked up at her he uncurled his tiny fingers and on his flat little palm, besides a few pieces of fluff and some biscuit crumbs, twinkled a little toy pendant made of gold-coloured foil.

"It's my precious treasure," explained Tekin in a whisper. "I keep it under my pillow, but now I'm giving it to you. It's for you to keep because you're such a pretty lady."

Celeste took the orphan's trinket and looked at it in her own hand, and she crouched down to hug Tekin and kiss his cheek.

"Thank you," she said. "It's beautiful."

She had tears in her eyes, because nobody had ever been so generous to her in her life before. She closed her fingers tightly round the foil pendant, the most valuable thing she had ever owned.

Leman and Celeste ate a quick lunch at the orphanage, which Celeste hardly touched. It was tripe soup followed by kebabs made from chickens' intestines, which the boys wolfed down with relish. They told her passionately how much they loved cook's food and one of them even revealed that he hoped to marry cook when he was older. As soon as they had finished eating, Leman hurried Celeste into the car to take her to the beauty salon where she had her appointment. While Leman drove through the city, Celeste managed, with some fiddling, to hook the foil pendant from Tekin onto the catch of her chain bracelet. Waiting at a set of traffic lights Leman glanced at her efforts disdainfully, but said nothing.

Walking through the glass and chrome doors of the beauty parlour, Celeste was greeted by a trio of women who looked like fashion models, immaculately manicured and with dazzlingly glossy, straight hair. Pictures of the world's most beautiful women hung on the salon's pale lilac walls; Marilyn Monroe, Audrey Hepburn, Kim Basinger, Julia Roberts. Perfume filled the air. The contrast between the glamour and luxury of the salon and the shabbiness of the orphanage left Celeste in shock. She suddenly felt ashamed of her clothes. She wore long, gathered skirts kept from her student days, like the skirts that Maryam wore. These women sported chic mini skirts and high heels. Their faces were made up with foundation, heavy lipstick and black kohl round their eyes. When they asked Celeste what she would like done to her hair, she was unable to answer, and in the end told them to do whatever they liked.

"Look what flawless skin she has," interrupted Leman, as if showing off her own daughter. Everyone agreed that Celeste had perfect skin, and a very 'natural' look.

"Are you ready for your waxing?" asked the tallest of the women.

"What?" exclaimed Celeste, panicking. "I'm here for a haircut."

"Full beauty treatment," said Leman.

Celeste was walked off to a small room with blue under-floor lighting by a calm, gentle girl, who invited her to lie on a couch like a doctor's examination table. Before she could tell the girl she was having second thoughts, she found her left leg smeared with hot, sticky wax like honey. It took twenty seconds to cover the front of her lower leg and a fraction of a second to rub a sheet of white cotton cloth over the wax and rip it off with a flourish, so fast that there was no time to feel pain. Much encouraged, Celeste relaxed as the girl repeated the process for the rest of her legs, finishing the whole procedure in less than three minutes. The girl waxed Celeste's armpits painfully and then made her almost cry by plucking her eyebrows with a piece of thread which she rolled against her skin, twisting it around the hairs.

"You aren't used to this, are you?" commented the girl. Celeste shook her head. "You're very pretty but I think you neglect yourself," the girl told her. "Men often treat us women like nobody. It's important to treat ourselves like somebody special. When we look good, they tend to remember we deserve respect. Leman knows that. She comes here every week."

Celeste pictured Ferhat at the breakfast table steadfastly contemplating his tablets while Leman strove to win a moment of his attention, but she said nothing.

At last Celeste was directed to the main salon for her haircut. After being shampooed by two girls at once, and given a scalp massage so relaxing that she almost fell asleep, she was placed in a black leather and chrome chair facing a mirror framed with light bulbs. A man appeared from nowhere, brandishing a comb and a pair of scissors. With a photograph of Demi Moore reflected over her shoulder, she sat back as the maestro started his work. Leman, whose black hair was now tinted with a blue sheen and set in waves, looked on throughout the process with apparent pride. The hairdresser flicked Celeste's long hair over her head to the left, then to the right, swiping the scissors above her head with grand flourishes. After a few minutes he snapped his fingers for the dryers, and then he was nowhere to be seen. Now Celeste was surrounded by five women, one wielding hairspray, another with a comb and three with brushes and hair-dryers. In a frenzied flurry of scent and hot air, working together as if performing a dance, the women dried and styled her hair as if preparing her for a catwalk show. Her head was pulled to one side and tugged to the other, until the blasts of hot air stopped abruptly and her chair was spun around for her to see her reflection in the mirror. She hardly recognised herself. Her thin, wavy brown hair had turned into a cascade of sleek, glossy satin. She felt she should have been pleased and yet she was ill at ease. This girl in the mirror was sophisticated and elegant, but she did not look like Celeste.

Next she was told that her nails would be manicured. She tried to protest this was too much, but Leman insisted she should have everything done. And Celeste wondered, more and more uncomfortably, why Leman was being so generous. While one woman attended to her nails, another gave her a foot massage and pedicure. Being pampered was undeniably pleasurable and should be relaxing, yet Celeste felt tenser by the minute.

Finally, with French polished nails, she was allowed to put her scuffed shoes back on and was escorted to the exit by five women, one of whom puffed her with perfume from a cut crystal bottle before opening the door for her to leave.

"How much of a tip should I give them?" she whispered to Leman in English.

"Nothing, I already took care of it," answered Leman.

Celeste and Leman arrived home late in the afternoon. Leman went straight into the kitchen to drink a shot of whisky while she thought nobody was looking, and Celeste headed for the living room. Levent was reclining on the sofa reading a book while Maryam, on her hands and knees, polished the parquet floor with a mixture of turpentine and beeswax. He leapt to his feet when Celeste walked in.

"Wow," he said. "You look like a film star."

Celeste laughed, and stroked her newly silken hair.

"It's true. You don't look like you!" commented Maryam, smiling cheekily as she peered around the legs of a dining chair.

"Listen, can I ask you a favour?" asked Levent, in a low voice.

"What is it?"

"Would you come to that university ball with me, please?"

"Yes, okay," agreed Celeste, surprised. "Aren't you inviting Nilüfer after all?"

"No, there's some guy at the university that she fancies and she wants to wait, because she hopes he'll invite her. I'm really grateful to you for saying yes. My Mother was giving me such a hard time."

"You don't have to thank me."

Levent suddenly spotted the white opal pendant around Celeste's neck.

"Why are you wearing that?" he asked.

"Not you, as well!" exclaimed Celeste. "Your mother gave it to me."

"I wonder why," mused Levent, sounding concerned.

"Because she broke the *nazar boncuğu* that I was given by someone else, so she gave me this as a replacement."

"Yes," repeated Levent, "but I wonder why."

After leaving a suitable pause for Leman to finish her drink, Celeste entered the kitchen to help herself to a glass of water. In the fridge she noticed that there was now a second jar of water with another scroll of paper inside. On the new one, she could see the Arabic writing more clearly, although it was very small and covering both sides of the paper.

"I was thinking, the orphanage boys are very well behaved, aren't they?" commented Celeste.

Leman hastily closed the kitchen cupboard where she thought her whisky bottle was well hidden.

"Too good. When they start being naughty we know that they are alright, in their psychology I mean."

"Oh."

"Did you enjoy?" asked Leman. "Would you like to go with me each week? Orphanage can't pay, but I think it can be fun."

"Yes, I would definitely like to go. I loved being with the boys, and I can practise my Turkish with them, too."

"Good. It is very kind of you to do that for them. It means so much for them. And for me too. I am grateful."

"Really, it's a pleasure. Leman, I've been wondering, why aren't there any girls?"

"There are some orphanages for girls too, mixed ones. But much less. They often is make to prostitutes."

"Even when they are little children?"

"Yes. It is more dangerous for girls living on streets. We don't find them for orphanage. Bad people finds them first. Then we can't do nothing."

"How do the children end up in the orphanage?"

"Sometimes they bring a group after a nature disaster."

"Natural disaster."

"Natural disaster, thank you. Like Tekin and some others. Other boys, police finds them on the streets in the city. Also, other childrens, they just find us by themselves. It's very unusual, but sometimes happens, they just walk in the door."

"What if girls come to you, would you take them?"

"No, send them to girls' orphanage in other part of city."

Celeste sat down on one of the chairs at the kitchen table. Leman put the kettle on to make some tea, and then went to take the milk out of the fridge.

"Maryam has finished all milk," she said into the fridge. "She's a lot bitch."

"You don't genuinely mean that, do you?"

Leman paused.

"No, not really. She only steal things for her children."

"How long have you known she was stealing things?"

"Always!"

"But you've never said anything to her?"

"No. She has been working for us here years, ever since she was fourteen and Levent was little boy. She have difficult life, with husband who hitting her..."

"He hits her?"

"Yes, once he hit her in mouth, that's why she have that nasty tooth. She never steal for herself. She only take for the baby. Her babies always hungry, she has too many. Five! It's ridiculous, how can she afford that?"

She took a cigarette out of the packet on the kitchen table and lit one.

"I told her to do abortion," she continued in her mellow voice, exhaling smoke and picking something off the end of her tongue with an orange fingernail. "You say do abortion, or make abortion?"

"Have."

"But she didn't listen to me. She is foolish woman. I have done three abortion after since Levent was born." She put the cigarette back to her lips and inhaled deeply. "I wanted my son to have the best life. That way we can have more money to spend on him, he can have all attention, all time, best education, more toys, more everything."

Celeste imagined herself growing up with more toys, a more expensive education and no sisters or brothers to share them with.

"Maryam, she should have done same thing, but she is simple woman, she have no self-discipline. She is a lot stupid."

Leman was so proud of herself, thought Celeste. She felt so clever, so progressive, so modern. She looked at Celeste smugly, and Celeste stared back incredulously at this woman who looked after other people's children, but had killed three of her own.

FOUR

The Baby Wrapped In Swaddling Clothes

Maryam stood on the third floor windowsill and leant out as far as she could to wipe the glass clean with a damp cloth, while her left hand firmly gripped the frame. In the distance behind her a vast, rusty Russian ship and several newer looking Turkish ones sailed majestically past while small fishing boats wove between them. The heat haze and air pollution reduced the mosques, warehouses and shops on the Asian shore opposite to a mere blur.

The only thing which spoiled Maryam's looks was a dead front tooth which had turned grey, but even that could not spoil the effect of her chocolate-brown eyes, which sparkled as she talked. She was only twenty-four, a year older than Celeste and Levent. In her flowery gathered skirt with a hole torn in one side, and with a scarf tied around her hair gypsy style, Maryam reminded Celeste of a chorus singer from a production of *Carmen*.

"Maryam, are you sure you have no idea what that egg is for?" asked Celeste. "You're such an expert on collecting gossip."

"I've asked all the clever people I know, and they have no idea," said Maryam. "I just know I'm not allowed to touch it. Leman has her funny ways. Look at all those newspapers! The thing I'm more interested in knowing about is what Ferhat was doing during the two years that Leman and Levent had lived alone in a flat in Nişantaşı."

"Isn't Nişantaşı very far from here?" asked Celeste.

"Miles away. The other side of town," answered Maryam.

"Leman told me Ferhat was working abroad, so she had decided to live closer to the city centre and take a smaller house for convenience. She said they let out this house just to avoid leaving it empty. I travelled by bus every day to clean and cook in the flat as usual, but I always knew none of it made sense."

"What do you mean?" asked Celeste.

"Leman would never willingly have let this house out to a stranger. It's her pride and joy. I could tell she hated being in that small flat. She hates modesty, she likes everything to be big, with gold on!"

"And they certainly didn't need the money," added Celeste.

"Ferhat used to telephone occasionally. Their conversations always ended in arguments, or else Leman stopped them abruptly when she realised I was close enough to hear her talking. There's definitely a secret being hidden. I want to know…"

Maryam used a word Celeste did not understand when explaining what she wanted to know. Celeste took her pocket dictionary from the desk and suggested Maryam could look the word up. Maryam sat down on the windowsill, took hold of the little red volume and cradled it reverently in her cupped hands for a few moments. Then, slowly and cautiously, she turned it upside down, opened it near the middle and gazed at the inverted page for a few moments, closed it gently and extended her hand back to Celeste with the book resting on her palm.

"*Çok Güzel*," she said, "very pretty," as she flashed one of her dazzling smiles.

"Maryam, how can you do things if you can't read?" Celeste asked as Maryam stood up and stretched as high up as she could in order to go over a particularly grimy strip at the top of the window again. Pausing to think, Maryam glanced out across the city, leaning so far off balance that her flowery skirt caught the wind and ruffled like the sail of a yacht. The hole torn at the side draped itself round the window catch and Celeste's heart skipped a beat as she released it for Maryam and caught sight of the drop from the windowsill.

"I thought you were about to fall into the Bosphorus," she gasped when Maryam's skirt was freed. Maryam poked her head into the room, laughing. Outlined against the sea and the panorama of the city behind her, she looked as if she were floating in the sky. The sun made some wisps of hair which had slipped out of her headscarf sparkle like silver threads as they fluttered against her cheek in the light breeze.

"Do you like it here?" Maryam asked. "I mean, it's beautiful, isn't it? Sometimes, when I need to get away from my life for a while, I just sit for ten minutes and stare at the Bosphorus."

"I fell in love with this view as soon as I saw it," agreed Celeste.

"You do know it's the sea, not a river?" asked Maryam.

"Yes, I know!" laughed Celeste. "Why does everyone say that?"

"Because it's true," said Maryam. "Anyway, to answer your question, I don't need to read. To be honest, I've never even thought about it."

"Yes, but I was thinking, when you buy things," persisted Celeste, "you can't read the instructions."

"What instructions?"

"Well, like, a washing machine or a food mixer or something. You have to find out how to use it."

"I haven't got anything with instructions. The only instructions in my life are from Leman," said Maryam. She was still standing on the window ledge, hugging the window frame thoughtfully.

"Well then," persisted Celeste, "how do you know what street you're in?"

"By looking at it."

"How do you know where the bus is going?"

"I ask."

"But, you can't fill in forms or read advertisements. You can't send anyone a letter."

Maryam smiled, tipped her head onto one side, and shrugged.

"I don't know," she said. "Reading is useful for rich people like you, but I don't need it for my life."

"What about when you have to sign your name on something?"

"Like what?"

"Like, at the bank, for example."

"I've never been inside a bank!" Maryam laughed, and sprang down from the window frame, agile as a cat.

"Let's have some tea," suggested Celeste.

"You've already made me breakfast," said Maryam. "I've had feta cheese, honeydew melon and black olives, soft-boiled eggs, toast and honey and four cups of tea."

"Leman's out all morning," said Celeste. "What's the problem?"

Maryam shrugged. Down in the kitchen Maryam fetched a newspaper from one of Leman's precious heaps, and placed it in front of Celeste.

"Why don't you read me something from this?" suggested Maryam as the water for the tea came to the boil.

"What would you like to hear about?" asked Celeste, turning the newspaper round to read the headlines on the front page. "Sport, politics…"

"No, not politics!" Maryam interrupted. "I wouldn't understand that, that's for men. Tell me about her."

She pointed at the photograph on the front page, of a plump, oiled belly dancer in a cerise, glittering brassiere, a filmy hipster skirt and pink, stiletto-heeled sandals. Her frosted pink lipstick contrasted so brightly with her dark skin that her mouth seemed to hover several inches in front of her face.

"I bet she has an exciting life," explained Maryam, and then looked at Celeste expectantly with her big dark eyes, like a puppy waiting for a chocolate button.

The dancer did turn out to have an exciting life.

Celeste had noticed that stories involving famous belly dancers were a regular feature of Turkish newspapers, but the belly dancer in this particular story was a man, the dancing partner of the portly lady in the picture. He performed in drag and was acclaimed as one of the best belly dancers in Turkey, but he had been stabbed by the husband of his portly partner after a particularly successful performance. The husband admitted he was jealous that the belly-dancing man might try to seduce her.

"Some people might think his cross-dressing proved he wouldn't want to make advances to the chubby lady," said Celeste.

"Especially as her husband's a psychopath," agreed Maryam, revelling in every detail of the story.

The enraged husband said later in court that they had been seeing each other every day and he 'was bound to have had the hots for her, even though he was a pansy'. The stabbed man was recovering in hospital but the gashes through his abdominal muscles meant he would probably never be able to dance again.

"That's sad. Maybe the husband could learn to dance with her instead," suggested Maryam after Celeste had finished reading.

"Maybe she could divorce the husband and marry the belly dancer," suggested Celeste.

"I told you her life would be exciting," said Maryam, finishing her tea. She stood up and carried the newspaper to the rubbish bin, tugging five other papers out from the bottom of a heap in the corner of the kitchen. She rolled them up as small as possible, shoving them under some carrot peelings so they were well hidden.

"I have to do this every day," she explained. "Otherwise nobody would be able to move around this house by now. Leman has never realised. She's so obsessed with her papers, she would never give me permission to clear them out. Ferhat and Levent complain all the time and she just snaps at them."

"Maryam, how did you get through school without learning to read?" asked Celeste. "I thought school was free in Turkey."

"Just because school is free, that doesn't mean everyone can afford to go. Food isn't free. Clothes aren't free. In my family we had seven children, and how can two adults earn enough to feed all those people? In England you're all rich, aren't you?"

"Compared with here, definitely," agreed Celeste.

"In Turkey, rich families like this one can support their children, but not normal people like me. Only babies get fed for nothing. As soon as you are old enough to understand what work is, you must do it!" laughed Maryam.

"Would you like to learn to read?" asked Celeste.

"Not really," answered Maryam "People who can read all have terrible memories! They write everything down then immediately forget it. I think they use paper instead of their brains."

Evil Eye

At this moment they heard the sound from the other room of the baby crying. Maryam brought her five-month-old baby boy Yakup with her when she came to work, and left him lying on the bed in the spare room, but her other four children stayed at home with their father or with Maryam's sister.

"I'll go and check up on him," said Celeste, taking off towards the bedroom at a sprint. When she reached the doorway of the bedroom she saw him lying, with his eyes wide open but still flat on his back, looking tiny and lost in the very centre of the king-size double bed. He was swaddled very tightly like a parcel, in a blanket which was wound round and round him, pinning his arms to his sides and secured with a dressing gown cord so he could not wriggle free. He rocked from side to side a couple of times and then gave up, lay stock still, and stared silently at the ceiling with no expression on his face. Celeste hesitated to see if he would start crying again, but he did not.

"I'll keep an eye on him for a while," Celeste called out to Maryam.

She sat down on the bed and glanced up at the grubby white ceiling, the only thing in his field of vision. She had told Maryam she thought swaddling was cruel. Surely it would dull his senses? What was he learning about the world? Babies were supposed to lie on their tummies surrounded by interesting toys to grasp and dribble on. She thought of the difference between this poor baby and her little brothers at the same age, who could already turn themselves over and lift themselves up onto their arms. Poor little Yakup had never even been allowed to try.

Maryam had said she had swaddled all her other babies for the first six months of their lives. She had explained to Celeste, seeming quite concerned, that when babies are inside their mother's belly their legs are all bent and squashed and they have to be straightened out when they are born, or else they grow up deformed. Celeste had dropped the subject, reasoning that she could not justifiably tell a mother of five how to look after her children.

Today she decided to release baby Yakup from his homemade straitjacket and play with him for a while. But as the folds of the blanket fell open she almost gasped in horror. He was dirty, horribly filthy. A ring of scum in the crease round his chubby little neck lined a bright red rash, with spots of blood oozing out. She found the same sores on his hands, and shuddered to think what she would find if she opened his nappy. How could Maryam do this? She spent all day cleaning someone else's house but she did not even clean her own baby.

"Maryam!" she shouted out. "I want to bathe Yakup! Is that all right?"

Maryam agreed happily, but as Celeste walked through to the bathroom to run him a tepid little bath, she realised her hands were trembling. Was she upset, or was she angry? Why didn't Maryam wash him? How could she not care? Celeste had no children of her own yet she knew how to look after them. It had been her life since her mother died. The job of mothering may have been forced on her, yet she had done it with devotion.

Her heart was pounding as she laid him on a pink towel on the floor, and took his nappy off while the water ran into the bath. She checked the water temperature with her wrist and gently lowered Yakup into the lukewarm water, knowing how much it would smart and sting his sore skin. He did not flinch and he did not make a sound. She remembered helping bathe the oldest of her little brothers like this when she was about seven years old, but he had always struggled and squealed like a piglet, and once he was in the water he made sure he splashed enough to drench everyone present. Yakup just lay blinking at her as if he were drugged.

She spent a long time trickling cupped handfuls of water onto his chest and neck and the back of his head. Throughout the whole process he did not utter a sound and hardly seemed to show any interest. When eventually he was clean, she carried him back into the spare room wrapped in a towel, and patted him dry. Then she put her hairdryer on its coolest setting and aimed it at his body, to make sure he was thoroughly dry all over. He seemed to like that and squeaked a couple of times.

She held him in her arms for a minute and kissed him, and then laid him naked on top of the quilt to kick about. She gave him a glove to gnaw on, which looked like a vast hand pinning his chest to the bed. Leaving him lying contentedly, she went through to the living room to talk to Maryam.

"Maryam, come and sit here please."

"I've nearly finished the floor, just a minute."

"No, please come and sit down. I've just given the baby a bath. He was really dirty and his skin is all red and terrible." She did not know the word for 'rash'. "I think you need to take him to the doctor."

Maryam looked scared. Celeste realised she had been worried about him too, but at the mention of the doctor she became uneasy. Celeste realised what a fool she had been. Of course Maryam would have taken him to the doctor if she could afford it. Maryam stared at the gold fringe round the edge of the chaise longue they were sitting on.

"He is very delicate, this little one," she said quietly, and pulled at one of the tassels on the corner of a plump cushion.

"I see," said Celeste, "I understand. But you must wash him every single day. His skin's like that because he's dirty," she said.

Maryam looked subdued, downtrodden even.

"I'll try to wash him."

"You have to do it every day," said Celeste firmly. Suddenly she felt like a horrible person. She was telling a mother of five how to look after her baby.

Celeste played with Yakup for most of the day and, when it was time for Maryam to go home, she offered to wrap him up again in his blanket. She went into her own bedroom first, and took several banknotes out of her bedside drawer, hoping the amount would be enough to pay the doctor. Then she went through to the other room and lifted the baby onto the blanket, and took hold of one of his feet.

"This little piggy went to market," she said, squeezing his big toe, "and this little piggy stayed at home-"

"What are you saying to him?" asked Maryam curiously, standing in the doorway.

"Oh, nothing. Why don't you make some coffee for us to have before you go?"

"OK," said Maryam and padded off to the kitchen.

Celeste finished the pig poem at a rapid whisper and then twisted the blanket around the baby, putting the money between two of the outer layers before she tied the dressing gown cord around his middle.

"This is for your Mummy to take you to the doctor," she whispered to him, "and I hope he can make you better fast."

As she stood up from the bed, Maryam reappeared in the doorway.

"You were talking to him, weren't you?" she asked.

"Yes. I was teaching him English."

"I think he needs to learn Turkish first!"

"He's so sweet!" commented Celeste. "He has such beautiful big eyes, like yours."

Maryam looked at her, without smiling. There was a horribly awkward long pause. Celeste had obviously committed some kind of blunder, but she did not understand what.

"We Turks don't usually compliment people like that, especially babies," Maryam said, eventually.

"Why not?" asked Celeste.

"We don't like to risk the evil eye. Envious people can invoke the evil eye if they admire your baby too much. Their jealous glances summon it, and it casts illness and death over the baby. That's why we have to protect babies, like this."

She picked up a tiny silver charm from the bed covers. It must have fallen out when Celeste undressed him. It was in the shape of a hand, with a blue glass eye on the palm. Maryam tucked it into the folds of Baby Yakup's clothes.

"I didn't mean any harm," apologised Celeste.

"It's no problem," answered Maryam with genuine warmth. "I know foreigners are different from us."

When they had finished drinking the coffee, Celeste told Maryam to leave the cups for her to wash up. She stood in the doorway to watch Maryam walk along the seafront towards the bus stop, hugging her baby tightly to her and kissing both his chubby little cheeks as she waited for the bus to arrive.

When Leman got home from work that evening and Celeste told her about the baby, she said that she had seen Maryam's home and it was a kind of shack with a leaking roof and no glass in the windows, just polythene stapled across them.

"She haven't no electricity and no taps water. In Turkey," she explained in her soft, deep voice, "there is a law saying if you build your own house or move into a falling down one, once you have put on roof, nobody can take it down or make you move out. Many people like Maryam live in old pieces of wood and rubbish inside buildings that is fallen down, and use anything what they can, to put walls and furniture on. It's dangerous for her to wash little baby Yakup, because cold wind comes in, she have no glass windows, and she doesn't have got hot water. Her first baby was died from" - Leman paused to light a cigarette - "What is it called, pneumonia, with coughing all the time and blood. That little baby had same thing when he was newly born. Her husband is very handsome but lazy man, and he never earned any money. Maryam has to support him as well as the children. He is so lazy, so lazy."

"She would be better off without him then, wouldn't she?"

"No. Life is very difficult for a woman without husband in Turkey, even a bad one," Leman stated, flicking her hair and running her fingers through it a couple of times as if it needed brushing. "When she had her first two babies I gave her a lot of things, I bought them clothes and vitamins and medicine when they were needed it. But she kept on having more and more children. I told her to stop! But she didn't take my advice. She's not my daughter. What can I do? You can't adopt a whole family."

Celeste sat back and watched her puffing on her cigarette, and thought about all those children and the handsome husband in Maryam's house with no glass in the windows.

That night Celeste dreamt that she was fighting and wrestling her way through swathes and swathes of pink plastic shower curtains, which were smothering her so it was hard to breathe, and tangling themselves around her arms so that she had to struggle to raise them up, until eventually she came to a bath filled almost to the brim, with a baby in it. Clouds of steam swirled above the bathwater like a witch's cauldron and the baby was struggling to keep its head above the surface. There were four adults, three women and a man, sitting on upright wooden dining chairs around the bath, all with their heads nodding forwards and their hands resting neatly on their laps, sleeping, while the baby was drowning. His cries and gasps could not wake them up, and however vigorously Celeste shook them they just slumbered on. She tried to scream at them, and woke herself up by making a strangulated croaking noise in her throat. She found that her blankets had got all twisted up around her arms and legs and she had to get out of the bed and remake it before she could go back to sleep again. But as she lay in bed drifting off, she realised that, for the first time since she had come to Turkey, she felt sure of herself and satisfied when she had washed and taken care of Maryam's baby. She had been in her element.

The following Friday, Celeste woke up late. She only had to work for the afternoon, so she was free to spend the morning relaxing. She found Leman and Ferhat already sitting at the table waiting for Maryam to serve their breakfast. Levent's place was empty; no doubt he was still in bed, as usual. Before she reached the doorway of the breakfast room, Maryam pulled Celeste's sleeve and led her into the spare bedroom where baby Yakup was lying. He was wearing a nappy and a little white vest. There was no blanket tied around him. Without a word Maryam reached into her bag and took out a big tube of cream.

"From the doctor," she said. "Thank you."
"Please tell me if you need more," said Celeste.
"*Tamam*," said Maryam. "All right."

When Celeste arrived home after teaching for the afternoon, she found Levent in the kitchen trying to light the gas ring. As he leant forward, a shock of hair from the top of his head slipped forward in front of his face, such an intense, glossy black that it shimmered blue as it caught the light. A large saucepan on the kitchen work surface gave off a faint smell of garlic.

"What are you doing?" she asked, surprised to see Levent in the kitchen.

"Maryam has gone home and my parents are out for their anniversary dinner..." he started to explain.

"Today's their anniversary?" asked Celeste in surprise. She thought of the blatant disinterest Ferhat had shown Leman during breakfast, as always. "Did your father remember this morning?"

"Of course. He always remembers, because his secretary reminds him. She books a restaurant every year and orders flowers to be delivered to

Mum at work. So anyway, I'm trying to reheat something to eat for dinner."

"Don't you know how to light the gas?" asked Celeste.

"Yes I do, but it's not working. It smells awful. That usually means the gas bottle is nearly empty, so the pressure isn't enough to make the flame stay alight."

"Gas bottle?"

Levent opened the cupboard beside the oven, which was filled by a dark grey metal canister, connected to the hob by rubber tubes.

"Didn't you realise it was in a bottle?" he asked Celeste.

"No! I just assumed it came though pipes, like it does in England."

"It does in some places, but it's dangerous if there's an earthquake. Anyway, this isn't solving the dinner problem. The gas man comes in the mornings."

"What's in the saucepan?" asked Celeste.

"*Mercimek*. Oh, I can't remember the word in English. They're small, red, elliptical objects used for making soup."

"Lentils?"

"Ah, yes! That's what I mean. Do you want to see what else is in the fridge?"

They looked in the fridge together and concluded that there was nothing much. The most prominent items were the glass jars of water containing the strips of paper that Celeste had seen the first day she came to see the house.

"What are they for?" she plucked up the courage to ask.

"My mother put them there. I don't know why," said Levent, picking a small, withered carrot out of the vegetable drawer and holding it to his lips like a cigarette.

"This fridge is a lot empty," he declared in a perfect imitation of his mother's strong Turkish accent, taking a long drag on the carrot with his eyes closed, "I want that you come to one restaurant with me today's evening. What do you think?"

Celeste giggled wickedly. His impersonation was all the funnier because he did physically resemble his mother to a certain extent. His facial structure was his father's, but he had his mother's nose; a nose too prominent for Leman, but attractive on Levent's larger, masculine face. Celeste accepted the invitation. She went upstairs to have a shower and, when she came out of her bedroom, Levent had changed into a crisply ironed white shirt and simple black trousers, and smelled faintly of aftershave. He told Celeste that he had already called Mehmet the chauffeur, who would be arriving shortly.

"Isn't he taking your parents out tonight?" asked Celeste.

Evil Eye

"No, Dad wanted to drive himself," said Levent. "Probably as an excuse to stop Mum trying to hold his hand in the back of the car."

Celeste said nothing, but found herself feeling deeply sorry for Leman. In the car, she realised that she had forgotten to put on the opal pendant Leman had given her. It would have been perfect with the blouse she was wearing.

"Where are we going?" asked Celeste."

"A hotel that my father likes a lot," replied Levent. "There's a very nice restaurant there. You can see the Golden Horn, you know, the channel of sea that divides the European side of the city into two halves"

"Isn't it going to be expensive?" asked Celeste.

"I'm paying, so it's none of your business," replied Levent, mock serious as he looked Celeste straight in the eye.

"We could just get a kebab or something," suggested Celeste. You don't need to splash out on me."

"What?" asked Levent, shocked. "A kebab? You can't eat a kebab! Which would you choose? Salmonella Surprise? Botulism in a Bun?" Celeste giggled at Levent's exaggerated show of horror. "You don't have the right immune system for kebabs," he continued. "We Turks have antibodies against all kinds of germs that would kill an English girl like you."

When they arrived it was already dark but the illuminated hotel lit up the street. They were escorted to the restaurant by a flurry of uniformed porters. The menu featured some European food and some Turkish dishes, which Celeste told Levent she would like to try, so he ordered stuffed peppers and lamb for her. The waiter stood to attention beside the table as he took the order from the young man half his age, his thin, bony face tensed into inscrutability. He had the crisp, controlled mannerisms of a man who had been providing silver service for two decades and had waited on the high and mighty, the modest and the downright unworthy without ever letting an expression creep onto his face. His uniform, consisting of a maroon, high-collared jacket and black trousers, seemed designed to look smart and formal yet was clearly made of polyester and fitted like a garment ordered from a work-wear catalogue. Celeste observed that the trousers had been ironed to a sharp crease down the front but without placing a damp cotton cloth over the fabric and had thus developed a shine which highlighted the edges of the seams. She also noticed that the waiter's highly polished shoes were so well worn they had fully adopted the contours of their owner's feet and had been re-stitched several times. As he walked away, she caught a glimpse of his socks, slightly threadbare at the heel.

Celeste told Levent about her family in England, and he told her about his degree, his friends at university, and how trying life could be living with his mother. He made her laugh constantly. A lot of his behaviour, which Celeste had judged as childish, started to seem more like survival skills. Maybe he distracted his mother with childish complaints and problems, to stop her prying more deeply into his personal life; to leave himself just a tiny space in which to breathe freely and live for himself. Celeste wished she had the audacity to ask Levent about the time he and his mother had moved out of the house for two years and rented it to the woman his mother called an '*orospu.*' She was sure she had not been told the real version of this story and, for that very reason, she dared not pry.

When the bill came, in a leather folder with gold embossed writing, Levent casually inserted a credit card without glancing at the total. The money came from his father's account, and Celeste realised that Levent had never had to consider the limit of funds in the account, or budget for any of his expenditures. The waiter, expressionless as always, placed the slip on the table for Levent to sign and proffered a gold pen produced apparently from nowhere. As Levent wrote his name carefully with his left hand, Celeste was struck by how soft and chubby his fingers looked, with the nails bitten right down into the nail beds. He had seemed perfectly at ease ordering an expensive meal and choosing a bottle of wine from the encyclopaedic wine list, yet it crossed Celeste's mind that some of his self-assured mannerisms were merely good imitations of his father - perfect mimic that he was - or perhaps it was just the incongruous sight of an American Express Gold Card in those podgy, dimpled baby-hands that looked as if they had never been used for hard work. When Levent snapped the lid back on the pen, his gold Rolex watch slipped down his wrist. He lazily pushed it back inside his jacket sleeve, throwing what looked to Celeste like a guilty glance at the waiter. The waiter thanked him for his choice of restaurant that evening with a dignified bow and walked away, as if he had had gold watches flaunted under his nose every day of his life.

FIVE

The Ladies Who Lunch

Celeste always left in good time to arrive at work. She usually found the journey an ordeal in one way or another, and liked to have time inside the peaceful haven of the school staffroom to relax and clear her mind before the morning's lessons. She also needed a few minutes in the bathroom to wash her face and hands, and clean the street's dust and grime from her shoes.

She liked her main class, a group of beginners who were all about her age. She taught this group three mornings a week, and various other classes and individual lessons four afternoons a week. This left her with several mornings and afternoons free for sightseeing and exploring the city with her drawing pad, sketching out quick impressions of the buildings and people she saw when she felt in the mood. Her favourite day of the week was Saturday, when she went to the orphanage with Leman and spent the morning teaching the boys English and playing with them. They revelled in every moment she gave them her attention, loving the spontaneous warmth she showed them; they certainly had no idea how badly she needed the trusting affection they showed her in return.

Today Celeste had left the house late. She tried to quicken her pace, coughing frequently in the oppressive hot air filled with traffic fumes, but could not make any more rapid progress because the cobblestones were loose and wobbly. In some places the holes in the pavement were more than three feet deep so, waiting for a break in the traffic, she had to pass them by stepping into the road.

As she left the rich area of Bebek and came closer to the school, she gradually entered a different world. Instead of sea salt and fresh fish, the air smelled of rotting cabbage and car exhaust. The buildings were grey and grimy cement tower blocks rather than graceful houses. Even the people looked different. Most of them were darker skinned, with black hair and heavy eyebrows, and Celeste felt menaced by the stares of men with large, droopy moustaches. In Bebek, only the maids covered their hair with flowery headscarves tied jauntily under the nape of the neck, like Maryam; now she was in a neighbourhood where nearly all the women pulled their scarves down to their eyebrows and tucked the sides inwards over their cheeks, pinning the fabric firmly under their chins so that every strand of hair was hidden. These women looked at Celeste askance, standing out like the pallid white foreigner that she was.

"*Orospu!*" growled one woman as she drew close to her, spitting at her feet.

Celeste sprang sideways to avoid her and carried on walking, somewhat shaken, until she reached the bus terminal. Under a large road bridge alongside the bus stop sprawled a heap of rubbish, higher than Celeste's shoulders and perhaps a little larger than the busses which drew up and pulled away continually. A few people were usually to be seen, picking through it in hope of finding something useful. On the pavement directly behind the bus stop was a small grocery shop where Celeste bought herself a carton of *ayran* every morning, a drink made from yoghurt and water shaken together with a pinch of salt.

The shop assistant laughed as she rummaged through the cartons looking for one with a *Nasreddin Hoca* story she had not read yet.

"You're getting obsessed, my English friend," he commented.

"I love *ayran*," she answered. "You know I have it every morning."

"I meant, obsessed with Nasreddin, our great Imam."

"He wasn't a real Imam, was he?" she asked. The man threw his head back and roared with laughter.

"Of course not! They're just funny stories."

"Some of them are very wise, too," said Celeste. Finally Celeste found a carton with a caricature of the pot-bellied Imam in long robes and a ridiculous turban as large as himself. "This is a new story," she said.

Back outside, she let out a rasping cough as she pulled the drinking straw off the side of the carton. She had been coughing for a while now, but only while she was outside. The smoke and fumes were so heavy and pungent in the early morning heat that they seemed to settle in her lungs, and could not be shifted. After a long swig of *ayran* she read the 'Nasreddin Hoca' story:

'Nasreddin Hoca had borrowed a cooking pot from his neighbour. When he didn't return it for a long time, the neighbour came knocking on the door.

'"Hoca Effendi, if you've finished with the pot, could I take it back? My wife needs it today." When Hoca handed back the pot, the neighbour noticed that there was a smaller pot inside it. "What's this?" he asked. "Well, my dear neighbour, congratulations, your cauldron gave birth to a baby pot," said the Hoca. The neighbour, delighted, thanked the Hoca, took his cauldron and the new little pot, and went home.

'A few weeks later Hoca came back, asking to borrow the pot again. The neighbour lent Hoca the pot with pleasure but, once again, it took the Hoca forever to return it. The neighbour had no choice but to go and ask for it again. "Hoca Effendi, have you finished with my cauldron yet?" "Ah neighbour, oh woe!" wailed the Hoca, "I'm afraid your cauldron is

Evil Eye

dead." "Hoca Effendi, that's not possible, a cauldron can't die!" objected the neighbour. But Nasreddin Hoca had his answer ready. "My dear fellow, if you believed it could give birth, why can't you believe it can also die?"'

As Celeste read, she felt a gentle pulling at her shoelace, and lifted and stamped her foot a couple of times, thinking it was somebody's bag or foot touching her on the crowded pavement. Finally she felt a stronger tug and looked down, aghast, upon a huge black rat. The end of her shoelace, in its mouth, was already partially eaten. Screaming out in disgust, she let her *ayran* carton slip to the ground as she kicked at the rat to scare it away. It scuttled off back towards the immense heap of dumped refuse which was evidently its home.

"Did you see that?" she asked some of the people nearest her, incredulous.

Nobody seemed particularly surprised or interested. One woman mentioned that rats were always to be found in large cities. Celeste thought of Maryam, who would have been thoroughly blasé about finding a rat feeding on her clothing, and tried to take the experience as calmly herself. Nevertheless she was greatly relieved when, moments later, her bus pulled up and she joined the other people boarding it.

As she raised her left foot onto the bottom step, she felt a gentle tugging at her skirt hem. Directing her gaze downwards with dread, she was already poised to kick out at the immense rat she expected to see when she realised that, instead, there was a boy of about seventeen years old, sitting on the pavement next to the bus, gazing up at her hopefully with huge hazel-brown eyes. Celeste noted that, with his sharply defined cheekbones and perfectly curved lips, his would be a very satisfying face to draw.

"Please would you help me onto the bus?" he asked, timidly.

It was only as he spoke that Celeste realised why he was down on the ground. Both his legs were amputated from the hip. Perched on a thick, rolled up wad of carpet, tied firmly to his buttocks, he clenched his rag-bound hands into fists and pressed his knuckles into the pavement to swing his body closer to her. Her stomach tightened in horror as she realised this boy had to do this repeatedly to propel himself along the pavement. She stood paralyzed, wordless in disbelief.

"I'll help you," a man cut in, stepping up behind the boy and inserting his hands under the boy's armpits. In one swift movement he hoisted the boy onto the highest step of the bus, and called out to the people already on board to make way and clear a seat for him. Climbing up the steps of the bus after them, Celeste guessed it was packed with more than seventy people. The smell of sweat and greasy hair hit the back of her nose and made her feel queasy, whilst the hot humid atmosphere unleashed a sudden volley of coughing she could not control. Once she had managed to clamber down the aisle, she realised she was standing directly in front of the legless boy, who was now on a seat and looking around contentedly. Celeste caught his eye and he flashed her a smile.

"Would you take my ticket up for me?" he asked, handing her the scrap of paper.

It took her several minutes to battle her way through the tightly packed passengers to the front of the bus. The bus made another stop before she reached the ticket receptacle behind the driver's seat and the surge of people boarding the bus helped to propel her forward.

The driver held the steering wheel with one hand while he used the other to play with another small string of beads, like the one hanging from the rear view mirror, flicking it first one way and then the other around his fingers. He had decorated his working environment with artificial flowers taped to the windscreen. A large *nazar boncuğu* hung from the rear view mirror along with a small necklace of beads with a tassel attached, a photograph of Kemal Atatürk was taped in the corner of the side window, and a small set of dolls in Turkish traditional costumes stood in lumps of glue along the dashboard. Below the *nazar* hung a silver cylinder on a chain, which presumably contained an excerpt from the Koran. All the buses Celeste had seen in Istanbul were decorated in a similar fashion, but this was probably the most elaborate she had seen. Celeste poked the two tickets into the ticket receptacle, trying to show them to the driver first but failing to catch his attention. The flame inside flickered through the slit and flared up more brightly when the two tickets landed on it.

The bus rocked and vibrated past a row of grimy grey tower blocks. Several storeys had windows with no glass and half the façade of one tower block, including several balconies, had fallen off; yet Celeste could see threadbare wet laundry hanging forlornly from makeshift washing lines attached to the windowsills and she caught a glimpse of faces inside one of the windows. Gazing from the bus window, Celeste clung to a steel bar and tried to maintain her balance as the driver careered maniacally along several more streets of houses which on first sight appeared derelict and abandoned, until she noticed children and toddlers playing in the gutter outside. Her pulse quickened with anxiety as they juddered alongside a large open space which, the first time she saw it, she had taken for a rubbish dump. Gaunt women and children concentrated intently as they picked through the refuse, selecting certain items to take home with them. On the far side of this desolate area two small bonfires burned outside the entrance to a tower block, its windows sealed off with opaque polythene.

Finally relaxing as she realised they had turned the corner into a busy main street close to Taksim Square, Celeste prepared to step off the bus, throwing one final glance at the legless boy. The moment her foot touched the pavement, she walked away so fast she was almost running. After a few yards, however, she had to stop abruptly. A lorry full of vast, jagged lumps of coal was parked diagonally in the road, its rear end blocking the pavement while several men lifted the coal, lump by lump, and dropped it down through an open coal hatch in the pavement. Their hands, wrapped in threadbare rags, were cut and bleeding from handling the rough rocks, but they continued working regardless. A river of people on the pavement flowed round the lorry and hastened on to work. Celeste's attention was drawn to a young boy among them selling bread from a round, flat basket which he held resting on his head. He could not have been more than nine years old.

"Ekmek!" he shouted out repeatedly to draw attention to his twisted bread pretzels and other fancy loaves. "Ekmek!"

Walking around the parked lorry Celeste turned her head to stare at the child and almost walked into a *hamal*, a street porter, coming the other way. His dark, shrivelled features were contorted from the exertion of carrying his load of firewood, propped on his back in a round basket the size of a kettledrum. Taking small and careful steps, he staggered along the pavement bent double, not looking ahead but keeping his gaze fixed upon the pavement; he knew the other pedestrians would clear a path for him.

Arriving at the school, Celeste greeted Mehmet, the greasy-haired receptionist and photocopying assistant, and headed up the two flights of stairs to the staff room. At last she was away from the noise and confusion of the busy city and could take a few minutes to compose herself.

Today, however, there would be no time to relax. As she emerged from the bathroom, feeling far better now that she had scrubbed her hands and face with some perfumed soap and cleanser, she was intercepted by the school principal, Sadberk.

"There has been a change," she hissed into Celeste's ear.

Sadberk had a habit of talking too quietly, forcing people to lean close to her and strain to hear what she was saying. She used it as a way of demonstrating her power over others; she was far too important to exert her lungs for the benefit of her underlings. Celeste refused to play along.

"Sorry, what did you say?" she shouted, taking a step back.

"Come into the office," hissed Sadberk, irritably.

In the office, Celeste was instructed to sit down, whilst Sadberk and the school secretary remained standing. Looking down at her sternly, they informed her that she would have a new class in the mornings as from today, since there had been a 'problem' with their previous teacher. Celeste wondered what type of a problem this could have been. Sadberk held Celeste's passport in the school safe, along with all the other foreign teachers' passports, to ensure that they could not disappear unexpectedly. The other teachers had told Celeste that English employees of the school had a habit of suddenly deciding they wanted to leave, and simply taking the first flight home without telling Sadberk their intentions. For the same reason, she paid the teachers a month in arrears, so, when Celeste's monthly salary was handed to her in an envelope, it was not for the month she had just finished working, but for the previous one.

Celeste's class had been reassigned to a new teacher called Heather, Sadberk explained in her customary intimidating whisper, to whom Celeste must give a list of all the topics she had taught so far. There were five minutes before the lesson was due to start, and Heather was waiting for her in the staff room, so she had better hurry up as the lesson must begin punctually. When Celeste found Heather, all that was visible was a mass of ginger ringlets on the top of her head as she rummaged through a cavernous brown leather shoulder bag. Coming up for air, she whipped out a cardboard folder which split open and scattered a flurry of papers all over the floor.

"Hello, are you Heather?" asked Celeste. Heather looked up at her with her startlingly intense, turquoise eyes. "Goodness, you have such blue eyes!" she exclaimed before she could stop herself.

"Yes, apparently they look like two swimming pools, I've just been informed by one of the students," Heather replied sardonically. "Are you the teacher of group 3C? You're not Turkish, are you?"

"No!" laughed Celeste. "Why on earth did you think that?"

"Because you have flat, shiny hair and you've made it stick up at the top."

"I was attacked by seven Turkish hairdressers, that's all," explained Celeste.

Celeste immediately liked the way Heather spoke to her as if they had known each other for years. Heather was older than Celeste and seemed full of self-confidence despite her scatterbrained clumsiness. Helping Heather to pick up her papers, Celeste hastily explained the grammar she had taught her class so far, and gave Heather the photocopies she had been planning to use for today's lesson.

"We can find each other at break to compare notes, after you've had a chance to meet them," suggested Celeste. "They're all very sweet. I don't know what I'll do with my new class, though. There's nobody to do a handover for me. I don't even know why Sadberk made me change group."

"She could have given me that new class," agreed Heather, "instead of making you change. Seems daft to me."

When Celeste walked into the new classroom she was struck by an atmosphere that could have been cut with a knife.

"Good morning," she greeted the students, *"Gŭnaydın."* Three of the fourteen students muttered a vague response, whilst the rest stared back at her in stony faced silence. "Let's try that again," she persisted, determined not to be beaten from the outset. "Good morning."

Silence. She stared around the room, wondering what to do.

There were only three male students. The rest of the group was young women, all of them heavily made up with frosted lipstick and their hair dyed artificial shades of aubergine or bright orange. They were dressed up to the nines in office suits, very high-heeled shoes and flashy gold and diamond jewellery. The only one different from the rest sat beside the door, her desk set slightly apart from the rest, as if ready to dash out of the room at any minute should the need arise. She was dressed entirely in black robes, her hair and face covered by a veil so that only her eyes were visible. Celeste had already learned that a girl from this strict Muslim sect was called a *dince*. According to Levent, they were hardly ever allowed out of the house without a male relative as an escort.

"I would like you each to tell me your name," Celeste announced decisively to the class, "what you do, that is, your job, and one thing you like doing in your spare time."

"What happen our other teacher?" asked a sullen looking girl in a leather mini skirt.

"I don't know," replied Celeste, honestly.

"You third our teacher in one month," one of the boys persisted.

Suddenly all the students were speaking out together in a mixture of Turkish and English, complaining that they were fed up of having new teachers, and asking how long it would be until she also left the school. Not long at all, if you carry on like this, Celeste wanted to reply.

"You need to ask Sadberk if you have questions like these," she announced as firmly as she could. "We need to start the lesson now. You first." She pointed to one of the male students on the extreme left of the room, who looked slightly less hostile than the rest.

"My name is Hakkan, I am engineer, and in spare time I like watch football," he responded obediently, to her immense relief.

"Good," said Celeste, encouragingly. "We say *'watching football'*. You next."

She indicated the girl beside him, dressed in a metallic bronze jacket with false nails to match. Her long hair had metallic highlights, and she swung it flamboyantly over her shoulder, towards Hakkan, as she nonchalantly crossed her legs before answering.

Veronica Di Grigoli

"I am Nezaket," she said lethargically, "and I don't work. I have husband. In my spare time, I like having hair coloured and nails painted and shopping."

"I see. Thank you. Good," commented Celeste. She caught the eye of the student beside Nezaket to invite her to speak next.

"My name Ayşe. I go shopping," was all she said.

"I see," commented Celeste. "You need to say "My name *is* Ayşe."

"Why?"

"Because you need a verb in the sentence," explained Celeste.

"Why?"

"Because all sentences have a verb," stated Celeste, patiently; but Ayşe was already examining her fingernails.

"Who is next?" announced Celeste, looking wretchedly at the clock. Less then five minutes of this torture session had passed..

"My name is Gul," said the girl beside Ayşe. "I go shopping."

"Original," commented Celeste.

She continued round the class, and every single girl gave the same answer, stating their name and that they went shopping. The only ones who gave a different answer were the two other boys, who were both students, and the *dince* who said that in her spare time she studied at home and helped her mother with the cooking.

Celeste looked at her watch at least three times a minute for the rest of the lesson as she worked mechanically through the exercises in the textbook. It would be pointless trying to organise any more interesting activity for this class. Conversations or games to practise grammar would be a guaranteed flop and any activity in which they were required to display some individuality would be doomed to failure. She found herself fingering Tekin's gold foil pendant hanging from her bracelet several times as she yearned for the clock to tick a little faster. When at long last the bell sounded for the end of the lesson, Celeste astounded herself and her students by being the first to flee the room. She found Heather in the photocopier room, waiting for Mehmet to copy some exercises for the next lesson. She described the class and the lesson to Heather.

"I'm sorry," sympathised Heather. "I feel as if it's my fault. I must say I'm surprised that 'dingy' is let out alone. You do know it's against the law for women to wear head coverings in public places, like state run schools and hospitals, don't you?"

"You're kidding!" said Celeste. "Why?"

"Turkey wants to be modern and secular," said Heather. "At least the richer ruling classes do. The poorer working class probably don't, since they voted for the Muslim fundamentalist party. I think they probably banned scarves as they think it should help their application to join the European Union."

"So what do the *dince*s do, then? If they can't go to school?"

"I don't know. Maybe they don't go to school at all. I just know they live in ghettos and they're usually kept on tight leads. I expect she has a brother waiting at the door to take her home after the lesson."

"You seem to know a lot about Turkey," commented Celeste. "How long have you been here?"

"I lived in Ankara for three years. I've just come here, where I hope they won't find me."

"Who's looking for you?" asked Celeste innocently.

"I don't know if they're actually looking for me. But I don't want to be found," answered Heather enigmatically.

"Didn't you want to just go back to England?"

"I can't go back there, after what happened."

It was clear Heather had a secret she did not intend to share, and Celeste realised it was time to change the subject.

"OK. How did you get on with my class?" she asked.

"Great," answered Heather, enthusiastically. "They're all very friendly, aren't they? Except for that Ahmet one."

"I like him. He's quite funny."

"He's dangerous," contradicted Heather. "Believe me, he's one to be careful of. He seems harmless, but isn't. Anyway, my favourite one in the class is that Kurdish girl with a giant nose, Itchy Anus."

"I'm sure that's not the right pronunciation!" laughed Celeste.

"Well, who wants to split hairs? What a fantastic name! Has she always been bottom of the class?"

Celeste laughed at the pun.

"Oh, yes. I gave her piles of homework," Celeste replied, grinning.

"So she got all behind," concluded Heather in delight.

Handing Heather the copies he had made, Mehmet silently took the books Celeste handed to him. She explained in Turkish the pages that she wanted copied. Mehmet, his skin pockmarked by severe acne in his youth, had particularly heavy eyebrows and hair so greasy that Celeste often wondered if it would actually drip onto the sheaves of papers he always seemed to be clutching in his hands. His fingernails, Celeste noticed with a jolt of squeamishness, were overgrown and black with dirt.

"Poor old codger," commented Heather, sympathetically studying his hand as he pressed the cover of the photocopier down over a book. "Working all day in this tiny room with no windows."

"You'd think they could find some space in the office upstairs for him," agreed Celeste, who had so far not thought about how life may be for Mehmet.

"I think Sadberk is too snobby to hang about with him," replied Heather. "I'm beginning to dislike her."

Back upstairs in the staffroom, they sat beside each other to sort out the exercises for the next hour's lesson. As Heather sat ruffling papers, Celeste suddenly noticed how profoundly sad her face looked when she was unaware that she was being looked at. It was an expression she had noticed countless times on her father's face since her mother had died. Celeste wondered how much of Heather's true character her saucy smile and barrage of schoolgirl jokes must be hiding.

"Now then, old fruit," announced Heather. "Do you want to come to my hovel for lunch? It's very near here, and I'm quite competent in the kitchen."

"That would be great," agreed Celeste.

The thought of having lunch with someone English, with whom she could share a joke, sustained her through the next two tortuous hours with her long-faced class of shopping maniacs. During the lesson she mainly set them writing exercises, not because they needed them but because it was impossible to induce them to talk, even when they knew all the requisite vocabulary. They seemed too arrogant to be bothered actually trying to learn anything new. She noticed that several of them stared hard at her opal pendant during the lesson, but nobody made any comment.

When the morning's lessons were over, Celeste spotted Bŭket chatting to Heather. One of the few Turkish teachers working at the school, Bŭket kept her hair short and dressed very simply.

"How was your last lesson with that miserable class?" asked Heather as Celeste approached.

"Miserable," replied Celeste. "I don't understand why they even bother coming to the school, since they don't seem remotely interested in actually learning anything."

"I have a class like yours," commented Bŭket. "They don't want to put in any work to learn English; they just want to buy it, somehow, the same as they buy everything else they ever covet. They're very rich and never do anything except shop for designer handbags and have beauty treatments. It's a fashionable status symbol to speak English at the moment, or to have an English friend as a kind of pet, so they book English lessons just so that they can point to their Gucci watch while they're having lunch with a friend and say 'uh oh, I'm afraid I have to go to my English lesson now.'

It's a way of showing off, the same as they show off their new designer clothes to each other."

"Yes, I noticed a lot of designer brands," commented Celeste.

"It's worse in winter," Bŭket went on, "They wear a different fur coat every day of the week. You walk into the class and there's a row of dead animals hanging up along the wall. Sometimes they're so rude to me. They look down on me because I wear Turkish-made jeans and my parents are just school teachers."

"I think they look down on everyone, actually," said Celeste. "They even try to look down on each other."

"They feel superior to me, but they're jealous because I can speak English properly. They're too lazy to actually learn a language, even though they could easily afford to go to England if they wanted to. One of them once said I couldn't possibly speak English properly because I've never been to England. They feel snobbish towards me, but this one thing makes them feel inferior, I suppose. They feel inferior to you in some way, because you're European."

"Fancy coming to lunch with us? At my house?" Heather cut in. "We're eating European food."

"That would be very nice, thank you so much," laughed Bŭket, "but my mother's expecting me at home today. She'll already have cooked something. Please, please invite me for another day."

"Tomorrow?"

"Oh, yes, thank you!" accepted Bŭket, delighted.

"By the way," asked Celeste, curious, "have you really never been to England?"

"I've never been outside Turkey," confessed Bŭket.

"Well, you speak perfect English anyway," confirmed Celeste.

"We must get going," urged Heather suddenly, "because if my fatmate arrives home before I do, she'll cook everything in the fridge and make it inedible."

"Don't you mean flatmate?" corrected Celeste.

"No, I meant fatmate. You'll understand when you see her."

Heather's flat was close to the school so they decided to go on foot, accompanying Bŭket to her bus stop on the way.

"Don't you worry about living in a dangerous neighbourhood like Cihangir?" asked Bŭket as they walked through Taksim Square together. "My parents don't allow me to go there."

"Is it that bad?" asked Heather. "Seems OK to me. The flat I live in is gorgeous."

"It's full of sleazy nightclubs, with prostitutes," said Bŭket.

"Who get men to buy them bubbly water, then they're given an exorbitant champagne bill at the end of the evening," added Celeste. "I've been warned against going there."

"Ah, that old trick," responded Heather. "I didn't realise the place was full of tarts. I suppose that's why I get hassled so much. This morning I was called 'Natasha' by some sleazy old bloke, and then another one called me the same thing."

"Someone called me the same thing this morning!" cut in Celeste. "Is that a code word for whore, or something?"

"No," explained Bŭket, "it's because there are lots of Russian prostitutes here, who they call Natashas. It even said in the newspaper recently that Russian housewives sometimes come over here for a kind of whoring holiday to save up money, and then go back to their husbands at the end of it and build an extension on their house, or whatever."

"Hmm," commented Celeste, and the three fell silent for a moment. Celeste noticed that Bŭket had fixed her gaze on the opal pendant.

"Do you like it?" she asked Bŭket.

"Well," replied Bŭket, evasively.

"What is it?" Celeste burst out, almost desperately. "Everyone keeps staring at this pendant but nobody will tell me what the big deal is."

"Didn't you know that many people consider white opals to be a curse?" asked Bŭket, opening her dark eyes wide in surprise. "In the past it was the stone of mourning, and was associated with sadness, disturbing dreams and quarrels."

"Do many people still believe that?" asked Celeste.

"Most people say they don't believe in that type of thing, but I know a lot of superstitious people. To be honest, I don't know anyone who would wear an opal, especially a white one. You'd never give one as a present, for example."

"That's odd, because this was a present," replied Celeste, wondering whether to feel offended by Leman's gift. Did Leman know about this superstition?

"The most unlucky type of opal was one which became milky while someone was wearing it," Bŭket continued. "It was believed to be sapping the wearer of their vitality and youth. People said the stone would give the wearer vivid nightmares that would gradually erode their emotions and soul, so they would descend into depression and desperation."

"You don't believe that, do you?" asked Celeste.

"No," replied Bŭket, "I'm Jewish and our religion is against superstitions. We certainly don't believe in all those old Ottoman black magic ideas."

"Are there many Jews in Turkey?" asked Heather.

Evil Eye

"About eighteen thousand, or so I've been told," answered Bŭket.

"And is it true that you all speak Spanish?" asked Heather.

"Not everyone, but in my family we do, and a lot of families do. But it's not real Spanish. Spanish people wouldn't understand us. There was a big influx of Jews from Spain in during the Inquisition in the sixteenth century, and the language we speak at home is derived from the Spanish they spoke then."

"I've read about the Turkish Jews in my guide book," commented Celeste. "They were Sephardic Jews, kicked out of Spain by Queen Isabelle and King Ferdinand of Spain."

"Yes," Bŭket continued. "People say it was in fourteen ninety-two, and that the Sultan Beyazit the Second gave them safe refuge. The Ottoman Empire always gave safe refuge to Jewish refugees, apparently."

"Say something in Spanish, go on," coaxed Heather. "I lived in Colombia for four years, I can speak Spanish."

Bŭket spoke, and Heather looked puzzled for a minute.

"Ah yes, I've got it! You said, here comes my bus."

"Well done," answered Bŭket. "Maybe it isn't such weird Spanish, after all."

"Well, I understood it."

Bŭket sprang effortlessly onto the packed bus and managed to secure herself a seat immediately. Heather and Celeste waved as the bus pulled away, then turned and headed down Istiklal Caddesi, a large shopping street reserved for pedestrians which led towards Heather's flat. The street was packed with vendors, shops which had laid out their wares on the pavement, cafés with tables and chairs crowded with people drinking coffee on the pavement outside, and buskers playing music. Celeste loved the bustling atmosphere and the explosion of vibrant colours that vied for her attention.

After taking a few side streets, they arrived at Heather's flat, which was on the third floor of an old, stone building.

"These old buildings look quite European," commented Celeste.

"Apparently this used to be the European quarter of the city. The European embassies were here when Istanbul was still the capital. That's why so many of the buildings are grand and swanky."

"What's it like inside?" asked Celeste, curious.

"You'll see."

Celeste was staggered as Heather opened the door to the flat. The apartment was spectacular. Celeste stepped onto the glossy white marble floor lit by two vast, antique chandeliers, in a room hung with very good oil paintings and furnished predominantly with antique furniture. The few modern pieces blended perfectly with the antiques, and the gentle yellow walls, brought to life by the shafts of midday sunlight beaming in through the three French windows, gave the flat a welcoming and lived-in atmosphere despite its imposing elegance.

"Not bad, eh?"

"Heather, you're so lucky to live here!" exclaimed Celeste.

"Do you fancy having a look around?" offered Heather. "Go for a wander, while I get to work in the kitchen."

A couple of novels, in French Celeste noticed, lay casually on a dark, carved wooden sideboard. She wandered along the main corridor leading from the living room towards the bathroom and bedrooms. The corridor was lined with large framed photographs of two little girls, both beautiful, with glossy black hair. In one the girls were playing together on a see-saw, in another they were by the sea. Celeste paused to look at several pictures of them when they were toddlers, and some baby photographs, presumably of the same two girls. In the first room along the corridor, Celeste found a sewing machine on a large table, festooned with fabric, ribbon, lace and beads. This was the type of room Celeste had always dreamed of having for herself, a den where she could sew and paint and study her art books in total peace. Her eye was caught by a square of yellow silk, edged with lace flowers. She walked across the room to pick the scarf up, and realised that each of the tiny flowers hanging from the rim of the scarf was a perfect miniature narcissus, woven with a needle and thread. Three sides were already filled with this exquisite lace, and the fourth was just begun. She played with the scarf, draping it one way across her arm and then the other, and was intrigued by the delicacy of the work and the way the flowers hanging from the edge of the fabric seemed to bob in an imaginary breeze.

Walking further down the corridor, Celeste peeped into a large bedroom with a four-poster bed, with soft green velvet covers and matching drapes. This flat was turning out to be her dream home. She suddenly felt envious of Heather. If only she had been lucky enough to find somewhere as wonderful as this to live!

"I'm jealous!" she shouted down the corridor to Heather.

"You haven't met Zelly, though," was Heather's reply.

"Who?"

"My flatmate, Zeliha. Go in the bathroom."

Celeste walked into the bathroom, large and spacious and decorated in black and white marble. She noted that there was some lime scale on the taps and the basin definitely needed a good clean. Looking at the shower, she found herself contemplating the largest pair of white cotton knickers she had ever seen in her life.

"Unlike normal people," explained Heather, back in the kitchen, "who put their pants in the laundry basket, Zelly Belly takes off her drawers in the shower, washes them with a bar of soap while she's in there, and then drapes them over the shower head to dry. You could sail a yacht with those things. She's got a derriere the size of Guatemala."

"Poor thing!" exclaimed Celeste. "But that doesn't mean she's a bad person."

"Of course not," agreed Heather. "I must try not to be so horrible about people. I've had such a stressful time lately that I have too short a fuse sometimes, and I seem to be turning all bitter and twisted."

What happened to you?" asked Celeste, half certain that Heather would still not be ready to tell her secret.

Heather seemed like a very nice woman and Celeste was surprised at some of her harsh comments about other people. They seemed out of character. And although she was naturally very witty, it was sometimes obvious that her barrage of jokes was a way of keeping people at arms' length.

"You mean, what happened to me in Ankara?" she replied. "It was so awful I'll probably never be the same person again."

"I'm so sorry," said Celeste simply, realising that Heather did not want to talk about it further. "What does Zeliha do that winds you up?"

"Oh, she means well, but she can already drive me nuts, and I've only been living with her for three weeks. Yesterday I got in and found she'd cooked all my food out of the fridge. She meant it as a nice surprise for me, but she'd gone and fried all the meat in margarine and smothered it in cinnamon. It was like eating the insoles from an old pair of trainers. Everything she cooks is like poo on a plate. And then there's the toothpaste all over the bathroom sink and taps, biscuit crumbs scattered all over the sofa, and her habit of slipping her smelly shoes off when we sit down to dinner."

"I suppose I can see those things would be unappealing," said Celeste, intrigued to meet this woman full of contradictions.

"I keep feeling guilty for finding her annoying," complained Heather, "because she tries so hard to please, and she has a lot of good qualities. Have you seen the things she makes? The clothes and embroidery?"

"Yes! It's wonderful stuff," confirmed Celeste. "What job does Zeliha do?"

"She designs clothes," answered Heather. "She works in some place with a French name like Maison du Polythene, or Maison du Pantaloons, something daft like that. I think she's good at her job. She brought home some clothes yesterday that were gorgeous. You can tell from this place that she has good taste. It's a shame she looks so awful herself, she doesn't wear the stuff that she designs."

"How old is she?" asked Celeste.

"About forty or forty-five, I reckon."

"Who are the girls in the photos? Are they her nieces?"

"No, her daughters. She's divorced, and their father has them. They live in some city really far away, so she only gets to see them about twice a year."

"How did her ex-husband get custody of the kids? She must have done something pretty awful."

"No, the man usually gets the kids in Turkey," explained Heather, "unless the wife has a very good lawyer."

"That's incredible! Poor old Zelly. Why do you reckon they got divorced?"

"I'm not sure, but I think he had an affair. I haven't liked to ask. She's so upset about not having her children with her. She knows their measurements perfectly and spends hours making them gorgeous clothes. Last night she spent all evening hand sewing beads onto a party dress for the older girl. She's embroidered their bed-covers by hand as well, and makes them all kinds of things. She showed me her albums of photos of the girls as soon as I moved in. Anyway, I'd better get cooking before she arrives. In fact, she's a bit late. Go in the living room and turn on the telly."

Celeste did as she was commanded, while Heather clattered around in the kitchen.

"It's the weather forecast," she called out to Heather, who immediately appeared in the doorway holding a tea towel. They watched wordlessly as the weather was foretold by a woman with bleached-blonde hair, dressed in nothing but highly revealing strips of black leather bondage gear held together by buckles and metal chains. She began the weather forecast by cracking a whip on the studio floor, like a circus lion-tamer, and then proceeded to describe the temperature and rainfall predicted for each region of Turkey in a falsely simpering voice.

"Whatever the weather may be tomorrow," she concluded, "it will be sunny for *you*."

With this she cracked her whip again, and the scene cut to a presenter announcing a lunchtime keep-fit broadcast.

"That was incredible," gasped Celeste.

"I know," agreed Heather, "and so is this. It's Zelly Belly's aerobics programme. She gets in front of the telly and follows this every day. I hope she gets home in time for you to see her."

The programme was presented by a man with an immense, bushy black moustache wearing green Lycra shorts with long narrow shoulder straps, revealing his chest full of thick black hair. He was surrounded by women,

Evil Eye

also dressed in Lycra, who followed his shouted commands and energetically copied his stretches and bends in time with the music.

"Look at that luxuriantly fluffy chest growth," said Heather. "He's so furry all over I bet he doesn't have showers. He could just get his wife to vacuum clean him instead."

Zeliha did not arrive in time to do her aerobics that day, and Celeste left without meeting her. But the meal Heather cooked was delicious.

Celeste remained intrigued and curious to meet Zeliha over the next few weeks, although most of her attention was taken up by her nightmarish class. Day by day the weather started to change. Autumn brought a chilly wind in from the sea and the humidity, instead of making Celeste sweat, started to dampen her bones and carry the bitter cold right through her.

Then something happened which made Celeste remember Zeliha and her daughters. She dreamt she was on Ferhat's yacht with Leman and Levent. They were stuck in the middle of the Bosphorus without a sail. How will we get to shore? she asked them, desperately. We are going to sail with Zeliha's knickers! came Leman's reply as, cigarette in hand, she hoisted the huge pair of knickers up the mast. As they billowed in the breeze, the yacht proceeded majestically down the Bosphorus. Let's cook dinner! cried Leman, picking up a vast cooking pot. Oh look, the pot has had a baby! Out of the cauldron peeped little Tekin, who struggled and struggled to get out, yet could not climb over the side of the pot. As Celeste reached in to free him, to save him, she realised in horror that he had no legs, just a wad of carpet tied to his little bottom like the legless boy on the bus.

Then the yacht began to rock violently, and a storm blew up suddenly and the sky turned black, and they were terrified that the yacht would sink. We need an anchor, said Ferhat. Celeste felt the opal pendant around her neck grow bigger and bigger, until it pulled her head down to the deck and she was trapped. I'll throw it in the sea! cried Leman, heaving at the massive opal. Suddenly Zeliha's two daughters surfaced from the turbulent black waves. Throw it away! Throw the opal away! they cried. Leman is evil and it is a dangerous gift! they called out from the stormy waters. But Celeste could not fight free of the heavy chain. Just as Leman heaved the gigantic opal overboard, Celeste woke up. Her heart was pounding and she was fighting for breath. She felt stifled in her stuffy room, so she opened the window wide and took several gulps of the fresh night air. She was so shaken by the horrible dream that she picked up little Bruno the bear and held him tightly in her hand as she leaned on the windowsill.

"What do you think, Bruno," she asked him, in a whisper. "Were the girls right? Is that opal a dangerous gift from an evil woman?"

As usual, Bruno said nothing, but reminded her of her mother and made her feel safer. When she realised that her feet were getting cold on the marble floor, Celeste climbed back into bed, and turned the pillow over to plump it up before lying down. Something inside the pillowcase crackled under her hand. She slid her fingers inside and felt a scrap of paper, which she pulled out. Turning on the desk lamp to see what it was, she was dumbfounded to see that it was covered in Arabic writing like the papers in the jars of water she had seen in the fridge.

For the rest of the night she lay awake, angry and frightened. As soon as she saw Leman tomorrow, she would confront her and demand to know what this was all about.

SIX

The Dancing Bear

Celeste came downstairs for breakfast at seven-thirty, but Leman had already left the house. Celeste had put the scrap of paper in her skirt pocket, and she showed it to Maryam as they made coffee together.

"I don't want tea today," explained Celeste. "I was awake half the night and I need something strong to wake me up."

"No problem," responded Maryam. "I know how to make coffee so strong you can polish shoes with it."

"Look what I found in my pillowcase," Celeste told her while she spooned coffee into the tiny, long-handled pot. "What do you think it is?"

"That's Arabic writing, isn't it?" asked Maryam.

"Yes."

"Then it must be a bit of the Koran. Arabic writing is always the Koran," stated Maryam confidently. "You have to treat it with respect. You mustn't leave it lying around, or let it fall on the floor."

"I'm not sure that's always true," said Celeste.

"Well, it's best to treat it with respect, just to be on the safe side," insisted Maryam. "You never know."

"But why would Leman put this in my pillowcase?" persisted Celeste.

"I don't know. It's quite strange," agreed Maryam. "Like the jars in the fridge. Why does she keep the Koran in the fridge?"

They laughed heartily at this idea, and Celeste settled down to read an article from the newspaper to Maryam, while she climbed up on a step ladder and started removing everything from the kitchen cupboards and scrubbing them inside with a mixture of ammonia and pine-scented detergent. When Maryam took her shoes off, Celeste noticed that the heels were worn down so far that her red woollen socks showed through holes at the back.

"What size are your feet, Maryam?" asked Celeste.

"Thirty-nine. Why?" asked Maryam.

"That's the same size as mine. Would you like some shoes? I have too many, I never wear them," she lied.

Maryam turned around on the step-ladder, tipped her head far back and made a 'tut' sound to say 'no.' She flashed one of her dazzling smiles and laughed, as if teasing Celeste. Celeste resolved to find a way to give Maryam some new shoes. Meanwhile she went upstairs to look in on baby Yakup, who was sleeping in the spare room as usual. Nowadays he cried for attention when he woke up and he had just started crawling that week, so Maryam had to put a barrier of chairs alongside the bed to stop him from falling off, should he decide to go exploring.

To her surprise Celeste found him awake and lying on his tummy, so she called down to Maryam that she was going to bathe him. She washed him almost every other day and was always satisfied to see that his skin was smooth and soft as a baby's should be. Before carrying him into the bathroom she played with him for a while on the bed, placing a toy monkey at the end of the bed and coaxing him to crawl towards it. He had quite a selection of toys at Leman's house, almost all of which Celeste had bought him. He pawed the bedspread and made his way rapidly towards the monkey, collapsing on his nose only when he had reached the toy.

"Well done!" exclaimed Celeste as she picked him up and kissed his chubby cheek. "Clever Yakup!"

When Celeste arrived cold and red-nosed at Heather's flat, the night's snowfall was still lying on the ground but already starting to melt in the winter sunshine. She climbed the two flights of stairs to the front door and was still catching her breath when Zeliha answered the door. Heather's florid descriptions of Zeliha's weight had been accurate. Zeliha was panting too, from the exertion of walking from the sofa to the door. Her obese hips swayed up and down with each step as she walked ponderously back to her seat. When she smiled at Celeste, her small eyes almost disappeared in the crumpling creases of fat surrounding them and the only feature which stood out from her face was her long hooked nose. Her shoulder length hair, forming a thin and fluffy halo around her head, had once been bleached, but now had more than three inches of black and grey roots.

While introducing herself, Celeste noticed that Zeliha was working on the yellow silk scarf that she had noticed in the little room when she had come to the flat for lunch with Heather.

"I love that lace," she commented. "Is it a traditional Turkish thing?"

Yes," answered Zeliha, suddenly glowing with enthusiasm. "It's called 'Oya.' It's traditional in most of Anatolia." She had started speaking English, which she spoke well, but as she warmed to the subject she switched into Turkish. "My mother and grandmother started teaching me to make this type of lace when I was about six years old, but it takes years of practise to make it well. Some people include beads or little pieces of material or even paper, but in my family we just use thread."

"Do you make a lot of this type of lace?" asked Celeste.

"Yes. The women in my village used to make them to show their feelings," answered Zeliha, obviously delighted that Celeste was so interested.

"How?" asked Celeste.

"Some of the different types of flowers have different meanings. For example, when a girl got married she would wear a pepper motif if she hated her new husband, or a pansy if she was happy. It's dying out now, but in the past this was how a woman could express what she felt, when women were completely repressed and unable to speak out. Some flowers have different meanings in different regions."

"What do those flowers represent?" asked Celeste, taking the scarf from Zeliha to scrutinise the tiny narcissi.

"This flower represents sorrow, loneliness and separation," replied Zeliha. "There are lots of Turkish myths where narcissi symbolise separation."

"Why are you making something with a sad meaning?" asked Celeste, suddenly realising this question would have been better unasked.

"My daughters," answered Zeliha simply.

She paused in silence and, looking at her eyes sparkling like two tiny black beads, Celeste wondered if she were about to cry. Suddenly Zeliha turned to take a biscuit from a large oval plate on the sofa behind her. Popping it into her mouth, she lifted the plate to offer one to Celeste.

"Oh, no thank you," responded Celeste. "I had a very big breakfast today."

Putting the plate back on the sofa, Zeliha took another two biscuits and put them into her mouth together, chewing them with urgency.

"Sorry about looking like Quasimodo," Heather greeted them as she rattled the front door open and dumped two plastic bags of groceries on the floor. Standing up, she flicked her ginger hair back and rubbed the small of her back as the curls bobbed back into place around her face.

"I went to a *hamam* yesterday afternoon," she explained. "Big mistake."

"What happened?" asked Celeste, noting that Heather did indeed seem unable to stand up straight.

"Well, basically, I was going to just wallow in the hot bath, and hoping to see some belly dancing, which the women tend to do at the baths when they feel perky. But some Australian woman in the queue convinced me to have a Turkish massage. It was wonderful, she said. My foot!"

"What happened?"

"I was grabbed by some scary wrestler type, all muscular with a massive moustache, who proceeded to thump and whack me about as if we were going several rounds in the ring. At one point he wrenched my legs open and got his hands right up towards my crotch, then pounded my muscles to a bruised pulp. Look at this."

Heather lifted her skirt and showed Celeste that she really did have bruises all over her legs. Zeliha, who had already seen the injuries, was continuing to eat biscuits with both hands.

"He must have had some kind of hatred of women, or something. He was just trying to pulverise me. I hurt absolutely everywhere."

"What about the Australian woman? Did she get the same thing?"

"No, she came out looking relaxed and saying she felt great. Either Australians like that kind of thing, or else she got a different masseur."

"Would you rather not go out today? If you can't walk properly, maybe I should just take Tekin out for the day on my own."

"No way!" protested Heather. "The walking will be good for me."

"Have a biscuit," offered Zeliha. "That'll make you feel better."

"No thanks," declined Heather. "I feel a bit queasy. It was so smelly out there. It's kind of smoggy. Let's just have a quick coffee and go."

While Heather put the shopping away, Zeliha made coffee and continued to eat the biscuits, which she had placed on the kitchen table. She had somehow managed to tip the plate and scatter a flurry of crumbs all over the tablecloth.

"Leman was cross that I'd promised to take Tekin out," said Celeste. "She said it was unfair to give special treatment to just one of the kids. I suppose she's right really."

"What is it about him that made you want to give him special treatment?" asked Heather.

"Well, he just asked me. He asked if I would take him out for day. How could I say no?"

That was not, strictly speaking, the whole truth. In reality, Tekin had been particularly quiet one day at the orphanage when Celeste started showing the boys photographs of her brothers. When she had taken him aside to ask quietly if something was the matter, he had replied that he used to have a lot of photographs of his auntie, the one who was coming to take him home to her house, but that they were all lost in the earthquake, so now he did not have a photograph of his parents, or his aunt, or in fact of anyone. Then he had repeated to Celeste, as he had done the first day they met, that she looked a lot like his aunt, who also had blue eyes and long, wavy brown hair.

Celeste had offered to draw pictures of his aunt and parents doing the things he most liked to remember about them. He described his mother knitting and chopping vegetables to make stew, which Celeste did her best to draw for him. She drew several pictures of Tekin helping his father while he sawed wood to do odd jobs around the house, and washed the car.

Then Tekin described his aunt playing with him on the living room floor and bringing presents from America, lovely exciting things with Mickey Mouse and Bugs Bunny on them; so Celeste drew his aunt arriving laden with bags and suitcases, in her red dress which was Tekin's favourite, and then a picture of her heating milk in a saucepan for Tekin to drink at bedtime. Tekin handled the pictures as if they were precious antique manuscripts and Celeste promised to bring a scrapbook for him to stick them all into next time she came.

"I wish I could go out in the city with my aunt," Tekin had said in his tiny voice as he stared at the picture Celeste had just drawn of her helping him do a jigsaw puzzle. "She used to take me to see lots of places when I lived in the old house, the one that fell down. She used to take me out for the whole day to see places that I didn't know."

"I'll take you out," Celeste had promised, impulsively.

No sooner had the words left her mouth than she had realised what a mistake she had made. This would be so unfair to the other boys. But how could she break a promise to a child now she had made it? Eventually, she had guiltily lied to Leman that Tekin had asked her to take him out, and that she had not known how to refuse, as he had seemed so upset at the time. Leman had agreed that she could not break her promise, but had warned her it broke all the orphanage's rules and she would certainly not allow it again.

"Coffee's ready," announced Zeliha, spilling some of it onto the hob as she poured it into the cups, and letting some drip onto the floor as she swayed towards the table.

"Oh, I forgot," said Heather, twisting the first empty carrier bag into a ball and dipping into the second bag. "There was a letter for you downstairs." She took a large envelope from the second shopping bag and passed it to Zeliha, who gasped with excitement.

"It's the photos of my daughter's birthday party!" she exclaimed in delight, tearing the envelope open hastily. "She was nine last week," she explained to Celeste.

Now that she was talking about her daughter, she looked different. Her face lit up, her smile looked genuine and happy, and she glowed. But as she flicked through the photographs, her demeanour changed. The transformation was truly distressing to witness as her face fell and her eyes crumpled into tears. Putting the photographs on the table, she said something neither Heather nor Celeste understood and tried to hide her face completely behind her hands as she sobbed uncontrollably. Suddenly she drew in a deep, shrieking breath as she fought to stop crying, but her shoulders shook and her whole torso started to shudder, the fat quivering.

Heather put an arm on her shoulder and leaned forwards, glancing at the photographs to try to understand what had provoked this reaction. When Celeste saw the way Heather looked at Zeliha, she knew that Heather understood exactly how Zeliha was suffering. She could feel her pain as if it were physically becoming part of herself.

"Oh," said Heather, sounding surprised and shocked as she looked at the pictures on the table. "She didn't wear the dress you made her."

Zeliha sniffed loudly, rubbing her hands across her red face to wipe away the tears and accidentally smearing a streak of mucus from her nose across one cheek. She tried to speak, but was still unable to control her voice, simply letting out shuddering gasps as the sobbing calmed down.

Celeste sat beside Zeliha and put a hand awkwardly on her arm. She had only just met her and did not know what to say. She had passed hours crying like this after her mother died, not immediately but after quite a few months, when the disbelief and anger had died down. She had always hidden herself alone in her room so that her brothers, and especially her father, would not have to take care of her; they had their own feelings to deal with. She normally felt the tears welling up in her for several hours, and could contain them and finish whatever job she happened to be doing, but all the while knowing that an eruption was building up inside her and, sooner or later, she would be unable to hold it back any longer. Finally the lid she held on her emotions would burst open.

"I planned so carefully to make her exactly the dress she wanted," Zeliha explained eventually. "She's wearing the dress that her stepmother bought her. She told me about it on the phone. I don't understand."

Heather had magically produced a box of tissues and was already suggesting that Zeliha telephone her daughter.

"You'll feel better if you speak to her, and maybe she'll tell you about the dress."

Zeliha took several biscuits with her and went to her bedroom to call her little girl.

"She worked for weeks on that dress," explained Heather, when she was out of earshot. "It was a real work of art, with hand embroidered flowers and handmade lace on the sleeves. She got the design from one of her French magazines. She asked her daughter what her favourite colours and flowers were and she slaved over it day and night. I can't believe her daughter didn't wear it. Can you imagine how rejected she must feel?"

"Poor, poor Zeliha," said Celeste.

When Zeliha came back into the kitchen, her eyes were still red but she looked far happier.

"She saved the dress I made for wearing to the professional photographer," explained Zeliha. "She didn't want to risk spoiling it while she was eating party food and playing with her friends. She told me she's having a poster photo made for me, but it was meant to be a surprise for next time I go over to see her."

Heather put a reassuring hand on Zeliha's back again.

"Do you feel better now, old fruit?" she asked gently.

Zeliha nodded.

"Would you like to come out with us today?" invited Heather. "It would be fun if you come with us."

"That's kind, but I have a few jobs I need to do," replied Zeliha. "I'll be fine on my own, really."

By the time Heather and Celeste were ready to leave the flat, Zeliha had emptied the plate of biscuits.

The journey to the orphanage took longer than they had planned, partly because it briefly began snowing again. They took two buses and had a long walk from the bus stop, which neither of them could face, so they decided to take a taxi for the last part of the journey. When they arrived, Tekin was outside in the front yard with a group of other boys, trying to teach Pazar the dog to stand on his back legs and walk. The taxi pulled in through the wide gates and as Celeste and Heather stepped out they were mobbed by the boys.

"He can take three steps now!" Tekin told Celeste excitedly. "We hold his front legs and he walks with his back legs, but he can do three steps all alone!"

"Yes!" confirmed Bŭlent, "we want to teach him to walk all the way from the door to the gate."

Celeste laughed at their enthusiasm, and asked if they knew who Heather was.

"This is your English friend," said Tekin, immediately. "Is she coming out with us?"

"Yes," confirmed Celeste.

She suddenly felt eaten up with guilt at the favouritism she was showing to Tekin.

"I'll take the rest of you boys for days out as well," she promised them. "A few at a time." Their beautiful, innocent eyes looked at her hopefully, but the boys said nothing. "I promise," she reassured them.

She kissed and hugged each of the boys before they walked off down the road, Celeste and Heather holding Tekin's hands between them. Celeste had to roll up the sleeves of his too large anorak to find his hands, hidden far inside. She turned back to wave to the boys every few steps, until they were out of sight round the corner.

After a brief bus journey and some more walking, Celeste's skirt hem was beginning to feel soggy. Her skirt was longer than her coat and the last four inches, which hung out below the hem, were splashed with dirty, melting snow every time a car drove past. They stopped to ask, for the second time, directions to the *Mısır Çarşısı* or Egyptian Bazaar, the spice market which they had been told was very close. The woman gave them different directions from the previous woman they had asked, but she reassured them that it was not far. They plodded on in the snow, Celeste coughing frequently and her feet gradually turning numb.

"Oh look!" said Tekin, "Look!"

He tugged at Celeste's hand. She looked around and there, walking along behind its owner was a huge brown bear, on a flimsy lead, just as if the man were out for a stroll with his dog. The bear tiptoed over the scattered patches of melting snow on the pavement, placing each paw delicately as if it were afraid of stepping on something which could hurt it. Its vast, soft sides rippled, the fat quivering under its shiny fur with each step, and its head hung down in a melancholy stoop. The man, carrying a drum on his back, was pulling at the lead to hurry the bear up which, although it was too lazy to walk any faster, was also too forlorn to bother raising its great paw and lashing out at him.

Celeste and Heather each held one of Tekin's hands and followed, until the man stopped in an open space, under the overcast sky, and waited for a crowd to gather. Before long a modest crowd had accumulated in drifts, and the man was satisfied that there were enough people to collect a reasonable amount of money. He unclipped the bear's lead, stepped back, and started to beat on the drum. The bear raised its nose and front legs high up into the air, until it stood more than seven feet tall, balanced on two impossibly tiny looking back feet, and then it started to hop and totter from one paw to the other. The bulk of its body did not move much, but each time it landed silently on the ground its whole adipose body jarred and shuddered, and its flesh trembled from shoulder to hip. The way it danced looked as if the ground were burning, as if it were trying in vain to keep both feet off the pavement at the same time. All the while it moved its head slightly, from one side to the other, as if it were afraid of every single person in the crowd.

"I wonder how they train a bear to do that" whispered Celeste to Heather, in English. "The poor thing looks so moth-eaten and unhealthy, I bet that bloke's horrible to it."

"Yes, I'm sure," said Heather, and then she suddenly looked mischievously at Celeste. "You know what it looks like?"

"What?"

"It looks like Zeliha doing her aerobics in front of the telly."

"You're so mean!" exclaimed Celeste, but she laughed. Then after a few moments she added "Come on, let's go. This is horrible." She bent down to Tekin and repeated to him in Turkish "Shall we go?"

"OK" he answered, and as she led him away by the hand he stared back over his shoulder at the bear, and craned his neck until they went round a corner and it was out of sight.

"Was the bear a boy or a girl?" Tekin wanted to know, after walking in silence for a couple of minutes.

"A boy," decided Celeste.

"Is the bear still there?"

"Yes."

"Has he finished dancing?"

"Um, yes, I think so."

"Does he like dancing?"

Were his questions ever going to end?

"Oh, yes, he does it because he enjoys it," she lied. "Wasn't he sweet?"

Tekin did not answer.

"Has he got a Mummy bear?" he asked after another pause. So that was what this was about.

"Well, he doesn't need a mummy now, because he's a grown up Daddy bear."

They were not as near to the Spice Market as the woman had said and, after walking for almost twenty minutes, all three of them felt frozen by the time they found it. Tekin sang a song on the way, to try to make Celeste feel better, he said. Celeste loved hearing Tekin sing, partly because the Turkish songs he sang sounded so exotic and strange compared to English children's songs that she was intrigued to hear them, and partly because his piping little voice was so clear and sweet. She was blowing her nose and sniffing constantly, and her ears ached in the cold wind. She turned her coat collar up as high as she could but still felt the chilly air against her neck. Despite feeling unwell her cold cheeks glowed such a rosy pink that she looked a picture of health. The humidity of the air had made her hair curl tighter than usual so her face was framed by a mass of wavy ringlets.

It was warmer inside the market. It was a single covered street, stretching as far as the eye could see and lined along each side with open-fronted shops. Each one radiated dazzling light and was crammed with barrels, baskets and sacks spilling over with foods and spices in warm and glowing colours, sprawling out onto the pavement. A hundred different aromas hung heavy in the air. There were huge bowls of dried dates and apricots, barrels of apple tea and lime tea, red peppers stacked on black peppers, jars of caviar from Russia, sweets like tubes which you could slice, every type of spice and herb, strange dried leaves and yellow flowers for herbal infusions, dark red rose hips in sacks and teetering powdery pyramids of sugar-dusted Turkish delight. The cries of the hawkers bellowed out from all sides and echoed back again from the tiled ceiling.

"*Buyurun*!" they called out, urging people to come and try their wares until all their voices blended into the bewildering melee of sounds and colours and smells and jostling crowds. Heather and Celeste again took Tekin by a hand each, sure they would otherwise lose him, and slowly made their way along the street. They stopped by one shop and the man gave Tekin a dried fig and some pink sweets to eat. He thought Tekin was Celeste's son, and told her the likeness between them was remarkable. Heather decided to buy a packet of *sahlep* from him.

"Have you drink this before?" he checked. "You know how make this?" He was proud of speaking English and wanted to practise.

"Yes I have, thank you" she answered, her ginger curls bobbing as she nodded her head. But the shopkeeper ignored her and explained it anyway.

"It is white tapioca drink, very good for you, in winter it's keep you warm and makes you strong against the snow. You make with hot water, and stirring a lot in cup. Then put also cinnamon on top. You have cinnamon? I can sell you cinnamon, best quality cinnamon in market, better than others shops. You want?"

"Oh, go on then," Heather answered, sounding a little weary.

"Go? You want me go?" he asked. "I go home and you work in shop? Good idea!" he joked.

"I meant go on then, sell me some cinnamon."

"Oh."

He poured some powdered cinnamon into a paper bag, and sealed it up by rolling the top over and over, then twisting the corners into little ears. He was intrigued by Tekin, and he also assumed Celeste was his mother. Celeste explained that Tekin was Turkish, and had no mother, but that she taught English at the orphanage as often as possible, to spend time with him and the other boys.

"And girls? No girls in the orphanage?"

"There are other orphanages for the girls," said Celeste.

"I think less homes for girl orphans. Terrible things happen to girls without parents, they end up not in orphanage but in other places. Really terrible things for woman - you understand? - even though they are very young. Many bad men don't care how young they are."

The man patted Tekin vigorously on the head, ruffling his light brown hair, and gave him another dried fig. Tekin waved at him as they left. As they walked on, Celeste began to feel dazed by the confusion of colours and voices around her. Her ears throbbed and her throat burned. A man standing by a shop to her left beckoned and called to her.

"You have a cold, I see you're not well," he said in Turkish. Then he repeated it in English. "I give you tea, can make you better."

She drifted over towards him, and he started asking about her symptoms. Did she have a sore throat? Yes. Did she have a runny nose? Yes. Did she sneeze a lot? No. Were her ears hurting? Yes, terribly. He was scooping small dried flowers, leaves and little closed buds, all in different quantities, out of barrels crowded at the front of the shop and tipping them into the bowl of a huge old set of brass weighing scales as she answered each question.

"This is Health Tea," he announced proudly. "It's make you very strong. Very good for you and your little boy. You leave in tea pot, five total minutes before drinking, not shorter time, no cheating."

He mixed everything together in the scales by plunging his fingers to the bottom and scooping up handfuls of the mixture, which he scattered back into the bowl. Then he poured it into two cellophane bags. He took a very long time writing 'Health Tea' in Turkish with a pencil on two white labels, before sealing the bags with them. He asked Celeste if she wanted one bag or both. When she enquired what the price would be, it was so low she almost laughed out loud. She took both.

They bought Tekin a bag of dates even though he said he did not actually want anything, and Celeste also bought a bag full of various sweets and dried fruit for Tekin to give to the other boys at the orphanage. When they emerged from the covered arcade of the Egyptian Bazaar, they realised that it was already dusk, and large flakes of snow whirled overhead in the dark grey sky. They decided to go back to Heather's flat in Cihangir so that Celeste and Tekin could warm up before she took him back to the orphanage.

Celeste wanted to try some of her health tea, so Heather duly produced the teapot. Celeste checked it carefully before putting her tea inside and could not resist washing it up before using it. The inside was slightly discoloured with tea stains which she knew she could remove with a bit of elbow grease. Tekin stood on a chair beside the sink to watch her, and play with the bubbly water.

"There," she declared with satisfaction when the pot was snowy white inside and out and looked like new.

"You're a bit of a maniac for cleaning, aren't you?" laughed Heather. "I wish you came round more often!"

"The tea will be much nicer out of a clean pot," insisted Celeste. "And it's much more pleasant using things that look as if they're new. Everything's more beautiful when it's clean."

Veronica Di Grigoli

She let Tekin put the health tea in the pot and then they watched the snow falling outside the window while it brewed. When four minutes had gone by Heather picked up the teapot to pour out a cup of the tea.

"No! He said 'five total minutes'," Celeste protested. "No cheating."

"Well, maybe it needs stirring then" suggested Heather, and so they took the lid off and, to their amazement and delight, saw a blossoming flower garden inside the teapot. Blooms which looked as fresh as if they had just been picked, in all the glorious colours of the rainbow, were piled on top of each other right up to the brim of the pot. The red buds had drunk up the water and swollen, the flower petals had opened up, yellow and orange and vibrant violet, and the leaves had gorged themselves on fluid and were as bright and juicy as if they were freshly picked. The tea poured a sparkling golden colour into the cups and they drank it slowly, savouring every sip. Tekin swung his little legs to and fro under the table as he drank his tea.

"I like this," he said. "My mother used to give me tea sometimes, when it was winter and we got cold going out."

"Did it get very cold where you lived?" asked Celeste.

"Really cold in the winter," answered Tekin. "She used to rub my hands and feet when we got in, to warm them up. My aunt always visited in winter, for New Year, and when she came she would sleep in my bed with me. Then it was lovely and warm! She cuddled me all night."

"It's nice having someone to cuddle at night, isn't it?" agreed Heather.

"It's nice having someone to do things with," said Tekin. "Sometimes I pretend Celeste is my aunt. She looks almost the same. Is it all right to pretend you're my aunt?" asked Tekin.

"Well, yes I think it is," said Celeste, "so long as you remember it's only pretending."

She kissed the top of his head and caressed his light brown hair, smoothing it down gently. Sometimes she had entertained the fantasy of taking Tekin home with her and looking after him with her brothers. She had managed to remind herself every time that this would be impossible and that she was only thinking such thoughts because she was homesick and missed her brothers almost all the time. Celeste decided to draw a picture of Tekin while they finished sipping the tea. She always kept a small sketch pad in her bag so she took it out along with some good pencils and drew a quick sketch. She even surprised herself at what a good likeness she managed to produce in so little time.

"Does Mr. Demirsar at the orphanage have someone to cuddle at night?" asked Tekin suddenly.

"I don't know. Why?" asked Celeste.

"He sometimes says strange things to us," answered Tekin. Heather and Celeste exchanged glances over Tekin's head.

"What type of things?" asked Celeste, trying to make her voice sound calm and casual.

"I don't know. Some of the boys say he does strange things," answered Tekin. "In the night."

Heather made a face at Celeste, who responded by standing up and making a cutting motion across her throat to tell Heather to drop it. She would mention this to Leman as soon as she got home. The three of them sat in silence for a few moments, drinking slowly while Celeste added a few finishing touches to her drawing of Tekin and slipped it back into her bag. Celeste noticed, just for a moment, the profoundly miserable look on Heather's face that she had seen in the staffroom the first day she had met her. She wondered what could have happened to her in Ankara that had affected her so much she was not only afraid to remain there, but even to return to England.

As the tea flowed down Celeste's throat she could feel it being soothed. Her ears stopped throbbing, and her cold seemed to go away. It warmed them all from the inside, and they sat together in the kitchen cosily watching the snow pile up on the windowsill.

"You'd better not hang around too long or you'll be stranded here," said Heather.

In a heavy snowfall at night the taxi drivers would go home and refuse to take any passengers, because driving conditions on the steep and narrow roads became too dangerous. There would be no way to get home after dark.

"Yes, we really have to go now, Tekin," said Celeste.

"Here, have some *ayran* to drink on the way home," offered Heather as they were leaving, taking two cartons from the fridge and inserting them into Celeste's bag.

They found a taxi after waiting long enough to make their feet go numb again and Tekin's little nose go pink at the end. The driver took a far longer route then normal, insisting it was the only way to avoid difficult roads in the snow. Celeste suspected he was taking advantage of the chance to work up a high fare since she was foreign and he had therefore assumed she had plenty of money, and also did not know the city very well. Her suspicions hardened when she realised he had driven her all the way to the coast and was following the scenic road along the shore of the Bosphorus.

"You know, this is sea not is river," he told her in his poor English, even though she had already demonstrated her fluent Turkish.

Veronica Di Grigoli

"I know," answered Celeste wearily. "It's very nice but I've seen it before. Please try not to waste any more time. Take the most direct route from here."

The driver performed a U-turn and followed the same road he had taken for about ten minutes before diving into a side road.

"You visit Turkey with your little boy?" the driver asked. "Where your husband?"

"He's not my son," said Celeste wearily. "He lives at the orphanage. And I live in Bebek. And my husband lives there too." She winked at Tekin, who grinned back.

When eventually they arrived at the orphanage, Celeste made the driver wait for her on the forecourt to take her on to her house in Bebek while she went inside with Tekin. She would very much have liked to find a different driver but she knew it may be impossible to find one by now.

It was not time for the other boys in the dormitory to go to bed yet but Tekin was tired and wanted to go to sleep early and, especially, to be tucked up in bed by Celeste before she went away. As she pulled the blankets up around his shoulders, he asked her about the dancing bear again.

"What's the bear doing now?"

"Sleeping."

"Is he happy?"

"Yes, I think so. I'm sure he's happy. He's probably at home with his wife."

"I don't think he's happy," said Tekin. "He looked at me, and he was telling me with his eyes that he was sad. I think everyone pretends he's happy so they don't have to worry about him."

And his words stabbed her in the heart, because she had been trying to pretend to herself all day that Tekin was happy, and he knew it.

When Celeste left the orphanage, the taxi driver told her she had accumulated a small fortune on the meter. By this time she did not care, as the snow was so heavy that she was simply relieved to have a taxi to take her home. She took out her *ayran* carton and drank it almost in one gulp, then tried to read the story printed on the reverse. She had to lean very close to the window and stare at it hard, picking out the words by the irregular bursts of light from the houses and shops they passed. Few of the streets had lampposts so, for much of the time, she could not read at all. But, eventually, she managed to decipher the whole story:

'A few people from another village were in Akşehir on business. At the end of the day, they knocked on Nasreddin Hoca's door. "Hoca Effendi, we were in town and thought we should pay you a visit. Here is a rabbit as a token of our respect for you." Hoca welcomed the guests as is the Turkish

tradition and asked them to stay for dinner. Hoca's wife cooked the rabbit and they all ate heartily.

'A few days later, there were people at the door again whom the Hoca didn't know. "Nasreddin Hoca, we are relatives of those folks who brought you the rabbit," they explained. They were passing through Akşehir and they thought they would drop by. Nasreddin Hoca and his wife welcomed them and served soup for dinner. "It's the broth of the rabbit," explained the Hoca.

'Another couple of days passed and there was yet another group of strangers at Hoca's door. "We come from the neighbouring village of the people who brought you the rabbit," they said. Hoca had no choice but reluctantly to let them in. When it was dinner time, he brought a large pot full of well-water to the table. "What's this, Hoca Effendi?" inquired the disgruntled guests. "It's the broth of the broth of the rabbit," Hoca snapped back.'

When she arrived at the house in Bebek, it was past nine o'clock and the family had already eaten dinner, so Celeste made herself a quick sandwich to eat in the kitchen. She brewed another cup of 'health tea' to drink with it. Her clothes were damp and she wanted to change, but she was so hungry she decided to eat first, and then soak in a long, hot bath. As she was washing the plate and knife, Leman came into the kitchen and asked about her day. She was still dressed in her work clothes; a lime green mini skirt and jacket, the pockets trimmed with narrow strips of black patent leather, and patent leather shoes to match.

"I loved the market," said Celeste, "and Tekin enjoyed being out for the day. I think everyone who saw him found him adorable."

"What is adorable?" asked Leman.

"It means, something or someone you can love very, very much," explained Celeste.

"Someone you love very much," repeated Leman, thoughtfully. "Adorable. All the boys love Tekin very much," she went on. "They protect him, because he is the youngest. But you are a adult, it's different for you. You must never favouritise one boy over the others. It isn't fair."

Celeste knew that was true, and felt guilty. But how could she not favour Tekin, when he favoured her?

"Leman, I have to ask you something," said Celeste suddenly, looking serious. "What do you think of Mr. Demirsar?"

"The caretaker? He is good at cleaning."

"Yes, but as a person? Tekin said something strange about him. He said he does strange things to some of the boys, at night."

"No way," responded Leman. "I understand what you saying. We check all staffs for that type of thing very carefully. Definitely not through."

"You mean, 'not true'?"

"Yes, not through. No way."

To show that the discussion was over, Leman stood up and took the box of tablets from the kitchen drawer beside the sink. She sat back down at the table arranging the various blister packs in rows, ranking and sorting them according to colour. Lighting herself a cigarette, she then started to rearrange them, with Ferhat's tablets in one platoon and hers in another, and finally a third squadron of general first aid tablets, mainly antibiotics sold over the counter and various cold and diarrhoea remedies. She would insist that Levent take a single antibiotic tablet every time she heard him cough, convinced that this was the best way to hold infections at bay.

Celeste sat down at the table opposite her and put the scrap of paper from her pillowcase on the table. She had decided to confront Leman.

"Leman," she began, "What's this? I found it in my pillowcase last night."

Leman snatched up the paper and immediately screwed it into a little ball. Celeste noticed that she took care to put it in her pocket, rather than throwing it into the ashtray as she would with most small items she wished to dispose of.

"It is nothing, just some rubbish thing."

"What, exactly?" persisted Celeste.

"It some piece of Koran, it's a prayer for Levent. I put in pillow case for him to bring protection. It's Turkish custom. Maryam must have been mistaking pillows and swapping. I must reprimand her. She is a fool."

So Maryam had been right. It seemed fairly harmless to place a prayer inside a son's pillow case. But had Maryam honestly muddled up the pillows? Celeste had spent so many sleepless hours of the night feeling angry and baffled, determined to find out what kind of sinister machinations Leman was plotting, and now, suddenly, the wind had been taken out of her sails. She must have let her imagination run away with her. And yet there was something that did not convince her. Why was there an egg in a bowl by Levent's bed? And what about the opal necklace? Celeste noticed Leman glance at her neck to check that she was still wearing it.

What you are drinking?" Leman asked, suddenly.

"It's herbal tea, from the market. It makes me feel better, especially my throat."

"From Egyptian Bazaar? Turkish tea?"

"Yes."

"That is good. Turkish tea better than French tea. Rubbish stuff from France."

"Hmm," responded Celeste.

Evil Eye

"You want melon?" offered Leman unexpectedly.

As was her usual way, she toddled to the fridge and removed a large yellow honeydew melon without waiting for Celeste's answer. She brought it to the table and strutted back across the room to fetch two plates and a very large knife. Sitting back down at the table, she started to hack clumsily into the melon's tough peel, the knife slewing sideways and making a crooked incision into the melon. Celeste fidgeted with impatience. She was very good at slicing and chopping fruit and vegetables. She knew she was not particularly good at cooking, but she could slice and dice anything with mathematical precision. She approached it as she would any one of her handicrafts or artistic creations, with calm control. Watching someone struggle to do something that she knew she could easily do for them could drive her insane with frustration.

"Let me do that for you," she suddenly heard herself say.

"OK" said Leman immediately, pushing the plate and the melon towards her.

Removing the knife, Celeste twisted the melon and started to make a clean cut straight down the melon from top to bottom. She lost herself in the work, becoming oblivious of everything around her. She was hardly aware of her hair slipping down over her shoulder as she bent over the melon, which was rapidly becoming a neat row of slices, all identical in size. Her mother had often said that Celeste would not have noticed a bomb going off beside her when she was concentrating on doing something with her hands.

When Celeste had finished, she looked up and realised that Leman had poured herself a shot of whisky and was using it to wash down her antacid tablet.

"I got something for you," Leman proclaimed suddenly, strutting out of the room with her cigarette still in her hand. She reappeared a few moments later holding a carrier bag. "It cold now and you don't have got clothes that are good for this weather. You only got house clothes. You can have these. They are things I don't wear now. If you want them."

Leman took a soft, cream mohair sweater from the bag, and a blue lamb's wool polo-neck jumper. They looked unworn, and were just the clothes Celeste needed. She had not anticipated such cold in Turkey and had not brought enough suitable clothing for this winter weather.

"These are lovely, thank you."

"You don't mind second hand?" checked Leman.

"No, they look good as new," said Celeste, wondering why she had never seen Leman wearing such tasteful clothes as these. "They're beautiful."

"They just old rubbish used things," contradicted Leman dismissively, "but you need something. You cannot go outside like this."

She picked up a small part of Celeste's still damp and mud-spattered skirt between her index finger and thumb, and let it fall as if it were too repulsive to touch with her bare hands.

When Celeste went up to her room, the first thing she did was prop up the picture she had drawn of Tekin against a pile of books on her desk. When she looked at the clothes Leman had given her, she realised that one of Leman's 'old rubbish used things' still had a label attached inside: it had never been worn. Why had she said those things when she had given it to Celeste ? Did she want to prevent Celeste feeling awkward about her generosity? If she wanted to avoid making Celeste feel like a scrounger, why give her anything at all? Or did Leman like handing out charity simply because it made her feel like a superior person?

That night Celeste had a nightmare. It was a dream she had had probably more than a hundred times as a child, a recurring nightmare which, for a long period of her childhood, had terrified her so much she would leave the light on all night for fear of falling asleep. The dream began with the little boy, Adam Miller, who had lived next door to her. They were born one week apart and always played together. There was a hole in the fence between their gardens and their parents knew that, if one of them went missing from the garden, they would be next door.

One day Adam had simply vanished. The police searched the neighbourhood and asked everyone questions. People made posters and everyone kept their eyes open all the time, but Adam was never seen again. His parents never found out if he was kidnapped, or murdered, or if he had simply run away and got lost. They lived day after day not knowing if he was dead or alive, not knowing whether to mourn or to search. Celeste, at her mother's suggestion, used to visit his parents sometimes, the way she did when Adam was still there. They kept his bedroom exactly as he had left it, with his school books on his desk and his toys cleaned and arranged on his bed, ready for when he came home. His clothes and primary school uniform still hung in the wardrobe long after the little ghost who had owned them would have been into his teens.

Celeste grew up seeing his parents living in a crisis that never ended. When her mother had developed stomach cancer, the family had lived in a crisis for a month, living on snacks and never sitting down to a cooked meal, going back and forth from the house to the hospital and hardly ever finding time to wash themselves or clean their clothes. Celeste had seen Mr. and Mrs. Miller live like this for fifteen years, turning into emaciated shadows of their former selves. Sometimes Celeste would look out of her bedroom window at night and see Mrs. Miller wandering round the garden, as if perhaps she were still looking for Adam there and, when she walked up and down like this at night, Celeste knew that she would always finish up sitting on the bench under the damson tree, at the end of the garden, weeping silently for most of the night.

Celeste's dream always began with Mrs. Miller under the damson tree. Celeste would go into the garden to console her, and would suggest that they go into the street to look for Adam. And a man with bristling stubble on his chin would come along and tell them that he knew where Adam was, and that he would show them. Celeste would wake up her family and they would all get into the family's Ford hatchback, with Mrs. Miller, and follow the directions of this man to where Adam could be found. They drove deeper and deeper into a dense, dark forest, too gloomy and thick even for the light from the car headlights to penetrate the murky blackness. Finally they would pull up beside a stagnant pond, so black and deep that nothing thrown in would ever reach the bottom.

"Adam is in here," the man would say to Celeste, his lip curling, "and you must get him."

Then he would throw Celeste into the black water and, as she struggled to stay afloat, to fight for air and swim to the filthy mud beside the bottomless pond, her family would calmly get back into the car and they would all drive away, as if they had forgotten her already, as if she had never existed. Just as she fought for breath, in the moment she found she could no longer stay afloat and was sinking beneath the black water, looking at her family disappearing through a layer of swirling water dark as ink, Celeste would wake up gasping for breath. She always found the sheets drenched with sweat and her heart pounded in terror.

When she had been at home, as a little girl, she would always run to her parents' bedroom crying and, after they had comforted her, she would sleep for the rest of the night between them. Once, she had been so terrified that she had been unable to speak and, standing by her mother's bed in panic, she had vomited into her sleeping mother's hair. Celeste still remembered with guilt the night her poor mother had awoken in shock as she realised what had happened and patiently shampooed her hair at three o'clock in the morning.

This time, Celeste woke up almost falling onto the floor and sat on the side of the bed breathing heavily for several minutes, clutching Bruno the bear tightly in her right hand. She wondered why she had had this dream again after all these years. Could it be the white opal from Leman? Büket had said the stone was thought to give the wearer vivid nightmares that would gradually erode their emotions and soul, so they would descend into depression and desperation. Celeste turned the light on and leafed through her Encyclopaedia of European Art for several hours, until the early dawn light was visible, tingeing the Bosphorus a rosy pink.

SEVEN

Knowledge Is Power

The Slap
Nasreddin Hoca was standing in the market place one day when a stranger came up and slapped him in the face, but then said, "Oh, do excuse me. I thought you were someone else."

This explanation did not satisfy the Hoca, so he brought the stranger before the local judge and demanded compensation. However, the Hoca soon realised that the judge and the defendant were friends. When the defendant admitted his guilt the judge pronounced the sentence:

"The settlement for this offence is one piaster, to be paid to the plaintiff. If you don't have a piaster with you, then you may bring it here to the plaintiff at your convenience."

Hearing this sentence, the defendant went on his way. The Hoca waited for him to return with the piaster. And he waited. And he waited.

Eventually the Hoca said to the judge, "Do I understand correctly that one piaster is sufficient payment for a slap?"

"Yes," answered the judge.

Hearing this answer, the Hoca slapped the judge in the face and said, "You may keep my piaster when the defendant returns with it," then walked away.

Maryam was pouring a bucket of water and ammonia onto the tiled hall floor when Celeste came downstairs in the morning. She had created a miniature tidal wave of foamy water with frenzied flourishes of the broom, sweeping it in front of her towards the front door as she sang a Turkish pop song that Celeste recognised from the radio. Celeste had never heard Maryam sing before and was surprised by how good her singing voice was.

"What are you so happy about?" Celeste asked, pulling her hands inside her jumper sleeves. She was glad she had the day off work today. Feeling vulnerable after her bad dream and spending most of the night awake, she had dressed in a vast, fleecy old jumper that her mother had bought for her when she was about to start university; the ultimate protective comfort clothing. She felt so well hidden from the world inside its billowing folds that she considered it the next best thing to staying in bed all day.

"Oh, you won't believe it!" answered Maryam, her warm brown eyes sparkling with glee as she paused from swishing her broom. "I've found out something so important!"

"Do tell me," asked Celeste. "I had a terrible night and I need something to cheer me up."

"This deserves a proper telling," insisted Maryam, letting in a gust of icy wind from the sea as she opened the front door to sweep the water down onto the doorstep. "Why don't you start to get some breakfast while I finish here?"

Celeste went into the kitchen. Little Yakup was lying on his tummy on a playing mat that Celeste had given him, surrounded by saucepans and plastic containers. Celeste was glad to find that she and Maryam had the house to themselves this morning. She was usually pleased to see Levent at breakfast as he made her laugh, but her private conversations with Maryam could only take place when nobody else was there. Celeste made toast and laid the table with feta cheese and black olives, pausing each time she walked past Yakup to show him how to put one plastic container inside another, or how to bang out a tune with a wooden spoon. Deciding that a large breakfast would probably be in order, she put on some extra toast and also laid a jar of honey and some fresh fruit on the table. Maryam finally came into the kitchen just as the tea was made and brewing on the table.

"*Afiyet olsun*," said Maryam as she sat down, wishing Celeste the equivalent of *bon appetit;* the real meaning, though, was 'May it contribute to your health.'

"*Afiyet olsun*," wished Celeste in return. "Right, then. Tell me everything."

"At last I've found out what was going on when Leman and Levent moved out of this house," declared Maryam, momentously. "That woman Leman calls '*orospu*' wasn't a tenant renting the house. She was Ferhat's lover, as we suspected. He brought her to live here, and he didn't go abroad on business; he was living here all the time! In this house! With her! For two years!" She sat back with satisfaction and smiled broadly at Celeste, her grey front tooth standing out among the perfect white ones.

"How did you find out?" asked Celeste, as Maryam sat on the floor to put some pieces of toast into Yakup's mouth.

"Ferhat's company chauffeur, Mehmet, was talking on his mobile phone outside the house, and I accidentally overheard him while I was leaning right out of the windows to clean them. He was talking about this woman whom Ferhat had living in the house, and how he kept it secret from everyone and paid Mehmet not to tell anyone. Mehmet's the only person who knows about her. I tried asking him to tell me more, but he refused to say anything."

"Well if he was being paid, I suppose he wouldn't risk it. What exactly did you hear him say?" asked Celeste, pushing up the sleeves of her jumper and buttering another piece of toast.

"He was saying that Ferhat spent a lot of money on her," answered Maryam, "and often bought her presents from France. He said she misses France. And he said that Ferhat was crazy about her and spent all his time on his mobile phone talking to her when he was at work."

"I wonder why Leman kept it secret, too. She must have known. She called the woman an *'orospu'* all the time and she also knew she was French. She told me that the first time I met her. Do you think she actually knows the woman?"

"No, definitely not," answered Maryam. "When I went to do the cleaning in that little flat, she would sometimes be on the phone to Ferhat and I could tell she didn't know who the woman in the house was. A few times she said things that made me wonder if Ferhat was having an affair, but she definitely didn't know who it was with."

"That still doesn't explain why she kept it secret from you and everyone else, though," observed Celeste.

"You know how she likes to look down on everyone else," said Maryam, after a sip of tea. "A lot of upper class Turkish people, like Leman, secretly think French people, and Europeans in general, are very sophisticated, better than us. They're richer and more modern."

"Being modern isn't necessarily better," disagreed Celeste.

"Being richer is," contradicted Maryam. "And also, Leman probably always hoped Ferhat would have her back."

"Which he did," said Celeste. "As soon as the French woman dumped him, no doubt."

"She made me take this house to pieces and clean every hinge and every keyhole when we moved back here," said Maryam suddenly, chewing a piece of cheese. "She wanted to eliminate every trace of that French woman. But she went over the whole house first like a detective, searching for clues about the other woman. I didn't realise at the time why she was doing it. She said it was because she wanted to clean up after the lodgers moved out."

"How do you think he met that French woman?" asked Celeste.

"I don't know, but there's a lot more to this story," said Maryam, adjusting her headscarf, which had slipped sideways revealing a cascade of glossy black hair. "Are you good at making snacks?"

"What?" asked Celeste, taken aback.

"Are you good at cooking?"

"Not really. Why?"

"Because Mehmet loves eating good food. He never gets to have proper meals because he's always driving around and waiting for people, so he lives on kebabs. If I can offer him some good home cooking to take with him in the car, I'm certain I can get him to tell me the whole story. He knows everything; I just need to find a way to make him tell."

"Why are you so mad to know?" asked Celeste. She enjoyed gossip, but it was not such a compelling passion for her as it was for Maryam.

"Because knowledge is power," responded Maryam enigmatically, returning to the table. She started to drink her tea at last, while Celeste poured herself a new cup.

"Shall we read the newspaper?" suggested Celeste. "We haven't done that for a while."

"Good idea," agreed Maryam, standing up again to fetch a newspaper from the corner of the kitchen near the fridge. She randomly pulled one from near the centre of the heap.

"Right, what shall we read?" said Celeste as she started to leaf through it. "Oh, what about this?"

There was a photograph of a man being put into an ambulance. Celeste turned the newspaper so that Maryam could see the picture for a moment and then read the headline aloud:

"*Judge Dies In Court Shooting Over Headscarf Ruling.* What's that about?"

"Some women went crazy when they banned wearing scarves in public places," said Maryam. "There were lots of protests and riots. Read me what this says."

"*A gunman shot dead a prominent judge,*" began Celeste, "*and wounded four others in the high court in Ankara yesterday morning. Judge Mustafa Yucel Ozbilgin died after six hours of surgery to remove a bullet from his brain.*

"*Judge Birden, also injured, has received death threats for ruling that teachers who are banned from wearing the Islamic headscarf at work, could not cover their heads on their way to school. He was shot in the stomach and following surgery doctors say his condition is stable. The other three judges were only slightly injured.*

"*The attacker, identified as Aslan Alpaslan, 29, was carrying false papers that identified him as a lawyer and passed security guards undetected. He burst into a committee meeting of the Council of State, the top administrative court, at 10 am shouting 'God is great' as he fired his weapon. Tansel Colasan, deputy head of the Council of State, said the attacker yelled "I am the soldier of God", and said he was carrying out the attack to protest against the court's decision on headscarves. He was arrested immediately.*

"The court's decision on headscarves has been condemned as illegal by Prime Minister Recep Tayyip Erdoğan, still loyal to the Islamist roots of his ruling party. Mr Erdoğan, though, was quick to condemn Wednesday's attack, and said the culprit would be severely punished."

"Those poor judges. I wonder if the rest of them survived," said Maryam.

"It would have to be in another newspaper," said Celeste, glancing at two of the piles of old papers side by side in the corner of the kitchen. "But I doubt we'd ever find it! Do you think this new law is just making people become more extreme? I mean, setting people strongly for or against women covering their heads?"

"Maybe," said Maryam. "But I think people were already becoming more extreme before this law. That's why they made the law. People like Leman are very against having a Muslim state and very keen to be European. Most ordinary people think religion is important and don't see why we can't stick to Turkish traditions."

"How did everyone react when the ban was first introduced?" asked Celeste.

"There were riots and things. There are still a lot of protests. Some girls from religious schools go to school every day wearing their headscarves, and protest outside school that they're not allowed in. They banned wearing scarves in religious schools a bit later than the general ban. The girls say they can't have an education if they don't uncover their heads."

"I think that's really wrong," said Celeste. "They should be allowed to dress in scarves if they like. If they made a rule like that in England it would be called racist. It would never be allowed. Would you ever go out without your scarf on?"

"No! It's says in the Koran women must cover their heads," said Maryam.

"Are you sure?" asked Celeste. "Leman told me there's nothing in the Koran about covering your head. She said it's just a tradition."

Maryam shrugged.

"Well, I've never read the Koran, but that's what I've been told," she stated simply. "I just know I'd feel stupid without a scarf on my head. I couldn't get used to it. Maybe it's strange for you to imagine, because you don't wear them in Europe."

Celeste was surprised, as she had been many times when talking to Maryam, at Maryam's instinctive understanding of Celeste's perspective as a foreigner and at her ability to understand an alien culture of which she had no direct experience. She was so good at seeing things from other people's points of view that Celeste often found she had far more insight than highly educated and widely travelled people. Her ability to put herself into other people's shoes was surely what made her such a persuasive character, so skilled at convincing people to do as she wished.

"For us Turks, if your mother gives you a scarf to wear from the day you have your first period," Maryam continued, "and the other girls see that you've become a woman, you get used to it as part of being a woman."

"But isn't it the men who make women cover themselves up?" asked Celeste. "I thought it was the husbands and fathers who want their women hidden."

"That's like saying the men make us wear skirts!" said Maryam. "Do you only wear a skirt because men make you? I mean, would you go out in your knickers if your father allowed it?"

She and Celeste both giggled at this idea.

"Of course not!" said Celeste.

"Well, wearing a scarf is the same for me," said Maryam. "It's part of getting dressed. Leaving it off would feel just like going out without a skirt on."

"So you don't agree with this ban?" said Celeste. "Do you think the girls should take off their scarves to go into school?"

"It's a real waste to lose an education," said Maryam. "I don't know."

"Do you think the ban was meant to help Turkey be accepted into the European Union?" asked Celeste. "That's what one of my friends thinks."

"What?" asked Maryam, laughing. "I don't know what you're talking about. You ask all these difficult questions. Why don't you have some more toast and read me the Nasreddin Hoca story?"

"Where is it?" asked Celeste.

"It's on the page with pictures," said Maryam, "near the back."

Celeste turned to the back pages of the newspaper, just before the sport section, and read out the story printed in the corner between several small cartoon strips and a crossword puzzle:

'Nasreddin Hoca's first marriage was an arranged marriage and, in keeping with tradition, he did not see his bride's face until the wedding ceremony. Unfortunately, she was terribly ugly. The next day when the bride was making preparations to go to market, she asked her husband, as was the custom, "Shall I wear my veil? I do not wish to show my face to anyone against your wishes."

'Nasreddin answered, "You can wear your veil to go out if you wish, or you can leave it at home. I don't give a fig if you show your face in public. All I ask is that you always keep your face covered when you're at home with me."'

In the afternoon, Leman drove Celeste through the centre of Istanbul to the orphanage. Pictures of Mustapha Kemal hung everywhere in the heavy smog. Immense banners covered entire tower blocks, posters of him clung to every wall and fence, his picture was suspended from ropes slung from one side of the street to the other, and coloured bunting was draped around every building, monument and lamppost.

"What's all this for?" asked Celeste.

"Today is twenty-ninth October, it's Republic Day," answered Leman. "It's anniversary of we became republic democracy."

"When did that happen?"

"It was 1923. All childrens learning this in school. Even the stupids who cannot read properly learning this. That man is called Kemal Atatürk, father of Turkish people. After we lose First World War, Greeks control us and he gets rid of them. Then he gets rid of Sultan and old style things and makes democracy and European style country."

"What did he do to make Turkey European?" asked Celeste, searching for signs of European culture around her.

"He makes Turkey a secular state, no Muslim government, that was most important thing that he done. He gives us European alphabet, not old Arabic one. He gives voting and equal rights to women. Long time before Europe women gets voting, Turkish women were given vote. No fighting for it like European women, we were just given it. Also, womans don't wear scarf on face or even head, and men doesn't wear fez hat any more. You know that funny hat, looks like flower pot?"

"Yes, I know the one. But lots of these pictures show him wearing a fez himself," protested Celeste.

"Yes, before he stopped it," snapped Leman impatiently.

Celeste pondered for a while.

"Why did he change the alphabet?"

"Arabic alphabet no good for writing Turkish. I know you think we Turks is Arabs, but we isn't nothing like Arabs. Iran people, they isn't Arabs either. We don't have Arabs' language and we don't have Arabs' oil either, unfortunate for us! We have different language and using Arabic alphabet doesn't work very well. Now we got European alphabet with extra letters which is perfect for our language. That new system was invented by Atatürk."

"So that's why Atatürk's picture is on the money and stamps," said Celeste, "and hanging up in the bank and shops and everywhere. He must be regarded as a real hero."

"He made Turkey. Without him we would be Greece."

They arrived at the orphanage slightly late for Celeste's English lessons. Bunting and streamers hung from the ceiling in every room and corridor, and a picture of Atatŭrk, the national hero who stopped Turks wearing the fez, was pinned prominently on the wall opposite the main door. In the art room Celeste noticed that the bunting across the windows even had a small picture of the great man's face on each triangle of paper.

Theoretically Celeste taught two groups at the orphanage, one class made up of the younger boys for an hour and then the older boys for the next hour, followed by an hour of playing time. In reality, the boys wanted to be with her the entire time she was at the orphanage, so she would divide them into two groups in the large art room and focus on teaching one half while she gave the other group pictures to colour, with the objects in the pictures labelled in English. She normally had greasy-haired Mehmet photocopy these at the school where she was paid to teach, pretending they were for the classes there, as the orphanage had no budget for copying teaching materials.

Today the boys were all in a state of high excitement and could not contain themselves enough to sit down. Eventually she made the hubbub of voices calm down enough to nominate a spokesman. Seven-year-old Ilhan explained their excitement.

"We went out for a day in the city with my school," he began breathlessly, "to see the beautiful Beylerbeyi Palace. We were looking at the sea near the place where we had to take the ferry and I saw a bottle floating on the water with a letter inside it!"

"We saw it too!" cut in Bŭlent.

"But I saw it first," stressed Ilhan. "The ferry men helped us get it and there really was a letter in there. It's in English. Look!"

Still clutching the green glass bottle tightly he handed Celeste a small piece of paper covered in large pencil writing.

"What does it say?" the boys asked her, so she translated for them:

'Hello. We are two German boys. Our names are Holgar and Frank. Holgar is twelve and Frank is ten. We like playing football and we both are learning playing the piano. If you find this letter, please write back us, and say us where you live and who you are.'

Their address was written at the bottom of the page.

"Can we write replies to them for this lesson?" suggested Ilhan.

Celeste thought this was a charming idea and the cries of enthusiasm confirmed that this was certainly how the lesson should be spent. She put all the boys together and suggested that they write letters together in pairs, to help each other with their English. She sat the youngest boys, who were still learning to write in Turkish, with some of the older boys and suggested that this way they could still contribute to the letters. She told them that if they needed to know any new words in English, they should ask her and she would write them on the blackboard.

The boys set to work with passion. They asked her to teach them dozens of new words, gripped with the excitement of telling these German boys about themselves and their interests. They wrote about their favourite subjects at school, their favourite foods, and the sports they liked doing. Some of them wrote about their dog and the tricks he could do. Some of them courageously told the stories of their previous lives and how they had come to live in the orphanage. Tekin and Bűlent worked together on their letter. Tekin suddenly shot his hand up and bounced on his chair waiting for Celeste to tell him he could speak.

"Oh Celeste, I've had such a good idea!" he said, breathless with excitement. "We can send the reply back by hot air balloon!"

"Yes!" cried several of the other boys at once. "We learned about hot air balloons at school. Could we fill a balloon with gas and tie the letters on, to send them flying to Germany?"

Their little faces lit up with with such delight at this idea that Celeste did not know how to go about explaining that it would not be feasible.

"The problem is," she tried, after a deep breath, "We can't control where the balloon goes. We wouldn't know how to make it go the right way."

"Couldn't we write the address on the balloon?" persisted Tekin, looking slightly crestfallen.

"Well, the wind might change direction, and then the balloon would fly the wrong way."

"Are you sure?" asked Tekin, his mouth beginning to turn down at the corners.

Celeste capitulated.

"You know what," she said, "I'll see what I can do about organising a hot air balloon."

As the boys continued writing, Mr. Demirsar came into the room with his bucket and mop and started splashing water around at the far end of the room. A few of the boys looked up and greeted him politely, then carried on writing. He did not acknowledge them, simply glaring hard at the floor, but he stopped working several times and rested his hands on his mop handle to stare intently and silently at certain boys in the class. Celeste felt distracted and uneasy and waited nervously for him to finish washing the floor. She breathed a sigh of relief when he finally left the room.

As the boys wrote, she went around the class correcting their mistakes and checking that they had copied the new vocabulary correctly into their exercise books. When the boys had finished writing, she gathered up their letters and reassured them that she would send the letters to the boys in Germany.

Veronica Di Grigoli

When Celeste arrived in Bebek the winter sunlight was so piercing that she had to screw her eyes up, yet there was a chilly wind blowing in from the sea that made her glad to be dressed so snugly in her baggy jumper. As she pushed the front door open, she could smell onion. She went into the kitchen, curious to see what Maryam was preparing for dinner, but there was no sign of any cooking utensils out, and there was no answer when she called Maryam's name. Yet the smell of onion was stronger than ever.

She pulled the oven door open and, sure enough, there was an onion inside. Strangely, it was just one single onion on a roasting dish, burned black so that the skin was flaking off. Something charred, like a black matchstick, poked out of the top. Protecting her hands with the tea towel, Celeste took the baking tray out of the oven and realised that the burned stick was a tightly rolled scrap of paper, wedged into the heart of the onion. She pulled it out carefully and unrolled it. The lower half, which had been rolled on the outside, was black and charred but seemed not to have anything written on it. At the centre of the upper half was a square divided into a grid, with numbers and tiny symbols or pictures in each of the squares. Written around the edge, spiralling around the square grid three times, was a long line of Arabic text.

Celeste knew that this piece of paper, with its strange number grid, could not possibly be a part of the Koran. And she knew better than to ask Leman what it was. Instead, she carefully tore the paper in half, pocketing the half with the writing, and took a scrap of paper from her bag which she placed against the blackened half of the paper. She carefully rolled this up again, until it looked exactly like the paper roll as she had removed it, and then inserted it back into the centre of the charred onion. Having placed the onion on its baking tray back in the oven just as she had found it, slammed the door shut and sat down at the table. The shaft of sunlight shining through the window warmed her up as she took the children's letters from her bag and leafed through the papers. She read Tekin and Bŭlent's letter to herself again, written in Bulent's neat but large handwriting:

'Dear Germans boys,

Our names are Tekin and Bŭlent we are 5 and 9. We come from Anatolia Turkey. We live in orphanage. Our parents dead in earthquack. We have got dog that knows walking and tricks. Very clevere dog. Have you got dog? Favourite our food işkembe çorbası is tripe soap.

Goodbye,

Tekin and Bŭlent.'

As she put the letter back into her bag, she heard Leman's high heels clacking across the hall floor. Grabbing her bag, she dashed up the stairs hastily to run herself a warm bath, not yet feeling ready to face Leman's company.

When Celeste came back down to the kitchen, Leman was already sitting at the small table by the window. She was surrounded by silver. The table top was packed with candelabra, a tureen, a large silver platter, the heavy, framed photograph of Ferhat, and countless other small items of silver.

"Good evening," greeted Leman, cheerily. "I polishing all silver. Maryam lazy and doesn't do polishing. Ferhat, he like silver stuff shiny."

Celeste had long ago realised how much effort Leman relentlessly made to please and impress Ferhat, apparently without acknowledgement. What she had only come to understand this morning, though, with the help of Maryam's discovery, was why Leman was so grovelling to him, when she took such a domineering attitude to everyone else. Leman suddenly stood up, throwing a grimy cloth onto the table top beside the silver.

"I can't get this silver clean," she complained. "Look these black smudges after I already polished it. This polish a load of rubbish."

"I had a Saturday job in a jeweller's shop when I was at school," began Celeste calmly, glad to have something she could chatter about while her mind was still preoccupied with burned onions and charred scraps of paper. "When we polished the silver trays and photo frames and babies' teething rings for christening presents, the jeweller taught us how to make things sparkle. You wash them in warm water with mild detergent to get all the polish off, then in clean water, and then quickly dry them and puff them with a hair-dryer, to make sure every part inside and out is dry as a bone. I'll show you."

Celeste sprinted off to fetch her hair dryer from the bathroom. Then she set about polishing and cleaning a tray of silver, an exquisite tray with engraved flowers and birds decorating the rim. She lost herself in the work, so that she was almost unaware of Leman observing her. She relaxed and daydreamed, feeling a profound sense of satisfaction as she removed all the dirt and grime, and simply enjoyed the beauty of the artwork she was holding. She washed it and dried it as she had described and, when she put it on the table beside the other silver, everything else looked dull and pathetic beside it. It shone so brightly in the piercing afternoon sunlight that it hurt the eyes to look at it. It reflected and refracted rays of light all around the room and, when Celeste looked at Leman's face glittering in that reflected sunlight, with that silvery sparkle scattered across her face, she knew that she had never seen silver shine like that in her life. And Leman said:

"Well, there are fifteen other silver trays and bowls and cups here, why don't you polish all them? You seem very good at this type of housework.

I don't like cleaning and housework chores, but you made for work like that type, I see," and she stood up and left the room.

Stunned at her rudeness, Celeste considered walking out of the room herself. But she could not help wanting the satisfaction of making that silver sparkle. She wanted a way to let out some of the tension she had built up all night, which had been passing, but which had come back at the discovery of the onion. And she had also realised something about Leman now, something which gave her some power over the woman.

So she polished all those things on the table. It took her two hours as she toiled at it, enjoying every curlicue and twirl, every gold rim, every burnished curve and engraved ornament as she smeared them with pink cream polish, and rubbed and rubbed until her brow sweated. She stroked their smooth surfaces under the soapy water as she got to know every curve, taking the same pleasure in their beauty, deriving just as much satisfaction from them as the man who had first made them. Then she rinsed and blew them dry with her eyes turned to one side to protect them from the blinding rays they gave off, she blasted them with the hair-dryer until they grew hot in her hands and it almost hurt to hold them, then she set them in a cluster on the table one by one, till the whole lot sat there reflecting light to and fro, back and forth to each other, from one surface to another, as if talking together. There was so much light bouncing around that kitchen that she could almost hear it as it beamed from one shiny surface and bounced off the next until it grew dizzy.

When Ferhat came home, he looked at all the silver glittering in the shafts of the late afternoon sun, and staggered back from the light as if he had been punched in the face, then he smiled and basked in the wonderful dazzling rays. He pointed at the silver tray, the first thing Celeste had polished, and he turned to Celeste and said,

"That belonged to my grandfather. I always loved it but I have never seen it shine so beautifully."

Then he turned to Leman, looked her in the eyes and thanked her sincerely for working so hard to polish his favourite possession, putting his arm around her shoulders affectionately to show his delight. Leman turned to look at Celeste, and Celeste saw in her eyes a bottomless lake of hatred, darker and angrier than the waters of the Bosphorus in a winter storm.

EIGHT

Husbands, Lovers And Boyfriends

Nasreddin's Donkey Dies
When Nasreddin Hoca's wife died, he didn't mourn for long. In fact he seemed fairly indifferent. Yet when his donkey died a few months later he was devastated, crying for days and bemoaning its loss to everyone he saw. The villagers were baffled.

"Hoca Effendi, when your wife died, you didn't grieve at all. But your donkey's death has moved you very deeply. You can't seem to get over it. What's the matter?"

"The night of my wife's funeral," explained the Hoca, "all my neighbours, friends and relatives gathered in my house and said: 'Don't worry, Hoca Effendi, we'll find you a younger, prettier bride, we'll wed you again, there are many good women out there, you won't be alone for long, we'll get you a better wife.' Now my donkey's dead, but nobody is telling me that they'll get me a younger, better donkey."

Having initially found a breakfast of feta cheese and black olives quite hard to stomach first thing in the morning, Celeste was becoming more and more used to it and even looked forward to it each morning. Today she was helping Maryam to clear the table, having had breakfast with Leman and Ferhat. Leman had hardly spoken a word to Ferhat, throwing him sulky glances and addressing all her comments to Celeste even when they were clearly for Ferhat's information. They had both gone to work and Levent had been driven to university by the chauffeur Mehmet, with a picnic breakfast of plum jam sandwiches to eat in the car, hastily prepared for him by Maryam as he had come out of the shower too late to eat before leaving. He had an exam today so he could not risk arriving late. Maryam had taken care to prepare sandwiches for Mehmet as well, which she took out to him in the car personally, wrapped in a lace-trimmed cotton napkin, stopping to chat about the sudden increase in prices and the ever more hectic traffic in the city.

"You won't forget about some tasty snacks for him, will you?" she said to Celeste, giving Mehmet a warm and friendly wave before vigorously slamming the front door shut. "I can't get him to spill his guts with rubbishy old honey sandwiches."

"Don't worry," reassured Celeste as she picked baby Yakup up from the floor and cuddled him on her lap, "My friend Heather has already made an English cake, which is fantastic, and she's giving it to me today. I'll bring it home tonight so you can give it to him tomorrow morning."

As Celeste finished speaking, the telephone rang.

"Have you got water?" asked Heather hastily when Celeste answered, without even waiting to say hello.

"Yes, why?"

"It's been cut off again and I was in the shower. I'm all sticky with soap and my hair's sopping wet."

"Get over here in a taxi right away," ordered Celeste. "Don't worry about towels, just bring your clothes. I'll fill the bath with water immediately just to be on the safe side."

Celeste told Maryam what had happened to Heather, and Maryam laughed and shrugged as she crammed a wad of Leman's newspapers into the rubbish bin. Celeste remembered that Maryam did not have running water in her house, or so Leman said. She put Yakup back down and went upstairs to prepare the bath for Heather. Heather lived in a neighbourhood where the water was cut off fairly frequently. Celeste was glad to live in a district where this problem was a rare occurrence. She could never cope with the type of problems Heather tolerated, and quite how Maryam lived with no water at all was impossible to imagine.

As Celeste started filling the bath with hot water, she heard the *Aygaz* van passing outside, bringing canisters of gas. Through loudspeakers on the roof like an ice-cream van it played a haunting melody in a minor key, sung by a woman with an eerie voice; the company's advertising ditty to let everyone know that it was passing. Celeste thought that the tune sounded profoundly melancholy and almost sinister, like the background music to a tragic film. Today she was determined to be in a cheerful mood, though. She was going to Topkapı Palace with Heather, Nilüfer and Büket. Heather and Celeste had asked Büket's advice about when it would be best to go, and Büket had been keen to join them, as she had last visited the palace on a school trip when she was nine years old. It had been Levent's idea to invite Nilüfer too.

"She can drive you," he had said, "and she loves old places like that. She knows a lot of history. In fact I'd love to come too, except for this terrible exam which I'm going to fail."

Hearing Maryam's voice summoning the *Aygaz* driver, Celeste turned off the taps and went downstairs to give Maryam a hand. The *Aygaz* man broke into a sweat and his face went a deep red with the exertion of carrying the full canister into the kitchen. Maryam had already opened the cupboard beside the oven where the empty gas bottle was still attached. She used one of her beaming smiles to persuade him to fit the new canister for her without paying the usual fee, just accepting payment for the canister of gas itself, and he whistled a cheerful pop song as he shouldered the empty cylinder and carried it back to his van.

"Men can be quite silly, can't they?" Maryam commented as she slammed the front door for the second time that morning and pocketed the remainder of the cash Leman had left on the kitchen counter that morning for the *Aygaz* man.

Before they had even reached the kitchen, Heather's taxi arrived and she emerged wearing a yellow bath-towel as a turban and her navy blue overcoat thrown over a pink bathrobe.

"Yes I know it's the bloody sea not a river!" she shouted angrily in English as she struggled to pull a large travel bag from the back seat of the taxi while her turban started to unfurl in the wind. She ran into the house without waiting for change from the driver and was already climbing the stairs to the bathroom as she greeted Celeste.

"Third time this week," she shouted, angrily. "I'm going to get pneumonia at this rate."

"This is turning out to be a busy morning," observed Maryam when Heather had disappeared up the stairs. "And I've got something important to do, that needs your help."

"What?" asked Celeste.

"Well, yesterday when I was dusting the living room, I couldn't open that writing bureau because the key was missing. I usually take everything out and clean the inside, with all those little drawers and compartments. When I asked Leman what had happened to the key, she told me not to clean inside there any more. She said it doesn't get dirty inside and there's no need to clean it."

"And so?" asked Celeste, beginning to realise where the conversation was going.

"Well, obviously she has something secret in there. So we need to get the bureau open and find out what."

"I see," said Celeste.

She would normally have objected strongly but, in the case of Leman, she felt like prying.

"Do you think the key could be in her room?" asked Celeste.

"I've already looked. I think she takes it to work. We have to find a way to break in. I think some people can pick locks with hair clips. Do you know how to do that?"

"Unfortunately not," apologised Celeste.

They tried in vain to open the lock using several of Celeste's hair slides and even a bent coat hanger while Yakup sat and watched, chewing frantically on a deep frozen carrot to relieve his teething pains. Celeste even sat on the floor to look underneath in the hope that there may be some kind of hidden opening, but there was none. They had just decided to take a tea break before continuing, when Heather came downstairs.

"*Canınız sağ olsun,*" said Maryam, laughing.

"What?" asked Celeste, translating: "May it last you hours?"

"Turkish people often say that when you've just had a shower," explained Heather. "Although with all the times our water gets cut off, I think it would be better to say 'may it last you days'!"

"We've only had the water cut off a couple of times here," said Celeste. "The electricity goes every once in a while, though."

"Apparently it happens all over the city but some areas are much worse than others," stated Heather, looking somewhat fed up. "What are you doing with all those hair clips and wires?"

Celeste explained their mission. Heather picked up one of the hair clips that Celeste had struggled with for several minutes and, making two swift circular motions she clicked the lock open and gently lowered the writing table to its open position.

"How did you do that so easily?" asked Celeste, amazed.

"I started breaking into my parents' booze cabinet when I was about thirteen," explained Heather. "I was such a tearaway when I was a kid. I gave my poor old parents hell, really."

"Phew, that's a strong whiff," Celeste commented, looking at the small oil lamp inside the desk. "Why fill an oil lamp with perfume?"

"And why keep an oil lamp hidden inside a writing desk?" added Heather.

Maryam pulled out the yellow wick and started to unroll it.

"Look," she said. "It's not a real wick. It's a piece of paper. Here, what does that say?" She thrust the piece of paper towards Celeste. It contained more Arabic writing and bizarre symbols, written in brown ink.

"Are you sure you know how to read?" teased Maryam when Celeste told her that she had no idea what it said.

"Let's take it with us," suggested Heather. "Maybe Bŭket or Nilŭfer know how to read Arabic."

"They should be arriving any time now," commented Celeste as she looked at her watch.

"Oh, I nearly forgot," said Heather. "I've got that lemon curd tart in my bag."

"Thanks, Heather. You're an angel," said Celeste.

"I reckon I owe you, since I stole your lovely class and left you with that horrible lot," said Heather.

When Maryam saw the tart, she took a long sniff before putting it in the fridge.

"Maybe Mehmet won't eat it all," she mused. "Then I can taste some."

Evil Eye

Nilüfer and Büket arrived at the same time; Nilüfer in her father's large Ford Mondeo and Büket on foot, having walked from the bus stop. Celeste introduced them to each other as she invited them into the house. Büket seemed slightly wary of Nilüfer as first sight. Celeste realised that Nilüfer was from the class of people who were sometimes snobbish to Büket; Nilüfer's mouse-coloured hair was highlighted with blonde streaks and she wore several gold bracelets as well as a diamond pendant on a heavy gold chain. She managed to make her jeans and three-quarter-length camel coat look eye-catchingly elegant. But when she laughed, she brayed like a donkey, and her chattiness soon put Büket at her ease.

Celeste took a carton of *ayran* from the fridge before leaving the house, offering cartons to the others as well. Only Büket accepted. Nilüfer played loud Turkish music on the car stereo as she drove through the city towards Topkapı Palace, and she and Heather sang along while Celeste and Büket drank their *ayran* together in the back.

"I can't work out if I'm more hooked on the *ayran* or the Hoca stories," said Celeste, almost apologetically. "This one's funny. Listen:

"Nasreddin Hoca was the local judge, and one day a woman and a man came to him with a dispute. The woman, who was the plaintiff, said `Kadı Effendi, I was on the street walking to the grocery store, when this man, a total stranger, approached me and, to my shock and dismay, he kissed me! I want justice.' Nasreddin Hoca agreed with the woman. `Good woman,' he said, `you will have justice. I authorize you to take your revenge now by kissing him back.'"

Büket laughed heartily, tipping her head back and screwing her nose up with pleasure at the silliness of the joke.

"Oh, I love Nasreddin Hoca!" she said. "He's so wise, in such a stupid way. Listen to the one on my drink. It's such a well-known story, this one, but it always makes me laugh:

"One day, Nasreddin Hoca and his friends were sitting at the coffee house. One of the men noticed a young boy carrying a tray of baklava. "Hoca Effendi, look! That boy's carrying a tray of baklava," he pointed out. "It's none of my business," the Hoca shrugged. "But, Hoca, look! He's taking it to your house." "In that case," said the Hoca indignantly, "it's none of your business!"

"What's baklava?" asked Celeste.

"What? You've never had baklava?" asked Büket, incredulous. "Nilüfer, we must find some baklava for Celeste. She's never tasted it."

Nilüfer was thumping her hands on the steering wheel in time to the drumbeat of the music, her gold bracelets jangling and glinting in the sunlight. Heather's mop of ginger curls was bobbing up and down beside her.

"You must eat baklava," she called over her shoulder, pausing in her song. "Everyone loves baklava."

Realising she had swerved, she hastily grabbed the steering wheel to drag the car back into its own lane, narrowly avoiding an oncoming lorry precariously loaded with rolled up carpets, a mountainous heap of them tied with blue nylon rope that looked ready to snap at any moment and leave the carpets to unfurl along the road. Heather glanced back over her shoulder at Celeste and mopped some imaginary sweat from her forehead.

Only now that Celeste had finished reading her *ayran* carton did she became fully aware of quite how terrible a driver Nilüfer was. She would constantly swerve into the oncoming traffic, oblivious of the evident swearing and angry threats of the other drivers. When the road was narrowed to a single lane by parked cars on either side, she would race along it in fourth gear, as if intending to terrify the other drivers into crashing into nearby parked vehicles to get out of her way. When she reached red traffic lights, she would slam the brakes on at the last minute, stopping so abruptly that she would throw her passengers out of their seats and against their straining seatbelts. Eventually she was stopped by a policeman, brandishing his pistol and a white lollipop to control the traffic.

"Your front headlight's broken," he said, nonchalantly.

"I'm very sorry officer," responded Nilüfer modestly. "Do you need to check my license?"

"Yes," he answered.

Rummaging in her Louis Vuitton handbag, Nilüfer found her driving license immediately but, to Celeste's surprise, did not hand it to the policeman straight away. Instead, she continued to rummage in her bag. Out came a tube of lipstick and an eyelash curler, a packet of cigarettes, some tissues and a bottle of nail varnish. Nilüfer started to laugh as she searched ever more frantically, muttering to herself what a mess her bag was.

"What are you looking for?" asked Celeste.

"Here it is!" exclaimed Nilüfer in response, finally lifting her Prada wallet out of the bag. She opened it and put a couple of banknotes inside her driving license booklet, and then offered it through the open car window to the policeman.

"It's not enough," he snapped, glancing inside and passing it back to her immediately. Silently, Nilüfer added another two bank notes and held the license out of the window again. Without a word, the policeman took the money and slid it into his trouser pocket, then gave the license back to her still without having looked at it, and waved her on with his white lollipop.

"Get that light mended," were his parting words.

"Was that a fine?" asked Celeste.

"Not exactly," laughed Nilüfer. "A bribe."

"Do all the policemen take bribes?" Celeste asked, incredulous.

"Of course," answered Büket. "They have to. Their salary is so low that nobody could live on it. More than half their income comes from taking bribes like that."

"It's illegal to drive around with a broken headlight," continued Nilüfer, "so they stop you, but instead of filling out the official form and so on, they take a bribe instead. It's better for me because they ask for less, and it means they can survive."

"That's amazing," said Celeste.

"It's just life," shrugged Nilüfer.

"Can either of you read Arabic?" asked Heather, suddenly.

"Why?" enquired Büket.

Celeste described the things she had found in Leman's house. She rummaged in her bag to find the pieces of paper she had saved from inside the burnt onion and the wick from the oil lamp in the writing desk.

"My God, she's a witch," concluded Nilüfer. "That's completely disgusting. I didn't know she was like that. I've never heard of anyone doing that before."

"I have," said Büket. "Some people believe in it, and even get obsessed."

"Look at these," said Celeste, offering the scraps of paper to Büket. "Can you understand any of what's written there?"

Büket scrutinised the paper for a few moments.

"That says 'man,' and that word means 'but,' I think!" she said finally, handing the paper back to Celeste.

"Can you read Arabic script?" Celeste asked Nilüfer.

"No," answered Nilüfer over her shoulder. "You need to find someone who goes, or who went, to a religious school. They study the Koran all the time in Arabic. They know the language and the writing properly. Nobody else learns it in Turkey."

"Do you know anyone who went to one of those schools?" asked Celeste.

"I'll have a think," said Nilüfer.

The music on the radio changed to a slow love song, which reminded Celeste to ask Nilüfer about the boy she had been hoping would invite her to the University New Year Ball.

"Yes, he's already asked me," she replied. "For the last two years I went with Levent. He told me that's why he didn't ask me sooner; he thought I would go with Levent again."

"Levent's invited me to the ball, actually," said Celeste. "His mother kept nagging him to invite someone. When he knew you wanted to go with this boy you like, he didn't have anyone to go with, so he asked me if I would be his date just so Leman would leave him in peace."

"Did he?" asked Nilüfer, failing to disguise her shock.

"He seemed really grateful to me, and said I was doing him a big favour," added Celeste. "But I'm sure it'll be fun."

"It's an incredible ball. Fantastic. But he..." Nilüfer's piercing voice trailed off.

"Why do you seem so amazed?" asked Celeste.

"Erm, didn't you know... well, nothing," said Nilüfer, uncharacteristically trailing off into silence again. "I'm really glad that you're coming to the ball, too," said Nilüfer, regaining her normal composure. "It'll be like a double date."

"Well, not exactly a date," said Celeste. "Levent's just a friend."

What did Nilüfer know that she was avoiding telling Celeste? She had known Levent all her life and would probably know any secret he may be hiding. Celeste decided to try to find an opportunity to ask her again when they were alone, wondering, however, if Nilüfer would be too loyal to him to reveal the truth.

"And?" asked Heather. "Don't try to change the subject. Tell us about this bloke who's asked you to the ball, Nilüfer. What's he like?"

"Well, we've been dating for a while, now," admitted Nilüfer.

"So he's a secret boyfriend?" asked Bŭket.

"Yes," admitted Nilüfer. "I don't think my parents would approve of him. He's not from a rich family at all, but he comes top of all the classes at University. He's really intelligent, and he's so nice. He makes me laugh all the time. And he's handsome, too." She let out one of her braying laughs.

"What would they disapprove of?" asked Celeste.

"They want me to marry someone rich, of course," said Nilüfer, suddenly serious.

"Isn't that a bit shallow?" asked Celeste.

"Not really," disagreed Nilüfer. "That way I'd have an easy life. It's not about being a gold-digger. They want me to have the best life possible. My parents worked so hard to give my brother and me a life with more freedom, without worries and problems. You can solve so many problems with money. You have so many more choices."

"That's certainly true," said Bŭket.

Evil Eye

"But isn't happiness more important?" asked Celeste.

"Sometimes happiness isn't about loving a good looking guy, it's depends on having someone who can take care of your needs and solve your problems," said Bŭket. "Money usually comes into it, sooner or later."

"I don't think I'd want to feel I was living off a man," said Celeste.

"We don't have free medical care here," said Nilŭfer, "we don't have state help for unemployed people, we don't have a lot of things that you have in England. You survive by yourself here. Being poor in Turkey isn't the same as being poor in England."

Celeste suddenly remembered the boy she had seen on the bus with no legs and no wheelchair. And she thought of Maryam, and her house with no windows where her baby had died of pneumonia. She thought of all the children of primary school age she had seen selling bread or cigarette lighters in the street, polishing shoes on the pavement, or working at petrol stations.

"Cheer up, Celeste!" commanded Nilŭfer, breaking into Celeste's train of thought. "Stop looking so sad! Tell us, have you got a boyfriend in England?"

"Not at the moment," answered Celeste. "I was seeing someone, but we split up after my mother died."

She thought about little Tekin giving her the gold foil pendant after she had told him about her ex-boyfriend.

"We weren't close enough for him to understand the way I felt after losing her. Or maybe he wasn't mature enough. He suddenly started to seem quite childish to me, and self-absorbed."

"I don't think anyone understands what it feels like to lose your mother until it happens to them," observed Bŭket.

"I think that's true," said Nilŭfer.

"Er, Nilŭfer! That was a red light!" cut in Bŭket. "Slow down here, this is a cross-roads."

"Oh never mind," said Nilŭfer cheerily, sailing across the junction unaware that a small van had performed an emergency stop as she cut in front of it. "But what about you, Bŭket? Have you got a boyfriend?"

"Yes," answered Bŭket, "but mine's secret, too."

"When do you manage to see him, you sneaky little thing?" asked Celeste, knowing how protective Bŭket's mother was.

"When I go out with groups of friends," answered Bŭket, shyly. "I always see him with other people." She blushed slightly and seemed almost apologetic, as if having a boyfriend were somehow naughty.

"Why is he secret?" asked Celeste.

"Because my parents would never let me marry him, and they'd stop me seeing him if they knew his secret. He had cancer in his.... you know, and he can't have children."

"That's really sad," said Celeste. "But it's no reason not to marry him."

"It is!" contradicted Nilüfer. "I think you should forget him. What kind of a life would you have with no children? And don't you think your parents deserve some grandchildren?"

Celeste was surprised at Nilüfer's opinion, but she was also surprised by Heather. She noticed that Heather was very silent. She had not contributed to the conversation at all.

"What about you?" she asked, leaning forward over Heather's shoulder. "What do you think of Turkish men?"

"No comment," said Heather, staring straight ahead.

"Have you ever had a Turkish boyfriend?" asked Nilüfer, not noticing Heather's mood.

"Unfortunately, yes," responded Heather.

"I didn't know that," said Celeste. "What was he like?"

"I dumped him at the altar," answered Heather.

"What!" cried all three girls at once.

Nilüfer performed an emergency stop, jerking the steering wheel at the same time so that the car swerved and partially mounted the kerb before coming to a halt as the engine stalled.

"You see why I didn't tell you before?" said Heather.

"Baklava!" answered Nilüfer, laughing raucously. "Look! Baklava for Celeste."

There, before them, and probably thanking providence that his stall was stall intact, was a man standing on the pavement beside a trestle table laden with small rectangular cakes. The girls stepped out of the car and gazed at the trays of baklava, made from fine strands of pastry soaked in honey. Some were topped with crushed pistachio nuts, some with hazel nuts, some were plain; and they all smelled delicious. Nilüfer asked the man to fill the largest box he had with some of every type, and carried them carefully back to the car. Once all the doors were shut, she twisted around in her seat and held the box in the centre of the car where everyone could reach.

"Eat!" she commanded.

So they each took a piece of baklava. Celeste was worried about her bad tooth which often hurt when she ate cold or sugary things, but she had to taste at least one piece of baklava to be polite. She selected a piece topped with crushed hazel nuts and the honey poured down her throat as she chewed slowly on the delicious filaments of pastry, savouring the taste.

"Aren't we going?" asked Celeste.

"No, we aren't going. I want more baklava, and I want to hear Heather's story before the car moves another centimetre," said Nilüfer.

"Well, all right then," said Heather. "I suppose sooner or later I've got to get used to talking about it." She took another piece of Baklava and chewed it for a few moments, as if taking time to decide where to begin. "I met him in England when he came over for an English course."

"What was his name?" asked Büket.

"Kağan. I moved out to Ankara to be with him, after we'd been dating for a few months. We were dating for three years before the wedding that never happened. I rented a flat for the first year, but then I moved in with him and his parents, so I lived with them for two years."

"What was that like?" asked Celeste.

"Irritating at times, but not as bad as you'd expect. His mother could be a bit of a sexist old bag sometimes, but she was quite nice to me. She used to tell me I should clear the table and not let him carry plates around, and she expected me to do all his ironing for him and all that but, to be honest, she and his father were quite open-minded for Turkish parents. They let us sleep together in the same bedroom, and they knew what we were up to.

"Hmm," commented Büket, making a face which Heather could not see. Celeste realised that Büket did not approve of this liberal attitude, and felt that they were evidently not a respectable family.

"Anyway, we started arguing a bit before the wedding. Nothing much, but we were trying to do a wedding that was a hybrid between a Christian and a Muslim ceremony, which wasn't exactly easy. Everyone in both families found something to be offended about. It was so stressful trying to keep everyone happy, I lost about a stone in weight. Kağan started getting grumpy moods and skulking around, sneaking out of the house and not saying where he was going. Sometimes he'd say he was popping out for a loaf of bread and then be gone for three hours, or else he'd go out for the evening with his friends and leave me at home with his mother watching garbage on the television, and eventually roll in smelling of booze at about three in the morning. His mother seemed to think her precious male offspring had a right to do as he wanted, and that I shouldn't complain."

"Did his father behave like that?" asked Nilüfer.

"No, he went out with his old cronies on a Saturday and often left his wife at home, but he never drank and he always came home before midnight. He came home when he was expected home. Anyway, two nights before the wedding, my whole family was there, cousins and aunts, the whole tribe, and about forty friends, too. They'd all flown out for this grand wedding, no expense spared and all that. They were all in a posh hotel near Kağan's parents' house. I went out with the girls for my hen night in a nightclub; it was pretty tame as they don't exactly do the wild hen party thing here. I felt a bit queasy so I came home earlier than I'd said I would. When I came back to the house, I slipped in quietly because the whole place was dark and I thought everyone was asleep. And I walked in on..."

She stopped and buried her face in her hands, curls of russet hair spilling over them and hiding her cheeks.

"He was in bed with another woman?" asked Nilüfer, breathlessly.

"With another man," answered Heather from behind her hands.

"More Baklava," announced Büket, decisively. "Have some baklava."

Heather looked at the sticky pastries but didn't touch them. She continued her story.

"Kağan's about thirty five, and the thing that disgusted me, more than anything, was that this boy he was with looked about sixteen. They were fully at it. He almost didn't notice me. He said I shouldn't be jealous because it had nothing to do with me, whatever that was supposed to mean. His mother got out of bed after a while, and I told her what I'd seen, but, literally as I was saying it, I realised that she already knew. Of course she already knew! The old bag had known all along."

"So why did she want you to marry her son?" asked Celeste. "Why didn't she tell you? And, more to the point, why did *he* want to marry you?"

"Respectability. And maybe she wanted grandchildren. She seemed to think I was being rebellious when she realised how upset and angry I was. It was like, well, 'why can't you just be a good woman and wife and accept it? You'll be the mother of his children. He won't betray you with another woman.'"

"So what did you do'" asked Celeste.

"I dithered and flapped around like an idiot, and spent a day at the hotel hiding out in a room all alone. I was so confused, I didn't know what to do. I felt humiliated. The whole of England had flown out to see me marry him. I even considered going through with it. I felt completely trapped. I didn't tell my parents right away, I felt ashamed to tell them. I'd had to put up such a fight to convince them that I was doing the right thing marrying a Turk and a Muslim.

"I got ready for the wedding in a daze. I was like a zombie. I didn't know what on earth I was doing. Then when the time came for the wedding, I just sat there and refused to leave the hotel room. It was just me and my Dad, and right when it was time to go, I told him. My Dad was fabulous, he was ready to go and stab Kağan if I wanted him to. But I still couldn't feel like that towards him. I thought I ought to tell him that..." Heather trailed off into silence, and Celeste thought she was crying and unable to speak. She had told the whole story so far staring straight ahead of her, not looking any of them in the eye.

"More Baklava," said Nilüfer, trying to insert another piece coated with pistachio pieces into Heather's mouth. "What did you have to tell him?"

Heather took the baklava with her hand and placed it back in the box.

"I was pregnant. I did the test about a week before the wedding. I'd decided to keep it secret and whisper it to him at the wedding, the moment we were actually getting married. I thought it would be so romantic. He always said how much he wanted children. Anyway, I had a miscarriage. It started right when I was with my Dad, telling him about it all. I'm sure it was because I was so upset. I bled on my wedding dress, and I ended up spending my supposed wedding night in hospital. And when my Turkish friends told Kağan what had happened, he didn't even bother coming to see me. Apparently he said, 'Well I bet it's wasn't really mine anyway.' I could have coped with losing him, but not... not my baby." At this she buried her face in her hands again and wept, first silently, then deep heaving crying that shook her body. "I wasn't ready to lose my baby..." she sobbed, her voice querulous and gasping.

Nilüfer put an arm around her shoulders and leaned across to hug her. Celeste leaned forward in the car and touched her arm, all she could reach. It felt like a long time that they sat in silence, all at a loss for words, but after what was probably only a minute, Heather stopped herself from crying, holding her breath for a few moments and roughly rubbing her eyes to wipe away the tears.

"Give me the rest of that stuff," she ordered, taking the baklava box and putting it on her lap. "It's so sweet it makes me feel sick, but I don't care," she added with her mouth full. "Anyway," she explained after a while, "that's why I'm here. I couldn't stay in Ankara and see the people we were friends with there, and risk bumping into Kağan all the time, constantly wondering which of them knew all along and didn't tell me. And I can't face going back to England yet, either."

"Wouldn't it be easier for you to be with your family?" asked Nilüfer.

"I know everyone would be kind, and try to help me get over it, and all that. It's just that nearly all my friends are married, and already have kids. I pictured myself being consoled by happy couples bouncing babies on their knees. I just couldn't face it. I'd rather lurk around here like a stray dog for a bit longer, even though I don't know what I'm doing here."

"Well, you're helping me, for one thing," offered Celeste. "I'd be finding that school unbearable without you around."

"Thanks, old bean," said Heather.

"Shall we drive on?" asked Nilüfer. "Are you ready to get moving?"

"Yes, let's get a move on," said Heather, as a policeman approached the car. He signalled to Nilüfer to open the window, tapping on the window with a podgy hand that sprouted thick tufts of black hair.

"What did I do wrong?" asked Nilüfer, innocently. "I wasn't even driving!"

"You can't park here," said the policeman from under his bushy black moustache.

Without hesitating, Nilüfer reached into her handbag and handed him a sheaf of tattered banknotes, without even offering him her license. He counted the money slowly and deliberately, licking his fingers to count off the notes. Celeste leaned forward in her seat to see him, incredulous at how blatantly he had accepted his bribe. His dark skin looked red and pockmarked, and he had several large moles on his chin and one on his cheek that was so large it hung down and wobbled when he spoke.

"Move along," he said, once he had pocketed the cash.

"Imagine going to bed with him every night," commented Heather, as Nilüfer started the engine with the car still in gear, making it jerk forward so suddenly that Heather's box of baklava fell onto the floor. "He's married, you know, look at that wedding ring."

"Ssh! I think he can still hear you," hissed Celeste, marvelling at how Heather could hide the pain she had just let them see, composing herself and putting up her defensive shield of jokes again.

"No, really," persisted Heather, her blue eyes still looking slightly red-rimmed but flashing naughtily as she turned around to look Celeste in the eye, "just imagine turning the light out and having him clambering on top of you, or worse still, leaving it on and -"

"Will you be quiet!" shrieked Nilüfer, making the policemen bend down to peer into the car as she pulled away with a screeching of the tyres on the cobbled road.

As Nilüfer drove on, the sea became visible ahead of them and Celeste realised that they were approaching the Galata Bridge. As the car rattled over the metal structure, Celeste turned her head from left to right and left again, unable to choose in which direction to look. The panorama of buildings along the seafront extending on either side of her was grand and exciting, with minarets rising from the mosques scattered along the coast and a haze of sea mist shrouding everything like a bride's veil. Once over the bridge, Nilüfer took them into an ever more confusing network of tiny streets lined with bars, restaurants, and shops of every kind. There was a street of shops selling rugs, a street selling nothing but copper and metal ware, and a shop offering plastic washing up bowls and buckets in every colour of the rainbow piled high on the pavement. Celeste was struck by how appealing such mundane objects could look when displayed flamboyantly. Nilüfer almost ran over the feet of a teenage boy as they passed a shop of pickled vegetables of every kind, floating in barrel-sized glass jars, from which the shopkeeper was decanting the pickles into smaller jars brought by the customers. The boy sprang back and held his hands up in a gesture of mock surrender as she speeded past him, hardly noticing.

"We're nearly there," commented Nilüfer. "I'll park round the corner here and we can walk the last bit."

Celeste was glad to stand firmly on her own two feet when the car was finally parked. They caught first sight of the walls surrounding the legendary Topkapı Palace as they were passing a street vendor's stall laden with jewellery beneath some trees.

"Oh, this is quite nice," said Bűket in English. "These are traditional Turkish designs of Jewellery. Look, Celeste, that turquoise in a silver setting is a classic style."

Celeste looked at a brooch, a large turquoise stone set in an elaborate silver oval with leaves and tendrils which curled inwards and over the stone like overgrown plants.

"Very good, very quality, I make best prices for you today," said the stall holder hopefully.

"What's that stone?" asked Bűket, pointing at a dark green stone set in a silver ring. The stone caught the light with a vertical stripe of bright green down its centre, exactly like the staring eye of a cat.

"It's called cat's eye," answered the stall holder in Turkish, "It's a magic stone that protects against witchcraft."

"Interesting," said Celeste. "Is that a well-known tradition, that this type of stone protects against witchcraft?"

"Pretty well known," said Bűket. "Certainly among people interested in that type of thing, like your landlady Leman. I thought it was cat's eye, but I wanted to be certain. People often wore cat's eye rings in the past to protect against witchcraft. A lot of people were afraid of witchcraft in the olden days, in the Ottoman Empire. They were Muslims but they retained a lot of the more ancient superstitions."

"They're unusual," cut in the stall holder, unable to follow the conversation in English. "You won't find another one easily. I'll give you a good price."

"How good?" asked Bűket, picking up the ring. "Try this on," she added, passing it to Celeste. Celeste placed it on her middle finger of her left hand, and it fitted perfectly. She studied it, turning it one way and then the other. The bright, iridescent line dividing it in two seemed to slide as she turned it, always there, blinking at her in the sunlight. It truly looked like a live eye. She was spellbound, unaware that Bŭket had paid for it until she took it off to give it back to the stall holder.

"No, keep it on," said Bŭket. "It's yours. I wish I could be there to see what Leman does when she sees you wearing it."

NINE

Mistresses, Mothers And Wives

The Older Wife
Nasreddin Hoca had two wives, one much older than the other.
"Which of us wives do you love the most?" asked the older wife one day.
"I love you both the same amount," answered Nasreddin, wisely.
Not satisfied with this answer, the older wife persisted, "Yes, but, if the two of us wives fell out of a boat, which one of us would you rescue first?"
"Well, my dear," replied Nasreddin, "you can swim a bit, can't you?"

They entered the Palace through a pair of tall, carved wooden doors. Within the area enclosed by the perimeter wall lay several gardens, all of them fairly sparse-looking in midwinter. Tall colonnades lined the courtyards, some of them with highly ornate pavilions at the centre and all of them leading to labyrinthine networks of exquisite rooms. Bŭket told Celeste the history of most of the halls and chambers they looked at, having a seemingly limitless knowledge not only of Turkish history but also of the Palace itself. They walked around the royal mint, hospitals, bakeries and the vast palace kitchens; then they toured the training school, the weaponry arsenal and the circumcision room; and finally they entered the chambers of holy relics which contained not only Mohammed's cloak, banner and swords but also sixty hairs from the prophet's beard, a holy tooth and even a sacred footprint.

"It's basically a whole city in here," commented Celeste.

"Exactly," confirmed Bŭket.

In the treasury, Celeste was delighted by the vast quantity of jewels; crowns and necklaces, rings, coronets and goblets of solid gold, all encrusted with red rubies, diamonds, green emeralds and other precious stones. There was even a throne, every inch of which was studded with pearls. The walls were lined with dozens of *'hookahs'* used by the women of the harem and other inhabitants of the palace to smoke tobacco or opium, each person having their own private bejewelled mouthpiece to fit onto the end of the tube as they took their turn for a drag on the heady smoke. Yet hardly any of the jewels were cut and faceted like European gems; they were polished smooth and set into the gold in their natural, amorphous forms. Treated in this way, they did not sparkle like the precious stones Celeste was used to seeing and they somehow looked fake;

indeed, some of the crowns and other jewellery reminded Celeste of stage costumes she had made at school using gold cardboard and coloured glass.

"Shall we go to the harem now?" suggested Nilűfer as Celeste examined a row of tall glass hookahs.

Everyone agreed, so Celeste, Heather, Bűket and Nilűfer set out across a garden. Celeste could see her breath forming vapour clouds in the chilly winter air as they followed the signs to the harem entrance. Eventually they entered the harem through an unimposing pair of dark wooden doors tucked away unobtrusively in one corner of a large courtyard. They had to wait outside to be taken in as part of a guided group, and it was stressed to them that on no account were they to stray from the group, touch anything, or try to remove any of the fixtures and fittings. Celeste had brought a small sketch pad, hoping to be able to stop and draw some quick pictures, but she realised with some disappointment that this would be impossible. When the whole group was assembled in the corridor, two guards bolted the doors ominously from the outside.

"I didn't realise they were still in business round here," observed Heather laconically.

Despite the exquisitely patterned royal blue and turquoise tiles which covered the walls, and the immense and ornate lanterns which hung from the arches of the colonnade to her left, it all struck Celeste as dismally stark and austere in the wintry drizzle. She tried to imagine a warm summer sun and some furniture with sumptuous cushions to sit on.

"These were the rooms of the black eunuchs" shouted the guide, pointing towards a pair of small wooden doors behind the row of pillars. "Move this way." He marched off over the rough flagstone floor, the metal tipped heels of his shoes making tapping noises at he strode. He led his loyal party on a route march through corridor after corridor and chamber after chamber, each lined with richly coloured tiles and fitted with stained glass windows. There seemed to be no grand halls, just endless narrow passages and secret little rooms like a rabbit warren. It was so vast that soon one corridor seemed like another and Celeste lost all sense of direction. With carpets on the floor and candles all along the way, the atmosphere could have been cosy, she imagined, but without them it seemed cold and forbidding.

The guide clearly had no intention of stopping to admire the surroundings, as he had seen them already. Celeste last sighted him ducking through a narrow doorway with a raised lintel and clattering out of sight with Heather and Nilűfer amongst the other tourists in hot pursuit. She took two steps to her left and emerged into an open-roofed courtyard which was completely deserted. The wooden gables protruded more than two feet over the doors and windows along the three walls, to shade them from the harsh summer sun and protect them from rain in the winter. A balcony-style walkway ran around the entire first floor, lined with more closed and tightly shuttered windows. The next tier, on the second floor, was the same but with smaller windows. Celeste thought it seemed like an old-fashioned girls' boarding school.

She walked across the open side of the courtyard and, when she leaned over the low railings, she saw the remains of a large Turkish bath far below her in a small garden. She suddenly became aware of someone behind her, and turned to see an old man, immaculately dressed in a smart black woollen overcoat and brilliantly polished black shoes. She presumed his job was to round up the stragglers. He must be at least sixty, she thought, but his round dark eyes and unusually large, smiling mouth contrasted with his white and grey hair and made him seem full of vigour and youthful energy. Celeste thought he was going to tell her to go and join the rest of the group, but then she realised that he was trying to show her something in the garden down below. She walked closer and leaned over the railings.

"Look," he said, "the swimming pool for the harem women. And there," pointing at a smaller, deeper pool over to the left, under a roof supported by an open portico, "that's the milk bath."

"Did they really have milk to bathe in?" she asked.

"Yes, I think so. At least, that's always been called the milk bath."

Celeste stared down at it and recalled oil paintings she had seen in museums, by the so-called Orientalist artists, the nineteenth-century European painters who first created fantasy scenes of middle-Eastern luxury and decadence which were later developed further by the Hollywood film industry. Their work portrayed comely maidens bathing in asses' milk, feasting on sherbet and Turkish delight in recumbent positions, or plaiting each other's golden tresses. Celeste started to picture a cluster of women down around the pool, herself sitting among them, taking shade from the sun and lolling around smoking opium in costly but transparent attire, awaiting their master's pleasure. One of them had flowing blonde hair into which another, with arms like lilies, was weaving white roses and orange blossom. Another took a jewelled casket, swept back her waist-length red hair, and started dabbing black kohl around her eyes and red ochre on her cheeks. Yet another emerged from the milk bath and anointed herself with sweet-smelling unguents before donning a robe of enchanting beauty, woven with threads of gold and silver which sparkled in the sunlight.

"Are you all right?" asked the man, sounding slightly worried. "Do you feel faint?"

Celeste lifted her gaze to the hazy view of the city with its domes and minarets, and then turned back to the flagstones and the boarding school shutters.

"Oh, I'm fine. Just a bit too much of a daydreamer," she laughed out of embarrassment.

"Everyone has had dreams about this place," the man answered. "It's fed people's imaginations all over the world, and been the focus of wild fantasies, for hundreds of years. And the reality of life here in the harem, all the plots and power struggles, was kept so secret that when it was closed, and the last women died, they took most of their secrets to the grave with them."

"When was it closed?"

"This particular harem, I'm not sure. They moved to other palaces along the Bosphorus, like Yıldız Palace. This place became a museum in nineteen twenty-four."

"Were the women ever allowed out of here, or were they kept inside like prisoners?" asked Celeste, curious to learn what else this man could tell her. Describing the history of the palace with spontaneity and passion, he was far more interesting than the other guide.

"They went out sometimes, but very rarely, always closely guarded because they were precious treasures. They were very expensive, especially the prettiest ones. They were never Turkish you know, always foreign, not Muslim. Where are you from?"

"England."

"You speak Turkish very well."

"Oh, thank you. I have Turkish lessons three times a week. I have a good friend whom I always chat to in Turkish," said Celeste, thinking of Maryam, "so I practise a lot."

"How long have you been living in Istanbul?"

"A few months, now."

"You're genuinely interested in our history, aren't you?" he asked, smiling as if pleased to have found someone who shared his interest.

"Yes," confirmed Celeste.

"Most people who come here just want to see a few pretty things and then go home. It's nice to find someone who wants to learn our history. We have wonderful history in Turkey. But it's cold out here. Come inside this room and I'll tell you some more."

She fleetingly wondered what the man's intentions may be. It was highly unusual for a woman to start a spontaneous conversation with a man whom she did not know in Turkey, and she hesitated on the threshold before entering the room after him. In the end, she decided to trust her instincts as he seemed harmless enough. She could hear the voices of another group of tourists who seemed to be approaching from behind, so soon enough there would be more people around them and, anyway, he did work here after all. They went inside a fairly large room which had delicate red flowers painted on the walls. There were low wooden seats and tables inlaid with mother of pearl in the elevated window bay, on a large rug draped so that it cascaded down two steps to reach the level of the main part of the room. The chairs were antique and not to be sat on, so they perched on the thick stone doorstep which stood almost a foot above floor level.

"Don't you have to get the other tourists rounded up?" asked Celeste.

"What?" asked the man, looking bewildered for a moment. "Oh! No, no, no, I don't work here. I'm a visitor, like you. How rude of me. Let me introduce myself. My name is Attila Zaman."

"Celeste Hamilton," responded Celeste, immediately feeling slightly uneasy.

"It's not really conventional to strike up a conversation with a respectable lady in this way," he said suddenly. "I don't want you to think I'm untrustworthy. Perhaps we should wait to join the next guided group?"

"I expect they'd prefer that," agreed Celeste. "They were very emphatic that nobody should split off from the group."

Pausing for a few moments, they heard voices echoing from the walls and suddenly a group led by a French-speaking guide rounded the corner and stopped in the courtyard outside. As the guide stopped to address her group, Celeste resumed her conversation with Attila.

"Is your name really Attila, like Attila the Hun?" she asked.

"The very same," he replied. "I know he's synonymous with destruction to you, but it's just an ordinary name in Turkey, you know. In some countries he's regarded as a great king and noble leader."

"Was he Turkish?"

"No, his empire didn't cover the land that's modern Turkey, but he led a collection of nomadic tribes which probably included some Turkic peoples."

"Are you a historian?" asked Celeste.

"No, I'm a bank manager, actually," answered Attila, his smile widening to show a seemingly endless row of perfect white teeth. "My mother taught me a lot of history and inspired me with a passion for it. She was born in the harem, you know."

"Really?" exclaimed Celeste.

"She left when it was finally closed. It was much diminished in size and quite a miserable and forlorn place in its last days, as she described it. When she was a little girl it was more lively, but still modest compared with the glory days that her mother and grandmother described to her, in

Veronica Di Grigoli

their tales of the past. A lot of the harem tales were handed down by word of mouth, probably mixing romance in with the real events. There was so much secret plotting and intrigue that I suspect even many of the women who lived through the major events in the harem's history didn't really know the whole truth."

"You were going to tell me more about the history of the harem," prompted Celeste, now so fascinated that she had stopped worrying about rejoining her friends. She knew they would wait for her in the courtyard outside the harem.

"Yes, where was I?" continued Attila. "The most valued harem women were from the Caucasus Mountains. They're blonde people there, and also supposed to be intelligent. Yes, they liked intelligent women," he added, noticing Celeste's sceptical expression. "How can a stupid woman have intelligent sons? But they brought women from everywhere to live in this place; Russia, France, maybe even England. The beauty of the sultan's harem women was legendary throughout the Ottoman Empire. I think that's why many Turkish people still have an idea that European woman are more attractive. Men fantasise about them, and Turkish women can be terribly jealous."

"Oh yes," interjected Celeste, "I know a bit about that."

"Some of the harem woman became very powerful, you know."

"How could they be powerful if they were never allowed out of the Harem?"

"Power happened inside the harem. The sultan controlled the empire; the sultan's mother controlled the sultan! Simple really."

Celeste thought of Levent and the way his mother exercised total control over his life.

"Did the sultan marry any of them?" she asked. "They weren't all his wives, were they?"

"No. The sultan didn't marry any of them. He had up to eight women who were something like wives. They were the ones who had sons for him and whom he chose as heirs. They were called *kadın*, which as you know simply means 'woman.' The Muslim religion allows a man to marry up to four women if he can afford it. That was the rule for everyone except the sultan. Nowadays we don't marry four wives in Turkey, only one! People think we're like Arabs but we're very different, you know."

"Would you like to marry more than one woman if it were allowed?"

"Are you joking? I've had one wife for forty-two years, and I've got three daughters as well. It's hard enough living with them all telling me what to do. I don't think I could survive having yet another woman in the house!"

Celeste laughed.

"You were telling me about the women in the harem. What happened to them when they were first caught, then?"

"They were often sold by their families, not caught. Many people around the Turkish Empire at that time were very poor, and selling a daughter could get enough money to keep the rest of the family alive. Also the girls could have a better life in the harem, with lovely clothes and education and good food. Sometimes they were caught in wars as well, of course, or by pirates who sold them if they were pretty. I don't think French families sold their daughters to Turks! Anyway, the original entrance to the harem was a magnificent pair of golden gates called the Gate of Great Happiness. When girls passed through that gate, when they entered the harem for the first time, they were told that those who pass through the gate would never return. And it was usually true; a girl who went into the harem would probably live there for the rest of her life. When they first arrived they were examined to check that they were healthy, with no diseases. Then they had to learn to speak Turkish, and to study the Islamic religion. They had to become Muslim women. If they were talented they could learn music or dancing as well. They could entertain the sultan like this and maybe attract his attention, so it was an advantage to have engaging skills like that. Remember, there were hundreds of women here. It wasn't easy to get noticed, but it must have been what the vast majority of them wanted. The closer to the sultan a woman could become, the more power she could get."

The French group started to move on towards the next courtyard, so Celeste and Attila followed them, still talking quietly at the back of the group.

"Some of the women had to bathe the sultan and attend to him as maids," said Attila. "They had the best chance of getting noticed and these jobs were usually given to the most beautiful girls. New women in the harem were called '*cariye*', which means 'someone who serves', but when they realised that the sultan favoured one girl she was immediately given a room of her own and some servants - other girls in the harem - and from that time she was called '*gozde*'. You understand that word?"

"It means 'in his eye', right?" asked Celeste, pointing at one of her own eyes and laughing.

"That's right. Can you see how the other women would begin to be jealous of her right away? Her position was terribly insecure. If the sultan called her to his bedroom one night, her slaves would dress her up for a night of passion and then she would be called an '*ikbal*', and she was secure with her room and her maids. But what if the sultan forgot all about her? After a while her room would be taken away from her. She would be an ordinary servant again."

"The treasurer used to keep a diary of all the various women the sultan slept with and when, to keep track of any potential babies' legitimacy and birth dates, as well as other significant incidents in the harem. Those diaries recorded some extraordinary events. The harem girls formed cliques, and often they would become jealous of one another and bitterly malevolent, especially if a girl from another clique was chosen to sleep with the sultan. Sometimes girls attacked other girls and mutilated their faces so the sultan wouldn't want them any more. There was so much at stake for them, that some even went as far as chasing girls off cliffs at the palace, poisoning their sherbets, strangling them in their sleep, or disposing of them in other ways: quite a few girls just mysteriously vanished, probably eliminated by the eunuchs who'd been bribed by a rival clique. That was why the poison tasters were always used. These girls, who'd been educated in the harem schools under a mistress to be a taster for a *kadın* or a *sultana*, tasted every drink, snack, meal, or anything else the woman whom they served would eat. Sometimes a taster really would die from poisoning, foaming at the mouth and writhing on the floor. They were taken to the Mistress of the Maladies, but nobody would ever hear of her fate. If the girl did survive, most of the time her liver or another organ would be destroyed and she would be of no further service, so she was sent home.

"The harem was such a dangerous world, and the girls had to develop real survival skills and always keep abreast of gossip. In the harem, you could say that knowledge was power. The more one knew about plots and lies being told behind one's back, the better one's chances of counter plotting and surviving. Sometimes women managed to involve the sultan in their schemes against other women."

"But what if a girl didn't want to go with the sultan. What if she found him physically repellent?"

"There are some records of women who said no to the sultan, and he allowed them their wishes. But I don't think it happened a lot, because the women could get so much power and money by saying yes. It was worth it to most of them."

"Money?"

"Yes. Some of them became incredibly rich. They opened hospitals, and built mosques and left fortunes when they died, to be used for charities to help people. Many of them sent money home to their families all their lives. One woman even had a military fortress built. My bank publishes books sometimes to give to our best clients. They're usually on some Turkish artistic theme with lovely photographs. We produced one last year which is full of reproductions of the written orders from the *valide sultanas*, the sultans' mothers, to set up charitable foundations on their deaths. They're all beautiful illuminated manuscripts. They specify the hospitals and mosques they want built and all the other public works they want carried out with their money." As he spoke, he reached into his pocket and handed Celeste his business card. "This is the address of the main branch of the bank where I have my office. If you're ever in the area, drop in and I'll give you a copy of the book. I've got quite a few spare copies lying around."

"That's very generous of you," said Celeste politely.

Attila laughed.

"I'm so pleased to meet someone who likes hearing my old stories. My daughters are about your age but they aren't particularly interested in this. They all took after their mother, and study science subjects."

"My mother studied science, too. She was a chemist. But anyway, you were telling me how the women gained power in the harem," said Celeste, eager to hear more.

"If they didn't want to be the sultan's wife," continued Attila, "they could work in the administration of the harem and still be quite important. It was like running a huge corporation. There were treasurers, a department of scribes, a team of housekeepers, and keepers of jewels, of robes, and all those things. But they would only be important in the harem, not important in the outside world."

"So," asked Celeste, "if a woman had a child, would she become a 'wife'?"

"Not so easy! If she had a child she was called a '*haseki*', but if she were lucky enough to have a boy, then she could become a *kadın*, but still only if the sultan chose her as one of them. It wasn't automatic. The sultan had to like her. The first of these was the *sultana* and her first son would be the next sultan. Once he did become sultan, she would be the *valide sultana*. The *kadıns* were numbered one to eight, and they had different amounts of jewels and clothing and accessories, and different sized rooms and numbers of maids, as well as sums of cash. Everything they had was graded according to their rank. Oh! So many things to fight about."

"You seem to think women are nothing but trouble," remarked Celeste.

"I know all about it," he sighed. "My three daughters gang up against me."

"You probably deserve it!" teased Celeste.

"I probably do," he answered cheerfully. "They devote their lives to improving me as a person. The sultans probably deserved it, too. The women were in control of the empire for a fairly long period of our history, which is called 'the reign of women'. It started with Roxelana, the woman whom Sŭleyman the Magnificent loved. He fell in love with her and never looked at another woman, a terrible mistake, terrible! Sŭleyman, he lived at the same time as your King who loved women, what was his name?"

"You mean Henry the Eighth? The one who got married six times?"

"You see, maybe he wanted a harem of his own. He was like Sŭleyman, supposedly a great King but actually rather a fool. Six wives, what a terrible life he must have had!"

"But he did have them one by one."

"Oh, even worse. If you're going to have six wives it's better to get it all over with in one go."

Celeste laughed. She knew he did not sincerely mean all the misogynistic things he was saying. He just wanted to tease her to see how she would react. And because she laughed, he said more outrageous things, to make her laugh even more. Celeste was used to being teased by her brothers, and she liked Attila's way of fooling around, because the joking and sheer silliness in her family had almost stopped completely after her mother died: Attila reminded her of happier days when the family was whole and they laughed together almost constantly.

"That was what Roxelana was called by Sŭleyman: '*Hŭrrem*'."

"What?" asked Celeste.

"It means someone who is laughing," Attila answered. "She was supposed to have a charming way of laughing, and to laugh all the time."

The French guide ahead of them had already moved on and the remainder of the group of French tourists was disappearing down a narrow corridor.

"Let's get a move on, so we can see some of the other rooms," suggested Attila. "They're very beautiful."

"I'd love to hear some more about Roxelana, if you have time. Then maybe I should look for my friends. They'll be worrying about me."

"I'm sorry, I shouldn't have detained you. Would you like to try and catch up with them?"

"Let's stick with this group," answered Celeste. "I'm sure they'll be waiting for me outside."

"Good idea," agreed Attila. "The harem is such a labyrinth, you could walk around for days and never find the way out! I come here at least twice a year to muse, so I know it well. Let's go this way, and I'll tell you the story of Roxelana while we walk."

"OK," said Celeste, standing up.

She brushed the dust off the back of her coat and stepped over the high doorstep into the narrow corridor, where she could hear French voices echoing against the flagstone floor and the wooden ceiling. Attila began telling her the tale of Roxelana as they walked side by side.

Evil Eye

"As I was saying, Roxelana the Russian redhead was born in a Ukrainian village around the year fifteen ten, if I remember correctly, and she was the one woman that Sŭleyman the Magnificent fell in love with. She convinced him to move his whole entourage into Topkapı Palace. She was the original genius of gossip gathering. She was such a smart lady, she truly understood how the harem worked. Anyone could be plotting against you and, even if someone was your best friend, they might turn against you in a heartbeat if they could see a way to further their own interests by betraying you.

"Nobody knows what her childhood was like, but her father was a Russian Orthodox priest, so I would guess it was fairly austere. She was captured by Turkish sailors as a young teenager – she must have been terrified. If she'd stayed at home, she'd probably have been married off to a lower-class landowner and lived her life as a housewife running a modest household. Anyway, at the time Roxelana arrived in the harem, Sultan Sŭleyman the Magnificent was a dashing young man in his late twenties, about to bring the Ottoman Empire to the peak of its power and prestige. He conquered Belgrade and Rhodes, beat the Hungarians and laid siege to Vienna. He conquered the coast of the Arabian peninsula, Mesopotamia, North Africa and parts of Persia. He was also a well-loved ruler, regarded as an able administrator and legislator, so he was also sometimes called The Lawgiver. He was quite a 'Renaissance man' in the European style, I would say, because besides all this conquering and ruling, he took great interest in architecture. He had the Sŭleymaniye Mosque built, which is still the largest mosque in Istanbul. He even rebuilt the walls of Jerusalem once it became part of the Ottoman Empire."

"So the harem girls definitely wouldn't have said 'no' to him, then?" said Celeste, smiling.

"I don't think so," agreed Attila. "Well, Roxelana became well-known in the harem for her intelligence and wit. She could tell entertaining stories, by all accounts, and her engaging social skills made her one of Sŭleyman's favourites even for official state occasions. This was unusual, as previously women tended not to be included in these men's affairs. Eventually he fell so deeply in love with her that he refused to be with any other woman, which was unheard of for a sultan.

"Even though Roxelana became Sŭleyman's favourite, the love of his life, she faced a terrible problem. He already had a first k*adın* called Gŭlbahar, who had a son, Mustafa. Obviously being Sŭleyman's first born son, Mustafa was the heir to the throne. But this, in itself, wasn't Roxelana's problem. The problem was the law at that time, which decreed that when a new sultan came to power, he had to put all his brothers to death. This was to prevent the internal power struggles and civil wars which could break out if there were disputes over who should take the throne, which in those days there always were. Poor Roxelana was very fertile! She churned out babies, one every year. I dare say she prayed they would be girls, but actually she produced boy after boy; Mehmet, Cihangir, Selim, Bayazıt and then finally a girl, Mihrimah Sultan. Can you imagine how desperate she must have been? So long as Mustafa was alive, there was a death sentence hanging over her four sons. But she had no intention of letting them die. She'd never allow her children to be taken from her. She was a tigress of a mother. I like to think this instinct to protect her children was what made her become so ruthless."

"What do you think could make a woman allow her children to be taken away from her?" asked Celeste, thinking of Zeliha.

"I don't know if it's a question of what, but rather, the type of woman she is. I think women come in two types, fighters and followers. My wife is such a fighter! That's why I admire her so much. She's a magnificent woman. Followers are women who obey men blindly, wait for men to sort out their problems and who accept what men do to them, whether they like it or not."

"Do men prefer fighters, or followers?" asked Celeste, intrigued by Attila's theory.

"It depends on the man. I feel sorry for men who want followers, though. I think they don't know what it means to truly love a woman. How can you fall in love like that with a woman who just passively waits for you to tell her what to do? Real love means letting go of control. Men who are truly in love will do anything for the woman they love, even make real idiots of themselves. "

"That's interesting," said Celeste. "So what makes a woman a fighter or a follower, then?"

"I think their mothers teach them. If a girl grows up in a family where their mother obeys their father, she learns that's the way for a woman to behave. She copies her mother."

"But what if a woman tries all she can, and simply can't keep her children?" persisted Celeste. She told Attila about Zeliha and her daughters, and how much she loved them.

"As I said, I think that lady is a follower. She's waiting for another man to come along and rescue her, and sort out her problems. Until then, she'll continue to suffer stoically."

Celeste pictured Zeliha sobbing over the photographs of her daughter's birthday party, and vowed she herself would always try to be a fighter.

"Anyway, what did Roxelana do?" she prompted Attila.

"Her first step was to get Gŭlbahar and Mustafa out of sight and out of mind. The sultan's sons were sent to govern provinces and learn military skills to prepare them for ruling the Ottoman Empire. Gűlbahar and Mustafa were sent to Manisa, which was quite far away, and that meant Roxelana could influence Sűleyman more effectively, as she was beside him every day.

"Her next job was to eliminate Sűleyman's best friend, Ibrahim. Ibrahim was against Roxelana because he realised how much influence she had over Sűleyman. Ibrahim wanted to be the only person who could control Sűleyman, and he was a supporter of Gűlbahar because she was not a particularly bright woman, and he could easily keep her under control. I'd say she was definitely a follower, not a fighter. Ibrahim had been Sűleyman's best friend since childhood, and had accumulated so much power that he rose from being nothing more than the royal falconer to becoming the Governor of Rűmeli, then *Vezir*, then *Sadrazam*. Sűleyman also showered him with money and gifts, married him off to his sister, and appointed him Commander in Chief of the armies of the Sultanate. Roxelana had to work on breaking this friendship for a long time. Ibrahim, being just a simple man, started feeling secure in his position of favour, whereas Roxelana never missed a chance to pick up on gossip and poison Sűleyman's mind against Ibrahim, reporting every little thing that could be interpreted as a sign of treachery and gathering a circle of loyal followers who would take her side. Eventually she brought things to a head by forging a letter which made Sűleyman think Ibrahim was plotting against him. So Sűleyman invited Ibrahim over to dinner and, after an evening reminiscing about the old times when they were always together, he had him strangled in his sleep."

"She sounds like an evil woman," commented Celeste earnestly.

"She seems like such an evil woman," said Attila, "but, remember, she was trying to save her sons' lives. The more power she could accumulate for herself, the better her chances. I think she had to be like that to survive in the harem. It was an incredibly backstabbing place. You were in constant danger."

"Do you think," asked Celeste, "that maybe we can't say that anyone's truly good or bad? Perhaps it's always a case of where you stand in relation to them," suggested Celeste.

"I think those are wise words from a very young lady," responded Attila. "I can certainly tell you that a woman fighting to keep her man or her children, a woman fighting to keep her position, can be a very dangerous creature indeed," said Attila.

Celeste thought of Leman and her constant struggles to secure Ferhat's attention and approval. To what lengths would she go, wondered Celeste. She buttoned her coat shut and turned the collar up against the cold wind as they walked into another draughty passageway, leading to a set of small chambers, again lined with elaborate tiles and set with niches lined with squares of translucent, pearly white mica and glowing mother-of-pearl.

"These were candle niches," said Attila, noticing Celeste stopping to study them. "The mica and mother-of-pearl are phosphorescent and would continue glowing in the night after the candles burned out."

"That must have been so beautiful," exclaimed Celeste. "I'd love to see them with candles in. But, anyway, did Roxelana manage to get rid of Mustafa after she'd had Ibrahim killed?"

"Well, Sŭleyman wanted to build a palace for the women, to separate his home and his office. This was a blow to Roxelana, because she knew that being sidelined with the other women meant she'd lose her influence over Sŭleyman, the way she'd made Sŭleyman start to forget about Gŭlbahar and Mustafa. Out of sight, out of mind. If she wasn't constantly by his side, she might lose everything she'd been cunningly building up over all these years. She managed to divert Sŭleyman's attention by urging him to build the greatest monument of his time, the Sŭleymaniye Mosque, which was constructed by the famous architect Sinan the Great. So, gradually, Roxelana Hŭrrem made herself Sŭleyman's adviser in matters of state. She was active in international politics, besides her interest in architectural works in the Ottoman Empire. I think she eventually established a fairly equal relationship with Sŭleyman because of their shared interests. Perhaps that's how she convinced Sŭleyman to officially marry her. This was a radical break with Ottoman tradition. No sultan before him had ever been married. It created a stir within the Empire, obviously, but even abroad as well.

"Even once they were married, though, the throne still wasn't secure for Roxelana's sons, and neither was life itself. So now she had to tackle the biggest challenge of her life; eliminating her husband's first born son. Sŭleyman's heir Mustafa was already very popular in the provinces of the Empire, so Roxelana decided to eliminate him the way she'd dealt with Ibrahim. She started inventing stories and lies to convince Sŭleyman that his son Mustafa was plotting to dethrone him, and she succeeded to a certain extent because silly old Mustafa never said anything to deny the accusations. He knew he was innocent, I suppose, and felt the truth was obvious. When Roxelana forged another letter, practically everyone realised it was a fake."

"What did the letter say?" asked Celeste.

"It was supposedly from Mustafa to the Shah of Persia, asking for help in dethroning his father Sŭleyman. Sŭleyman went to battle against Mustafa at Ereğli. They say he almost turned back several times. He loved his son and I think deep down he didn't believe his son was guilty. Mustafa certainly trusted his father to realise he was innocent. He went to his tent alone and unarmed, to show he was no threat. He was led through the four partitions of the tent until finally, in the innermost partition, where nobody could hear his cries, he was strangled. Sŭleyman cried bitter tears, they say, not only for the son he'd killed but also for himself, the father who could kill a son."

"Why do you think Sŭleyman had his son killed, if he didn't really believe he was guilty?" asked Celeste, captivated by the story.

"Maybe he was so heavily under Roxelana's influence that he couldn't see any alternative," mused Attila. "As I said, they call it the 'reign of women.' Roxelana was in charge, not Sŭleyman."

"Is this the exit to the harem?" asked Celeste, catching sight of her original, English-speaking guide waiting impatiently by a small pair of wooden doors while tourists milled around inside.

"Yes," confirmed Attila, "and we must look for your friends. I'm afraid with all my ramblings I'll have made them worry about you."

"There she is," Celeste heard Heather exclaim from outside the doors. "We thought you'd been kidnapped and sold off into the white slave trade."

"She's fooling around," contradicted Bŭket earnestly. "But what did you get up to? You missed the whole tour."

"I think I had a much better one," said Celeste, glancing at Attila. She introduced him to the girls while he nodded politely to everyone. "So, did Roxelana's oldest son become the sultan after Sŭleyman died?" persisted Celeste after the formalities, not wanting Attila's story to finish.

"No," said Attila. "Mehmet died before Sŭleyman, from natural causes. Roxelana chose her third son Selim as the next heir. She died eight years before Sŭleyman as well, but he was still succeeded by Selim."

"Who was a terrible drunkard," added Bŭket.

"So the empire must have gone downhill when he ruled?" asked Celeste.

"It took a long time," said Bŭket, "but things degenerated until eventually the whole royal household forgot what it existed for. The sultans got distracted by all those beautiful women at their disposal, and forgot there was an empire outside that needed governing."

"Also," added Attila, "the custom of putting the new sultan's brothers to death was replaced by another tradition, which was even more barbaric in my opinion. They would put the boys, from early childhood, in a cage in the harem called the '*kafes*'. They were locked in there literally all day and night, and grew up never being allowed to leave and see the rest of the harem, let alone the outside world. In one case, there was a wall built in front of the door with a tiny slit to poke food through. They usually turned mad as hatters. Sometimes, when a sultan died unexpectedly, they would have to go and fetch some poor lunatic out of the *kafes* to declare him the next sultan. You can't get away with governing an empire like that for very long."

"And I don't think we can get away with hanging round here for much longer either," added Heather. "Look at that tour guide. He's virtually got steam coming out of his ears trying to shoo everyone out of here."

Attila said that he should be getting home to his wife, and said goodbye to Celeste.

"Do drop in for that book," he reminded her, "if you find yourself in the area."

Celeste wandered around the rest of the palace in a daze of daydreams, enjoying the beauty of her surroundings and pondering on Roxelana's life and Attila's observations.

When she slept that night, strangely enough she dreamt about Nasreddin Hoca rather than Roxelana. She saw him as a little man with a bulging pot belly dressed in a full-length kaftan and a gigantic turban, as big as his body. His little feet protruded from the bottom of his robes in slippers with curled-up toes, just like the picture of him on the *ayran* cartons.

"I'm having *baklava* and *halva* and Turkish delight and lemon curd tart!" he cried merrily. "And it's all for me, none for you!"

"Why are you eating all these things, Hoca?" asked Celeste.

"Because I'm being bribed by women," he answered, and as he looked at her she realised he had the face of Attila, the bank manager, smiling with his long row of dazzling white teeth. "They are being sweet to me, and giving me sweets, to make me do as they want. The sweets are stronger than me. They make me weak, they lower my defences and they break me. I'm going to tell the women everything. I'm helpless against their witchcraft."

"Well, I suppose it doesn't matter," said Celeste, as Nasreddin the Bank Manager tucked in to his treats. "I mean, witchcraft doesn't work, so it's harmless really."

"It's not harmless," disagreed Nasreddin. "It doesn't matter whether it works or not. What matters is the mind that wants it to."

TEN

The Dog

Levent and Celeste were sitting at the table in the morning room, having a late breakfast. Since Levent had been curious to know what people ate for breakfast in England, Celeste had toasted thin slices of bread and soft-boiled some eggs, and was teaching him how to dip 'eggy soldiers' into their runny centres. Meanwhile Maryam was laboriously cleaning the living room under Leman's supervision, the smell of beeswax and turpentine wood polish mingling with the smoke of Leman's cigarette and gradually pervading the hallway until it was strong enough to reach the morning room. Yakup, good as gold as usual, sat on the rug in the living room among a collection of toys.

"You've honestly got pictures of Leman with an asymmetrical, ginger haircut in the family album," said Celeste to Levent, "dressed like a pirate?"

"Not only that. She's had every fashionable hairstyle that's ever existed, as well as every colour."

"What's her natural colour?" asked Celeste.

"She hasn't got one," replied Levent.

"I have to see this. Go and get the album right away," instructed Celeste. "Please."

"Only if you butter this toast for me and put some honey on," bargained Levent.

"All right, you big baby."

"Two slices?" asked Levent, gazing at her with his blue eyes opened wide.

"Deal."

He came back after a few minutes, slowly opened the heavy album at the page where his soft finger had been inserted, and pointed with a bitten nail at a photograph of Leman, looking younger and slimmer, with carrot-coloured hair. One side was cut in short layers close to her head whilst the other hung down long and straight, covering one of her eyes. She wore a pair of knee-length black satin breeches, a waistcoat with large gold buttons, and a white blouse with very full sleeves and a floppy white lace collar and cuffs.

"That was fashionable in the eighties, wasn't it?" commented Celeste, remembering other photographs she had seen of the New Romantic look.

"If Mum had it, then, yes," answered Levent.

In the photograph, Levent was peeping from behind one of Leman's legs and holding onto her trousers. He looked about four years old. Celeste was intrigued and worked her way through the album, laughing at Ferhat with about twice as much hair, still mostly black, and Levent on a red and blue tricycle sticking his tongue out at the camera.

"My aunt took that," he explained. "She used to smack me if I didn't finish all my food. Nobody has to force me to eat nowadays, but I still hate her."

There were more pictures of Levent, in many of them playing with a very thin little girl.

"That's not Nilüfer, is it?" asked Celeste.

"Yes. We used to play together all the time when we were little. We used to draw pictures together, like a comic book, inventing stories to tell each other and taking turns to draw the characters in the cartoon strip. She kept all the books we filled up. She's still got them all in her house. Once, I made her a penguin out of plasticine and she was so pleased, but she didn't know I put ketchup inside it and, when she was playing with it, I suddenly attacked them and killed it, and all the 'blood' came out and squirted on her dress. It was so funny. It worked perfectly. She couldn't help being a girl sometimes, but mostly she was great."

"I'm glad my brothers never thought of that one!" exclaimed Celeste, who thought she had seen every horrible trick a little boy could turn his mind to.

On the next page were some pictures of Levent in a tiny grey suit, like a miniature businessman, and when Celeste saw them she burst into laughter.

"How sweet! What on earth were you dressed up like that for?"

"Oh, that? That was a special occasion," said Levent, hastily trying to turn the page. Celeste turned the page back again.

"Yes?" she asked. "What special occasion?"

"Oh, nothing really."

"How can a special occasion be 'nothing really'? Don't you remember?"

"Of course I remember. I'll never get over it."

"What?" asked Celeste again, insistently.

"Well, ….do you know what 'circumcision' means?" he asked coyly. His face was blushing pink.

Celeste smiled, "Oh, I see. You had it done when you were ….How old are you in this picture?"

"Ten. Let's move on to some more interesting pictures" he said, turning over four pages at once.

Evil Eye

"I think these are interesting pictures," insisted Celeste, turning them back again.

After a couple of photographs of Levent at home wearing his immaculate miniature suit, there were more pictures of him with the rest of the family and some other people outside a mosque. Then there was an outdoor party, in a garden with a fountain, full of little children and their mothers and dozens of other relatives. The sunlight was very strong, and in all the photographs the people screwed their eyes up as they smiled at the camera.

"Wasn't your mother there?" asked Celeste, searching the photographs for Leman.

"Of course!" exclaimed Levent, surprised. "There she is."

He pointed to a woman with long, platinum blonde hair, ballooning out around her head like a lion's mane. She wore an electric blue jacket with immense shoulder pads and gold buttons, and a matching mini shirt. Her shoes, also the same colour, seemed to catch the light so dazzlingly in several of the photographs so that they were not clearly visible.

"Look at those shoes," commented Levent, as if reading Celeste's mind. "They were patent leather, but they were so shiny they looked like plastic. They were horrible. Dad used to be so embarrassed when she went round in them."

In one photograph, Celeste spotted a man with a long beard who glared directly at the camera, dressed in full-length white robes.

"Who's that?" asked Celeste.

"He's a kind of priest," answered Levent, "and look what he did to me."

He pointed at the next picture. It showed a small Levent, looking very nervous in his suit, sitting on a chair balanced high on top of a plinth which was draped in deep red velvet. The various relatives who stood around were drinking what looked like cocktails and nibbling party snacks. Celeste could quite clearly see Levent's little pink penis cowering under the gaze of the huge and hairy-knuckled priest, wielding a sparkling pair of nail scissors.

"When little boys in Turkey are naughty, their parents threaten them by saying 'The circumciser's coming.' It's very effective. It made me truly try to be good. But then, one day, he actually did come."

"He didn't do what I think he did with those scissors, did he?" asked Celeste incredulously.

"Yes, he did."

"But you said he's a priest, not a doctor."

"That's right."

"What, out there in the garden in front of all those people? At a cocktail party?"

"Yes. He didn't just do me. Also him and him." He indicated two other boys at the party by jabbing his finger into the photograph.

"It must have been agony!"

"Not at the time. There was some other man who injected my…me, with a pain killer. I couldn't feel anything until that wore off. And by that time, I was at home and it was too late."

"Too late for what?"

"To kill him," Levent answered, not entirely in jest, Celeste thought.

He turned the page over quickly and there he was in bed, looking exceedingly happy and relieved. By the side of the bed was Nilüfer in a pair of blue shorts, with skinny little legs and her hair in bunches, and standing behind her, stooping so that her head would not be cut off at the top of the picture, was Leman sporting a pair of tight ski pants with low-heeled white pumps, and a large cerise blouse with a very wide white belt sitting on her hips. Her mane of blonde hair hung around her shoulders. Levent heaved a sigh of relief as he looked at the photograph.

"This was afterwards," he explained, tapping the photograph with his finger, "and that duvet was a present for the occasion." Celeste looked at the photograph more closely, and realised that the duvet featured pictures of formula one racing cars all over it.

"You still use that! I've seen Maryam putting it in the washing machine!"

"Of course, I'm not getting rid of that! It's my best one."

"How long were you in bed for?"

"I can't remember, a few days I think. What I do remember is the first time I had to pee. Mum was ten times more nervous about it than I was, of course, and she insisted on coming into the bathroom with me, and holding the seat up while I did it. But at the critical moment she was so distracted by anxiety that she let the toilet seat and lid slam down on the thing she was trying to protect. Ouch! It hurt so much, and some little drops of blood appeared. I hadn't cried till then, but it was too much. Nilüfer was really nice. She gave me her sweets and things that week." He turned over the page, and there were some pictures of him with a bucket and spade at the beach. "Phew, that's the end of them. This was our Summer holiday in Italy." Levent left the album where it lay on the corner of the table and turned back to his breakfast, picking up a piece of toast.

"Do you mind if I ask you about something a bit personal?" asked Celeste.

"What, more personal than circumcision?" asked Levent wryly.

"No!" laughed Celeste. "I just wanted to ask why you and your mother moved out of this house for two years. Was it really because your father went away on business?" She had already heard the chauffeur Mehmet's version of events via Maryam, but she wanted to know if Levent knew what had happened.

"I don't think so," answered Levent, apparently quite willing to speak openly with Celeste. "I don't really know, but I'm pretty sure he was having an affair, and wanted to get Mum out of the way. Mum's totally convinced he had an affair, but she still denies it to everyone, so you must never mention it. Never. Dad simply told us he was going away on business and, the next thing we knew, he was arranging for removals men to pack virtually everything up. He'd rented a flat for us and found a lodger for the house, without even telling us till it was already arranged. Mum was furious. You know how she has to control everything personally."

"Did you ever ask him about it yourself?"

"Yes, but he denied everything. He sounded hurt when I mentioned it, as if I was wounding him in the heart by even suspecting. He never left us a phone number of where he was, as he said he was always moving to different hotels, so he would phone us."

"Did he phone?"

"Every Sunday. He came to see us in the flat every few weeks, too, but it was quite weird. Dad can be very secretive. Anyway, in the end, I don't really know." He stuffed the last of his toast into his mouth and licked his fingers as he stood up.

They cleared the table together, Celeste doing most of the work although Levent showed willing. Leman reproached her son when she saw him carrying two plates into the kitchen.

"You shouldn't be doing women's work," she scolded in Turkish, staring for slightly too long at Celeste, as if she were at fault.

She commanded Maryam to continue cleaning the framed pictures in the living room and sent Levent upstairs to his room to study. Then she strutted into the kitchen to take things in hand herself. Celeste decided to join Maryam in the living room and play with Yakup for a while. Maryam had cleared the side table, where a selection of framed photographs was usually ranked, and was setting them back in their places one by one, first wiping each frame and glass with a moist cloth. She held the heavy, silver-framed photograph of Ferhat in her hand; the one Celeste had polished until it hurt her eyes to look at it, and smiled at Celeste as she smeared her damp cloth over frame and glass alike.

"Oh Maryam, don't use that cloth on the silver ones," Celeste pleaded before she could stop herself. "I'll clean that one," she offered.

Veronica Di Grigoli

But as she reached out to take the frame, it slipped from Maryam's fingers and smashed to the floor. The glass shattered into shards which skidded to every corner of the room, the silver frame bent slightly, and the photograph of Ferhat fluttered across the floor and settled under a tasselled couch. Both of them instinctively sprang towards Yakup on the rug at the other end of the room and Celeste, reaching him first, lifted him onto a sofa where he sat happily with a toy car in each hand, making 'broom broom' noises. Luckily none of the broken glass had reached him. Maryam took a newspaper from one of Leman's heaps beside the couch and laid it on the floor, to gather up the broken glass. As Celeste bent down to help Maryam pick up the larger pieces, their eyes simultaneously came to rest on something else that had remained wedged inside the frame. It was another photograph, folded into a small square, which Maryam lifted out and opened excitedly. As she did so, Celeste realised that the photograph was defaced with a scrawl of writing. Maryam looked at it curiously then turned it over and tilted it towards Celeste to show her that the face was covered by lines of Arabic text, laid out like a poem. After staring at the photograph for a few moments they both realised at the same time that the photograph was of Leman.

But this was not the only thing that interested Celeste.

As Maryam had unfolded the paper, something else had slipped across Celeste's arm, the way it tickled her skin revolting her. She picked it up off the floor gingerly, realising that it was just a lock of brown hair tied with a red thread. Then suddenly she caught her breath in her throat, startled and shocked. She looked at the hair for another moment, and held it against her own hair which cascaded in waves over her shoulder, turning toward the window to scrutinise it in the natural daylight. The colour and the wavy texture blended perfectly. This was, without a doubt, a lock of her own hair.

Hearing Leman stomping back toward the living room, probably at the sound of the breaking glass, Celeste hastily folded the lock of hair back inside the photograph and hid it inside her jumper sleeve, hoping it would not slip out. She had no intention of letting Leman take this away too, the way she had taken the paper Celeste had found in her pillowcase. This time, she would find out, in one way or another, what was written on the photograph. Celeste's mind raced wildly while Leman's eyes scanned the floor, appraising the damage and searching for the photograph, clearly wondering if they had already found it. Leman must have taken Celeste to the beauty salon because she wanted to obtain a lock of her hair. But why had she put it inside the silver frame? And why had she taken Celeste to the salon not just once, but several times? Celeste, her heart pounding, went and sat on the sofa beside Yakup to stop him crawling too near the edge and falling to the floor.

"That's it," Leman was saying. "Maryam, you're fired. Get your things, and get out of my house. I never want to see you here again."

"You're sacking me?" asked Maryam, shocked. It was only now that Celeste realised Leman was utterly livid.

"Yes, you stupid fool! I've had enough of you stealing things, breaking things, being lazy. I need a decent cleaner and servant. You heard me. You're fired."

"But that's not fair," protested Celeste, mildly, as Yakup crawled up her body, apparently trying to reach her shoulders. She was about to tell Leman that she had broken the picture. Leman could not fire her. Even if she threw her out of the house, Celeste would not really care. But Maryam cut in first.

"If you fire me, I'll tell everyone about the French woman your husband had an affair with," she said. As she spoke, Celeste could hear the emotion in her voice, yet she was surprised at how controlled Maryam seemed. Leman stopped in her tracks, her mouth lined with scarlet lipstick hanging open. Levent had appeared in the doorway, drawn by the sound of shouting, and stood behind his mother listening to Maryam's declaration. "If you let me keep this job, I'll tell you all the things you want to know," Maryam went on, grasping a handful of her own skirt with whitened knuckles. "I know who that woman is. I know her name. I know where she lives. Did you know your husband still sees her? I know where they meet. I know everything," she finished. She glanced around the room, catching Celeste's and Levent's eyes as if recruiting witnesses. Celeste was astonished at Maryam's audacity, yet reasoned that, if Maryam lost her job, she had nothing to lose. So why not try using the only weapon at her disposal? Leman stared at her for several seconds in silence, during which time Levent silently slipped back out of the door. Then, finally, Leman spoke.

"Finish cleaning up this broken glass, and then carry on cleaning the living room," she instructed in a voice that sounded harder than usual, and she turned on her heels and walked out of the room without looking back.

"There," whispered Maryam to Celeste, her voice quavering as she could no longer hide her fear, "I told you knowledge is power."

Yakup, sitting in Celeste's lap on the sofa, realised his mother was upset and started to cry, his loud wailing drowning out the sound of Leman's footsteps as they clacked against the parquet floor in the hallway.

Leman hid for most of the day, spending part of the time in her bedroom and the rest in Ferhat's study, pretending to sort through family paperwork. Ferhat had been working every Saturday for several weeks now, and Celeste was used to him hardly ever being at home. She wondered what thoughts were going through Leman's mind as she sat in her absent husband's study. Eventually Leman summoned Maryam into the study to quiz her on all the information Maryam had said she knew about Ferhat's mistress. The interview was short and when Maryam was finally released, looking white as a sheet, Leman announced from within the dimly lit room that she did not intend to eat lunch. Celeste and Levent both decided that they were not in much of a mood for eating either, but they invited Maryam to join them for some *ayran* and fruit. She declined, saying she had too much cleaning to get through and might have a snack later in the afternoon, if there was time. Celeste wanted to talk to her alone, but Maryam was exceptionally withdrawn all day and made it clear she did not want to talk to anyone, not even Celeste. She just thanked Celeste for looking after Yakup and asked if she could keep an eye on him until she left for the school, so Maryam could get more work done. Whilst Maryam may have been stung by Leman's criticisms of her cleaning standards and aimed to be above reproach from now on, Celeste knew that Maryam could usually work with Yakup nearby and that in reality she wanted him to stay with Celeste so he would not cry or become tetchy in reaction to his mother's distraught mood.

"Why don't we make fresh *ayran*," suggested Levent, "instead of having this stuff in cartons? There's more than enough yoghurt."

"I love those cartons," protested Celeste, taking Yakup's play mat out of the corner cupboard in the kitchen and sitting him gently at the centre. "I like the Nasreddin Hoca stories."

"That's no problem," exclaimed Levent. "I've got a book of them, from when I was a kid. I'll get it." While Celeste sat opposite Yakup and tried to teach him how to clap his hands, Levent sprinted upstairs and reappeared, panting slightly, just a few moments later. He left the book on the table and scooped the yoghurt into a large glass jug and topped it up with water from one of the five-litre glass bottles of purified water kept under the sink. Then he tipped some salt into the jug and, as Celeste stood up to look at the book he had just fetched, he handed her a spoon and told her to stir the mixture.

"Aren't you going to stir?" she asked.

"No, that's women's work," he teased, flicking his hair the way his mother habitually did, and then breaking into a broad grin.

"Do you feel all right?" asked Celeste, as Levent leaned over her shoulder watching the *ayran* swirl around in the jug. "I mean, after those things Maryam said?"

"Yes, I'm OK. She only confirmed what I think I knew already, deep down. My mother deserved it, to be honest. She's a witch, my mother." Celeste wondered how literally he intended this comment to be interpreted.

Sitting down at the table, Celeste reached towards baby Yakup and pulled him up onto her lap. She opened the Nasreddin Hoca book and started to flick through it. It was illustrated with cartoons showing a man in an enormous turban riding a donkey, very similar to the pictures on the *ayran* cartons. Yakup seemed slightly interested in the pictures Celeste showed him, but far more interested in crumpling up the paper of each page between his sweaty little fingers.

"Can I show you my favourite story?" asked Levent. Celeste passed him the book and he flicked through the pages for a moment before pressing the spine open when he found the right page, and turning the book back around on the table for Celeste to read.

"Would you mind reading it aloud?" Levent asked. "I like having stories read to me, and I love hearing you talk in Turkish."

"So you can laugh at my mistakes?" she asked.

"No, because hardly any foreigners learn Turkish. It's so unusual for us to hear people talking Turkish with a foreign accent. I find it mesmerising."

"All right," said Celeste, and started to read, holding the page down firmly so that Yakup would not rip it. "*One day the Hoca was invited to a grand feast in an important and wealthy family's home but, when he arrived, neither the hosts nor the other guests paid any attention to him. They made him sit at the corner of the table, nobody spoke to him, and they did not ask his opinion on any of the matters they were discussing. Worst of all, they even forgot to pass him the dishes of food being served. Nasreddin Hoca was completely left out. Nobody was showing any of the respect due to an Imam. Even the servants were passing him by and forgetting to fill his drinking goblet. After half an hour of this, the Hoca had had enough of being ignored, so he quietly slipped out of the house. He went back to his home and changed his clothes, putting on the best and the newest garments he owned. Then, he borrowed a very nice coat with real fur trims from one of his better-off neighbours. With this new attire, he headed back to the house where the banquet was being held.*

"*This time around, everyone noticed the Hoca. The hosts and the servants welcomed him warmly and enthusiastically, and the other guests gave him their undivided attention and treated him with great respect. They gave him the best spot at the table and plied him with food and drink. Nasreddin Hoca was very pleased with this new reception. He tucked into the food with relish and joined in the conversation enthusiastically. However, the guests and the hosts soon noticed that, every now and then, the Hoca would dip the hem of his coat into the food on his plate and mutter to it, 'Eat up, my fur coat, do eat! You must eat, too.' Everyone was baffled.*

"'Hoca Effendi," the host finally inquired, 'why are you dipping your coat into the food? And what is it that you're murmuring?' Nasreddin Hoca had been waiting for this opportunity.

"'I'm feeding my dear coat,' he was glad to explain, 'and I'm telling it to enjoy the food. After all, it's entirely thanks to its fur trims that I'm being offered all these delicious treats.'"

Levent laughed as Celeste finished the story and reached across the table to put a tiny piece of pear into Yakup's mouth.

"*Ye, kurkum, ye!*" he repeated, "Eat, my coat, eat! Have you heard that phrase used?"

"No," replied Celeste.

"It's a common phrase. It's a way of pointing out to people that the way they get treated just depends on the amount of wealth they're showing off."

As Celeste and Levent were finishing their fruit Leman walked into the kitchen, reeking of cigarette smoke. Celeste was surprised at how quietly she could walk in her high heels when she wanted to. She had changed her clothes and was now sporting a black leather mini shirt and a yellow silk blouse, with golden-coloured glossy tights and matching gold metallic nail varnish. She looked slightly red and puffy around the eyes, but she had renewed her make-up with black mascara applied more heavily than usual.

"Ferhat, my husband," she announced in her deep, resonating voice, emphasising the word 'husband' as if Celeste may be unaware of their relationship, "has made a telephone to invite all us to eat dinner in a restaurant this evening. It is a lot elegant. He wants take out the family and Celeste for dinner. So please be ready at seven-thirty, because Mehmet come for us. Ferhat he will meet us there." Celeste's nostrils were briefly stung by the smell of alcohol beneath the suffocating reek of cigarette smoke as Leman turned to leave.

Celeste spent the afternoon at school teaching her unfriendly class with Maryam constantly on her mind. The students seemed to have made no progress at all despite her best efforts but she was beyond caring. They were unwilling to put in any hard work and they also seemed unconcerned that they were not getting ahead. Celeste usually arrived home as Maryam was leaving, and today she put her folders and books into her bag before the bell rang for the end of the lesson, so that she could sprint out of the door and be sure to arrive home before Maryam left. She reached the house more than twenty minutes earlier than usual and immediately went into the kitchen to make herself some tea to warm up. When she was due to go home, Maryam came to find Celeste after she had already put her coat on and thanked her in a slightly croaky voice for looking after Yakup for the morning. She seemed calmer than she had done earlier but still declined to talk to Celeste. She told her she just wanted to get off home right away, but would look forward to a good talk with her the next day.

At seven-thirty on the dot, Celeste and Levent were waiting in the entrance hall. Celeste had made her best efforts to look smart, with a cream silk blouse and the opal pendant Leman had given her. She wore the cat's eye ring from Büket, too, which Leman had not noticed so far. Her hair was fixed up loosely, some of the curls around her hairline loosely framing her face. Leman came down the stairs after they had waited a couple of minutes. She had changed her outfit again, this time sporting a tight-fitting green velvet dress which to Celeste's surprise looked very tasteful. She waited for Levent to take her fur coat from the coat cupboard and hold it out for her to slip her arms into the sleeves. As Celeste watched her do so, Leman seemed to become four inches taller, she palpably grew into a better person and, as she stroked the costly mink with its pink satin lining, the feeling of that expense, of its monetary value, made her realise her real worth as a person. She looked at Celeste in her threadbare three-quarter-length overcoat and she relaxed, the tension in her brow and shoulders physically melted, and she felt safer and more secure as she realised that, even though Celeste was European, like the French woman her husband had preferred over her, and, even though she had a degree and spoke French and Italian, Leman was superior. She walked across the hall and looked at herself in the mirror, wrapped around and enveloped in that expensive fur garment, and she felt shielded and protected from critical or competitive eyes by it, the way the *nazar boncuğu* by the front door protected her home from evil; for that coat was like a huge price label encircling her and proving to all the world, whatever direction they might be looking at her from, that she was worth more than they were.

"I hope she remembers to give that something to eat tonight," whispered Levent in Celeste's ear as he held the car door open for her to climb in.

The restaurant Ferhat had chosen turned out to be in an ancient Roman water cistern, a vast underground tank constructed to store and supply drinking water to the citizens of Constantinople. Celeste paused by the balustrade behind the reception area and looked down on the interior before descending the long flight of stairs to the restaurant below. The whole restaurant was lit exclusively by candlelight, the tables laden with black iron candelabra supporting heavy white church candles, and the

Veronica Di Grigoli

ceiling hung with iron hoops on chains, nearly five feet in diameter, each laden with perhaps a hundred candles. Six colossal white marble columns supported the domed ceiling and Celeste could just make out, in the flickering light, the walls and arches overhead built from Roman bricks, much flatter and longer than modern ones.

They were seated at a table directly in front of the brick and marble fireplace, in which a fire was blazing brightly and emitting snapping and crackling sounds from time to time. Celeste was intrigued to see that even the table settings were in the ancient Roman style, with large thick plates and drinking goblets of terracotta glazed in dark green, earthenware jugs for water, and heavy knives and forks which looked like pewter.

"This place is wonderful," commented Celeste, still looking around her, enchanted.

"I thought you would like it," replied Ferhat, pleased that he had managed to impress. "It was used as a car repair workshop until the years of the nineteen-eighties. It was bought and restored by a, what's the word, an association, that also restored a street of Ottoman houses very close to here. They run the whole street as a hotel."

"We could take a walk down there after we've eaten, couldn't we, Dad?" suggested Levent.

"That would be very nice," agreed Ferhat, as Leman snapped her menu shut and laid it on the table.

"You all still haven't even looked at food," she chided. "Waiter will coming, and you slows don't know what you eating." Levent picked up his menu and started to read it thoroughly, checking that Celeste understood each item as he went through the choices line by line.

"You know, they have leaflets in various languages, that tell the history of this cistern," said Ferhat, apparently oblivious to his wife's growing impatience. "Let me bring you one."

"No, no, I'll get it," said Celeste, springing to her feet. As she walked towards the small stand of leaflets she prodded her hairdo a few times. She did not fix her hair up very often and hoped it had remained reasonably tidy. The women she saw around her were dressed very elegantly and she felt a little self-conscious in her simple blouse and black trousers, but then she remembered the story of Nasreddin Hoca's fur coat and reassured herself that the substance of the person matters, not the clothes. She looked at the leaflets in various languages, but the English ones were all gone. There was only one French leaflet and a few German ones left, so she picked up the French leaflet and started to read it as soon as she was back at the table. After a moment, a waiter walked near their table but, since Ferhat and Levent were still buried in their menus, he turned to walk away.

Evil Eye

Leman snapped her fingers at him, beckoned him to the table imperiously, and brusquely demanded an English leaflet.

"Really, it's not necessary, this French one's fine," protested Celeste.

But Leman said to the waiter that it was no good, Celeste needed to read the text and he must fetch an English one. Even as Celeste was reading when the cistern was built by the Romans, just as she had come to the date that it was constructed by the labourers of the Emperor Constantine to bring fresh drinking water to his loyal citizens, Leman plucked the leaflet from her fingers and threw it on the fire, grumbling to the waiter what bad service he was giving, since he could only provide leaflets in languages nobody understood. Astonished and infuriated, Celeste said nothing. She dared not look at Leman, for fear of what she may say if her real feelings took her over. She noticed Ferhat and Levent exchange meaningful glances, when they thought Celeste was not looking. Celeste was disappointed that, now, she might never find out about the cistern's history, from the time it was built to the time it became a restaurant with green china and real candles hung from the ceiling on vast iron hoops two metres across. Yet it was still wonderful; the golden firelight flickered warmly and left the corners in such comforting gloom that the room seemed to have no angles, no edges, just smooth surfaces curving infinitely around them.

Ferhat suggested they all order soup as a starter, which was a speciality of the restaurant. To follow they ordered wholesome meals of meat and fresh vegetables, and finally a large platter of fruit. Leman spent much of the evening interrupting her husband or speaking to him rapidly in Turkish, clearly hoping and sometimes succeeding in making the conversation impossible for Celeste to follow. After a while, Ferhat and Levent stood up without exchanging a word and swapped places as if by telepathic agreement so that the table could split into two conversations, Levent chatting to Celeste in English while Leman talked in Turkish to Ferhat. Celeste noticed that, without slowing down in her talking, Leman would frequently look around to compare herself to other women sitting nearby. Celeste noticed her frown several times as she looked at a middle-aged couple at a table beside them, who occasionally touched hands for a brief moment across the table. Celeste wondered if it was the evident warmth in their relationship that occasioned her displeasure but, after observing her carefully, she realised that her glares were reserved just for the woman. She was dressed in a black evening dress with a diamond necklace, not just a pendant on a chain but a mass of diamonds set in circles like flowers and, even more eye-catching, her left hand was adorned with her massive engagement ring. Celeste realised it was a replica of the ring Prince Charles had given Lady Diana when they were engaged, a truly immense oval-shaped blue sapphire surrounded by a ring of glittering diamonds. This couple must have been married shortly after the Prince and Princess of Wales, Celeste surmised, and the lady's husband had bought her this replica ring as a magnificently romantic gesture. Leman seemed never to have seen a gem as large as this in real life and her eyes were repeatedly drawn to it in uncontrollable envy. Celeste slid her fingers inside the cuff of her blouse under the table and held the gold-coloured foil pendant Tekin had given her between her finger and thumb for a few moments. How ironic that Celeste had a piece of jewellery worth more than anything Leman would ever own, and it had been given to her by a little orphan!

Despite almost constantly striving to attract Ferhat's attention, Leman actually allowed her mind to wander to that gigantic ring a few times and consequently had to ask her husband to repeat himself. She was so focused on that spectacular piece of jewellery that she didn't even notice the cat's eye ring Celeste had worn deliberately to see how she might react. Her mind was eventually dragged away from the mesmerising gemstone when her mobile phone rang. She answered it and suddenly looked very serious. After talking for a moment, she snapped the phone shut and said,

"That was orphanage. The dog is dead."

"Pazar? How did it happen?" asked Celeste, horrified.

"Right this minute, a car came in for turning around on front playground area, even though it said no entry. He was nobody business with orphanage, just a public person. The Cook tell me, he came so fast, he hit dog and then drove away. He didn't even stop."

"Were any of the boys there?" asked Celeste.

"Yes, some of them were out there playing with the dog. Tekin was there and was nearly hit. The dog cried a few times and then died after a few minutes."

"Those poor boys," said Celeste. She could hardly bear thinking about how the children must be feeling.

"They all so upset," said Leman. "Tomorrow morning very early I will going there to them."

"I'd like to come too, please," said Celeste.

"Yes, you can coming," said Leman. "Oh, I'm so furious. If I had that man in front of me now, I would kill him. I would really kill him. Those boys had nothing. They made something out of nothing, and now he's taken that away from them."

Ferhat looked at his wife without speaking and Celeste could see his dull eyes coming to life. He sat up straighter and he looked at her with respect. He spent several moments gazing at her in sheer admiration. If only Leman herself had noticed it, thought Celeste, yet her eyes were

Evil Eye

inexorably drawn one more time to the gigantic blue sapphire ring she so badly seemed to covet. If only she could have enjoyed that brief moment of the one thing she truly craved in life. If only she could understand what her husband really wanted from her.

As Ferhat ordered the bill, Leman took her packet of cigarettes out of her bag so that she could be ready to smoke one the minute she walked out of the door. With the bill, the waiter brought two leaflets about the history of the cistern.

"This one is for Madam," he said, giving the Turkish one to Leman. "And this is for the young lady from England," he added, giving another leaflet, in English, to Celeste. Celeste hastily read the leaflet while they waited for the waiter to bring their coats, half fearing Leman might snatch it away again and throw it on the fire. When the waiter held Leman's fur coat up for her to slip her arms into it, she relaxed a little. She pulled its soft collar up around her cheeks and looked back, hoping to see the woman with the immense sapphire on her ring finger. And, by some strange coincidence, the lady did happen to look up from her plate at that moment and turn her head in Leman's direction. And Leman flicked her hair and turned on her heels, swinging her coat as she walked and making sure it caught the light of those hundreds of candles so that everyone could see she was a superior person.

That night Celeste dreamt she was serving Romans at a banquet. They lay on couches, placed in a semi-circle around a warm, blazing fire as Celeste brought them platters of fruit and plates of steaming food. They wore wreaths of real gold leaves, set with imitation fruits made of precious gemstones. The headdress of the Emperor himself was decorated with grapes made of huge, oval blue sapphires. He was draped in a fur wrap. After the first course, the guest of honour arrived; Nasreddin Hoca, with the face of Attila the bank manger. Beneath his huge turban, he wore Leman's fur coat, which he refused to take off even when he sat down to eat.

"Poor Celeste," said the Emperor. "She needs some rich clothes, too! Bring her a fur coat!"

So the other servants went to bring her a new garment and, when she unfolded it to see what it was, she realised it was made from very short fur like velvet.

"Yes!" cried the Emperor. "It's the fur of the dog, Pazar! You can wear this dog's fur so that you deserve respect, like us."

"That's disgusting," said Celeste, appealing to Nasreddin Hoca. "And isn't it evil?"

"It's very sad," he contradicted, his broad face looking grave. "Fur coats and riches aren't what merit respect. It's sad, to be so misguided. Very, very sad." And he took off Leman's fur coat, rolled it into a bundle, and threw it into the fire. "The only thing to do with things that people don't understand," he explained, "is to throw them into the fire."

ELEVEN

Tulips And Water Lilies

A Holy Man's Advice
"Hoca Effendi, you're supposed to be a man of religion, but you never talk about the verses of the Koran and you never participate in discussions of the Islamic faith. What kind of a Hoca are you?"
"Well, I'll talk to you about Islam if you like. Do you know the Great Holy Man Ikrimah? Do you know his two most important teachings for the Muslim Brotherhood? Holy Ikrimah Effendi preaches two very important rules that all Muslims must know by heart."
"So what are these two teachings, Hoca Effendi?"
"One of these teachings, the Holy Ikrimah Effendi forgot to tell me. The other one he did tell me, but it's slipped my mind!"

Leman drove through the city in silence. Celeste had telephoned the school pretending to be ill as an excuse to take the morning off work. Feeling tense and angry as she thought of the boys at the orphanage, she twisted a lock of hair nervously around her left index finger and glared out of the window at the city in the greyish haze of early dawn. Her pale white face, reflected in the car window, looked drawn and her cheekbones seemed sharper than usual.

As Leman's car pulled up outside the orphanage, Celeste caught sight of Tekin with about ten other boys standing in the front yard, watching Mr. Demirsar, who was bent double under the only tree in front of the building. When Celeste got out of the car she realised that he had a spade in his hand and was digging; digging with a maniacal frenzy, digging as if his life depended upon it. He seemed unaware of all the eyes watching him, and paused only occasionally to wipe the sweat from his brow and then continue attacking the soil at his feet. It was as if he had some vendetta to carry out, or else some type of punishment he had chosen to inflict upon himself through physical hardship. After watching him for a few moments, Celeste noticed that the dog's body lay on the far side of the tree. Laid out limply on the ground, Pazar looked thinner and bonier than he had done when alive.

Celeste and Leman greeted the boys, Celeste kissing them on the cheek one by one.

"Good morning, Leman. Good morning, Celeste *Abla*," they said, without showing their usual excitement at Leman and Celeste's arrival.

None of them cried but after a while Tekin began to sing in his clear and piping little voice until gradually the rest of the boys joined in, a slow and haunting song in a minor key that sounded appropriate for a funeral. Little by little more boys appeared outside until almost all the boys from the orphanage were crammed into the yard and then, finally, the cook appeared in her apron and a thick, bobbly cardigan, along with the rest of the staff.

Having completed his back-breaking work, Mr. Demirsar stood up slowly and rubbed his back, carefully staring at the ground to avoid eye contact with anyone. Then he walked around the tree to pick up the dog without a word. After the frenzy of his digging, Celeste was surprised by how tenderly he held the lifeless animal in his arms and how carefully he climbed down into the deep hole to place it at the bottom. Once he had done this, he jumped out surprisingly nimbly and hid behind the tree.

The fat cook stepped forward, and spoke to the boys.

"Pazar was a very good dog, and a brave dog," she announced, wiping her hands on the front of her apron. "You adopted him and loved him, and I want you to remember all the love you gave him, and give that love to each other. Remember you are brothers, and you must always help and love each other. Don't be sad for Pazar. You gave him the happiest life a dog could ever have."

Then she grunted a single word to Mr. Demirsar, who was now peering at her curiously around the tree trunk, and made her way towards the back of the crowd of little boys, watching from behind them as Mr. Demirsar flung spades full of earth onto the dog's body. Celeste found the fact that none of the boys cried more upsetting than if they had been wailing and sobbing. After her months of working to bring them out of their shells and help them to express their feelings spontaneously, they seemed to have withdrawn again and reverted to their stoical little adult selves.

Once Mr. Demirsar had finished his work he walked away without a glance at any of the boys and disappeared around the corner of the building. The boys stood, as if wondering what would happen next, until Leman and the cook started herding them back inside the building, scolding some of them who had come outside without putting on jackets or any warm clothing. Cook told the boys that she wanted them all in the dining room, immediately, for biscuits and warm milk. Their reaction was a mixture of delight at the unprogrammed treat and sombre gravity as their thoughts remained with their lost dog. Celeste made to follow the boys, but Leman took her hand and pulled her into her office.

"I'm need cigarette and company," she said, by way of explanation.

Sitting at her desk, she opened the bottom drawer and removed a bottle of *rakı*, a Turkish liqueur based on pure alcohol with liquorice to flavour it.

It was normally drunk in a tall glass diluted with water, but Leman proceeded to remove two tiny shot glasses from the same drawer and filled them both with the neat liqueur. She pushed one across the desk toward Celeste, and dipped her hand into her pocket as she took hold of the other. With one hand she popped a tablet out of its blister pack and dropped it straight into her mouth, immediately tipping the whole glass of *rakı* after it and slamming the glass down on the desk as she turned to dig her cigarettes out of her handbag.

Celeste was tempted to try the *rakı* but managed no more than to moisten her lips with it as it burned like fire. She put it back on the desk, apologising to Leman that she was simply not in the mood. Without a word Leman took Celeste's glass and drained it as she had the first. As Leman lit her cigarette, Celeste made an excuse and left. She could not decide if she respected Leman more now that she had shown how much she sympathised with the boys, or despised her for her behaviour at the restaurant the night before. Irritated and confused by her conflicting feelings, she simply wanted to get away from Leman so that she could avoid thinking about her any more.

In the dining room she found the boys singing a song together and accompanying themselves by clapping a complicated rhythm, led enthusiastically by the cook, who was beating time with her rolling pin on one of the tables. No wonder the boys loved Cook so much, thought Celeste; she seemed to know exactly what they needed. Her eyes scanned the room looking for Tekin, and when she spotted him she realised that he had already been looking at her, hoping to catch her eye. She sat next to him for a while, then asked if he thought the other boys would like an English lesson with her.

"I've got a special surprise for you all," she added, patting her bag.

When a few more songs had finished, Celeste announced that all her English pupils could come to the art room if they wished for a special lesson. When they were all sitting down, she took out a large envelope from her bag. It had arrived early that morning, just as she and Leman were leaving the house; a reply from Holgar and Frank, the German boys who had put a message in a bottle. The envelope was large and bulging, but she had resisted the temptation to open it before arriving in the class.

"Who would like to open it?" she asked, holding it out to the nearest boy. He took it and passed it back to Ilhan, the boy who had spotted the green glass bottle bobbing in the sea.

"You should open it, Ilhan," he said. Ilhan very slowly and carefully picked along the top of the envelope with his finger, making the exciting moment last as long as possible. Then he tipped the envelope to spill all its contents onto the desk in front of him. Out came a sheaf of postcards, stickers and a letter. The boys waited patiently in their seats, until Celeste told them to gather round and see what the German boys had sent. She picked up the letter, and read it out to the class.

'*Dear Turkish boys,*

'*Thank you for everyone for all your letters. We were so excited when arrived your answer. We never imagined our bottle could travel so far and get an answer. We are sending you photographs of us and our familys. We think you are very brave boys and we are sad that you don't have parents.*

'*Holgar also has got a dog and we are sending you a photograph of him. His name is Bonzo. He often runs away but he always comes back. Have you got a photograph of your dog? We are also sending postcards of our city and stickers of our football team and some other stickers. What is the name of the your football team that you are fans to? We have a football tournament in our town now for all schools and we won three matches already.*

'*Please write us more letters. We like your letters. We take them our school and all our friends read them.*

'*From Holgar and Frank.*'

Celeste spread the postcards and stickers out on the desk to find the photographs. One showed a large blonde-haired boy in football kit, standing with one foot resting on a football between a fairly portly blonde-haired couple. On the back was written 'Holgar and parents.' Another photograph showed both boys with a German shepherd dog, crouching in a large garden full of flowers. In the background was a sprawling white house, immaculate and adorned with red flowers in window boxes. A photograph of Frank, smaller and darker than Holgar, showed him seated at a grand piano, turning to smile at the unseen photographer. The postcards showed views of an immaculate modern town with white houses and beautiful mountains in the background. Celeste pinned the photographs and postcards onto the notice board and shared the stickers out amongst the boys. As they set about replying to their new German friends, Celeste resolved to write the German boys a letter as well. She wanted to thank them for their reply, but wondered whether she could explain to them quite how much it had meant to these little boys, in a far away Turkish orphanage, who had just suffered another loss.

The time flew by relatively cheerfully despite the fact that all the boys wrote about why they no longer had a dog, and explained that they did not have any photographs of him. Celeste suggested they drew pictures of him, and that they could decide which ones to send to Germany and which ones to fix up on the wall. They welcomed this as a wonderful idea and set to work with a passion and attention to detail which Celeste found so touching she feared at one point she might start to cry. She was staggered by how good many of their pictures of Pazar were and immersed herself so thoroughly in chatting with the children that she was taken aback when Leman peered round the door and told her that the lesson should have finished ten minutes ago.

"You want me leave you at your work after lunch?" Leman offered.

"Thank you," replied Celeste, not wanting to go to the school, but feeling guilty about having lied. Her timetable had been changed so her morning class, the one she dreaded teaching, now had an extra lesson after lunch and today she would have to teach them all afternoon.

Celeste ate at the orphanage and sat at a table with Tekin and Bŭlent and some of the other boys who had spent the most time playing with Pazar. Tekin ate nothing and did not say a word during the meal. When the other boys left the table to queue for pudding, Celeste beckoned to Tekin and he slipped out of the room with her.

"Are you all right?" she asked him, sitting down on a bench in the corridor to lower herself to his level and look him in the eye. Without answering, he reached up to be pulled onto her lap. Rummaging in her bag, she found a pack of dried dates, but Tekin shook his head.

"I don't feel like eating anything," he explained. He sat on her lap in silence for a few moments. "This feels a bit like when my Mummy and Daddy died," he went on. "I was so hungry when I was under the ground, I thought about the things my mummy would cook for me. But when they got me out and offered me food, I didn't want to eat it. I just wanted my Mummy. I tried to eat, but I couldn't."

"I know what that feels like," said Celeste, softly. "My Mummy died recently. I know what it's like when you can't eat, and the world feels empty."

"I used to play with Pazar and cuddle him when I felt like that," Tekin went on. "I could cuddle him and he always understood how I felt."

Celeste held Tekin tightly for a while. He was almost the same size as her youngest brother, whom she had spent a lot of time holding like this when her mother had died. Thinking of her mother made it hard not to cry. She had cried out a lot of her feelings of grief already, but she knew it was a job that would never really be finished. Right now, she wondered if she needed the comfort of holding Tekin more than he needed the comfort of holding her.

"I've had an idea," she said. "I have to leave now, to go to work. But I'm going to come back at bed time to see you again. I'm going to bring you something important."

Tekin nodded.

"It's something very special for you to look after," she added.

As soon as Celeste entered the class she wished she had simply stayed away all day.

"Why you not here in morning?" asked Ayşe, accusingly.

"I was ill," explained Celeste.

"Don't do it again," responded Ayşe in Turkish.

Celeste had planned a lesson in which the students could practise using past tenses by writing each other questions and pulling them out of a hat. It was a lesson she had taught several times before and which usually resulted in the students telling each other entertaining anecdotes. This class virtually refused to speak, and Celeste resorted to filling the repeated stony silences with leading questions and sometimes anecdotes of her own to try to stimulate some kind of reaction or enthusiasm from her class.

"This very boring," whispered Nezaket loudly behind her hand while Celeste was speaking, and several of the other students seemed to mutter agreement.

"What would you like to do instead?" asked Celeste, immediately. "Would you like to do written grammar exercises, or vocabulary? Or something else? You tell me."

A few of the students shrugged, but nobody spoke. Celeste was overwhelmed by a desire to be back with the little boys in the orphanage. In the end she simply ended the hour's lesson ten minutes early. During the break, she searched for Heather and was immensely relieved to see her sitting by the window in the corner of the staff room staring at the traffic in the busy street down below. Celeste told her about the dog, her morning at the orphanage, and the problems she was having with her class.

"I know just what to do," said Heather, grinning slyly. "Leave this to me." She trotted downstairs to Mehmet's dingy little room and returned to the staff room three minutes before the start of the next lesson. "Here," she said, thrusting a sheaf of papers into Celeste's hands. "This'll keep them busy for the next hour."

Celeste looked at the papers. The instructions at the top of the page explained that it was a reading comprehension. The text was about Dutch elm disease, copied very small so that it occupied less than half the page. The questions were on the other side of the paper, also very small and oriented sideways, so that to read each question the students would have to turn the paper over and then twist it around through ninety degrees, then turn the paper back and re-orientate it to search for the answer in the text. Celeste handed the papers out to the class in silence, and told them to let her know when they had finished. They read in dismay for nearly twenty minutes while Celeste composed a letter to Frank and Holgar, and then the frantic paper turning began. Celeste pictured Heather and her wicked laugh as she had devised this hideous lesson to torment Celeste's students. She dipped her head down until it almost touched the desk so they could not see her sniggering childishly to herself.

In the staff room during the break, Celeste gave Heather a gleeful report on the effect of the exercise.

"That should teach them what boring really means," observed Heather, looking satisfied.

"Listen, can I come to your place for a while after my last hour?" asked Celeste. "I'm going to the orphanage this evening, but I don't feel like lurking around at home if I can avoid it."

The death of the dog and her conversation with Tekin had stirred up feelings about her mother that she had been managing to keep at bay since she had arrived in Turkey. She could not face Leman when she was in this mood.

"What do you think of going out instead?" suggested Heather. "I still haven't seen the Blue Mosque or the Ayasofya Museum."

"The Blue Mosque is the Sultanahmet Mosque, isn't it? I'd be up for that," agreed Celeste. "I've been reading about it in my guide book."

"I'll meet you outside Ayasofya after your last lesson," said Heather. "I'm setting off now."

After the lesson finished, Celeste passed her time in the taxi by reading about Ayasofya, first an Eastern Orthodox basilica, then a mosque and now a museum. She was glad to escape into history and get away from thoughts of her horrible class at the school, the orphans' dead dog and unfathomable Leman, even if only for a few minutes. She arrived before Heather did, and screwed her eyes up in the piercing sunshine to gaze at the huge domed roof and minarets of the former greatest cathedral of the world. The building was so large and sprawling that it looked squat despite its immense height. It was painted a patchy ochre red, as if it were covered in powder paint that had been partly washed away by rain. The four minarets were a mismatched jumble, two in white marble, one a thicker structure of red brick and one snow white and thinner than all the others.

As soon as Celeste entered with Heather her mouth fell open. Viewed from inside, the sheer dimensions of the basilica stunned her but the real impact was from the mosaics high on the ceiling. The beautifully portrayed figures were set against a background of dazzling gold tiles which reflected the sunshine with such an intense yellow light, multiplying the rays and sending them beaming in so many directions that the face of Jesus seemed brighter than the sun itself. The atmosphere was mystical and unearthly. The people in the mosaics looked so realistic, the shading on their faces and the drapery of their clothing depicted so cleverly, that the tesserae seemed to blend into each other until the pictures looked like Renaissance oil paintings. Celeste imagined the people turning their heads to talk to each other. She and Heather stood side by side for almost ten minutes without speaking.

"You know there are lots more of these mosaics under that plaster, don't you?" commented Heather eventually. "Zelly told me about it. Apparently there are lots of arguments about whether to pull the plaster off, because it would mean destroying the Islamic art painted on top."

"It's such a pity when people paint something pretty on top of something else that's also beautiful," sighed Celeste, looking at the delicate Islamic calligraphy painted on the walls and ceiling. "And it often turns into a nationalistic fight."

"Can you imagine how stunning it must have been, with these gold mosaics from floor to ceiling?" asked Heather.

"It must have been the most magnificent building in the world," said Celeste, without taking her eyes from the mosaic of Christ and John the Baptist high above them. "According to my guide book there's been a long-lasting dispute over whether to pull the plaster off the dome, where that Arabic writing is up there, because there's supposed to be a mosaic of Jesus as Pantocrator, the Master of the World, underneath. The mosaic was written about in ancient times as an unforgettable sight."

"So the Islamic calligraphy could be considered vandalism, really?" said Heather.

"It was already damaged when the Ottomans arrived, actually," said Celeste. "There have been lots of earthquakes so there may not be many mosaics left, in reality. It probably wasn't the Ottomans who ruined them, but an act of God himself."

"That would be ironic," commented Heather.

"There's something even more ironic. In the thirteenth century the crusaders from Venice vandalized every Byzantine church in the city, including the golden mosaics here. So perhaps it was the Christians who trashed it, not the Muslims. Most of the things the Italians didn't ruin were shipped off to Venice after that crusade. Those famous lions in St. Mark's Square in Venice were nicked from Istanbul."

"How do you know all this stuff?" asked Heather. "You're like a professional tourist guide."

"Well, I did study history of art," laughed Celeste. "I ought to know a thing or two."

"All right then, when was this place built?" asked Heather, reaching to take Celeste's guide book from her hand.

"Sixth century," replied Celeste immediately. "Oh, and by the way, it wasn't really dedicated to Saint Sophia but to the holy wisdom of God. Its full name is the Church of the Holy Wisdom of God."

"When did it become a mosque then?" asked Heather.

"You've got me there," admitted Celeste, opening her guide book where she had been marking the page with her finger. "When the Ottomans invaded in the fifteenth century. The book says they took away the Christian features and plastered over the mosaics. Lots of other mosques in Istanbul, including the Blue Mosque, were modelled on Ayasofya."

"So all the most famous mosques were basically modelled on a cathedral?" asked Heather.

"Yes. Shall we head off to the Blue Mosque now? Time's getting on a bit."

They walked the short distance in a few minutes and arrived at the Blue Mosque as the sun was beginning to go down. The sky was already a blaze of red and orange at the horizon, fading into deep blue high in the sky above. The sundown prayers were taking place, so they had to wait in the outer courtyards before they could go inside. They wandered from one white enclosure to another, looking at the arched colonnades of white marble and filigree stone carving glowing a warm rosy pink in the dying sun.

When the prayers were finished and they could enter, they pulled their scarves up over their heads and went into the entrance area where the wall was lined with shelves divided into small sections, each designed to hold one pair of shoes. Most of the shelves were empty as the prayers had now finished. Three old men waiting just inside the doorway wanted to know where they came from. Was it Australia? Yes, said one, he could tell from their accents. What was that perfume Celeste was wearing? Did they live in Istanbul? Where did they live? Was Heather a natural redhead? Then they asked for money.

"Are you really Muslims?" asked Heather suddenly, her blue eyes flashing with anger.

"Yes," they declared, "of course we are."

"Well, why are you disgracing yourselves here in your place of worship?" she demanded to know, aggressively. "What does your religion mean to you?"

Celeste had never seen Heather lose her temper. She was furious. And she was terrifying. The men fell silent and stood by sheepishly as Celeste and Heather put their shoes on the shelf and walked inside. The mosque was vast and the floor was covered in layer upon layer of hand woven prayer rugs piled one on top of another in a spongy, soggy cold heap which bounced when they stepped on it. Some of the carpets looked very old, some were new, and many of them were exquisitely beautiful. The whole lot oozed water as they trod, so that their socks instantly became soaking wet.

"Just think of all the verrucas and athlete's foot we're going to catch in here," said Heather.

"Oh, don't say that!" hissed Celeste. "You know I'm neurotic enough about hygiene already. Did you know this is the only mosque in Turkey with six minarets instead of four?"

"Yes, I did, as a matter of fact," answered Heather.

"Aha, but do you know why?" persisted Celeste.

"No, but I've got a feeling you're going to tell me."

"I won't," said Celeste, "if you're going to be a smarty pants."

"I'm sorry," insisted Heather, "I do want to know really."

"Well, Sultan Ahmet the First built it," began Celeste, "some time in the seventeenth century, and he wanted it to be the most impressive mosque in the world. So he decided to give it six minarets, because the only other mosque at the time which had six was some Mosque in Mecca. It was called the Haram Esh-Sharif, or something like that. After this mosque was built, the Arabs added a seventh minaret to the one in Mecca, just because they couldn't bear to be outdone by a bunch of Turks."

"Quite right," agreed Heather vehemently. "I couldn't bear to be outdone by a bunch of Turks." Her turquoise eyes glanced around furtively, as if checking in case any bystanders knew enough English to have understood her irreverent joke, but nobody was taking any notice of them.

They walked around the mosque slowly, looking up at the building. The walls and the huge ceiling high above were entirely covered in tiles with intricate designs in white and different shades of blue. The last beams of dusky sunlight coming in through the high windows were fading rapidly, but from the ceiling far above hung glass oil lamps on long chains reaching down to just above their heads. Heather and Celeste walked off in different directions at one point and stood by themselves in silence for almost twenty minutes. Celeste watched some of the men who were still praying inside. Their mood of complete concentration and inner calm seemed to expand and fill the whole mosque with an atmosphere of peace and supreme serenity. It became so pervasive that it suffused the fabric of the building itself and even penetrated Celeste's tense, brittle shell and started to melt her anxiety away. She memorised every detail and every hue so that she could paint the scene later at home. The sun was going down so rapidly that she could watch the colours inside the building changing before her eyes, from green to pink and finally a short blaze of orange before fading into shadows.

When Celeste found Heather again and they went outside, the old men were no longer in the entrance hall. Heather and Celeste crammed their wet feet back into their shoes, which now felt freezing cold. The sky had

Evil Eye

turned pitch black but the outside of the mosque was floodlit and shining white, with hundreds of seagulls circling around the domes and minarets. Celeste felt calm now, and was ready to go back to the smoky, beeswaxy house in Bebek.

When Celeste pushed the front door open, Levent was sitting at the bottom of the stairs polishing his shoes. He was sweeping a brush to and fro across the shiny leather in a steady and businesslike manner.

"Don't you usually ask Maryam to do that for you?" she asked, perhaps sounding a little too surprised.

"We all know I hate working," answered Levent good-humouredly, "but I had no choice."

"Where's Maryam?" asked Celeste, hoping to take refuge with her in the kitchen over a cup of tea. Celeste was worried about Maryam and had hoped to be able to speak to her alone. She was also curious to hear what had been said in her conversation with Leman in Ferhat's study the previous day.

"I sent her home early. Her oldest son's ill, so I raided Mum's medicine cabinet and told Maryam to go and take care of him. Also, I thought it was better for her to be out of the house for a while after what happened between her and Mum yesterday."

"Does your mother know Maryam's gone early?" asked Celeste.

"No way!" exclaimed Levent. "And she's not going to find out, all right?"

"Isn't she here either, then?" asked Celeste.

"Oh yes, she's here. But there'll be no sign of her until Mehmet arrives to collect us. She'll be in her room trying on twenty different dresses and different types of perfume for this evening. She's already changed her nail varnish twice."

"Where are you guys going?" asked Celeste.

"To the Freemasons' dinner, and you're coming too," answered Levent. He tipped his head to one side and contemplated Celeste with a slight smirk. "You'd forgotten, hadn't you?"

Celeste said nothing, but let her mouth fall open as she slapped her hands to her cheeks. Ferhat had mentioned this evening to her personally several weeks ago. It was clear that the annual Freemasons' family dinner was a very important occasion for him, and he was being extremely generous in choosing to invite her along. She had been flattered that he wanted to treat her so kindly. Unfortunately, it had escaped her notice that the long awaited evening had arrived.

"Don't worry. You've got till eight thirty to get ready," Levent reassured her.

"I have to go to the orphanage tonight, I promised one of the boys."

"That may be a problem," said Levent, patiently.

"Just for a minute, to say good night. Is the dinner anywhere near that area?"

"I don't know, but if it's really important, I'll call Dad. Anyway, have you got something fancy to wear?"

"Erm," said Celeste. "I'll figure something out." Levent looked hesitant, as if debating something to himself.

"Everyone will be very dressed up," he said at last, placing his now gleaming black shoe beside its partner on the bottom step. "Maybe..., can I give you your Christmas present early?"

Celeste had not been expecting a Christmas present from Levent and would certainly not have expected clothes. Ignoring the surprised expression on her face, Levent started up the stairs and called to her to follow him. He dashed into the bathroom to wash the shoe polish off his hands and then disappeared into his bedroom for a moment, reappearing smiling in the doorway to present her with a stiff, shiny carrier bag with red cord handles.

"I think this could be the right type of thing to wear this evening, if it fits," he said casually. "Only if you like it, of course."

Celeste retreated into her room and opened the large box inside the carrier bag. As she lifted the dress out, she almost gasped. It was exquisite; a bias-cut dress made from a deep red silk, very simple in style but of immaculate quality. She slipped it over her head, desperately hoping it would fit and, as the folds of fabric fell about her legs, she caught sight of herself in the mirror and realised that the size was perfect. She decided to leave her hair down the way it was and, with a light touch of red lipstick, she was ready.

"Thank you," she called to Levent as she stood outside his bedroom door. He came out, dressed in black tie, with his bow tie draped loosely around the collar of his shirt. Used to seeing him wearing jeans, Celeste was startled by how handsome he looked dressed so elegantly. Despite being so young, he looked fully at ease in these formal clothes.

"Are you any good at tying these?" he asked her, twiddling the ends of the bow tie. "I keep getting it crooked."

"No problem," said Celeste, who had had plenty of practise tying bow ties for the boys from her university, struggling to prepare themselves for the university ball.

"Do you like the dress?" Levent asked as she tucked one end beneath the other and pulled it through. Celeste felt his warm minty breath on her cheek as he spoke.

"It's wonderful," said Celeste. "But you didn't have to get me this. You've been far too generous."

"No problem," he replied, looking happy. "But be careful of Cengiz. He might have a heart attack."

"Be careful of who?"

"Cengiz. Named after the Great Khan, but not like him at all, I'd say."

"Who's the Great Khan?"

"Don't tell me you've never heard of Cengiz Khan! In America they call him Ghengis Khan with a hard 'G' instead of a 'J' sound. He was feared across half the world. He invaded from Mongolia, and his empire was ruled from Xanadu."

"Oh, I know who you mean," said Celeste.

"Anyway, the Cengiz you're going to meet is a little guy at my university who's going to be at the dinner tonight," said Levent, patting the now neatly fastened bow-tie beneath his chin.

"Why, exactly, would I give him a heart attack?" asked Celeste.

"Well," said Levent, "he's very nerdy. He studies Arabic and has his nose in some Arabic book or other all the time. He goes to the mosque every day. He wants to be an Imam but his father isn't into it. Anyway, the sight of you like that might just be too much for him."

Celeste laughed.

"I've just remembered something I need to bring with me," she said to Levent, turning back towards her room again. She opened her large shoulder bag and took out the scraps of paper with Arabic writing that she kept hidden there; the yellow wick from the oil lamp in Leman's writing desk, the photograph of Leman from behind Ferhat's portrait photograph that she had found folded around a lock of her own hair, and the rolled-up scrap of paper she had extracted from the burnt onion in Leman's oven. Putting these into a smaller handbag, she turned and sat on the bed, picking up Bruno, her beloved teddy bear. She looked at him for a moment and stroked the fur on his tummy.

"Bruno," she whispered almost silently. "There's a little boy who needs your help. He's going to look after you for a while."

She held his furry head against her cheek for a moment and then squeezed him into her bag.

Leman appeared to have dressed in absolutely all her jewellery for the evening. Her evening dress was long, made from turquoise satin with gold lace laid over it. It had a train at the back made of lighter blue chiffon lined with yellow satin. She had clearly spent the afternoon at the beauty salon, because her hair was dyed a strange shade of orange, somewhere between blonde and ginger. Her face was heavily made up, with turquoise eye

Veronica Di Grigoli

shadow and foundation which looked powdery and the same orangey colour as her hair. Celeste concluded that the make up colours had been carefully selected to coordinate with her dress and her new hairdo. Seeing Leman without her usual black bob was disconcerting, but the smell of perfume mixed with cigarette smoke was reassuringly familiar.

Leman initially objected to Celeste's request, on the way to the Freemason's dinner, to stop briefly at the orphanage.

"You getting obsession with boys," she said. "You not their mother. You can go tomorrow. This dinner most important for Ferhat."

Ferhat's response, meanwhile, had been to ignore his wife and lean forward to Mehmet and ask him to make the brief detour.

"There's plenty of time, so long as you don't take too long there," he said to Celeste with a kind smile.

Mehmet made rapid progress through the dark city. The car seemed to glide when he drove, in surprising contrast with the abrupt stopping and sudden starting which jolted Celeste in her seat whenever Leman or any of the city's countless taxi drivers were behind the wheel. When they pulled up outside the orphanage, Leman told Celeste not to take longer than five minutes, as she laid her podgy hand, adorned with a ring on every single finger, on Ferhat's thigh. Celeste ran up the stairs of the orphanage and straight into Tekin's dormitory. He was already in bed, looking very anxious. Most of the other boys were already asleep.

"I thought you forgot me," he said, his reedy voice sounding slightly tremulous.

"I'm sorry I'm late," said Celeste, sitting down on the side of his bed. His threadbare and obviously second-hand bedspread was a faded pink and had what looked like a burn mark near the corner. "But anyway, I didn't forget you. And I've brought something very special, as I promised you." She opened her bag and produced Bruno, the bear. "He always looks after me when I need my mother and, for a while, he can stay with you and look after you, now that you don't have a dog. You will take good care of him, won't you?" Celeste hoped Tekin would treasure her bear. Foolish though she felt, she was not ready to part with Bruno for good. She definitely needed to know she would get him back. "I'll try to find you a dog, maybe a puppy who needs to be looked after, then you can give Bruno back to me."

"I'll look after him very well," said Tekin, already cuddling Bruno to his chest. "When will you come back? When will you come to see me again?"

"I'm not working on Saturday, so I'll come then. I'll ask Leman if I can take you out somewhere nice for the day. But anyway, even if she says no, I'll spend the day here with you. That's a promise."

Evil Eye

Tekin nodded silently, biting his lower lip. Celeste remembered her little brothers trying to be brave like this when their mother had been ill, trying to believe in her father's words of optimism. She felt utterly helpless, knowing that nothing she could say would really change how this scared little boy felt inside.

"I love Bruno. He smells like you," Tekin told her. His tiny hands slid into the long fur and Celeste saw that they were too small to reach fully round the bear's torso. She remembered when Bruno had been that big for her, too. "I'll give him back when my aunt comes," he promised.

Celeste pulled the covers up to Tekin's chin and kissed his forehead, wondering if that meant she would never get her bear back again.

The Freemasons' annual dinner was held in a grand hotel on the Asian side of Istanbul, up on a hill overlooking the sea. A string quartet played chamber music quietly in one corner of the grand atrium as armies of white gloved waiters and waitresses, dressed in black and white uniforms, plied their way among the guests, holding silver trays laden with glasses of champagne and Russian caviar high above their heads. At the centre of the atrium, water trickled silkily down a three-tiered fountain, dripping in turn from one white marble basin to another, each shaped like cupped bouquets of petals and leaves hanging languidly in the air. The pool at the bottom had been filled with cut water lily flowers and small floating candles in the shape of flowers, which drifted around in the slow currents created by the cascade from the fountain. The building dated from the Art Nouveau era and still had its original windows, tiles, light fittings and even copper door handles, decorated with swirling patterns in rich, sumptuous colours. Celeste was dazzled by the beauty all around her and noticed that some of the patterns in the tiles and windows were images of water lilies just like the exquisitely beautiful pink and white ones floating in the fountain. She hardly knew which way to turn among the bustle of busy waiters and all the elegant guests.

Ferhat beamed with happiness and looked more relaxed than Celeste had ever seen him before. She had not realised until now how much tension he usually carried in his face, and how much this seemed to age him. He appeared to know every single person present and proudly introduced her, along with Leman and Levent, to everyone he greeted. Leman followed him like a bodyguard, linking her arm through his at every opportunity and butting into his conversations whenever she could. For once, he seemed not to mind, and even gave her more attention than usual. Meanwhile Celeste's mind was increasingly occupied with when she would be able to meet Cengiz and how she would get him on his own to show him the scraps of paper she had brought. She unconsciously patted her bag several times as she thought of its contents. Finally she had her chance to meet him when Levent took her by the elbow and steered her towards the next room, beyond the atrium with the fountain.

"Look, let me introduce you to my geek friend," he said.

Cengiz was shorter than Celeste and very thin. His suit seemed too loose for him and his bow tie somehow looked overly large, drooping downwards below his Adam's apple as if it were wilting in the heat. He had a round-shouldered, stooping posture and peered up at Celeste through a pair of thick, black framed glasses which made his eyes look like two tiny points of light at the end of long tunnels. While speaking, he looked at Levent and avoided making eye contact with Celeste, even when answering one of her questions. Her heart fell as she wondered whether she would manage to enlist his help, especially without involving Levent.

She decided to try to draw him out of his shell by asking him about the Koran and the Muslim faith. Perhaps talking about his pet subject would break the ice. He answered her questions briefly and continued directing most of his attention towards Levent. Celeste was about to give up trying, but then she thought of how Maryam would react in this situation, when she had a mission to accomplish. She put on her best smile and asked him about his university course, about his father's membership of the Freemasons, about his interests, and about anything else she could think of which might lure him into conversation. He persistently gave her one- or two-word answers and averted his gaze. Eventually, deeply disappointed, she followed Levent back to the atrium and sat on the base of the fountain watching the water lilies floating on the water. Their tips were white but at the bases of their petals the heart of each flower was a deep pink, which gave them a translucent glow as it was reflected by each opalescent petal and then onto the rippling surface of the water.

"I was right," said Levent. "You nearly gave him a heart attack."

"I don't think so," laughed Celeste, hoping she was succeeding in hiding her disappointment. "He practically ignored me."

"That's the longest and most lively conversation I've ever seen him have with a girl," said Levent, his easy smile spreading across his face as he looked teasingly into Celeste's eyes. "In fact, I think it's the only conversation I've ever seen him have with a girl. He's probably planning his marriage proposal speech right now."

He dipped his hand into the water of the fountain and lifted out a water lily. He shook the dripping water from its short stem and held it out to Celeste, who took it in her cupped hands. He was about to say something else to her, when his mother called to him shrilly from across the room to come and meet one of his father's friends. She was beckoning wildly and holding her glass of champagne recklessly high in the air, tipped so far onto its side that she looked as if she may accidentally spill it down her sleeve.

"I'll be back in a moment," apologised Levent as he stood up reluctantly and made his way towards his still frantically beckoning mother. Celeste glanced back to where she had spoken to Cengiz, and realised he was looking at her. The moment he saw her look at him, he turned away. How could she approach him now and ask him to do some translating for her? As she set the water lily Levent had given her back in the fountain she glanced across the room and saw Levent deliberately walk past Cengiz instead of heading directly for his parents. Passing close to Cengiz, he said a word in his ear. Cengiz, timidly and reluctantly, came towards the fountain and asked if he could sit beside Celeste.

"Levent said you're alone and suggested I keep you company," he said, shyly.

Good old Levent, thought Celeste.

"That's kind of you," she said. "Levent tells me you're very good at reading Arabic. I was wondering, could you translate something for me?"

"My Arabic isn't all that great," he protested modestly. "What did you want translated?"

"To be honest, I don't know what it is. And it may not even be in Arabic. I think it could just be Turkish written in Arabic script." She dipped into her bag to pull out the scraps of paper and the photograph. "As I said, I've no idea what these are, but I'd really like to know."

Cengiz pushed his glasses up his nose before taking the pieces of paper, and held them so close to his nose that they almost touched it, hunching down towards the water of the fountain so that he could see better by the light of the candles. He spent several minutes reading all three papers before he spoke, turning the number square and the strange symbols around so that he could study them upside down and from every direction. Behind his heavy glasses, Celeste could see his dark eyebrows knitting together into a frown. Eventually, she could wait no longer.

"Well, what do..."

"Where did you get these?" Cengiz interrupted her, looking suspicious.

"I just found them," replied Celeste, warily. "What are they?"

"They're weird, and nasty," he replied. "They're like something between prayers and curses; magic spells, I suppose you could call them. This one," he explained, holding the very creased paper Celeste had found inside the burnt onion, "seems to be the least malicious of the three. It's supposed to be burnt inside an onion, to make the heart of the person you desire become inflamed with passion. The onion is supposed to symbolise the different layers of a person as you get to know them, and the love is supposed to burn at the very core. The Koran specifically forbids practising magic, but in the olden days people were very superstitious and this type of thing was quite commonplace. It's a very old Ottoman belief that died out long ago."

"Except for some people," said Celeste, glancing hastily around the room to check in case Leman or Levent were approaching. When she saw neither of them, she asked Cengiz, "What about the symbols and numbers? What are they for?"

"I've no idea," Cengiz replied. "I've never seen symbols like these before. I can only translate what's written here. I do know that number squares were used for doing so-called magic in Ottoman times, so maybe that's what these are."

"What about the other ones?" asked Celeste. She realised her palms were becoming sweaty in anticipation of finding out, at last, what Leman had been trying to achieve with her bizarre objects and rituals.

"This one," said Cengiz, holding the creased photograph of Leman that had been wedged behind the photograph of Ferhat, "Is a curse. Or rather, you could call it a beauty stealing spell." To Celeste's relief, he seemed not to have noticed that it was written on a photograph of Leman.

"What exactly does it say?" she asked.

"It's not easy to translate accurately because it's written a bit in old Turkish and a bit in Arabic, which is full of mistakes. But the gist of it is something like, 'may the beauty and youthful vigour of the person enfolded in this spell be taken out of them, and become the possession of the writer of the spell, the person who encloses.'"

"So, if it was wrapped around something from another person, say, a piece of their hair, for example, then the magic was supposed to steal that person's beauty to give it to another person?"

"Exactly. The person who has made their mark on this paper," confirmed Cengiz, holding out the photograph so that Leman's smiling face stared smugly up at Celeste through the writing. "Her, I guess." As Cengiz looked up at Celeste the lenses of his glasses reflected dozens of tiny points of light from the candles floating among the water lilies in the fountain, so that she could no longer see his eyes behind the thick discs of glass. Had Cengiz realised that this photograph was of Leman? If so, he was not giving anything away.

Celeste was stunned. Was Leman seriously trying to make herself more beautiful and attractive by taking Celeste's youth and beauty, and trying to make her husband fall back in love with her by slow roasting an Arabic magic spell inside an onion? Was this why she sometimes took Celeste to the beauty parlour with her? Not for company, not to be generous, and not simply to get at a lock of her hair to perform creepy magic rituals with it, but because she wanted to make sure Celeste had as much beauty as

Evil Eye

possible for her to steal? The opal necklace must have been intended to help the spells work, thought Celeste. She was glad she had left it at home today. She resolved never to wear it again, even though she did not believe in these idiotic superstitions. She remembered Bűket's words about white opals. Many people consider white opals to be a curse, she had said. A white opal was supposed to sap the wearer of their vitality and youth. They were said to have bad dreams that would strip them of their emotions and soul, so that they would gradually descend into desperation. Celeste took the photograph and the paper from the onion out of Cengiz's hand, tucking them hastily into her bag as she asked him about the last piece of paper, the yellow one from the oil lamp in Leman's desk. He held it by one corner, as if he wanted to avoid touching it.

"This one is gross," he stated simply. "It says that these symbols are written in blood, these brown signs here."

Celeste looked at the symbols she had thought were written in brown ink, and wondered how many times she had unwittingly touched them. A feeling of dread built up before she managed to ask Cengiz,

"What does it say?"

"It's meant to be used for taking possession of someone," he said.

"In what sense?" asked Celeste, feeling as if her heart had stopped beating in suspense.

"In the sense of owning their thoughts and controlling their every feeling, controlling their every decision and being able to make them do your bidding. It says that burning these blood symbols in the magic oil will activate the power of possession and capture ownership of the object's heart."

"But does it say who it's supposed to possess?" asked Celeste.

"Well, down here, 'The person who consumes the possession compound,' is what it says. Whatever that's supposed to mean."

Celeste thought of all the times she had eaten or drunk with Leman and wondered if Leman had ever slipped some horrible substance into her food or drink. Could that be what those glass jars containing swirls of paper in the fridge were for?

"Does it say anything about this possession compound?" she asked. "I mean, as in, what it is, or what it looks like?" she asked, hastily. Cengiz studied the paper again.

"No," he replied flatly. "I can't tell you anything else," he went on, "Except to warn you that whoever wrote these spells, or had them written, meant a lot of harm."

Celeste tucked the yellow paper into her bag, feeling somewhat repulsed and, like Cengiz, not wanting to touch it. She leaned a little closer to thank him.

"You've been really helpful, and so kind to help me out like this," she said. "I'm really grateful." As she spoke, she became aware that he was leaning back and had frozen rigid in embarrassment. She realised she had leaned too close and he had thought she may be about to touch him. She had made him feel uncomfortable just when she wanted to express her gratitude, and suddenly she felt mortified. She decided to try starting a new conversation to defuse the atmosphere.

"Levent has told me that you were hoping to become an Imam," she began, desperately. To her immense relief, he threw his head back and guffawed with laughter.

"He's such a tease, that Levent," said Cengiz, still laughing. "That's not true at all!" Celeste laughed too, still a little nervous and deeply distracted by the things she had just learned about Leman. "If I were so religious, would I drink champagne?" Cengiz went on, standing up to take two glasses of champagne from the tray of a passing waiter. At last seeming to throw off some of his crippling shyness, he handed one of the glasses to Celeste. "You do know that the Koran bans taking alcohol or any other mind-altering substance, don't you?"

"Yes. I did know that, although I've noticed quite a few people don't take much notice of it in Turkey."

"It's not like the Arab countries where alcohol is illegal," said Cengiz, "and that's a very good thing. I believe deeply in personal choice, and in personal freedom. But a great many people here in Turkey do choose not to drink alcohol at all."

"The people I live with drink all the time," said Celeste. She would previously have avoided criticising her landlord and landlady this openly, especially as Ferhat was her host this evening, but she felt so deceived and furious with Leman that this was the way the anger welling up in her found its outlet. "Not Levent, he hardly ever drinks," she added, "but his parents do all the time." Their cocktail cabinet was the most important feature of the house, for Ferhat as well as for Leman. It was their succour in times of stress and unhappiness and their friend during periods of loneliness. Despite its generous proportions it achieved a complete stock turn at least once a fortnight. There was always a bottle of Napoleon brandy and peach schnapps on the top shelf which Ferhat sometimes had to replace after only a week. Did Leman keep her 'possession compound' in there as well, Celeste wondered, in disgust.

"Leman habitually washes her antacid tablets down with a shot of whisky," she confided.

"Not likely to be very effective medically," commented Cengiz, still smiling. Now able to see his teeth properly for the first time, Celeste noticed they looked quite yellow, but she felt grateful to this shy boy who had at last resolved a major mystery for her. She wondered whether she might have been better off not knowing. She suddenly remembered a dream she had had recently, about Nasreddin Hoca in the form of the kind bank manager, Attila. In her dream she had said that magic was harmless, since it didn't work, and he had contradicted her. *'It doesn't matter whether it works or not,'* he had said in her dream, *'What matters is the mind that wants it to.'*

"Oh look," Cengiz interrupted her thoughts in a whisper, "here come the drunkards in person."

"You won't say anything to them, will you?" pleaded Celeste hastily, suddenly panicking in case she might have to pay for her moment of indiscretion.

"Of course not," he hissed back, standing to shake Ferhat and Leman's hands.

"They are calling us in for dinner," said Ferhat, happily. "We have taken a place at the table beside your parents, Cengiz, so we can all sit together."

"Off we go then," said Celeste, trying to sound casual but realising as she spoke that her voice sounded exaggeratedly flippant. She felt as if they all knew what she had been saying to Cengiz. She was also afraid to look Leman in the eye. What should she say to a witch who wanted to steal her looks, make her waste away with illness and possibly take possession of her soul?

The dining room was painted with a tulip motif, small coral red flowers with pointed petals like the wild Turkish tulips painted delicately on traditional Iznik pottery. Their curling green leaves, rendered in classic Art Nouveau style, gave the Turkish flower an unusual lightness which made the room seem intimate despite its grand dimensions. Ferhat noticed Celeste studying the design and looked pleased.

"Have you noticed these little tulips woven into Turkish fabrics and rugs?" he asked her. Celeste admitted that she had not. "We Turks experienced tulip mania before it reached Holland and bankrupted the country. Tulips grow wild all over Turkey and were cultivated with a real passion for a long while before they reached Europe. They're almost a national symbol."

"That big rug in the living room has got tulips all over it," put in Levent. "I'm surprised you haven't noticed. You're so observant."

"I'll have to check when we get home!" joked Celeste.

Ferhat pulled out a chair for Celeste as he continued speaking. She was concentrating on his conversation yet she could not help noticing, out of the corner of her eye, that Leman seemed angry to have her own chair was pulled out for her by her son, rather than her husband.

"We Turks infected the Flemish ambassador with Tulip mania," Ferhat went on. "He was sent to Istanbul by the Austrian Emperor to negotiate peace at the end of the Ottoman siege of Vienna."

Celeste started to wonder if he genuinely was as oblivious to his wife's moods as he seemed. Perhaps he was far more cunning than she had realised. Could this be his strategy for avoiding confrontation and irritation? Levent managed to manipulate the seating arrangement so that he was between his mother and Celeste. In this way Celeste was neither beside Leman nor opposite her, for which she was immeasurably thankful.

"When was this ambassador sent to Turkey?" Celeste asked, hoping Ferhat had not already told her whilst her attention was wandering.

"He was a contemporary of Sŭleyman the Magnificent, so that would be the late sixteenth century," answered Ferhat, beaming with delight that not only Celeste but also Cengiz' parents seemed fascinated. "He started the cultivation of tulips in Vienna, and they spread to Holland from there. Among the Europeans the diseased and mutated tulips, the ones with striped petals, or those ones with wavy edges, were worth a fortune. People would pay the equivalent of thousands of pounds just for one bulb."

"Oh Ferhat, I love listening to you! You always tell us such unusual and interesting tales," commented Cengiz' mother, sitting between Ferhat and her husband. Dressed in an elegant silvery-grey gown and with her grey and white hair fixed up in a French pleat, her beauty seemed effortless. She wore almost no make-up, yet the clean and youthful radiance of her skin made her glow, her beauty all the more impressive for its simplicity.

"When people went wild on speculation," resumed Ferhat, "a simple tulip bulb could be worth more than a house. People invested their life's savings in them."

"How stupid of them!" commented Leman, dismissively.

"Why did they do that?" asked Celeste.

"It started because a simple tulip bulb could suddenly mutate and sprout a rare coloured flower, or a bloom with striped petals, or some other magical surprise," said Ferhat. "At first people were bewitched by the wonder of such unexpected natural beauty. Everybody who could afford a tulip bulb wanted to plant one in the garden and hope it would do something amazing. Then people realised it was a way to speculate and make a great fortune and the mad prices got out of hand. Then one day people suddenly came to their senses and the bulbs were worth nothing."

"So, did the Turks start going bankrupt like the investors in Holland?" asked Celeste.

Evil Eye

"To a lesser extent, yes," said Ferhat. "Sometimes I think it's a real pity people stopped valuing beauty so highly. There aren't many things truly worth very much in this world."

Celeste was relieved that the conversation had started so easily and, like Cengiz' mother, she enjoyed the fact that Ferhat's conversation was above the mundane level of domestic arrangements or hairstyles and clothing, which seemed to interest Leman above all else. Celeste hid the turmoil and distress that she still felt inside, after learning from Cengiz what was written on Leman's scraps of paper, by continuing to chat to Ferhat on topics she knew would not interest Leman. She asked him if he knew the history of the hotel. Then she asked him if the Freemasons performed the bizarre rituals that they were believed to, and he teased her, saying that if they did, he certainly would not reveal the truth. He also complimented her on her new dress, which he apparently did not know had been a gift from Levent.

"If I may be permitted to say so, you look radiant in that dress. Red is definitely your colour, it flatters you very much."

Celeste felt Levent beside her stiffen with tension, and realised that Leman had heard and was not pleased.

"Perhaps my wife has also helped you blossom out from a girl into a young woman," Ferhat continued, "as she loves the beauty parlour and I know she has been introducing you to their secrets. You see, it's not only the Freemasons who keep closely guarded secrets!" This observation produced a tinkle of polite laughter from Cengiz' parents and the others sitting nearby.

"You're right," said Celeste slowly and deliberately, "some of Leman's secrets regarding beauty have certainly come to my knowledge."

"Although real beauty comes from within," added Cengiz, looking down affectionately at his beef mignon. This observation was followed by a lull in the conversation, which lasted an uncomfortably long time until Cengiz' mother filled it by asking Ferhat,

"Tell me, are you still taking your frequent business trips to France?"

At this Levent gasped and started to choke on some food, so Celeste tried to help by patting him on the back. Her hand was slapped away by Leman, who insisted that she was hitting him too hard and would bruise him, and that he had to drink water with some lemon squeezed into it to 'calm his throat.'

"I'm fine, Mum" he protested, still red faced and spluttering, as behind his back Leman glared at Celeste through her newly auburn hair. Celeste noticed that while she was thumping Levent on the back, her cat's eye ring had caught Leman's attention. As she turned back to face Ferhat and

Veronica Di Grigoli

Cengiz, she reached for her glass and was glad that Cengiz' mother commented on it.

"It's very unusual," she commented admiringly. "What type of stone it is?"

"Oh, this is called cat's eye," responded Celeste immediately. "It's traditionally regarded as a protection against witchcraft."

"Something like a *nazar boncuğu,* then?" suggested Ferhat.

"Well," explained Celeste, choosing her words carefully, "the difference would be that a *nazar* protected against the jealously of innocent people whose harm was unintentional. This type of stone was supposed to guard against the evil doing of malicious people who deliberately set out to do harm by using magic spells and rituals."

Levent turned his head to look at her as she spoke and, as she looked up into his eyes, she realised that this was the first time she had ever seen anguish on his soft baby face. Did he know exactly why she had said those words? She was filled with remorse when she felt the intensity of the pain she saw in his eyes.

The next morning Maryam did not come to work at Leman's house. She telephoned from a public payphone to say her eldest son was still very ill and she was sorry, but she could not leave him. Celeste was frantic with nervous tension. Feeling shocked and bewildered the day after she had made the discovery that her landlady was genuinely trying to perform magic up on her, she was desperate to talk either to Maryam or to Heather, but Heather was also unavailable as she had to work all day. In the end, she decided to seek the soothing calm of the bank manager Attila's intelligent and rational company. She telephoned the number on his business card to check whether it would be convenient to visit, and was given an appointment for ten-thirty by his secretary, who seemed unable to understand that she merely wanted to make a social call.

Celeste entered Attila's office hesitantly, wondering if he would have forgotten her after all this time and whether she had made a mistake in deciding to visit him. She started to fear that all her dreams in which Attila appeared as Nasreddin Hoca might have made her think she knew him better than she did. She started to convince herself that he was not really the kindly avuncular man she remembered him as. As she rounded the door, her doubts faded instantly. She was welcomed into a large office almost as cosy as a living room, and Attila stood in front of his desk waiting to greet her with his warm smile. Immaculately dressed, as he had been the previous time she had seen him, he shook her hand gently and introduced her to the tall smiling lady standing beside him.

"This is my wife, Berna" he said proudly.

Evil Eye

So this was the magnificent woman he had told Celeste about. Like her husband, she was dressed simply but elegantly. Her face looked kind but Celeste had no doubt she would take nonsense from nobody. Attila beckoned Celeste away from the desk to a corner of the office where two leather sofas stood facing each other on either side of a glass-topped coffee table. Below the glass of the table was a layer of polished wood, upon which were laid out different crystals, lumps of metal ore and fossils. The two walls behind and sofas were lined with dark wooden fitted cupboards with sliding doors, filled with a mixture of books and more fossils, creating the atmosphere of a cosy gentleman's club. Attila invited Celeste to sit down, and picked up the phone to ask for some tea to be brought up.

Impatient to move on from the initial polite chatter, Celeste found she could contain herself no longer and suddenly started to blurt out the news she had learned the previous evening. She told Attila and Berna everything, all jumbled up, stumbling over her words and finding her Turkish deteriorating as she grew more agitated. She became increasingly aware of grammatical mistakes and pauses as she tried to remember the right words.

"Do you believe that this magic works?" asked Berna finally, when Celeste paused for breath.

"No," she answered, almost convincing herself.

"That's the important thing," said Berna. "It can't hurt you if you know it isn't real. If you believe in it, if you let yourself be overcome by fear, then maybe it really could make you ill."

A young girl tapped on the office door and placed a silver tray very carefully on the coffee table. It was set with a plate of different types of *halva* cut into cubes, and three small glasses of tea, in the centre of which was a small silver bowl of sugar cubes. Wearing a black and white waitress-style uniform, the girl looked sixteen years old at the most and seemed nervous about serving someone as important as Mr. Attila Zaman. Her hand trembled slightly as she arranged the coasters carefully on the table and placed a small gilded glass of tea in front of each person. Berna smiled at her and thanked her warmly, inducing a smile of relief from the girl as she stood up and tiptoed out of the room hastily.

"My wife is right, you know," said Attila. "Belief in magic has generally been associated with a lack of education and low social status. I knew a clever young lady like you would never let herself get fooled by such nonsense." Celeste smiled and took a piece of *halva*. "In the past, in Ottoman times, it was perhaps more widespread because women rarely received an education. Did I mention, the first time I met you, that Roxelana was widely believed to be a witch?"

Veronica Di Grigoli

"No, you didn't," said Celeste, sitting herself more upright on the slippery leather sofa.

"People said she'd put a spell on Sŭleyman with black magic incantations and potions. That was quite an accusation, as women believed to be witches were generally chucked in the Bosporus to drown. That was the fate of quite a few women from the harem over the course of history. I've got a book about her here," he said, opening a dark wooden cupboard and taking out a small blue book, which he started to flick through. "An Austrian ambassador wrote that his informants had assured him there were women in the city of Istanbul who supplied Roxelana with pieces of hyena skull, which were believed to be a very strong aphrodisiac. Ah, here it is: '*But none of them*,' says Busbecq - that was the ambassador's name - '*agreed to sell these bones to me saying they were meant exclusively for Hŭrrem Sultana who, they said, made the sultan constantly addicted to her by making love potions and by other magic means.*' It was widely believed at the time that Sŭleyman was so obedient to his wife because of the magic spell that she put on him." Attila glanced up at his wife and winked at her affectionately. "They said that was how she managed to make him decide to have Ibrahim, his closest friend and vizier, and Mustafa, his first-born son, put to death."

"But of course it was a load of nonsense," commented Berna. "Attila, please would you read out that love poem he wrote to Roxelana. It's beautiful. You can't make someone love you like that using magic: his was real love."

Attila turned to the front of the book and read aloud:
"*I have given my orders -
make a gown for my beloved.
Use the sun to make the bodice,
Use the moon to make the lining,
Use the white clouds
for the trimmings,
Use the blue sea
to make the threads.
Use the stars for buttons,
And make the fastenings
out of me.*"

Berna had closed her eyes as she listened, rapt by the beauty of the words. Attila opened the same dark wooden cupboard again and, putting the book away, took out another very large book bound in white leather with the cover tooled with gold writing, which he handed to Celeste.

"This is for you," he said. "It's the one I promised you before."

The book, the one Attila had told Celeste about when they had first met in the harem, contained reproductions of exquisite illuminated manuscripts in Arabic script, with multi-coloured border decorations. On the page opposite each photographic reproduction was a translation of the manuscript into Turkish, English and French. The manuscripts dated from the seventeenth century onwards, and were the orders from the sultans' mothers, the *valide sultanas*, and other important women of the Harem, for the establishment of charitable foundations on their deaths, using their personal wealth. Each manuscript, which was essentially a last will and testament, was beautifully bound and bore the signatures and seals of the woman concerned, her scribe and a slave witness.

The wills specified exactly how the foundations were to use the money bequeathed, ranging from the building of hospitals for the poor, mosques and a military fortress to defend the city from foreign pirate attacks, to drinking water fountains and bird baths. One of them described a hospital, to be built and managed after the *valide sultana*'s death by her trusty chief black eunuch. She stipulated not only how much money she was leaving, but also listed every man to be employed, ranging from doctors to porters, door-keepers and cleaners, cooks, candle-lighters and wood-choppers. She detailed how many loaves of bread each man was to be paid each day, and stated which of the more important posts were also to be paid with coins.

'*Let a man chosen for his reliability be appointed door-keeper,*' Celeste read, '*and let him be paid three loaves a day for his work. Let a man chosen for his strength be appointed wood-chopper for the hospital fires, and let him be paid three loaves a day for his work.*'

And so the list went on. Most of the women, in bequeathing their funds, required that their descendants should, for all eternity, be entitled to live off the surplus profit made by the establishments to be created.

"You're like my husband," commented Attila's wife Berna. "He relaxes when he's upset by sinking into history. He goes off somewhere else nobody can follow him, and comes back feeling calmer." She picked up a cup of tea and placed it in Celeste's hand. "I'm very pleased to have met you. Attila told me all about you. Just keep on reading," she added slowly, as Celeste took a sip of the hot, sugary apple tea. "Take your time."

Celeste knew Berna really meant what she said, and she felt comfortable enough in her company to continue reading the book and ignore her hosts for a while longer. She carefully placed the small glass of tea back on the coffee table and turned the page. The manuscript described at length how the honest Muslims living along the Bosphorus were repeatedly prevented from worshipping or carrying out their trades because of pirate raids by infidels in their ships. For this reason the *valide sultana* wished to leave absolutely all her money for the building of a fortress on the Bosphorus to protect the citizens of Istanbul.

"Is this fortress still standing?" Celeste asked after reading out the last sentence referring to the fortress.

"Not that one, but there are others," answered Attila.

"You can see them from our yacht," added Berna. "We sometimes go sailing in the Bosphorus or out into the sea. The city seems a relaxing place when you're out at sea and viewing it at a distance from the shore." She smiled and then added, "We'd love you to join us for a day sailing. Our skipper's very good at catching fish and he cooks them for us himself. So we could make a day of it."

"That's sounds wonderful," said Celeste.

"Next time we plan to go out, we'll let you know," Berna concluded.

Celeste picked up her tea and took another sip. It was already tepid but she decided to finish it in one gulp.

"You know," said Attila, philosophically, "These stones in here are millions of years old. Doesn't that comfort you? We humans get all worked up for a few brief moments with anger, or fear, or love, and then it all passes as if it never happened. I look at these stones to remind myself that most of this world stays the same for so long that it hardly notices one human life."

"This is the same as his love of history and the comfort he takes in the oldness of things," added Berna. She pointed to a stone at the far side of the table. "He especially likes that lump of gold, there in the corner. That one will never corrode or deteriorate. It'll still be perfect and shiny new looking long after we're both dead."

TWELVE

Zeliha's Visitor

Delivering a Sermon
Once, Nasreddin was invited to deliver a sermon. When he got into the pulpit, he asked the congregation gathered in the mosque, "Do you know what I'm going to say?" The gathered people replied "No." At this, the Hoca declared "I have no desire to speak to people who don't even know what I will be talking about," and he left.

The people felt embarrassed and called him back again the next day. This time, when he asked the same question, the people all shouted "Yes." At this, Nasreddin said, "Well, since you already know what I'm going to say, I won't waste any more of your valuable time," and he left.

Now the people were really perplexed. They decided to try one more time, so once again they invited the Hoca to speak the following week. Once again he asked the same question: "Do you know what I am going to say?" This time, the people were prepared and so half of them called out "Yes" while the other half called out "No." Hearing this, Nasreddin said "The half who already knows what I'm going to say, tell it to the other half." And with that, he left.

As soon as Celeste walked into the *Kapalı Çarşı*, the Grand Bazaar, she felt sure she would get lost sooner or later. This was not because she had taken the wrong bus three times on the way there. Nor was it because she had dreamily walked past Heather without noticing she was there, leaving Heather screaming at her to turn around while she chased her almost the entire length of a side street full of butchers' shops whose windows distractingly displayed skinned sheep's heads with their tongues lolling over their teeth. No, it was because here, her every sense was bombarded and her consciousness was overwhelmed with new sounds, smells and sights. In the market's vast labyrinth of countless alleys and tunnels, archways and cupolas, each one looking the same as the rest, each corner resembling the last, her ears were filled with the sound of hundreds of voices echoing against marble and tiles. The smell of smoke, cured leather, metal polish and a thousand spices stung her nostrils. Glowing lights reflected from every surface and movement in every colour of the spectrum dazzled her eyes as bright clothes, sparkling metal ware, pottery, rugs and paintings vied for her attention. The walls and ceiling seemed to be closing in on her as the place thronged with people, all in a frenzy of

Veronica Di Grigoli

activity; wizened old men carried vast baskets of wool, little boys sat on the ground polishing shoes beside elaborate carved wooden boxes containing over twenty different colours of shoe polish, men waddled under the burden of stacks of rolled up leather hides they were delivering to the tanners in the heart of the market, and everywhere shoppers pushed past, jostling for space as they hauled their shopping bags through any gap they spotted and pressed on, hungry to make more purchases.

Heather took Celeste firmly by the hand and led her along an arcade to their right, Celeste stumbling after her while gazing back over her shoulder like a small child.

"What's wrong with you?" asked Heather. "You're like a zombie today."

"There's just so much to see," answered Celeste. "I'm fine. I'm a bit tired but basically I'm just rather overwhelmed by all this bustle."

"Well let's just focus," said Heather. "What are you aiming to buy?"

"I need a pressie for Maryam's birthday," said Celeste. "I'd like to get her some shoes. Apart from that, I just want to see what there is."

"Has she told you anything about Ferhat's secret lover?" asked Heather.

"Nothing," answered Celeste. "She was adamant that she couldn't tell me anything because of the way Leman threatened her. She's really scared of Leman. She won't speak to anyone about it."

"I thought it might all blow over after a few weeks, and then she'd tell you the secret scoop."

"She's not breathing a word," said Celeste. "Whatever Leman's threat was, it's working."

"Let's try this way," said Heather, pulling Celeste down an alley to their left. "If I remember rightly, the shoes are down here."

Immediately recognising them as foreigners among the many tourists, the shop keepers tried calling out to Celeste and Heather in every language they knew.

"Hey, you Yankees, good price, Güten tag!"

"Prego, parlo Italiano, bonjour, we make deal."

As they slowed down in front of a shop full of jugs and plates, the owner poured forth his entire English repertoire without pausing for breath:

"Hey sexy chicks, you are dollars money, coca cola rock and roll! Look, welcome my shop! Look here, look, look, all real antiques, good price."

"If we see any Americans," Heather responded in Turkish, "we'll be sure to tell them about you." With that she gave him a pitying look and marched on as fast as she could. A couple of shops further along, Celeste heard a shopkeeper saying to his assistant,

"Look out, here comes money." Then, without pausing for breath, he continued in English. "Hello ladies, I make special price for you, only for you!"

"I bet you will!" answered Heather, without even turning her head as she strode past. "Zeliha told me this is the worst section for ripping off tourists," she explained as they walked on. "She told me where to find the better places to buy things. Apparently most tourists experience sensory meltdown and don't manage to penetrate to the inner part. They wander around here for several days deliriously wondering who they are and why they came."

"Just like me!" exclaimed Celeste, laughing.

They walked past a workshop making carpets, with large vats of dye and long, thick skeins of wool on wooden stakes which men were dipping into the liquid to colour them and then laying out carefully in rows to dry. The foul smell of the dye stung Celeste's nose and Heather quickened her pace, holding a large white handkerchief to her face.

"Do you reckon those fumes make them hallucinate?" asked Heather. "I can just imagine them coming up with freaky psychedelic carpet designs under the influence of whatever poison they've got brewing in there."

"If that's bad, what about the stink of this lot?" gasped Celeste. They were now passing through the alley of tanners, displaying vast arrays of coloured leather items in their windows, ranging from jackets and coats to tooled picture frames, briefcases, covered boxes and even furniture. Inside the shops lay waist-high stacks of raw hides awaiting treatment. Pressing on, they passed countless jewellery shops and fabric wholesalers, small boutiques selling river pearls which their owners said came from Japan, shops selling nothing but blue glass *nazar boncuğu* in every size and of every type, an arcade of sellers of silverware, their shop fronts festooned with silver jugs, pots, candelabra, platters, serving dishes and ornaments, and an alley filled with thousands of copper pots polished until they reflected the lights overhead as rosy red sparks and star-bursts of pink. They walked along arcades of carpet shops, more fabric shops with bales of cloth and rolls stacked against their windows, and ceramics shops selling beautiful handmade pottery in traditional styles as well as modern looking plates decorated with scenes of Turkey for tourists.

Heather spotted a coffee shop so they decided to take a pause and have a drink. The air inside the café was clouded with cigarette smoke so thick that Celeste could only just make out the Ottoman style painting decorating the walls, depicting fat men smoking hookahs and ladies dressed in old fashioned costumes of slippers with curled up toes peeping out below baggy harem trousers and knee-length embroidered velvet coats. All around Celeste and Heather sat Turkish men drinking small glasses of stewed black Turkish tea and intently playing board games with numbers, dice and cubes. Occasionally, when one made a move he was particularly pleased with, he would shout out and raise his hand in the air, or all his friends at the table would pass comment together on his luck in rolling the dice.

Heather asked for the full menu, saying she felt hungry.

"I bring to you Ingiliz menu," offered the owner, proudly.

The dishes on the menu included 'rubbish kebap', 'kebap in paper', 'eats from meats', 'small bits of meat grilled,' 'lamp staeck' and 'wedding soap.'

"What on earth is wedding soap?" asked Celeste, chuckling.

"That's what they call tripe soup," explained Heather. "Actually, they usually call it wedding soup rather than wedding soap, but I'm sure that's what he means. I don't fancy any of this. I've decided I'll just have a drink."

The menu offered Turkish coffee and also 'Nest coffee,' which Celeste had by now learned was one of the endless variations of the spelling for Nescafé for those too weak to face the blast of caffeine in a traditional Turkish coffee. Fancying neither type of coffee, both Heather and Celeste ordered freshly squeezed orange juice, and sat sipping their drinks as they looked out upon the relentless mayhem of the market.

"So when exactly is Maryam's birthday?" asked Heather.

"It's today," replied Celeste. "I only found out this morning. She didn't tell me anything, I just heard Leman mention it casually to Levent, saying that she's decided not to give Maryam her usual birthday bonus pay this year. That's how I found out."

"Is Leman still sour over the photo-breaking incident?" asked Heather, deliberately mispronouncing her name by stressing the first syllable to make it sound like '*lemon*'.

"Probably," agreed Celeste. "It's not Maryam's fault there was some nutty magic spell behind the photo. Lemans' directing all her resentment about Ferhat's affair towards Maryam at the moment. I hope it gets forgotten soon. The atmosphere's horrible when Leman's on the prowl. As soon as she goes out of the house and there's just Levent or Ferhat, it seems like a different place."

"Why don't you move out?" asked Heather.

"I've thought about it, but the rent is really low and I don't think I could afford anywhere else in a nice area. I'll stay put for the time being."

"Anyway, what do you want to get for Maryam's birthday?" asked Heather.

"She desperately needs shoes," replied Celeste. "I sneaked a look when she took them off, and she takes the same size as me, thirty-nine."

"Right then, are you ready to set off again?" said Heather decisively.

"Let me get a carton of *ayran* to take with me," said Celeste. "I'm getting a bit hungry."

Tucking the *ayran* into her bag, Celeste linked arms with Heather and accompanied her further into the market, until they reached a perfume shop.

"Well it certainly smells like a tart's boudoir in here," said Heather, as they entered through the low doorway. The short, elderly shopkeeper wore a woolly grey cardigan buttoned to the neck. His large, hooked nose and stooping posture gave him the look of an eagle or some other bird of prey, perched on a branch waiting to swoop.

"I see he's got a special advantage in this profession," observed Heather, glancing down at his beaky nose benevolently. He took his hands from the pockets and, without a word, started to wave bottles under their noses. Celeste so loved the succession of flowery perfumes and heady scents that she demanded more and more.

"Stop!" the man suddenly shouted. "Go outside and clean your nostrils! Otherwise your noses won't understand a thing." They trooped out and took several deep breaths of the now chilly air in the arcade outside before rushing back into his shop for more. Celeste chose to buy a perfume called '*Bahçe Gűl*', Garden Rose, while Heather picked a musky scent called '*Ruh Zahar*'. Once they had decided on the perfumes, they had to choose from a vast selection of bottles, each a tiny phial in coloured glass with a twisting stopper like a candle flame. Some bottles had swirls of different coloured glass like marble, others were embellished with golden bands and gilt stoppers, whilst others were of a single, intense colour. They made such a beautiful display it was impossible to choose which one seemed most pleasing and Celeste and Heather gazed at the bottles until they had taken as long to chose them as they had to select their perfumes. The little eagle man roosted on a stool behind the counter, happy for them to take as long as they liked. Eventually they left clutching their carefully wrapped tiny bottles and set out again, following the man's directions to the area which sold shoes.

When they found it, Celeste was disappointed. The first few shops she saw seemed the same; full of men's shoes, all made of plastic, the vast majority of them tassel loafers in black or a lurid orangey-tan colour. One of the shopkeepers stood outside proudly modelling a pair of his own tassel loafers, with sparkling snow white socks showing proudly beneath his too-short stonewashed jeans. His black hair was cut fairly short, but with strands deliberately left longer than the rest at the nape of his neck, which hung over his collar. Flicking a short string of beads ornamented with a tassel to and fro around his fingers, he dragged the smoking stub of

Veronica Di Grigoli

a cigarette from his lips and invited them to come inside to look at the rest of his stock. The smoke wafted from his mouth and his nostrils as he spoke.

"I can show you many interesting things inside," he offered, hopefully.

"I bet you can," replied Heather. "But we need shoes for women."

"Do you think he got his trouser hems taken up deliberately to draw attention to his feet?" whispered Celeste, turning away and searching ahead for any sign of women's shoe shops. Eventually they found a shop which looked more promising, and Celeste asked if she could try on a pair of shoes which were similar to Maryam's old pair, in black leather with low heels. Celeste knew that Maryam was on her feet all day and so comfort was more important to her than looks. Heather managed to haggle so effectively to reduce the price that Celeste decided to buy Maryam a second pair, this time more dainty and in deep red leather which would match one of the skirts she wore fairly often. Satisfied at last that she had bought the gift she was searching for, Celeste asked Heather if she wanted to look at anything else.

"No, I'm ready to head off home," said Heather.

When they emerged from the market, it was only six in the afternoon but it was already pitch dark. The bustling activity showed no sign of relenting. They found themselves in a fruit and vegetable market illuminated by street lighting. They were surrounded by stalls of which there had been no sign when they had entered the market. The stalls were not general greengrocers' stalls but instead each stall sold one specific fruit or vegetable. They passed one stall piled high with bananas, several groaning with pyramids of oranges and another stacked with kiwis. Amongst all of them stood a man selling plastic fruit from a tray.

"I hope that's organic," said Heather in English as she walked past him. He smiled and held out his hand, perhaps thinking she intended to stop and buy something, but she just turned her bouncing head of ginger hair to smile back and then walked on. A horse and cart rattled past, laden with more fruit, followed by a boy pushing a trolley piled with bread snacks and a posse of seven *hamals*, porters bent over to carry their huge round baskets like kettle drums on their backs.

"Can we stop for a minute?" suggested Celeste. "I want my *ayran* now."

Heather bought a bag of tangerines and they found a marble plinth to sit on as Celeste drank and Heather peeled a tangerine.

"Read me the story," said Heather. "I know you're obsessed with them, and you're getting me addicted as well."

"I was just going to," answered Celeste. "*'One day the Hoca did lots of shopping in the Akşehir market place, so he found a porter to carry his purchases.'*"

"Oh, how topical," said Heather.

"*'Nasreddin loaded everything into the large basket the porter carried on his back. They headed towards the Hoca's home, Hoca walking in front and the porter following him. However, the dishonest porter chose to make off with Hoca's purchases rather than receiving his porter's fee. Hoca searched for him, and complained to his friends and neighbours, but the porter was nowhere to be found.*

'*Ten days later, as the Hoca and his friends were sitting in the coffee house, someone spotted the thieving porter. "Look Hoca Effendi, isn't that the porter you lost?" Hoca's friend pointed out. To his surprise, instead of going up to the man and confronting him, Hoca tried to hide. Everyone in the coffee house was amazed. "Hoca Effendi, why don't you go and face the man?" they asked. "What if he asks me to pay him the whole ten days' worth of porter's fees?" answered the Hoca.*' Do you reckon these *hamals* really do nick stuff sometimes?" asked Celeste as she inserted the straw into her *ayran*.

"Well, not that one," answered Heather, pointing out a *hamal* staggering sideways under a burden of what appeared to be firewood. "If he wanted to pinch that, I can't imagine him running fast enough to get away from anyone. The poor old geezer can hardly walk."

When Celeste arrived home, Maryam was ironing a large stack of bedding. It was heaped so high on the sofa that she was scarcely visible behind it. Celeste wondered if this had been a deliberate ploy to hide from her employer. Leman repeatedly entered and left the room to check that Maryam was working without a pause. She had been wearing orange and tan coloured clothes all week, apparently to coordinate with her new hair colour. Today she looked vaguely like Calamity Jane in a tan suede waistcoat and a matching suede skirt, the hemline of which was cut into a deep fringe so that her dimpled knees and chubby thighs showed when she walked. She had teamed it with a turquoise blouse with a deeply pointed collar and folded back cuffs. The heels of her cowboy boots were far higher and more pointed than normal cowboy boots and their tops were trimmed with stones which looked like real turquoise, a theme she had echoed in her choice of jewellery; a turquoise bead necklace with a silver pendant in the shape of a horse, and a ring set with a very large oval of turquoise. Celeste half expected to see a ten gallon hat in her hand but, instead, there was just the customary cigarette.

"Would you be able to take me with you to the orphanage tomorrow morning, please?" Celeste asked her. Her cheeks were still blushing pink from the cold air outside, giving her young fresh face a glow even more radiant than usual. "I promised Tekin I'd spend the day with him and the other boys."

"Of course," said Leman coldly, staring at Celeste as if she had said something utterly bizarre. Celeste waited patiently in silence for Leman to leave the room before putting her bags on the floor and picking up the one containing Maryam's shoes.

"Happy birthday," she said, holding the bag out. "I hope you like them."

"What's this?" asked Maryam, putting the iron down.

"Your birthday present, silly!" said Celeste. "Come on, open it right away." Maryam opened the box of shoes and held them as if they were precious gems.

"They're lovely, but which pair is for me?" she asked.

"Both of them," replied Celeste. "By the way, where's Yakup?"

"I left him with my sister today. He's getting bigger and she can cope with him along with the other children now. But Celeste, I've only got two feet. How can I wear four shoes?" Celeste laughed at the absurdity of Maryam's joke.

"Now you can choose which pair you want to put on each day."

"Like Leman," giggled Maryam. "I've never had two different pairs of shoes at the same time before. Thank you."

Celeste was pleased that Maryam had liked her gift, but she remained disappointed not to see baby Yakup. She thought he was too young to be left all day without seeing his mother, and wondered if Maryam had left him with her sister at Leman's insistence.

Celeste dreamed in the night that she was lost in the Grand Bazaar and could not find her mother, whom she had taken there. She ran down arcade after arcade, along street after street, calling to her mother constantly; but she was nowhere to be seen. She stopped a jewellery seller to ask if he had seen her. He said he had no recollection of seeing the woman Celeste described, and told her to buy some jewellery instead. All the time Celeste felt a growing sense of presentiment as she desperately turned one way and another among the endless alleyways and arcades, hoping to catch a glimpse of her mother but realising that she had no idea how to get back out of the market and no idea where she had been. Then she realised that Tekin had been with her too, and that she had let go of his hand in her desperation to find her mother. "I've lost Tekin, too!" she cried out in

Evil Eye

desperation, the words choking in her throat. "He's a tiny little boy, and I've lost him."

"You'll never find them," said the shopkeeper. "Buy some jewellery instead. This will protect you against cowboys." And he held out Leman's turquoise necklace with the horse-shaped pendant. The sight of it made Celeste's breath stop in her throat and her heart started to pound against her ribs.

"Oh, how will I ever find them?" gasped Celeste, ignoring him and desperately pressing on, deeper into the heart of the market. Then she felt hands grabbing her, squeezing her so tightly she could not breathe and dragging her along, pulling her up into the air and up through the ceiling.

"Celeste, Celeste! Are you all right?" Celeste woke up with a shudder and realised that Levent was holding her arms, sitting her up in bed and then brushing her hair away from her face. She suddenly felt bitterly cold, shivering violently in her damp pyjamas and bedding. The hair at the nape of her neck was drenched with sweat and she felt a wet trickle running down her back inside her pyjama top. "Are you all right?" Levent repeated, his voice betraying panic. He pressed the palm of his hand to her forehead. "You've got a fever," he said. "I'm so sorry to come into your room when you were asleep. I could her you shouting and choking. I was really scared. It sounded like you were suffocating. I didn't know what to do."

"I'm going to be sick," announced Celeste.

Levent hastily sat her up in bed, putting his arm around her body to raise her to her feet and help her across the dark landing, lit by a shaft of light from the full moon. They staggered into the bathroom together and she reached the toilet just in time, falling to her knees and vomiting several times. She realised Levent had withdrawn and was waiting just outside the open door, on the landing.

"Shall I come in, or do you want me to leave you alone?" he asked when she had been silent for a few moments.

"Can you help me get back to bed?" asked Celeste, realising she felt too weak to stand alone. Levent carried her back to her room and laid her on the still damp mattress. She lay dizzy and confused as she heard him disappear downstairs and return a few minutes later with a cold wet flannel, a glass of water and two paracetamol tablets.

"Take these if you can," he said. "You've got a very high fever."

Celeste knew that if she tried to swallow the tablets she would be sick again, so she just drank some water then lay back down on the bed.

"Shall I leave you alone now?" asked Levent. He had moved the chair from Celeste's desk so that he could sit where he could see her. "I'll stay here if you like, but if you want to be alone, I'll leave you."

Celeste desperately wanted her mother. She was ashamed to realise that she also wanted her teddy bear, Bruno, to grasp in her hand. She felt like a lost child. The feeling of nausea had not subsided and she felt excruciating pains in her stomach every time she tried to move. She also felt dizzy with the fever and so desolately cold that her body was racked by violent shivers and she wanted to wear all the clothes she had, and to light a fire beside her bed as well.

"I can't ask you to spend the night on a chair," she protested feebly, as Levent drew back the curtains to let in some silver moonlight.

"You can," replied Levent stubbornly.

And he did spend the night on the chair, bringing her glasses of water and dabbing her head with fresh cold water when she needed it, the rest of the time sitting in his dark blue pyjamas at her desk leafing very quietly through her stacks of art books by the faint light coming in through the open curtains.

Celeste finally fell asleep as the first shafts of sunlight were rising over the horizon and in her fitful, delirious sleep, she dreamed that she was a patient in a hospital, the hospital where Nilüfer's parents worked. They had insisted that Nilüfer helped them by working as a nurse, and she was waiting beside them in her light blue nurse's dress and crisply starched white hat and apron. They were a few beds away from her, but she could overhear them talking about buying and dealing drugs. They were drug dealers! Nilüfer and her parents were trafficking drugs and using the hospital as a cover. Celeste needed to call the police, to tell them that these respectable people were really criminals! She tried to stand up, to call out for help from the other patients, but Nilüfer helped her parents tie Celeste down. They were still talking about her. They were talking about her dying, about her death. They were going to kill her! She had to escape, but suddenly she wasn't on her bed any more, she was tied to a hard, cold stone slab and they were holding a syringe above her head. They were going to inject her with drugs! She tried to scream but it was too late; they had filled her veins with drugs that would confuse her, that would silence her, that would make her hallucinate.

Then she found herself back at home with her mother and father. She was about seven years old and she was standing by the kitchen table, showing her mother a picture she had just painted of a phoenix flying over a mountainous landscape carpeted with rainforest. It was a wonderful phoenix. She had painted it in every colour of the rainbow and even in some special colours that nobody else had ever seen before, that humans normally cannot see. Could her mother see them? These shimmering feathers that whispered on the breeze and started to beat against the paper they were trapped in? The phoenix glowed, he shone, not with normal earthly light but a special light from another dimension. Little Celeste put her palm against the back of the picture and felt his heart beating rapidly and furiously against her hand, and felt the paper warming up, and she suddenly took pity on the magnificent creature she had trapped in this two-dimensional prison so she decided to release him. She punched against the back of the paper, using all her force to make him burst free of the now scorching hot paper and she was flying with him, over the rainforest, clinging to his back as his wings beat like drumbeats against the hot humid air and hundreds of feathers fell from his wings and tail, fluttering to earth and filling the jungle with their happiness. Where each feather landed sprang up a flower, a blossom which filled the air with its divine scent and lifted Celeste's spirit, sent her soaring into a joy of an intensity she had never known a human could feel. Every part of her body tingled with the ecstasy of the lightness and power she felt herself imbibing from this jungle, but the phoenix wanted to lead her on, to show her greater wonders than this.

They reached the people near the top of the highest mountain and Celeste knew they were not human because their golden skin looked metallic, their hair seemed to give off a healing light and their eyes were so loving she could have drowned in them. They were tall and muscular and their happiness was so exuberant that it filled Celeste and made her feel even lighter than before.

"How old are you?" she asked them. "Are you immortal?"

"I can remember back to times before you were born, to before your grandmother and even her grandmother lived. We are the golden people; we have gold and silver in our veins, in our bodies. You humans have mundane base metals in you, tarnishable substances like iron, zinc and copper which are corroded and corrupted. Think of something made of iron, think how rusted and weak it becomes in a short time. How can you hope to live long when you are made from these perishable minerals? The gold in our bodies lasts forever, it is perfect and immortal. But the trace of silver in us tarnishes eventually. That is why we do not live forever. But the gold, this eternal substance, gives us our magical abilities and keeps us alive for more than a thousand years. We have time to learn things you humans do not. And when it is time for us to go, the phoenix takes us to a place where we burn with him and are reborn again. We come back to life with him and we re-awake with a deeper wisdom, ready to understand the world better each time we come back."

When Celeste walked again through the beautiful forest she felt its calmness and carefree lightness as the butterflies did, and the perfume of each flower lightened her until she felt as if she had no physical body left. As she floated onwards she realised she was in a garden and the flowers now were ones she knew, the ones her mother tended and watered. Then she saw her house again, and realised she was in her own garden and she was at home again with her parents, her mother embracing her and telling her how much she loved her, would always love her.

Celeste finally awoke at midday. Her fever had passed and she was glad to realise that she felt less nauseous. She saw she was alone in her room. When she stood up she felt her eyes blacking out, so she sat back down on the bed to wait for the blood to reach her head.

"Are you there, Levent?" she whispered, not expecting a reply.

"I'm here," he answered from the landing. He must have been waiting out there for her to wake up, she thought, as he entered her room and sat on the bed beside her. Celeste was shocked to see him. He looked gaunt, his cheeks seemed hollow and his eyes were lined with dark rings, but he seemed overjoyed to see her awake.

"Do you need anything?" he asked her, sounding concerned.

"Not really. But I was supposed to go to the orphanage to meet little Tekin today," she explained. "Your mother knows, but would you mind calling her? Just to ask her if she'll tell Tekin that I'm ill, but I haven't forgotten him."

"Are you sure you were supposed to meet him today?" asked Levent, looking anxious. "You do know what day it is, don't you?"

"Yes, Saturday of course," answered Celeste, starting to feel uneasy. "I promised him last week, the night of the Freemasons' dinner."

"It's Friday," answered Levent. "That dinner was two weeks ago. You've had a fever all week," he added, gently resting his hand on hers. "Don't you remember Nilűfer's parents coming?"

"What?" asked Celeste weakly.

"They came to see you three times. We were all so scared for you. I didn't dare leave you alone at all. Nilűfer sat with you for two nights, so I could sleep a bit," he added, almost apologetically. "They didn't know what was wrong with you. They took blood samples and everything. Are you sure you don't you remember it at all?"

"I..." began Celeste, faltering. " Maybe I do."

"They didn't know what treatment to give you. They couldn't work out what illness you had. At one point, they even said there was a possibility you might...." Levent looked terrified as he pronounced the word "possibility."

"A possibility I might...?" she asked. Celeste realised there were beads of sweat on Levent's forehead and his hand tightened around hers.

"That we might lose you."

She decided to have a shower in the evening. She did not want to eat dinner, but instead asked Levent if he would help her go downstairs to eat some fruit in the kitchen. Leman sat at the table sorting out her blister packs of tablets. Celeste was strangely relieved to see that her hair was black again, her fringe slightly shorter than usual but essentially the same old Leman Celeste now knew so well. She was using a small pair of nail scissors to cut away the parts of each blister pack where the tablets had already been used, making a pile of empty blisters with the cut away parts and sorting out the remaining, irregularly shaped foil cards by pharmaceutical category. She had removed her make-up and Celeste, who had never seen her before without heavy black kohl lining her eyes, was surprised by how small and red-rimmed and watery her eyes looked.

"You better now?" she asked, staring at Celeste with no sign of emotion as she sat at the table opposite her. She reminded Celeste of the chickens she had seen when her family had visited a farm when she was little: you could stare into their beady eyes, but you saw nothing behind them. She stood up holding the empty blisters in her cupped hands and crossed the room to toss them into the rubbish bin, while Levent brought Celeste a plate of plums and grapes and a glass of *ayran*.

"Yes, thank goodness," replied Celeste as Levent sat down beside her, rolling his eyes at the sight of the blister packs spread out before them.

"You don't never eat properly," Leman told Celeste from inside the fridge, "that's why you have stomach problems. You only take *ayran* for breakfast. Fruit isn't food. You should real eating."

Hearing this, Levent imitated his mother throwing an antacid tablet down her throat and flushing it down with a shot glass of whisky.

"You should listen to my mother," he said, winking at Celeste, "she knows all about stomach problems."

Hearing this Leman removed her head from the fridge and slammed the door shut, looking proud and smug at her son's endorsement of her opinion. Celeste took a small sip of *ayran* and said nothing.

The next day Celeste stayed in bed, feeling too weak to get up. On Sunday she awoke feeling slightly better. Her appetite had returned at last, and her stomach no longer hurt at all. She ate toast and honey for breakfast and suggested going out to do some sketches for the day with Levent, but he had to revise to retake an exam and his mother had ordered him to stay at home and study all day. Celeste was so profoundly grateful to Levent for his devoted care when she was ill that she felt awkward when she tried to thank him; but he reacted with a joke and his usual teasing smile, as if it were nothing. He seemed to treat everything in this effortlessly relaxed way, regarding any situation, however strange or unusual, as simply another experience in life. Celeste often wondered how he could be so different from both his parents; his deeply intellectual but anxious father who kept so many secrets hidden in his heart, and his acerbic mother who was desperate to control everyone around her and have her own way at any cost.

"You still look very pale, you know. I think you'd get tired going out sketching," Levent added. "You'd do better to stay in and rest for the day, if you don't mind me giving you my advice."

"I'm just really keen to get out of the house for a while," explained Celeste.

"I can certainly understand that," said Levent.

Celeste telephoned Heather to ask if she could spend the day at her flat. Levent insisted on calling Mehmet to ask if he was available to take Celeste there so that she would not have to go outside and look for a taxi. By the time Mehmet reached Heather's building in Cihangir, Celeste felt very weak again and wanted to lie down. Mehmet insisted on accompanying her up the stairs, even though he did not permit himself to help her up by actually touching her. He told her there was no way he would leave her standing around alone in this type of neighbourhood even if she felt perfectly well. Inside the flat, she went straight to Heather's room and lay on the double bed with a selection of drinks and snacks prepared by Heather on the bedside table, while Heather sat propped up against a pile of cushions beside her, drinking a cup of tea and leafing through an English language text book.

"Now then," announced Heather, in a businesslike manner. "I have news."

"Go on," prompted Celeste.

"Sadberk is taking that nice class away from me. Your old class."

"Why?" asked Celeste.

"That Armpit bloke, you know, Ahmet, the one who you thought was harmless..."

"Oh yes," said Celeste.

"Apparently he complained that I 'should wear taller skirts.'"

"What's that supposed to mean?" asked Celeste, baffled.

"I wore an over the knee skirt a few times, and he objected," said Heather.

"But everyone wears mini skirts in that school!" exclaimed Celeste, astounded. "How come they didn't just tell him to lump it?"

"Because that silly Sad Berk thinks the customer is always right and the teacher is always wrong. You know she didn't even want to tell me why she was giving me a different class?"

"So how did you find out?" asked Celeste.

"I just refused to leave her office until she gave me the reason. I said I'd hand in my notice if she wasn't honest with me."

"That was a bit risky, wasn't it?"

"Not too risky. I know they're having trouble finding teachers at the moment. Those two Canadians have done a runner. They asked her for their passports so they could change some Canadian dollars into Turkish Lira, and never reappeared."

"How is it that you know all the gossip, and I miss everything?" complained Celeste.

"Probably because I have no qualms about eavesdropping and spying on people," stated Heather calmly. "Talking of things you've missed, I found out that Ahmet was the reason Sadberk took that class away from you in the first place, when she gave them to me."

"You're kidding?" asked Celeste. "Why?"

"It seems he complained that you were too funny and you made jokes. He thought the lessons should be more serious."

"The little swine!" exclaimed Celeste. "But you make far more jokes than me, anyway."

"Not ones he can understand!" answered Heather. "I just say things to entertain myself. Oh, did I mention what Nezaket said in the last lesson? I was teaching them how to describe people, and she told me her boyfriend 'is two metres long.'"

"What did you say?" asked Celeste.

"I said 'Oh, lucky you.' This is all drivel," Heather went on, flipping the English textbook carelessly onto the bed-covers. "Sadberk says I have to follow this book lesson by lesson, but it's useless. There's no speaking practise in it, it's just grammar exercises and comprehension."

"Who's that?" asked Celeste suddenly, half sitting up on the bed.

"Who?" asked Heather.

"I heard a bloke's voice," said Celeste.

"It's only Zelly Belly," said Heather. "She's probably grunting from the exertion of her aerobics training." But then Heather heard it, too; Zeliha's voice coming through the bedroom wall and another, deeper male voice, talking softly. "You're right! She's got a man in her bedroom!" exclaimed Heather, her eyes lighting up with glee as she crossed the room to press her ear against the wall. "What a dark horse!"

Celeste slowly got up from the bed, sitting for a few moments before standing up as she felt slightly dizzy. She stood near the wall beside Heather. She was not really interested in the man Zeliha had invited into her room. As far as she was concerned, Zeliha could keep company with whomever she wanted and it really was no business of theirs. But Heather's delight in following other people's private lives like a gossiping schoolgirl reminded her of Maryam, and her relentless sense of fun. She realised, as she looked at Heather pressing her ear against the wall and sniggering silently from beneath her shock of curly ginger hair, that both of them used their gleeful enjoyment of prying into other people's private lives as a distraction from their own; in Maryam's case to forget that she lived in a house with no windows and a husband who beat her; and in Heather's to avoid thinking of the fiancé who had betrayed her so cruelly before their wedding and the baby she had lost through grief.

Celeste pressed her ear to the wall beside Heather, facing her so she could see her expression as she reacted to the snippets of conversation they overheard. Before she could pick out any words clearly, Celeste realised that Zeliha was crying.

"I'm so sorry, you know I love you, and I always will," the male voice said.

Heather's mouth was wide open and her eyebrows were raised so high they almost seemed to be disappearing off the top of her head. Celeste smiled back at her, half laughing at the way Zeliha had managed to keep this lover secret from her flatmate, and from everyone, for so long. Heather pressed her hands over her mouth so that only her bright blue eyes peeped back at Celeste, opened wide in an exaggerated expression of shock.

"I can't keep this going any more," announced the male voice, quite clearly audible now. He seemed to be no more than a foot away from the wall between the two bedrooms, which meant he must be standing beside Zeliha's dressing table. "I've thought about it for a long time. It was a far from easy decision, but I have to do the right thing. I have to take responsibility for my family. I owe it to them." There was a long pause, in which Celeste was not sure whether Zeliha were replying. Then she heard her voice more clearly.

"I think you're just using them as an excuse," she heard Zeliha say. "You're a coward. You've been lying to them for so long, and you've lied to me too. How many times did you tell me you wanted to leave her and marry me?" she protested.

"Did you hear that?" mouthed Celeste to Heather. "She's been dumped."

"Yes," Heather mouthed back. "But who is he?"

"I'm so sorry," the male voice said, somewhat lamely Celeste thought.

"I don't understand what's made you suddenly decide to end it like this," Zeliha continued, sniffing. There was a trumpeting sound as she blew her nose noisily.

"My son's struggling with his degree," the male voice went on, "and he needs more encouragement and support from me."

"What he really needs is a brother or sister," contradicted Zeliha. She was getting angry and had raised her voice so her words resonated through the wall. "Being an only child means he bears the weight of his parents' problems all by himself. He's too closely involved with you and your wife, and your family life together." She spoke the words 'wife' and 'family' in a sarcastic tone. "But it's about twenty years too late to resolve that problem properly," she added, indignantly.

The male voice's reply was too muffled and faint to make out. He must have turned away and walked to the opposite side of the room. Celeste and Heather looked into each others' eyes, waiting patiently.

"I think it's time I gave my wife a second chance," the male voice suddenly said, very close to them again and crystal clear. "As you know, she's never made me happy, but I did marry her, and she's the mother of my only child. It's time I thought of them rather than my own happiness."

The voices became muffled again, and Zeliha seemed to be crying and pleading, although Celeste was not sure as she had moved across the room. Celeste wondered if she were sitting on her beautiful four-poster bed with its green velvet drapes as she pleaded with her secret lover to take her back. Suddenly Celeste and Heather both jumped as Zeliha's bedroom door clicked open. Heather, reacting with lightning speed, dashed across the room in her socks and opened the door an inch, holding her hand against the door jam so that the catch would not make a noise as it opened. Celeste followed her more slowly and peered over her shoulder, hoping to catch sight of Zeliha's ex-secret lover as he walked briskly along the gloomy corridor. He strode rapidly, his shoes clicking on the polished parquet floor, pausing momentarily when he had reached the living room to look back at Zeliha's bedroom door, which was now closed again. In the split second before he turned the corner and disappeared from sight, Celeste saw Ferhat in his customary light blue weekend shirt and black trousers, his white hair shining under the yellowish light from the electric light bulb and his big, black eyes two pools of infinite sadness. In three steps he reached the entrance hall, grabbed his coat with a clacking sound as the buttons tapped against the wall and slammed the front door shut behind him.

And with that, he was gone. Celeste and Heather contained themselves in total silence until Heather had very gently and silently closed the bedroom door. Then she turned on her stereo quietly, rotating it to face the wall adjoining Zeliha's bedroom, took Celeste by the hand and pulled her toward the window.

"What? How? When? How on earth?" hissed Celeste, amazed at what she had seen. "How do they know each other? When did they meet? How come he's with her?"

"You mean you know who he is?" asked Heather calmly, for once the serious one.

Veronica Di Grigoli

"What?" gasped Celeste. "He's Ferhat. He's my landlord! Leman's husband. He's Levent's father."

"Oh you're joking!" spluttered Heather. The discovery was so titillating it almost left her at a loss for words. She sat on the bed as if digesting the revelation carefully. "Well it's a bit too much of a coincidence, isn't it?" she concluded finally. "How come these two people we live with just happen to be having a secret affair?"

"Exactly," said Celeste. Her reaction to the momentous discovery was somewhat dulled by the fact that she felt dizzy again and realised she was also very hungry. Her mind could not process the information. She reached for one of the fairy cakes which Heather had placed beside the bed for her, and took a small bite.

"Where did you see the advertisement for your room at Leman's?" asked Heather, frowning as an idea started to form in her head.

"On the school notice board," answered Celeste.

"Which is where I saw the advertisement for this flat," said Heather. "So either Leman found out that Zeliha was advertising for an English lodger and copied her, or vice versa," she pondered.

"But how would either of them find out?" asked Celeste.

"Maybe Ferhat let something slip," suggested Heather.

"Or maybe they know each other," said Celeste, thinking aloud. "Just because Leman doesn't know Ferhat's having an affair with Zeliha, doesn't mean she's never met the woman."

"I can't imagine Zeliha being capable of being that deceptive," said Heather. "She's drippy enough and got low enough self esteem to be 'the other woman' for years, but I don't think she could be so brazen about it. You have to enjoy laughing at people behind their back to spend time with your secret lover's wife, or to start an affair with someone whose family you already know."

"I bet Zeliha would be scared of Leman if she met her," added Celeste. "I used to be scared of her."

"Not any more?" asked Heather.

"No," said Celeste, dreamily. "When I was ill I realised that, for all her domineering attitude, I'm a stronger person than she is. I know how to be happy with what I've got. She'll never have what she wants, and she'll never be happy with what she's got."

Heather considered these words for a moment. "But why do you think Leman, or Zeliha, would want to do something so weird as to get a lodger from the same school?" she asked.

"Maybe whoever copied thought it could be a way to spy on the other," proposed Celeste. "If they both had flatmates who were colleagues they might pick up a bit of gossip."

"It sounds like a long shot," said Heather. "Maybe it was a status symbol thing, as in, if she can have a pet English person to learn English from, then so can I."

"It could have been a bit of both," concluded Celeste. "Leman is genuinely keen for the whole family to practise English with me all the time, more so than Zeliha, I'd say. And Leman has never tried to extract information from me about you or even asked about your flat mate. Has Zeliha ever asked you about the family I live with?"

"No, not really," said Heather. "She listens when I talk about your mad landlady but she's never seemed to dig for more information than I was letting out by way of conversation."

"Well I suppose it's probably the status symbol thing then," concluded Celeste.

"I agree," said Heather, "but we'll probably never find out for certain. And for sure we'll never find out who copied whom. Anyway, something else I really want to know is, how long has this been going on for? And even more mysterious, what, in the name of Genghis Khan's underpants, does that man see in Zelly Belly?"

Celeste told Heather everything that Maryam and Ferhat's chauffeur, Mehmet had told her about Ferhat's secret lover: "Mehmet thinks, or at least told Maryam, that she's French."

"Why would he have said that?" mused Heather.

"I suppose with Zeliha's French obsession it could have been easy to come to the wrong conclusion about her nationality, if he's never actually spoken to her. Apparently Ferhat buys her endless gifts from France."

"Oh yes!" concluded Heather. "That must be where all her French fashion magazines come from, and those herbal tea bags and the French books."

"I think they probably have quite a lot of interests in common," said Celeste, thoughtfully. "They're both very keen on art and antiques. They like learning about foreign cultures. They're also both quite weak and indecisive people. They're both quite easily manipulated, I think."

"That would explain why they've been faffing around having a secret affair instead of making a bold decision and sorting their lives out," said Heather.

"Yes," agreed Celeste, thoughtfully. "As if they've both been waiting for the other one to take control of the situation. They're both followers, not fighters."

"But it still doesn't explain," objected Heather, "why he would be interested in a woman who neglects herself the way Zeliha does. I mean, wouldn't you think he'd want someone whose hair is all the same colour from the roots to the ends? Someone who's seen their own toes in the last decade? I know she's a very sweet person, but I also know how men think. This may sound really callous, but I've never met any man who'd want to have illicit rumpy-pumpy with a woman whose rear end is large enough to be considered for inclusion in the new edition of the Times World Atlas."

"Maybe he didn't just regard it as illicit rumpy-pumpy," said Celeste, bemused. "I can't say. He may be reacting against Leman and her obsession with fancy clothes and beauty treatments. Perhaps he was just looking for the opposite of her in every way. Because that's what Zeliha is."

Celeste arrived at the house in Bebek in a pensive mood that evening and went straight to her room. She wrote a letter home, mainly aimed at her younger brothers. She told them about the things she had seen in Istanbul lately and drew them some little sketches of scenes of the city from memory, including the Blue Mosque and the Grand Bazaar. She drew caricatures of some of the people she mentioned and told them when she would be flying home for the Christmas holidays. Thinking about Christmas was fairly distressing. One the one hand she could not wait to see her brothers and was determined to do everything in her power to make Christmas as much fun for them as she could. On the other hand, the idea of being back in the family home to try to celebrate Christmas without her mother was a horrific prospect. Her mother had paid so much attention to every little detail that made Christmas fun, putting herself into everything they ate, every decoration, every present, every ornament hung on the tree, that her mother actually *was* Christmas. It was as if the event was a physical manifestation of her mother's persona.

The first Christmas without her mother had been impossible to contemplate and the entire family had fled in different directions, her father going to his sister's house, the boys staying with their grandmother and Celeste visiting a Hindu friend for the day and having a simple family meal at her house with, thankfully, no presents and no tree. This year the boys deserved a real Christmas, Celeste had resolved. They were still children and it was up to her to create a new way of celebrating Christmas which would let them enjoy the excitement and delight her mother had surrounded her with each Christmas, but without making her feel haunted by the ghost of Christmas past. She and her father would work together this year to help each other find a new way of enjoying Christmas, and start moving forward. There was no way to go back.

Once she had finished her letter and sealed it in its envelope, Celeste sat on her bed with her feet up and flicked through the Nasreddin Hoca book that Levent had lent her. His name was written in messy, childish handwriting in green pencil inside the front cover. What kind of festivals had he enjoyed as a child, she wondered. Had he ever experienced anything like the wonder and thrill of Christmas the way she had as a little girl? He would have spent each holiday alone, she thought. An only child, as Zeliha had said, perhaps overhearing his parents arguing, or else feeling their stony silences during the long periods when they ignored each other and went off sulking in different rooms, feeling the burden of their problems all by himself. His relentlessly sunny outlook seemed all the more remarkable when Celeste contemplated how melancholy much of his childhood must have been.

Celeste came to a page in the book that Levent had marked with pencil, underlining the title of the story and working a rectangle around it several times. She leant back against her pillow to read the tale:

'A foreign scholar and his entourage were passing through Akşehir. The scholar asked to speak with the town's most knowledgeable person so, of course, the townsfolk immediately called Nasreddin Hoca. The foreign intellectual didn't speak Turkish and the Hoca didn't speak any foreign languages, so the two wise men had to communicate through sign and gestures, while the others stood around and looked on in fascination.

'The foreigner, using a stick, drew a large circle on the sand. Nasreddin Hoca took the stick and divided the circle into two. Then the foreigner drew a line perpendicular to the one Hoca drew, so the circle was now split into four. He motioned to indicate first the three quarters of the circle, then the remaining quarter. At this, the Hoca made a swirling motion with the stick on the four quarters. Then the foreigner made a bowl shape by cupping his hands together, and wiggled his fingers. Nasreddin Hoca responded by cupping his hands palms down and wiggling his fingers.

'When the meeting was over, the members of the foreign scientist's entourage asked him what he had talked about with Nasreddin Hoca.

'"That Nasreddin Hoca is really a learned man," he said. "I told him that the earth was round, and he told me that there was an equator in the middle of it. I told him that three quarters of the earth was water and one quarter of it was land. Then he said that there were undercurrents and winds. I told him that the waters warm up, vaporize and move towards the sky, to which he responded that they cool off and come down as rain."

'The people of Akşehir were also curious to know how the meeting went. They gathered around the Hoca to hear his retelling of the conversation in Turkish.

'"This stranger has good taste," the Hoca explained. "He said that he wished there was a large tray of baklava. I said that he could only have half of it. He said that the syrup should be made with three parts sugar and one part honey. I agreed, and said that they all had to be mixed very well.

Next he suggested that we should cook it on a blazing fire, and I added that we should pour crushed nuts on top of it."'

Celeste smiled at the ending to the story, and lay back against her pillows with her eyes closed, the book resting on her knees. She still felt slightly weak after her severe illness and welcomed any opportunity to rest. She thought about Leman and it struck her that the story she had just read was an analogy for her relationship with Ferhat. They shared their lives, but each seemed to be living in their own separate dimension, unable to take in what the other was thinking or trying to communicate. They could have the same experience together but each have a perception of it so radically different that they might as well have lived on opposite sides of the world. Essentially, they had lived their lives together at cross-purposes. How had Ferhat and Leman ever ended up married to each other? Celeste wondered if this analogy had ever crossed Levent's mind. There must have been some reason why he had underlined the title of the story so many times.

Closing the book, Celeste realised she was hungry and noticed that it was past nine o'clock. She went downstairs to ask what time the family planned to eat dinner, and found Leman in Ferhat's study poring over some letters at his desk.

"How was Tekin?" Celeste asked. "I hope he wasn't too upset when I was too ill to go and see him."

"What?" asked Leman, looking up blankly. She was wearing her reading glasses, which Celeste suspected she did not need as she always set them very low on her nose and peered over them rather than looking through the lenses. Celeste wondered if she put them on simply to look the part while she was 'doing paperwork' as she always called it.

"I told Tekin I would visit him, but then I was too ill to go," explained Celeste patiently. "Did he ask you where I was?"

"Oh, boys asked about English lessons, but I don't remember Tekin in among them," replied Leman casually. She noticed Celeste's worried expression and straightened up in her chair, pressing her hands against the small of her back. "Children forget things like that," she explained confidentially in deep, soothing tones. "Anyway, doesn't matter, he not there now."

"What do you mean, he's not there now?" asked Celeste, half hoping, though not daring to believe, that Tekin's aunt really had come for him.

"He gone," said Leman casually. "He run away last evening. Disappear. We don't know where he is."

THIRTEEN

Mr. Demirsar's story

Celeste thought she might faint when Leman told her the news. She sat down heavily on the carved chair beside Ferhat's bookcase, but then stood up again immediately. Her blood boiled at how casually Leman had mentioned Tekin's disappearance, as if it were of no consequence. She felt gripped by an urgent need to go to the orphanage, to start searching the streets for Tekin. She began to bombard Leman with questions. What did the other boys say? Had Leman spoken to all of them? Where did they think he had gone? Had she told the police? What did the other staff say? Could they get his photograph in the newspaper to alert more people to search for him?

"He not a celebrity," answered Leman finally, after wearily answering some of Celeste's questions and ignoring others. "People not that interested in one boy." She sounded bored by the whole affair and carefully took her glasses off, pausing to disentangle the gold chain from one of her blouse buttons before carefully placing the glasses on top of the papers she had read, as if to underline the fact that she had been irrevocably interrupted when she had work to do. "He probably will come back when he get tired and hungry. I got boys at orphanage to look after. I can't waste all time for others ones that decides to leave."

"How do you know he decided to leave?" asked Celeste, suddenly horrified by a new thought even worse than her previous ones. "What if he was kidnapped?"

Leman ignored this comment. What was it Tekin had told Celeste about Mr. Demirsar at the orphanage? 'He sometimes says strange things to us,' Tekin had told her. 'Some of the boys say he does strange things, in the night.' Celeste decided to go to the orphanage immediately and start asking the boys about Tekin, and Mr. Demirsar.

"It's the night, boys asleep, nobody there," said Leman. Celeste found the calm, gentle tones of Leman's husky voice deeply irritating. "Police been told he is missing. I already speak people. Why you think you can find more out than what I did? You doesn't need worrying." She put her glasses back on and pushed them up her nose to signal that the conversation had ended. Realising that trying to reason with Leman was simply wasting time, Celeste decided to talk to Levent, at least to let off steam even if for no other reason.

"Mum never even mentioned a boy had gone missing," he said when Celeste explained the situation to him, sounding bewildered and slightly indignant. His normally relaxed face formed a frown and for a moment he closed his soft, full lips tightly. "You're really fond of this kid, aren't you?"

"Yes," replied Celeste simply.

"Look, I really have to study for this exam because my father is going to go nuts and have a nervous breakdown if I fail yet another one, so I can't leave the house tonight. And it's far too dangerous for you to go wandering round alone. What I can do is call Mehmet and ask him to take you to the orphanage if he's available, stay with you there, and then bring you home when you're ready. I have to do this exam tomorrow morning, but after lunch I'll come with you wherever you want to go, to look for this kid... what was his name? Tekin?"

"Yes, Tekin."

"So, shall I see if Mehmet's available?"

"Yes, please. I can't just sit here doing nothing."

Celeste hastily changed into jeans and flat-heeled boots, and fixed her hair back into a pony tail. She felt most comfortable dressed like this and wanted to feel she could move freely or run easily should the need arise. She had no idea where she might end up, even though she had promised Levent that she would only go to the orphanage to talk to the people there. Mehmet arrived after twenty-five tense minutes in which Celeste had paced around the landing outside her bedroom like a wolf prowling for prey and then violently attacked some lime scale around the bathroom plughole with a powerful de-scaling product and a scouring pad. She muttered Leman's words to herself under her breath as she worked, whipping herself up into an ever more fulminating rage as she contemplated the casual effrontery of the woman.

"*Children forget things like that*," she muttered angrily under her breath, rubbing the scourer back and forth frantically. "*Anyway, doesn't matter, he not there now.* How dare she be so indifferent?"

She was so absorbed in the scrubbing and eradication of unwanted dirt that she lost awareness of her surroundings, as she tended to do, and consequently jumped out of her skin when Levent touched her arm and told her that Mehmet was waiting downstairs.

"You shouldn't sneak up on me like that," she snapped.

"Didn't you hear me calling your name all the way up the stairs?" asked Levent, genuinely surprised.

Mehmet was waiting with the car engine revving as she sprinted downstairs.

"Levent said I should come inside the orphanage with you," he mumbled as he drove through the city, his hair ruffled and his eyes looking puffy with sleep. "He said not to leave you by yourself."

"Thanks," said Celeste. "I'm sorry to have got you out in the evening like this, but it's an emergency."

"Don't worry," answered Mehmet. "Levent told me what's happened. I hope they find the poor little kid. Anyway, I've been working so many nights lately that I'm getting used to it." He laughed and turned on the radio, loud Turkish dance music with a drum beat that made the windows of the car vibrate.

"I thought you were working daytimes," said Celeste.

"Yes, days too," replied Mehmet phlegmatically.

They reached the orphanage quickly and Celeste sprang out of the car before Mehmet had even stopped the engine. Her hands and legs trembled, but was unsure whether this was caused by anger or still the effect of the illness she had had. She felt drained of all her strength yet unable to relax or even keep still. Her distress was all-consuming. She had decided to go directly to Mr. Demirsar and she marched into the orphanage far more boldly than she felt inside, Mehmet following her and waiting patiently as she was greeted by several boys in their pyjamas.

"Shouldn't you be in bed?" she asked them.

"Nobody can stay in bed," they replied. "We're afraid. We heard Mr. Demirsar so we got out of bed. He's very strange."

"Where is he," croaked Celeste, her throat seeming to dry up and close shut.

"Outside, I think," answered the tallest of the boys, "In his shed."

Celeste strode outside and around the building to the wooden hut where Mr. Demirsar stored his tools. There was a faint light coming from the window and the door was closed. Without hesitating she barged directly up to it and pushed it open without even breaking her step, standing on the threshold as the door smashed against the inner wall of the hut. Mr. Demirsar, who has been sitting on a wooden crate in the far corner of the hut, alone with his head buried in his hands, sprang to his feet in sheer terror at the sudden shock. When he saw it was Celeste, he almost fell back down and held his hands to his head, shocks of his unkempt greasy hair hanging about his thick, rough fingers as he stared at the floor. The hut was almost entirely lined with photographs of little boys, some toddlers, some older, some as much as seven years old. Celeste scanned the room in an instant, taking in scenes of a little boy with a rounded tummy at the beach in a red bathing costume; a boy aged about five, standing in a street with a football tucked under his arm; an older boy sitting on a doorstep looking over his shoulder into the room behind him. Mr. Demirsar sat motionless for several long seconds before he turned his head to look Celeste in the eye. His swollen, blotchy red face was almost unrecognisable. He looked ashamed and afraid, his eyes searching through the gloom to look into hers like an animal caught in a trap. At first Celeste thought he had been beaten, until she realised that he had been crying.

"Where is he?" she demanded. "You know were Tekin is, don't you?"

"I'm so afraid he's dead," said Mr. Demirsar, in a voice so faint Celeste could hardly hear it.

"What did you do to him? Where did you leave him?" demanded Celeste, her voice rising hysterically.

"Me?" he responded. He seemed utterly terrified. "I don't know."

Mehmet pushed gently past Celeste to enter the hut and stand beside Mr. Demirsar. He introduced himself politely.

"What do you know about the boy, my friend?" he asked gently. "We want to try and find him."

"The other boys told me he went to look for his aunt," said Mr. Demirsar.

"Did he speak to you or see you before he went?" asked Mehmet, still calmly. Celeste wanted to interrupt, to accuse Mr. Demirsar of lying, to scream that he knew exactly what he had done with Tekin. Could Mehmet not see all these photographs of little boys all around them? Did he not realise what that meant? But she held her breath and waited for Mehmet to continue questioning him.

"He's never spoken to me. I never speak to any of the boys," said Mr. Demirsar, glancing for a split second at Celeste through his puffy red eyes. "I can't."

"Why not?" demanded Celeste, losing her patience. "And who are all these boys? Why've you got pictures of boys all over your shed?" She threw a meaningful glance at Mehmet, her temper rising in frustration at his far too calm attitude.

"He's only one boy," answered Mr. Demirsar.

"Who?" demanded Celeste, taken aback at his directness.

"My son," replied Mr. Demirsar. Celeste looked around her. She stared carefully at one picture after another. And she realised to her utter mortification that, as he had said, the pictures were indeed all of the same boy, taken at different times as he grew older. "I've never cried for him until now," added Mr. Demirsar.

"What happened to him?" asked Celeste. She took a step back, the storm of rage that had been brewing up inside her suddenly passing and deflating her so completely that she wondered if she still had the strength to remain on her feet.

"He disappeared when he was seven," answered Mr. Demirsar, his voice sounding hoarse as if from lack of use. "Look, that's the last photograph we ever took of him. We never found out what really happened." He indicated a picture which showed the boy standing beside a woman, presumably his mother, reaching up to hold her hand. But Celeste had an image in her head of Adam Miller, the little boy from next door who had disappeared and left his mother weeping under the damson tree for years, searching for him forever, never knowing when to stop looking. "He was such a good boy," said Mr. Demirsar. "My wife couldn't have any more children after he was born so he was quite spoiled. He was always at my wife's side. When he disappeared the police said he'd probably run away. But we knew he couldn't have run away. He was far too good, and anyway, he'd have been too afraid. Why would he want to run away? My wife was a wonderful mother and he never wanted to leave her side."

Mehmet had sat on a narrow bench opposite Mr. Demirsar and was listening intently, showing his concern by his attention. Celeste stood in the doorway, feeling like a phantasm that had drifted in on a scene that was none of her business and in which she had no right to participate.

"I couldn't express any feeling at all, I just froze up," Mr. Demirsar confided in Mehmet. "Sometimes my wife accused me of not caring. She thought I had no heart. Maybe she was right. I had no feelings at all, no emotions. I never tasted my food, I never even knew if I was asleep or awake. I wandered the city all the time, all day and sometimes all night as well. I used to go round all the orphanages hoping he would turn up, and that's how I ended up working here. I liked being near these boys. Even if my son was still missing, I wanted to be near other people's lost children to protect them. I prayed every day that someone, somewhere, was looking after my lost boy for me. But Allah willed it otherwise."

"So he was never found?" asked Mehmet.

"Oh, yes, they found him. It was after two years had passed, two years of searching and of my wife crying constantly. One day I went to the police station to ask for news, and they said they had found a body of a boy aged about seven. It had been in the sea, in the Bosphorus. It was just bones, but they said it was definitely him.

"We had a funeral eventually. They made us wait a long time before they would let us have the body. And after he was buried, my wife killed herself. She..."

"It's all right, you don't have to tell us," said Mehmet. He took his cigarette packet from his breast pocket and held it out for Mr. Demirsar, who took a cigarette and waited while Mehmet lit it for him. There was a long silence as Mr. Demirsar smoked and rubbed his coarse hands roughly over his face several times, as if trying to erase the expression, obliterate the feelings he had just shown there.

"I never cried for my wife and I never cried for my son," he said, eventually. "I wanted to work here in this orphanage to be near the boys, but I could never actually be near them. I could never speak to them. But I liked to be close to them, to listen to them, to imagine what my little boy would be like if he were growing up somewhere." He let out a rattling cough and shifted his position on the wooden crate. "Now tiny, tiny Tekin is missing, and suddenly I can feel my heart beating again inside me. I have to find him. What can I do?" He looked pleadingly from Mehmet to Celeste, as if begging them for a solution.

Celeste asked him if he had asked the boys what they knew. He said that he had tried to, but he was so shy he did not know where to begin.

"Whenever I try to speak to them my tongue freezes up. I don't know what to say at all. I used to play so naturally with my boy, but now I can only watch the children and leave them to play by themselves. I did try to ask them..." he trailed off despondently.

"Come with us if you like," said Celeste. "I'm going to talk to them."

She wanted to talk to Bŭlent first, as he was usually with Tekin, particularly when they had played with the dog. She ended up speaking to all the boys together in a large group, as they were all desperate to tell her everything they knew about Tekin and to ask her if she would start looking for him. They confirmed her worst fear; that he had been deeply upset the day he had expected her to come and she had not turned up. But that was not the reason he had decided to run away.

"Leman told him off," they recounted to Celeste. "She was very angry and she shouted at Tekin a lot."

"What had he done?" asked Celeste.

"We were running around at bedtime and didn't want to get into bed," said Bŭlent. "Leman told us to go upstairs immediately and Tekin laughed, so she got very, very angry and her face was all red when she was shouting. We were very scared. When we were going upstairs to bed, Tekin said to Hakkan that he would be able to stay up as late as he liked when his aunt came for him, because she always let him stay up till she went to bed."

"Yes," continued Hakkan, "Leman was so angry she ran up the stairs and shouted that his aunt wasn't coming, that his aunt would never come for him and he must stop telling lies. She said he must stop dreaming and wishing he had someone who would never really be by his side."

"What did Tekin do?" asked Celeste.

"He cried," resumed Bŭlent, "and he went to bed crying and went to sleep crying. He said to me that his aunt was real and he would find her, but I didn't imagine he would run away to look for her. In the morning he was gone."

"He took his teddy bear with him," added Hakkan. "The one you gave him with funny eyes."

Many of these boys had experience of living on the streets and sleeping rough. The concern and sheer panic on their faces was more alarming to Celeste than any danger she herself could imagine Tekin would be in. They knew from first hand experience what little Tekin must be suffering now, if he were still alive.

"Tekin doesn't know how to look after himself," one of them with a long scar on his cheek told her. "His mother and father looked after him very well and they had lots of money. He was from a very rich family before the earthquake. They did everything for him. He doesn't know how to live on the street."

"That's the main thing I'm worried about," said Celeste. "It's too cold to sleep outside."

The boy exchanged glances with some of the other boys, as if they were all wondering how to make themselves clear to Celeste. As on so many occasions, their pinched faces and grave demeanour made Celeste feel like the youngest one there.

"No, that's not the real problem," he said eventually. "That's not what we meant. When it's cold you can find other children, or a dog to sleep with. The problem is that Tekin doesn't know how to steal. He doesn't know how to beg for food, where to go and who to ask."

"That's right," confirmed another boy. "He trusts everyone. He doesn't know that lots of people want to harm you. He's just a baby. He doesn't know about danger."

"Otherwise he wouldn't have run away," concluded Bülent, his dark, chocolate eyes glistening with tears. Celeste anxiously rubbed the tips of her fingers over the foil pendant Tekin had given her as if it were a magic talisman that could summon a genie to answer her wishes.

Celeste spent every day searching the city in her free time, wandering aimlessly or convincing Mehmet to drive to some of the areas near the orphanage to help her search. She sometimes thought of the old woman who had read her palm when she first came to see Leman's house. 'You have some to search for a missing person,' the woman had said. Levent accompanied her whenever he could spare the time from his studies, although he constantly tried to tell her, as gently as he could, that she must brace herself for the fact that Tekin might never be found and that this was not the way to find him. Yet he understood that she had to do this, that she was physically incapable of sitting at home or doing anything with her free time other than searching for Tekin. She taught her lessons in a trance and sometimes drifted through them hardly aware, by the end, of what she had actually said or taught. Heather helped her by planning the lessons and having the photocopies done for her.

Celeste developed a nervous habit of holding her left hand around her right wrist where she could feel Tekin's pendant, as if she were checking it was still there or perhaps protecting it from the outside world. She put the little pencil portrait she had drawn of Tekin in her bag and carried with her wherever she went, looking at it often as if it helped her feel closer to him. She gradually grew used to the knot in her stomach and the fact that she would lie awake for hour after hour at night, feeling exhausted and enervated but too agitated to sleep, and to the fact that she felt physically as weak as a piece of straw yet so tense she would snap pencils in her fingers if she let her mind wander. She grew accustomed to the feeling of the acid in her stomach burning a hole right through her torso and out of her back, and the way the sudden sharp pain of making just a slight change of position could take her breath away. And at night, every night, when she finally fell asleep she had the recurring nightmare she had had so many times as a child. She would go into the garden to console Mrs. Miller under the damson tree and suggest that they go into the street to look for little Adam, her lost son. And the man with bristling stubble on his chin would come along and tell them that he knew where Adam was, and that he would lead them there. Then suddenly one night, it was Mr. Demirsar who told them he knew where to find the lost child. The child they were searching for was now Tekin, not Adam. Celeste woke up her family and they all got into the family's Ford hatchback, with Mrs. Miller, and followed Mr. Demirsar's directions to where Tekin could be found. They drove into the dense, dark forest, which now seemed even gloomier and denser than before. Finally they pulled up beside the stagnant pond, so black and deep that nothing thrown in would ever reach the bottom.

"Tekin is in here," Mr. Demirsar said to Celeste, his eyes filling with tears, "and nobody can get him. He's down there with my dead boy. That's where all the lost, dead little boys are. And nobody can get them."

When Celeste peered down into the murky water she caught sight of countless tiny faces swimming around under the surface, drifting up towards her and then gliding back down out of sight in the inky depths; but they were not dead, they were struggling to reach the surface, their tiny white hands reaching and grabbing at nothing as they battled to save themselves and escape from the water, just as she had done so many times in her nightmares. Then with horror she saw Tekin's face drift into view, so close she was sure she could reach in and pull him out. So she crouched down and dipped her arm into the water and then suddenly the world was upside-down and she was freezing and suffocating in the black, peaty water and, as she nearly struggled back to the surface, she lost her grip on Tekin's hand and he slipped down to the depths, to the bottomless infinity of water beneath her. And as she battled to stay afloat, to fight for air and swim to the filthy mud bank beside the bottomless pond, she could her Mr. Demirsar's voice saying sadly,

"Nobody can get them. That's where the lost little boys stay."

And then he went with her family and they all calmly got back into the car and drove away, as if they had forgotten her already, as if she had never existed, as if Tekin had never existed, as if all the lost little boys had never existed. And as always, just as she fought for breath, in the moment she found she could no longer stay afloat and was sinking back beneath the black water again, looking at her family disappearing through a layer of swirling water dark as ink, Celeste woke up gasping for breath.

After she had had the same dream for two weeks, Celeste's father telephoned. Ferhat happened to answer the telephone in his study and called her in to take the call there. He wandered off into the hallway to leave her in privacy.

"It's already the nineteenth," Celeste's father said. "I can't wait to see you! Have you packed yet?"

"Well, I've been thinking...." Celeste began reticently.

"What's wrong?" he responded immediately. "Are you ill again?"

"I'm OK, Dad," said Celeste. "It's not that. It's this little boy, Tekin. He's still missing. I can't face leaving the city knowing he's still lost. I've decided I have to stay here to keep looking for him."

"What! But what about your brothers?" asked her father, sounding angry and hurt. "They're so excited about seeing you."

"I've thought about it so hard, and changed my mind so many times, Dad," pleaded Celeste. "I know it's not fair to them, or to you. But I'm so tense and upset, the only thing that calms me down when the tension builds up inside me is to go and look for him."

"You go wandering the city alone?"

"No, I always go with Levent or Mehmet."

"Do you really think you can find this kid?" he asked, as if trying to make her see reason. She wondered if he was thinking of little Adam Miller.

"That's not the point," she said. "I just have to keep looking."

"Sweetie, I'm really worried about you."

"I'm so sorry, Daddy," said Celeste, beginning to cry.

"Are you sure about this decision?"

"Really sure, Dad," said Celeste, drying her eyes and bottling up her feelings again.

"Well, I trust you and I know you haven't made this choice lightly. You know the effect it'll have on the boys and, just for that reason, if you still feel this is what you have to do, I'll back you up." He did not sound at all comfortable with Celeste's choice or at all sure about what he was saying. But Celeste understood that he wanted to treat her like an adult and that he had realised she would not be convinced to change her mind. "I know you haven't decided this without thinking it through."

"Thanks, Dad."

"You know I always support you in whatever you choose. I love you Celeste."

"I love you too, Dad. I'll call you often."

When Celeste put the receiver down she went to look for Ferhat to tell him that she had finished the call so he could return to his study. She found him sitting hunched in the large sitting room, simply staring out of the window.

"Are you all right?" she asked, surprised.

"Perhaps a little overstressed and tired," he replied, turning his head slowly to look at her. His face looked drawn and gaunt. "And how are you?" he asked, forcing a smile. "You have lost weight, I think. I'm worried about you. You look unwell, if I may be permitted to say so. I think your father might worry, if he saw you."

"I think I'm a little overstressed and tired as well," said Celeste.

Ferhat looked at Celeste for a moment, clearly knowing that, like him, she was feeling worse than she wanted to admit. Suddenly Leman burst into the room wearing her black leather mini-skirt and a tight top with the word 'kiss' written across the chest in silver and pink sequins, exuberantly singing a popular love song that was played constantly on the radio. In the original version the singer seemed to screech to be heard above the loud and frenetic drumming; Leman had no such competition, yet she raised her voice all the same and danced happily across the room to her writing desk, which she opened using the ornate key she held in her hand. She caught Ferhat's eye and winked at him as she belted out the line '*I'm going crazy for a beautiful boy, he knows I love him and I know he loves me.*' Ferhat forced himself to smile back at her as he slowly stood up and headed towards his study.

Celeste turned to leave the room as well, but glanced at the opened desk as she did so. The small oil lamp in which she had found the magic spell twisted up into a wick was no longer there. Leman must have removed it, Celeste realised, now she knew that its magic had worked. Leman's pride over her successful domination of her husband suddenly made Celeste regard her as demonic.

Feeling shaken after her conversation with her father, Celeste wanted to go out and be alone somewhere to think over her decision. She knew if she allowed herself simply to go for a walk she would look for Tekin in every side street and every passing car, and in the face of every child she set eyes on, so she decided to sink down into the depths of the Yerebatan Sarnıcı. She had visited this huge underground water cistern three times already and loved the almost supernaturally calming effect it had had on her each time. Built by the Romans in the sixth century, it had once stored clean drinkable water for the entire city, brought in by two separate aqueducts, yet above ground the only visible sign of it was a small square structure that looked like a public toilet. Having paid for her ticket Celeste found that, descending under ground in mid-winter and out of tourist season, she had the entire cistern as large as a subterranean cathedral to herself.

Although it had originally served the same purpose, it felt so different from the underground cistern restaurant which Ferhat had once taken her to. The floor was three metres deep in water and Celeste stood on a wooden platform looking out as far as she could through the forest of marble columns, listening to the classical music played very softly from hidden speakers. The columns were lit from their bases so that the shadows they cast were an inverted version of natural lighting and the cistern seemed like an upside-down version of the normal world. Celeste loved the cistern mainly because it was constructed from salvage and left-overs of other buildings. Some of the columns were smooth and Doric in style whilst others were Corinthian, fluted and with leafy curlicues at the top. One was the pediment of a temple or some other structure stood on its end and the original Latin inscription was still visible running up its side. Two particularly large pillars had massive stone heads of the mythical demoness Medusa used as their bases, one of which was turned on its side. Her wide open eyes stared madly and her was hair was a mass of writhing snakes seeming to squirm under the water.

Celeste thought about how many people must have built this cistern, digging every bucket full of soil out by hand to excavate the vast empty space and then gathering any lump of stone they could find around the city to make the huge number of columns necessary to support the roof, which would become the pavements on which generations of people would unwittingly walk, assuming they stood on solid ground. The way the salvaged marble had been thrown in randomly gave the impression that the cistern had been built with a reckless urgency. Yet the atmosphere was so serene Celeste did not want to leave. She walked to the farthest limit of the wooden platform raised above the water and looked down at the head of the formidable Medusa of Greek mythology, the demon so powerful that one glance from her would turn a man to solid stone. Even she had been

Veronica Di Grigoli

rendered harmless eventually, her head for all eternity tipped sideways and pinned under water by the weight of a column of stone while hundreds of people walked over her every day without even giving her a second thought.

FOURTEEN

An Unusual Christmas

Celeste was woken up at ten past eight on Christmas morning by the sound of the *Aygaz* man playing his melancholy ditty outside the living room window downstairs. She remembered having her usual nightmare and waking at around four in the morning, but she must have fallen back to sleep and managed to doze for a few hours in dreamless peace. In the distance she could hear the tinny sound of the recorded call to prayer from the closest mosque and the babble of a group of fishermen hauling buckets of live fish up from their boats moored in the sea across the road. The sun was already warm and it looked set to be a bright, mild day. As she sat up in bed she felt the usual stabbing pain of heartburn in her chest and back, so she hastily pulled on her jeans and a light sweater and went downstairs to drink some milk, which was the only thing that seemed to calm the pain of her over-active stomach acid.

She waited impatiently to telephone her father and brothers two time zones away, even though she was sure that at ten past six there was every chance her excited brothers would already be awake. By the time she had spoken to each of them in turn she felt agonisingly homesick and was thoroughly regretting her decision not to go home for Christmas. She tormented herself with the thought that she could have booked a brief trip home for Christmas and been back in time for the New Year ball with Levent, thus being absent from Istanbul for a week at most. Celeste decided to call Attila and his wife to ask them if they could think of any way to help her find Tckin. She knew it was a long shot but she had to try something. She had to keep trying, to keep moving, to keep herself busy. Attila and Berna invited her to meet them that morning at the bank again.

Berna made Celeste feel safe and as welcomed as the first time they had met in Attila's calm and cosy office but, when Celeste tried to return her warm smile, she found she could not drag her face into the right position; all she managed to force out was a kind of grimace. She said "Hello" and stared at a cobweb near the ceiling for a few moments. She was hardly aware of Attila asking his young assistant to bring up some tea or, when it arrived, of Berna placing the glass in her hand. Berna sat beside Celeste patiently. Somehow her presence, the strength of her as a person, gave Celeste courage. Celeste desperately wanted to apologise for her behaviour. She was sure she seemed rude and completely unfriendly to these kind, generous people. But she found herself simply unable to speak.

"Tell me again about this little boy," said Attila, coming straight to the point. "I want to know what we can do to help."

Celeste retold the story of Tekin, this time giving them all the details she knew. She was surprised at how easily she told them how she felt for him, and how much his disappearance had affected her.

"I realised it was something very serious when you told me you were still here in Turkey today," said Berna. "It's Christmas Day, for heaven's sake! So we know what this boy must mean to you."

"There have been moments when I've thought I was losing my mind," said Celeste simply.

"I could ask a friend of mine who's a journalist to print an article about him in the newspaper," suggested Berna. "Have you got a good photo of him?"

"Not one," replied Celeste wretchedly. There was a slight pause in which she studied her fingernails as if hoping to find inspiration. "The only picture I've got of him is one I drew myself."

"I have an idea," interrupted Attila, emerging from his own thoughts. "I think I shall ask another friend to have this little boy mentioned on air. He owns a broadcasting station and one of his channels is very widely listened to in Istanbul. If he describes the child, who knows whether it could lead to some information?"

"That's a very good idea," commented Berna, looking at Celeste as if trying to encourage her to feel more optimistic at the prospect. "Meanwhile, bring me that picture of yours. Is it a good likeness?"

"I've got it here," said Celeste, slightly embarrassed. She opened her bag and slipped the drawing out of her hard-backed sketching book. She passed it to Berna.

"That's a very good picture," she commented, impressed. "And it's a good likeness, you'd say?"

"Definitely," said Celeste.

"I'll ask my journalist friend if he'll get it printed in the newspaper. Even though we don't have a photo, I'm sure a drawing would be better than nothing. You see," she added, resting her hand affectionately on Celeste's forearm, "you must try to feel stronger now we're doing something concrete to find Tekin."

When Celeste stepped outside, she was surprised how much the temperature had dropped while she had been inside the bank. It was now so gloomy and overcast that the cars were all driving with their headlights on, even though it was still only eleven in the morning, and the bitterly cold air stung her cheeks and made her ears burn. Unsure how to spend the rest of Christmas day, which was one of her days off work, Celeste wandered around for half an hour alone, wishing she could see Heather.

Every time a small child came into sight she would scrutinise him to see if he could be Tekin. Every time she passed a side alley she glanced down it, convinced she would catch sight of Tekin's light brown hair and see his innocent green eyes looking back at her. Every time a car stopped near her, her heart skipped a beat as she hoped and prayed that he would jump out, running up to greet her. She gazed hopefully into every shop doorway and peered into the porch of every closed building, all the while hearing Heather's voice telling her she was making herself ill like this, that she could not go on living in this state, that she had to get a grip on herself.

Heather had flown to England for a long break with her parents, leaving the day before Christmas Eve and returning in mid-January. Until Heather had left, Celeste had not fully realised how dependent she was on her, not only for company and morale but even for practical things like advice on how to manage difficult students in the class, explanations of aspects of Turkish culture which baffled her, or tips on where to shop. Heather had a superhuman instinct for sniffing out bargains; she seemed to have memorised every bus route and ferry timetable in the city; and she was also a type of walking Turkish-English dictionary whenever Celeste needed help. Now that Celeste was in Istanbul on her own, she felt as if she were a newcomer to the city again, even though she now knew it well.

She saw a small grocer's shop and decided to buy something to eat, not because she felt particularly hungry but more for something to do. She wandered round the shop, constantly thinking of what Heather would probably say, and as always chose a carton of *ayran* and a small pack of dried figs. Before opening the *ayran*, she looked for a place to sit so that she could read the story on the back:

'Everyone Is Right.

'Once when Nasreddin Hoca was serving as the local judge, one of his neighbours came to him complaining about another neighbour. The Hoca listened to the charges carefully, and then concluded, "Yes, dear neighbour, you're quite right." Then the other neighbour came to him. The Hoca listened to his defence carefully, and then concluded, "Yes, dear neighbour, you're quite right." The Hoca's wife, having listened to the entire proceedings, said to him, "Husband, both men cannot be right." The Hoca answered, "Yes, dear wife, you're quite right."'

The story made her think of Ferhat, who seemed to take this attitude to the two women in his life, and perhaps to everyone. Then she thought of Levent and the Nasreddin Hoca book he had lent her, and suddenly hoped he were at home and that he had some free time to spend with her.

"What am I doing here?" she said to herself out loud.

She took a taxi home and found Levent in the kitchen reading a folder of photocopied notes. He slammed it shut the moment she entered the room and greeted her with,

"I've been worried about you. I thought you'd gone wandering off into some dangerous neighbourhood by yourself."

"No, I went to see a friend."

"What do you usually do on Christmas day?" he asked, suddenly changing the subject.

Celeste explained that the extended family would get together for a big lunch, followed by opening the presents in the living room by the Christmas tree, some games with her little brothers and lots of playing with their new toys.

"It sounds really nice," said Levent.

"It was nice when my mother was there," said Celeste quietly, and bit her lower lip as she looked down at the floor.

"I meant, having brothers," explained Levent. "To play with."

"Oh, yes," said Celeste.

"You must miss them terribly," he added.

"Yes, I do."

"That's why you love the boys at the orphanage so much," commented Levent. "I think we should go there for Christmas."

"Hmm," said Celeste absently.

"I know you want to find Tekin, but you won't find him today and you shouldn't forget all the other boys," cajoled Levent. "Otherwise you'll only go on one of your guilt trips afterwards. You can't spend Christmas - what was that word you taught me? - *moping* around here." Celeste took a deep breath as if about to object. She could think of nothing to say.

"You're right," she agreed.

"So let's go immediately," said Levent decisively.

They threw their coats on and started walking along the pavement to look for a taxi. The weather had turned even nastier, with a chilly wind blowing in from the sea and flecks of white all over the water as the wind churned up waves and ripples on the surface. Some of the yachts' sails flapped loudly, the canvas making slapping noises against the masts. When Levent spotted a yellow taxi approaching, he let out the loudest whistle Celeste had ever heard and seemed to have the door open before the car had even fully stopped. She sprang in and Levent followed her, telling the taxi driver where to go as they pulled away from the kerb.

"Why don't we stop off at a department store on the way and get some presents for the kids?" Levent suddenly suggested. "Would that make it feel more like Christmas for you?"

"There are so many of them," said Celeste. I don't think I could afford that."

"You always worry too much about money," laughed Levent. "I have American Express."

"It's easy not to worry about money when you have plenty of it," retorted Celeste.

"You're right," agreed Levent, looking more serious. "I'm very spoiled, you know."

"I didn't mean that," Celeste objected. "I wasn't trying to criticise you."

"But it's true," insisted Levent. "I am spoiled. I think my mother tried to bring me up to be like her."

"What do you mean?" asked Celeste.

"My mother always wants her own way and can't deal with being told 'No.' She can't handle being told she can't have something."

"So what did she do to make you like her?" asked Celeste, intrigued to hear Levent criticising himself and his mother in this way.

"She decided not to have any more children, for a start, so I never learned to share things when I was little. She justified it by saying that I could have all the toys I wanted and all the money would be for me, as if that was somehow better than having company and love. Then she would always nag my Dad to spend money on whatever she decided I needed, or anything I vaguely expressed an interest in. When he suggested it might be good to teach me a sense of proportion, she would accuse him of not loving me, or not loving her."

"Did they have discussions like that in front of you?" asked Celeste, shocked.

"Oh no, but I always listened in," explained Levent.

"But it sounds as if you have turned out more like your Dad," said Celeste. "You're definitely not like your mother."

"I hope I'm not like my Dad either," said Levent, thoughtfully. "He's so weak. He always capitulated and gave in to whatever my mother wanted. It seemed as if he was too lazy to bother arguing. He just hid at work all day long, and then went off and found another woman for consolation without ever trying to solve the problems at home."

"That was pretty mean to your mother," said Celeste.

"That was also pretty mean to me," added Levent. "In their different ways, they're both selfish, my parents. They're both obsessed with money. Dad's obsessed with earning as much as possible and Mum's obsessed with having it and spending it. They both think money can make you into a better person." Levent paused and looked out of the window for a moment. "I'm just as messed up as they are when it comes to money, only in a different way. I'm determined not to worship cash they way they do, but

Veronica Di Grigoli

that means I'm a spoiled little rich kid who takes it for granted. I can't win."

He suddenly told the taxi driver to take a turning to the left and stop outside a department store. When the taxi pulled up he sprang out, paid the driver and ran behind the car to open the door for Celeste. Inside the shop, Celeste felt a pang of homesickness when she saw the dazzle and bright lights of the impressive Christmas trees and lavish decorations.

"Do you like the New Year decorations?" asked Levent. "They've put up trees, the way they do in England."

"Trees are for Christmas, not New Year," said Celeste, feeling even more homesick.

They rode the escalator up to the toy department, which they reached by walking past the furniture and then the children's clothes.

"How many kids are there in the orphanage?" asked Levent. "Do you know the exact number?"

"No, but I reckon about a hundred and twenty." Minus one, thought Celeste, looking around her at all the excited children shopping with their parents.

"Right, then," cut in Levent hastily, sensing that the progress he had made in lightening Celeste's mood was slipping. "Look, toy cars."

They decided to buys lots of different small toys and give them to the children as a kind of lucky dip. They found miniature toy cars, no more than an inch long, which came in boxes of twelve.

"Oh, cool, they have a dynamo," said Levent, beaming with pleasure. "Look." He placed one of the minute cars on the floor and dragged it backwards, releasing it and watching it shoot across the floor and disappear under a display cabinet. "We could get quite a few of these and open the boxes to give the cars out individually," he suggested.

"Good idea," agreed Celeste.

They added transparent rubber balls with insects inside them and highly elastic rubbery monsters to the shopping basket, and left it at the counter while they went to collect more toys. They found some board games and other toys designed to be played with in groups and decided to buy a selection of these for the boys to share. Celeste constantly spotted toys that would have delighted her little brothers, and consequently felt guilty about the fact that she was not with them. Her guilt made her regret the toys she had posted to them for Christmas, partly because she had made her decision not to go home too late so the gifts would probably not arrive on time and partly because, now, she kept seeing better toys she wished she had sent instead. Worst of all, she obsessively scrutinised every child in the shop who seemed about the same height as Tekin, as if certain she would spot him among the other children if only she looked hard enough.

She was unaware of the fact that she spent long periods gazing at little children as if she were going into a trance, rather the way Mr. Demirsar tended to stare at the boys at the orphanage.

"We've got a huge amount of things and I don't think we can carry any more," said Levent, finally.

"You're right," said Celeste. "Let's pay and get a move on."

Levent nonchalantly handed his father's credit card to the cashier and refused Celeste's offer to contribute what cash she had. He carried as many of the bags as he could handle down the escalator. As they left the shop it was started to snow. Despite being laden with carrier bags, Levent sprinted to the line of taxis waiting outside the shop entrance and managed to open a door and throw all the bags in before Celeste reached the taxi.

"Oh no, I hope the snow stops soon," he said as he bundled Celeste's bags into the taxi and waited for her to clamber in on top of them.

"I don't," said Celeste. "It's supposed to snow at Christmas."

"Why?" asked Levent, innocently.

"It's more Christmassy," Celeste explained earnestly.

The boys were overjoyed to see Celeste with Levent at the orphanage and Celeste immediately realised that, in insisting that she came here for Christmas, Levent had done exactly what she needed. The boys were very excited when Celeste told them that they had brought Christmas presents. She had taught them about Christmas in their English lessons and they had been particularly excited to learn about Christmas stockings, which were filled in the night by Father Christmas.

"Should we bring our socks to put the presents in?" suggested one of the boys. Celeste laughed aloud.

"That's a great idea!" she said. She had not had time to think of wrapping the presents or how exactly she would distribute them, but now the children themselves had come up with the solution. While they ran to their dormitories to fetch a clean sock each, Celeste and Levent took the bags of toys into the dining room and heaped everything onto one table, setting aside the board games and the larger toys for sharing. The cook came out of the kitchen to see what the commotion was about and her delight when she realised that they had turned up with toys for all the children was truly infectious. She dabbed her sweaty forehead on a corner of her floury apron and clapped her huge hands together as she examined the heap of toys.

"The only thing lacking is a Father Christmas," said Celeste. "Usually a man dresses up as Father Christmas to give out the toys," she explained.

No sooner had she spoken than in walked Mr. Demirsar, wearing a red boiler suit. Celeste had only ever seen him wearing his old dark blue dungarees with holes in the trouser legs and a threadbare bottom. This boiler suit was clearly brand new, without a trace of a stain. Celeste and Levent exchanged glances, realising they had both had the same idea. Celeste explained to Mr. Demirsar what they were doing and, in his own undemonstrative way, he seemed even more delighted than the cook. The cook produced a red towel and Mr. Demirsar was able to come up with two large packs of cotton wool and a roll of thick black insulating tape, all of which Levent used to transform Mr. Demirsar into an Eastern style Santa Claus with a red turban trimmed in white, a long white beard below his black moustache and a black belt and white fluffy trimming around the trouser legs of his red boiler suit.

"You have to say 'ho ho ho,'" explained Celeste.

"Ho ho ho," repeated Mr. Demirsar, gravely. "What does it mean?"

"It's laughter," explained Celeste, feeling silly. "That's the way Father Christmas laughs," she added.

"Oh, I understand," said Mr. Demirsar, looking as if he did not understand at all. When Mr. Demirsar stepped out of the dining room door, the boys broke spontaneously into a cheer.

"He's being Father Christmas, isn't he?" asked Bűlent, looking at Celeste in delight.

"Yes, Father Christmas has come from the North Pole to bring your Christmas presents," she answered. "And the snow followed him all the way here!"

"Ho ho ho," added Mr. Demirsar, fairly quietly. "That's how Father Christmas laughs," he added, by way of explanation to the children. "Ho ho ho."

Celeste told a group of boys to give their socks to Father Christmas, who in turn handed them through the doorway to Levent. While Celeste and Mr. Demirsar chatted to the boys in the entrance hall, Levent and the cook rapidly filled each of the socks with a selection of the toys. As the boys dipped into their socks and delightedly showed each other what they had been given, Celeste called up a new group of boys. Mr. Demirsar started out very taciturn and subdued as always, contributing the occasional "ho ho ho" as instructed, but as he listened to Celeste chatting to the boys and as he sensed their happy reaction to seeing him dressed as Father Christmas, he gradually warmed to the role and started to speak to the boys himself, asking them if they liked their presents or making comments about the things they had received. As he gradually relaxed and opened up, Celeste began to see hints of the warm and attentive father he must once have been. Inhibited as he was, there were occasional flashes of spontaneity when he seemed completely relaxed with the boys and knew just what to say to them.

After a while Levent came out of the dining room and Celeste took his place, helping the cook to fill the socks he passed through the doorway to them. With Levent beside Mr. Demirsar Celeste heard peals of laughter from outside the door; shrill giggles from the boys and, for the first time ever, spontaneous laugher from Mr. Demirsar as well. He had a deep throaty laugh which sounded unexpectedly infectious.

When all the socks had been filled, there were still quite a few toys left.

"What shall we do with these?" said Celeste to the cook.

"If you don't mind, I'd like to save them for when the boys have birthdays," said Cook. "We always try to find something to give them from the clothes that get donated, but it would be wonderful to give them a proper presents like these toys."

They scooped all the remaining toys into two of the carrier bags for cook to set aside, and then placed one of the board games on each table. Celeste invited the boys into the dining room and told them they could sit at the tables to play in groups. Levent threw himself into the game, joining in with a group of boys with genuine delight. Celeste repeatedly heard his laughter again above the general hubbub and the room seemed to echo with the laugher of the boys on Levent's table. Mr. Demirsar refused to remove the cotton wool or any other part of his Father Christmas costume and sat at another table while Celeste and the cook moved around the tables helping the boys to read the instructions and to understand how to play the games when they needed help. This was so unlike any normal Christmas Celeste had ever experienced and yet somehow she was enjoying herself. She and Levent had not only brought happiness to the children but also to Mr. Demirsar, it seemed.

"You loved playing with the boys today, didn't you?" she asked Levent in the taxi on the way home.

"Ho ho ho," he replied, and then broke into a laugh that sounded almost like Nilüfer's. "Yes, I did."

"But you never go to the orphanage," commented Celeste. "Haven't you ever been curious to go before?"

"I used to want to go when I was little," Levent replied. "I pleaded with my mother to take me every day. I couldn't understand why she made me stay at home with a babysitter when she went to a place full of other boys that I could have played with. She always refused, and managed to make me feel guilty just for wanting to go."

"How did she make you feel guilty?"

"She would say that I had all these wonderful toys she had bought me and a beautiful house and why didn't I appreciate them? When I said I wanted friends to play with, she would tell me that those orphans were not good enough to be my friends and when I asked why not, she said they spoke bad Turkish with a low class accent or that they were ignorant or that they had diseases and I would get ill if I played with them. It was a new excuse every time. In the end I gave up asking."

"I suppose she thought she was doing what was best for you. I've noticed your mother's very protective of you," commented Celeste as tactfully as she could. "I mean, she really seems to dote on you."

"Hmm," responded Levent. "Yes."

"At least you had Nilüfer to play with when you were little," suggested Celeste. "You two were together all the time, weren't you?"

"Only after my grandmother insisted that my mother let me have a play mate."

"Your father's mother?"

"Yes. She was a really domineering and scary woman but she knew what was best for me. She always took good care of me. She was the only person my mother never managed to stand up to. Everyone did what my grandmother said. Grandmother had huge hands and a hairy mole on her cheek that pricked when she kissed you. Anyway, once I started school it was fine because I had loads of friends there. Though the best two years of my life so far were when I lived in America."

"What?" asked Celeste, flabbergasted. "I didn't know your family used to live in America."

"Not, not the family. Just me."

"By yourself?"

"Yes. I stayed with an American family who had an enormous kid called Scott. I lived with them for two years on an international exchange programme."

"How old were you?"

"They sent me out when I was eleven and I came home when I was thirteen."

"They just left you there alone for two years?"

"Yep," answered Levent. "It was the best time of my life because I lived with a family where there weren't any secrets. Scott's Mum stayed at home and gave us help with our homework, and took us to do things after school like baseball club, and she used to sit down after school and talk with us. I found it really difficult to adjust when I came back here. I grew up a lot there and when I came back home I felt like a foreigner."

"Well, at least now I know why you talk English with an American accent," said Celeste. "But I don't understand how your mother could have let you go on your own. She..." Celeste's voice trailed off.

"Go on," prompted Levent. "What were you going to say?"

"I was going to say that she really fusses over you," said Celeste.

"You don't think she was happy about sending me, do you? Dad insisted," said Levent. "It was one of the few times he has ever stood up to her. They were arguing so much it was awful. I got this weird rash on my skin that I think was psychological. The strange thing is that even though Mum is so fussy, I felt better cared for by Scott's mother. She actually listened to me. She used to ask me what I wanted, instead of telling me. But anyway, I've got something more interesting for you to think about," Levent continued, changing the subject. "A present." He slipped his hand into the inner breast pocket of his overcoat and pulled out a small rectangular package, gift-wrapped in paper from the department store where they had bought all the toys for the children.

"How on earth did you manage to buy this right under my nose?" exclaimed Celeste, incredulously. She felt embarrassed, as she had been so absorbed in choosing presents for the children that she had not thought to buy anything for Levent.

"You can be quite a daydreamer, you know," said Levent.

"But you've already given me a beautiful dress for Christmas," Celeste protested.

"Go on. Open it," said Levent.

Celeste tore open the paper and took out a wooden box, the lid inlaid with different colours of wood making a pattern of flowers framed with a ring of tiny leaves.

"It's beautiful," she exclaimed, holding it closer to the car window to see better in the fitful light of the city's illuminations.

"You haven't even opened it yet," said Levent.

She slipped the catch open. Both the bottom and the lid were filled with coloured squares of watercolour paint. At the centre was a furrow holding four brushes of different sizes. Levent had given her such a thoughtful gift, so perfect for her.

"It's wonderful."

"It's nice to see a smile on your face from time to time," Levent replied.

Celeste held the paint box in her hands for a while and studied it as the taxi drove on in silence. The driver was not a skilled chauffeur like Mehmet, who seemed able to make his car glide smoothly no matter how bad the road surface. This taxi threw Celeste and Levent constantly from one side of the car to the other, shook them out of their seats with every hole in the road and vibrated furiously even when it was stationary at junctions and traffic lights. The driver lurched into a side street with no lampposts and in the pitch darkness, lit only by the car's headlights, Celeste felt immensely relieved to be with Levent rather than travelling in the taxi on her own.

"Are you still in touch with Scott, the huge American kid?" asked Celeste suddenly.

"We e-mail each other and chat on line nearly every day," answered Levent. "He's my best friend. And he's still huge, by the way. Really tall and pretty fat, too."

"I was just wondering about something else as well," mused Celeste. "Why does your mother work in that orphanage?"

"What do you mean?" asked Levent.

"It's not as if she needs the salary. I've had the impression lots of times that she really does care about the children. Until Tekin disappeared, anyway," she added, almost under her breath. "But most of the time it seems so out of keeping with her character that I can't understand her at all."

Levent was silent for a while, and Celeste wondered if he thought she had been rude to ask such a question. He could criticise his own mother but it was different if someone else criticised her.

"She definitely does care about the children," stated Levent. "She loves to fight for them. My Mum loves winning and so she needs things to fight about. It's also about control. She has total control over the lives of the children there. And then there's the fact that she gets a kick out of feeling superior to people. So there are lots of reasons."

"You mean she likes to feel superior to the kids in the orphanage?" asked Celeste, baffled.

"In case you hadn't noticed," said Levent, "my mother divides the world into people to envy, and people she thinks envy her. She prefers people she feels superior to, the ones she thinks envy her. She likes helping people because it makes her feel superior. That's why she's happy at the orphanage."

"You have a low opinion of your Mother," said Celeste, partly to hide the fact that she thought Levent had just summed up his mother's character so well.

"I love her," said Levent. "She'll always be my mother. But I have to admit, I don't really like her."

Celeste was woken up late on the morning of Boxing Day by a telephone call from a journalist who said she was a friend of Berna Zaman and would like to ask Celeste for some information regarding a missing child. She worked for one of the national newspapers and explained that her editor had instructed her to conduct a telephone interview and write an article about Tekin. Celeste told her all she could about Tekin and the journalist said she would also like to talk to the director of the orphanage from which he had run away. Celeste gave her Leman's mobile number, hoping she would not be angry. The journalist sensed Celeste's reticence when talking about Leman and asked for the reason.

"I'm just not sure how she'll react to your call," explained Celeste.

"Don't worry, I'm used to uncooperative people," laughed the journalist. "And anyway, she'd be a pretty strange woman if she didn't collaborate actively with someone trying to help find a child who went missing from her care. I mean, it doesn't make her look very good, does it?"

This was when Celeste realised that Leman had taken Tekin's disappearance as a sign of personal failure. He had completely stepped out of her control and the very fact that he was missing was a blemish on her, a sign of her imperfection, a reason to feel inadequate.

Shortly afterwards, when Celeste was having breakfast, she was interrupted by another call, this time from a man who said he was an assistant to a radio disc jockey. His manner was witty and lighthearted and he cracked a number of jokes which Celeste didn't really understand, while taking down some details on Tekin. He told her which radio station to tune in to and said that they would start making announcements immediately. Celeste managed to find the radio and tune in to the right wavelength just in time to catch the end of a piece on Tekin. The announcer played three songs before repeating the announcement, which he continued to read more or less between every three to five songs for the rest of the morning. He used the same scripted announcement every time, describing Tekin's looks and height, giving his name, and telling listeners to contact the orphanage if they had any information that could be relevant. Each time Celeste heard the message read out, she felt a tiny bit more optimistic. Each time, more people would have heard about Tekin and more people would be keeping their eyes out for him. She felt, as Berna had said, that something concrete was being done at last. Celeste kept the radio on quietly all day in her room. When a different announcer came on air she continued listening and was surprised and very pleased that the announcements continued. She heard announcements about Tekin at least once an hour throughout the day. The owner of this broadcasting station must be a very good friend of Attila, she thought.

Celeste bought a Turkish newspaper for the first time the next morning. She had read so many of them but they had always been old copies of Leman's papers. She flicked open the first page, ready to leaf through it frantically, and felt a surge of excitement at the sight of her picture of Tekin low down on the third page. Beside it was a brief article repeating almost verbatim what she had said and quoting Leman, Orphanage Director, making a personal appeal to the public to be vigilant and do anything they could to look for Tekin.

"Don't make the mistake of thinking this child is unloved just because he has no living family," she was quoted as saying. *"Little Tekin is sorely missed by many people who are desperate to see his safe return."*

Over the next week, Leman came home from work late every day but one. On the Thursday evening, Ferhat asked her at dinner how things were going at the orphanage.

"How things going?" she repeated, raising a carefully plucked eyebrow at him. "We getting new boys every day. There is a rumour in the city that there is reward moneys for Tekin, so they brings any boy they find called Tekin. Most brings boys much older than him, not called Tekin, and they makes big fuss asking for money. One even was bringing a girl! We wasting so much time to send away these stupids. We got three new boys living in orphanage now that was brought to us, that was stray children on streets. One man, he bring own son, and ask reward! Like he was trying to sell boy to us!"

"What did you tell him?" asked Levent.

"I ask him why does he think there is reward money? He says because there is articles in radio and newspaper and so there must be one reward. So I say to him, Oh so you know how to read? That's a surprise. Well you should learn better because nothing is written in newspaper about reward."

"What did he say after that?" asked Levent, laughing.

"He didn't speak because I didn't permit him to. Then I said him to go and look for job instead of showing his son how much he is idiot," answered Leman. "You know, parrot in entrance hall learned to say 'I found Tekin, give me reward money,' and he say it all day. I don't know if really he learnt from these smelly fools that come in, or if boys teach him that for joking. But he make me getting nervous when hearing it all day. I make Demirsar put him in art room."

Celeste remained silent, while Leman fretfully stroked her hand along the brown fur collar of her burgundy red mohair twin-set, as if trying to smooth out the ruffled hair of a scruffy child.

"That's sounds very stressful," said Ferhat, unusually attentive. "But I suppose it's good if those three boys are living safely now."

"Good, but where we get the money for others?" said Leman. "I send away five boys that need home. I all day telephoning to other orphanages to find if they can take these boys. I all day finding homes for boys that not Tekin. *I* need reward moneys for help these boys! Why is everyone so stupid?"

"Have some water, Mum," said Levent, filling her tumbler with mineral water.

"Levent my darling, put in some *rakı* please," asked Leman, pointing to the bottle of concentrated liquorice flavoured liqueur at the opposite end of the table.

"I'll see if I can get one of the secretaries from the company to spend a bit of time at the office to help out," suggested Ferhat. "Do you think that would ease things a bit?"

"Yes, could be helpful a bit," agreed Leman, stirring the *rakı* and water together as they turned a cloudy white.

Ferhat's attitude to his wife seemed gradually to have transformed since the conversation Celeste had overheard at Zeliha's flat. Leman's behaviour was suffused with a new confidence and - was it happiness? Not exactly, Celeste concluded. She looked very well, satisfied and somehow triumphant. Instead of striving to prove in every little way that she was superior to anyone around her, she now seemed effortlessly to take the fact for granted.

The next day was New Year's Eve and the day of the University Ball. Celeste did not feel in the mood for going out to a large party and even considered telling Levent she did not want to go. Nilüfer called her during the afternoon and convinced her that the ball would be the ideal thing to cheer her up.

"If you don't come, you'll ruin my evening," she protested. "And what about Levent? Does he deserve to have a ruined evening?"

"You're right," admitted Celeste.

"What are you going to wear?" asked Nilüfer.

Celeste described the red dress Levent had bought for her.

"Oh! That's funny!" screamed Nilüfer with her usual braying laugh. "I've got a red dress to wear as well! It was a present from my parents, because I got the top grade in my exam this time. I mean, the highest in the University."

"Congratulations!" said Celeste. "Levent had an exam as well, didn't he?" she suddenly remembered.

"Don't say anything to him," warned Nilüfer hastily. "He failed it again, for the second time. He got into big trouble. He's got real problems with his degree now."

"Poor Levent," commented Celeste. "Why does he keep failing? Does he find the course too difficult?"

"No," said Nilüfer. "He's lazy but he's not stupid. In fact he's one of the cleverest on the course, when he decides to work. At the moment, his problem is that he can't concentrate. He's got things on his mind. He's getting an obsession."

"Obsession with what?" asked Celeste, intrigued. This sounded most unlike the Levent she knew.

"I can't say!" guffawed Nilüfer raucously. "It's private!"

Her girlish manner and constant laughing worked a treat on Celeste's mood and she realised that going to the ball with Levent and Nilüfer probably would distract her somewhat from her own obsession with finding Tekin. She took a long time in the shower and did her hair and make-up carefully to keep herself in the mood for going out. When she put on the red dress that Levent had given her for the Freemason's dinner she realised that she had, as Ferhat had noticed, become thinner. The dress was loose around her waist and hips but the fabric was so flowing and clingy that it flattered her all the same.

Mehmet was due to collect her and Levent at eight-thirty, but Celeste was ready by eight o'clock, so she went downstairs to read one of Leman's newspapers. Leman had already called to tell Ferhat, who was going to take her out to dinner, that she would be later than planned as another boy, who appeared to have been badly beaten, had been brought to the orphanage and she was waiting for the police. Celeste felt guilty for all the trouble the announcements on the radio and the newspaper article were causing for Leman, but she still felt it was worthwhile as she hoped that it would lead to someone finding Tekin in the end. Ferhat, who had been watching television but switched it off as soon as Celeste entered, came to sit in a low armchair near her and asked her how she was getting on generally. He clearly knew how difficult it had been for her to decide to stay in Istanbul over Christmas. As he spoke, Celeste noticed that his breath seemed tight and he continued to wheeze even when he was sitting down. He slid his hand into his jacket and held it against his chest for a few moments, and then took it out and gripped his left arm tightly.

"Are you all right?" she asked him. "You look as if you're feeling pain in your chest."

"It's just a little heartburn, I think," he replied, forcing a somewhat unconvincing smile. Celeste still felt the searing pains of nervous heartburn in her own chest, especially when her stomach was empty, but she had the impression Ferhat's pain was different.

"You're rubbing your arm, though," she persisted, suddenly very worried. "Does it hurt there, too?" She was probably panicking about nothing, just because she was so tense these days.

"It does hurt, actually," Ferhat admitted.

"Have you ever had angina?" she asked.

"What is that?" asked Ferhat.

"Pain in your heart," explained Celeste. "I think we should call the doctor. You have a cardiologist, don't you?"

"Oh, that won't be necessary. Leman will be home soon, and once I start eating, my stomach will settle down," he insisted.

"If you say so," said Celeste.

Celeste's mother had insisted that she had nothing wrong with her, right up until it was too late. They had believed her and respected her wishes, Celeste asking herself a million times afterwards why she had not made more fuss over her mother's symptoms. Celeste had no intention of making the same mistake again. She decided to mention her concerns about Ferhat to Levent, so she went upstairs and called to him through the bathroom door.

"Is it urgent?" he asked her. She heard the shower stopping and a squeak as one of Levent's feet slid on a floor tile.

"It could be," she answered. "I don't know." Unexpectedly the door opened and Levent was standing in front of her, dressed in a white bath robe with his hair dripping wet. Celeste hastily told him that she was worried his father was having some kind of problem with his heart and that she thought he should be checked by the doctor. "I'll go back downstairs and sit with him while you get ready," she concluded.

When she reached the living room again, Ferhat was leant against the back of the armchair and his face looked almost as pallid white as the wall behind him. Celeste sat beside him and touched his forehead, as if checking his temperature. Why was she doing that? She had no idea. She knew nothing about heart disease other than that heart attacks often began with angina or pains in the left arm. She also knew that Ferhat took a great many tablets for his blood pressure, fibrillation and cholesterol, amongst other things, and was evidently not in good health. The doorbell rang and she sped to open it, knowing it would be Mehmet.

"Do you know where Ferhat's cardiologist is?" she asked him, immediately. "I mean, how we could contact him?" Mehmet walked into the house, looking around the entrance hall as if he felt slightly awkward there, and asked Celeste where Ferhat was. Celeste was immensely relieved that he was immediately taking charge of the situation, the way he had when he had accompanied Celeste to the orphanage and she had started to accuse to Mr. Demirsar.

"Where are Leman and Levent?" he asked her. "We should take him to the American Hospital of Istanbul. There is a brand new cardiology unit there."

"Stop talking about me as if I'm not here," protested Ferhat, breathlessly. "I just need a rest. We can't go out before Leman gets here."

"Is it a good hospital?" asked Celeste. She had been told some very worrying things about Turkish hospitals by Nilüfer and her parents.

"It's excellent," said Ferhat, "It's a private hospital. Everything is very modern and well-equipped."

Levent came dashing downstairs, his hair still wet. He was dressed in his black tie suit, without the bow tie, and was hastily buttoning up the last few buttons of his shirt. He and Mehmet helped Ferhat towards the front door while Celeste sprinted to the kitchen drawer where Leman stored her stash of pills. She took out the metal tin containing all Ferhat's medicines.

"We should take your tablets with us," she said to Ferhat as she climbed into the back of the car beside him. "They always ask to have your tablets."

On the way to the hospital Ferhat finally admitted that he was starting to feel unwell, and that he would be glad to be checked up by a doctor. Levent called his mother on his mobile to let her know where they were going.

"Yes, it could be his heart," he repeated, raising his voice. "Yes, it *is* necessary to take him to hospital." He looked at Celeste, exasperated. "She'll be at the hospital as soon as possible," he told his father as he slid the small telephone back into the breast pocket of his jacket and placed his hand against on father's arm to reassure him.

"That's good," replied Ferhat, sounding as if he meant it.

As they stepped out of the car and headed towards the hospital entrance, with Mehmet one side of Ferhat and Levent the other, Ferhat seemed to faint. His legs buckled beneath him and he fell forward, his arms hanging awkwardly. Celeste shouted for help, and Levent and Mehmet joined in, hoping someone from the hospital would hear them and come out. Suddenly there were about five paramedics around them with a trolley on wheels, lifting Ferhat from the steps and laying him on his back whilst they were already wheeling it in through the large double doors. Celeste followed the trolley at a trot, ahead of Levent and Mehmet, unaware of the corridors they took. When they came to a halt in a large, white room full of medical equipment, Celeste tried to disappear into a corner while Ferhat was attached to a heart monitor so his pulse was displayed as a moving green line on a screen beside the trolley. After a few minutes, a doctor told Levent that he seemed to be stable so they would leave for a few minutes and come to check on his condition every ten minutes.

"Where's Mehmet?" asked Ferhat. "Tell him to park the car properly or else we'll get a huge fine," murmured Ferhat.

"I'll go," offered Celeste immediately, but Levent said he wanted to go.

"I need the toilet," he added. "Stay with Dad."

As the door swung shut, Ferhat turned his head slightly to look at Celeste.

"Thank you for insisting on bringing me here," he said. "It was kind of you be so concerned about me. Although, I'm glad it wasn't necessary. I actually feel fine now."

"That's good," said Celeste.

"I just feel tired," he added. "I think I'll lie back and close my eyes for a minute."

As he spoke, everything seemed to go into slow motion for Celeste. She watched his eyeballs drifting upwards and rolling back ghoulishly. His eyelids sank sleepily closed as his head fell back onto the pillow, his mouth lolling open. The wavy green line on the screen beside Ferhat went flat and the monitor sounded a piercing alarm. Ferhat's hands started to slip apart. His right arm brushed Celeste's hip as it slid lifeless from the stretcher and dangled limply. The high-pitched buzzing noise of the alarm seemed to numb Celeste's brain. She felt as if she stood dumbly for several minutes before she started to scream, though in reality she took just a split second to react.

"Help! Help! doctors! Anyone! Please come, anyone!"

The next thing she knew, she was being swept back into the room by a tidal wave of white coats and Ferhat was surrounded by doctors. At least twelve of them bustled around with syringes and bags of medicine which they were connecting to narrow tubes, all of them shouting to each other in an organised frenzy. One doctor was up on the trolley, straddling Ferhat and thumping him in the chest as if trying to break his ribs, counting out a type of shouted rhythm between each time he beat his fists down together on Ferhat's chest. The force he used was so great that his flushing face broke into a sweat and, of all strange details to notice, Celeste stood and stared, transfixed, at a raised vein in the doctor's temple. Another doctor was standing by holding large black pads in each hand. Among the throng of doctors standing around Ferhat, Celeste could make out one cutting an incision just below his collar bone and another inserting a fine tube, which seemed to go on and on inside him. At that moment Levent appeared in the doorway and froze. Celeste stood beside him. She thought she understood the doctors saying the tube had reached the heart, and one of them was holding a bag of clear liquid up over his head so it would flow down the tube and directly into Ferhat's heart, and then there was blood everywhere; Ferhat's blood was flowing so much that the sheet on the stretcher was bright red and shiny and wet and it ran dark and sticky down the leg of the trolley and spread in an oval shape on the floor. And then two doctors approached him again holding the large black pads to deliver another electric shock, and a nurse was holding Celeste by the shoulder and gently telling her she and Levent had to leave. While the door was closing in front of them she realised she was holding Levent's hand and his soft fingers twitched and clenched around hers tightly as they heard a loud, deep howl coming from Ferhat, from his unconscious lungs as the power of the voltage running through him made his lungs jerk into a spasm that made his whole body jump up from the trolley he was lying on. When a nurse led them away they heard another two wrenching groans reaching them down the corridor, and then they could hear no more from that room where the doctors were trying to bring Levent's father back to life.

And as they sat in the tiny waiting room on a flowery sofa, Mehmet found them and said he would wait outside in the entrance, and Levent was to call him if he needed anything at all. Celeste gave Ferhat's medicines to the nurse who came in to offer them some news.

"His condition is still unstable," the nurse told them. "That's all I can tell you."

"That means my father's dying, doesn't it?" asked Levent, and the agony of his anguish made Celeste feel selfish, made her want to think only of her mother and the hours she had spent terrified in hospital knowing that one day, one hour, the minute would come when a doctor would come and tell her that her mother's suffering was all over, that the inevitable had finally happened. And then she wanted to hold both Levent's hands and tell him she knew exactly how he felt and she wanted to help him, but she knew there was no way to make him feel better.

"I want my mother," he said eventually. "I wish she was here."

"She'll be here soon," reassured Celeste automatically. When Leman did arrive she bustled into the room and, ignoring Celeste completely, she commanded Levent to tell her exactly what had happened.

"Why can't we see him?" she asked. "They won't let me see him." Celeste waited in uncomfortable silence while Levent explained everything to his mother. His bow tie still hung loosely around his shirt collar and his mother took it off and carefully placed it in his coat pocket as he spoke. When Levent had finished speaking, Leman placed her hands on her son's cheeks, her orange-varnished nails slipping through his black hair, and looked up into his eyes. "My darling son, I need you to look after me now," she said. "My son, I promise I'll look after you forever."

Then began a wait which seemed interminable, perhaps because they had no idea when it would end. They sat mostly in silence and spoke sporadically, Leman wiping her eyes and blowing her nose on the multi-coloured tissues from the box at the centre of the coffee table, the only object in the room, and directing gestures of affection towards her son. The dark kohl around her eyes ran down her cheeks and into lines which followed the crows' feet at the corners of her eyes. When eventually she acknowledged Celeste's presence, she allowed her to remove the smudges of make-up with a fresh tissue. Levent took off his coat and dinner jacket and paced back and forth behind the sofa, his long legs crossing the room in three strides so he was constantly having to turn on his heels to change direction. Celeste felt cold in her red silk dress and sat hunched in the corner, her arms wrapped around her body over her aching stomach.

Eventually the nurse told them that a doctor would be coming shortly and that Ferhat's condition now seemed to be stable. When the doctor came, accompanied by the same nurse, he said that they were finding Ferhat a bed for the night and that his wife could accompany him up to the ward. Celeste offered to go home and prepare an overnight bag of toiletries and pyjamas for Ferhat to send to the hospital with Mehmet, so that Levent could stay near his father, but Leman told Levent he should go home with Celeste and prepare the things for his father.

"If you can't stay with him, it's better you stay with Celeste. At least you won't be alone," she said, stroking her son's shirt sleeve affectionately. The soothing tone of her deep voice made her sound incongruously serene, even though Celeste knew she was not.

"Please, come with me, Madam," invited the nurse, leading Leman out of the door. "You can wait with your husband while they prepare the bed."

As Leman tottered along the corridor behind the nurse, the doctor held up the metal tin of Ferhat's medicines.

"Are these all the medicines your father takes?" he asked Levent.

"Yes."

"I just want to go through them with you," explained the doctor, sitting on the sofa and indicating to Levent that he should take a seat beside him.

"My Mother puts everything in there. She's quite obsessive about his medicines," explained Levent, wondering why the doctor was being so meticulous. Celeste hovered in the doorway.

"This one," said the doctor, holding up the small brown glass jar, "What's this for?"

"I think that's his cholesterol tablets," said Levent. "I don't understand you're asking me. Doesn't it say on the bottle?"

"It does," confirmed the doctor, "but the tablets inside the bottle are not what it says on the label. Tablets for lowering cholesterol are white, but these are brown. Look," he said, opening the childproof top and tipping a few tablets into his hand. "They're very large, these tablets, and they look like vitamin pills or some type of herbal remedy. Cholesterol tablets are white, as I said, and they're very small." Levent turned his head to look directly at the doctor, as if asking him what this could mean. "Is you mother ever absent-minded?" asked the doctor. "Could she possibly have got his medicines muddled up without realising?"

"Not a chance," said Levent.

"Is it worth asking her?" persisted the doctor.

"No," insisted Levent, emphatically.

"In that case, with your permission, I'd like to get these analysed," concluded the doctor. "If, as you say, all his medicines are here, then we can probably deduce that your father hasn't been taking any medication to lower his cholesterol. It could be very important to know what these tablets are, even if they are just a herbal remedy. They're not always safe, to be honest."

"Please get them analysed as quickly as you can and tell me the result." said Levent. "And please don't say anything to my mother."

"Not a problem," said the doctor.

Mehmet was waiting for them in the chilly night air, smoking a cigarette as he leaned against the car door opposite the entrance to the hospital. Most of the traffic had now dissolved away and they made the journey home very quickly. Levent said nothing and Celeste could not think of anything to say to console him. When they arrived home, he disappeared into his father's room and prepared the bag for him while Celeste brought him Ferhat's toothbrush and toothpaste and then waited awkwardly on the stairs. The most ordinary things, like a toothbrush or a clean pair of socks, suddenly seemed so pointless and so excruciatingly poignant when faced with the fact that their owner may be about to die. The agony of disposing of her mother's hairbrush and tights, of her clothes and her everyday trivia had been perhaps the most intensely painful of all the painful moments after Celeste had lost her mother. Trapped in no-man's-land, she had been faced with the choice of leaving everything as it was and feeling as if the ghost of her mother had never left the house, or removing it and facing up to the fact that her mother was gone for good and would never, ever come back to touch her or hold her again.

She looked at her watch. It was eleven-thirty: half an hour until the New Year. Levent's mobile phone rang three times while he was preparing the bag and Celeste was glad each time to overhear him talking to his mother, thus taking her mind off the thoughts that ran freely though her head when her mind was left to wander.

"Mum says Dad's asleep now and she's going to sit with him for the night," said Levent. "She said to come in the morning, there's no point waiting around at the hospital for the night. So I'm going to give this to Mehmet to drop off."

Celeste followed him downstairs and, when he had given the bag to Mehmet, Celeste asked Levent if he would like a drink of water or tea.

"It's half past eleven," she added, pointlessly.

"Let's open a bottle of champagne," said Levent.

"Are you sure?" Celeste asked. "We're not exactly celebrating, are we?"

"It's still New Year. And we should celebrate that Dad is alive," said Levent, managing a brief, weak smile. "Which is thanks to you. He could have died."

"Right then, you get some wine, and I'm going to boil some pasta," said Celeste, suddenly feeling decisive and realising that now it was her turn to try to be positive for Levent. "Are you hungry?"

"Not very," said Levent. "But I suppose it would do me good to eat something."

Celeste set a saucepan of water boiling ready for the spaghetti and opened a tin of tomatoes and tipped them into another pan, which she seasoned with herbs and oil to make a simple sauce. Levent seemed distracted and for the first time ever Celeste saw him looking serious and without a trace of a smile on his handsome face. They both spoke very little, yet Celeste did not feel uncomfortable in the silences. When the food was ready, they decided to sit in the breakfast room rather than the kitchen, as they usually did when eating together. Levent fumbled while trying to open the champagne, running his fingers through his glossy black hair several times before fiddling again with the wire holding the cork in the bottle. Celeste wondered if his soft baby hands had ever actually opened a bottle of champagne before. He hardly ever drank alcohol and even when he did, there was normally a uniformed waiter to open the bottle and pour the drink for him.

Eventually Levent poured the champagne into the two glasses and proposed a toast to his father. Celeste was still holding the glass to her lips when Levent placed his glass back on the table and said,

"I think she poisoned him."

"You mean she wanted to kill him?" asked Celeste.

"No, definitely not," answered Levent immediately. "I think those tablets were supposed to do some kind of magic on him, but they contained something poisonous." At the mention of the word magic, Celeste's hand froze holding a fork full of spaghetti in mid air. "My mother used to go to a fortune teller, a horrible woman who's basically a *cadı*, a witch. She would tell Mum her destiny, supposedly, by looking at the coffee grounds in the bottom of her cup or reading her palm, and also give her magic spells written on bits of paper and tell her to do weird things that were supposed to get what she wanted."

"Is that why she keeps those bottles of paper in the fridge?" asked Celeste.

"Yes, they were supposed to make me get better grades in my exams. There's an egg in my bedroom beside my bed, too. She won't let me move it. But anyway, I'm terrified of touching it."

"Why? Is it some really magical thing?"

"No! It's been there for about a year. If it breaks the stink could kill me," Levent replied. Celeste laughed. "Those jars of water, she first put one in the fridge two years ago and I threw it away. She went completely mad and got a new one, so I just left them there. The egg is supposed to be a protection against the evil eye; you know, harm caused by other people's jealousy. She seems to think everyone would be desperately jealous of me. What have I got to be jealous of?" Celeste stopped eating altogether and put her fork down on her plate. Levent looked so desperately unhappy that she wanted to walk around the table and hug him. "In the Koran, magic is condemned and I tried to convince her to stop by copying a passage down and leaving it on her dressing table, where she would find it. We're not exactly religious in this family, but I thought it might have some effect. She just sat me down and explained, like I was a tiny kid, that there are two types of magic, white magic and bad magic."

"What's the difference, then?" asked Celeste, intrigued.

"White magic uses passages of the Koran to do good things like curing illness or protecting against evil, and bad magic uses other methods to achieve your own ends."

"How, exactly, would you use the Koran to cure an illness?" asked Celeste.

"One example of supposedly good magic would be to copy a quotation on the inside of a bowl, then pour water in to rinse the writing away, and get the ill person to drink it," said Levent.

"Is that what it says in the Koran?" asked Celeste.

"No," answered Levent. "I'll tell you exactly what it says in the Koran." He jumped up from the table and sprinted to his father's study, reappearing in a moment with a piece of paper covered in his own handwriting. "Here," he said as he sat down again at the table. "This is what I left for my mother to find. Dad keeps it in his desk. I don't know why."

Celeste read the passage:

'The devils were disbelievers. They taught the people sorcery, and that which was sent down through the two angels of Babel, Haroot and Maroot. These two did not divulge such knowledge without pointing out: "This is a test. You shall not abuse such knowledge." But the people used it for evil schemes such as the breaking up of marriages. They can never harm anyone against the will of God. They thus learn what hurts them, not what benefits them, and they know full well that whoever practices witchcraft will have no share in the Hereafter. Miserable indeed is what they sell their souls for, if they only knew.'

"So it basically says that if you do magic, you'll go to hell," concluded Celeste.

"Pretty much," confirmed Levent. "My Mum's definition of 'doing good things' means making everything the way she wants. She's done some incredibly gross things," he went on, playing with his spaghetti as if ashamed to meet Celeste's gaze. "Before you moved in with us, well, until about three months before you came, we lived in a flat in Nişantaşı. Dad made up some story about work, which I believed at the time, but it was because he'd decided to move his mistress in here with him. He said he'd rented the house out, just to stop Mum coming here and finding the woman. I'm sure Mum already knew he was having an affair, even though she always denied it when I asked her. I trusted my father to tell the truth, but I guess she knew him better." Levent covered his eyes briefly with his hands and Celeste thought she saw him wipe away a few tears as he took them away. "Just before we moved out, Mum left those stupid magic spells everywhere. I saw her pull open the fabric on one of the chairs in the lounge and put a dead rat inside the stuffing, with a piece of paper that must have been from that fortune teller. She didn't know I saw her, and I never said anything to her about it. But I'm sure it was supposed to do harm to the other woman."

Celeste wondered whether to tell Levent about Zeliha. Finding out would obviously be very upsetting, and she wondered if it were better to leave that episode in the past as it was now over, especially since Ferhat was seriously ill. Yet Levent seemed so upset to have been kept in the dark. He had spoken several times about all the secrets and lies in his family. She decided to tell him the truth.

"I found out who that woman is, that your father was having an affair with," she blurted out hastily, before she could change her mind. "He finished the affair a little while ago."

"How do you know?" Levent asked, so astonished he spoke with his mouth full of pasta.

"She's my friend Heather's landlady," Celeste stated simply. Levent's piercing blue eyes studied Celeste in disbelief for a moment.

"Are you sure?" he quizzed her, eventually.

Celeste told him the story of how she had seen his father at the flat. She even confessed to the details of how she had managed to hear the conversation.

"I know it was really nosey," she admitted. "I didn't know it was going to be such a private thing. I wouldn't have listened if I'd known it was your father."

"What's the woman like?" asked Levent.

"She's the opposite of Leman," said Celeste. "In every way."

"You mean tall and thin, and not a witch?" asked Levent.

"No, she's actually very fat. I meant that she's very into art and history and the things that your father likes, and also she's not a very decisive person. She's..."

"You mean she's not a control freak?" asked Levent.

"She gives the impression of not being truly in control of anything, to be honest. But I think she has a lot of interests in common with your father."

"Unlike my mother, who had none of his interests," commented Levent in a matter-of-fact tone of voice.

"I couldn't help noticing that," agreed Celeste. "I've wondered what they originally saw in each other."

"Money, in her case," answered Levent immediately. "Dad's family was always wealthy and you must have spotted how my Mum adores money. I think Mum knew how to act quite cute when she was younger. She wasn't bad looking in some of the photos. My Grandmother reckoned that she got her claws into him and he was too weak willed and lacking in initiative to resist. She sometimes hinted Mum had used some kind of magic spell to enchant him. My grandmother said that Mum managed to make Dad marry her, but he never loved her, and she spent the rest of her life trying to make him."

"That's quite sad. It makes me feel sorry for her. It shows she's not just interested money, doesn't it?" concluded Celeste. "She does actually want love, too."

"Yes, you're right," said Levent. "I wonder what Dad really wants. Do you think this woman he was seeing could have made him happy?"

"I can't answer that," said Celeste. "I don't approve of extra-marital affairs but, putting that aside, I'd say she seems to be a kind woman."

"I wonder why he dumped her," mused Levent, more to himself than to Celeste. "I mean, why now, after all this time?"

"He said he was worried about you failing your exams and stuff, and that he had to dedicate himself more to his family," answered Celeste spontaneously, immediately wishing she could swallow her words. Why had she blurted this out? She was normally so measured and so good at weighing up what she planned to say before speaking. Suddenly Levent had her spilling out every thought in her mind with no consideration for the effect it may have. She had probably drunk too much champagne, she thought; she was glowing warm and her body, so tense these days, now felt far more relaxed than it had done for weeks. But perhaps it was not just the champagne. There was something about Levent's suffering this evening that made her feel she was finally seeing inside him. His constantly optimistic demeanour, always so appealing and attractive, somehow masked a lot of what he really felt. Today Celeste felt she had been invited in to meet the whole person.

"I bet Mum thinks her magic worked," said Levent, wringing his napkin in his hands.

"I think I might know what your mother was trying to do with those tablets," said Celeste.

"What?" asked Levent, looking concerned.

"I've found a few of her magic spells around the house," she began hastily. She had started so she may as well tell him everything. Somehow she was enjoying telling all the secrets she had harboured for so long. Pouring everything out with no consideration for the consequences felt like finally sitting down to rest after an exhausting day that never seemed to end. "They were spells that were supposed to make Ferhat fall back in love with her. There was also a spell that was aimed at me."

"What kind of spell?" asked Levent, a worried frown forming on his face.

"It was supposed to be stealing beauty from me, and giving it to the person who made the spell."

Levent paused for a moment and breathed deeply as he took this in.

"That must be why she broke your *nazar boncuğu* and gave you that opal pendant instead," he concluded. "I guessed she was trying to do something when I saw you wearing that pendant, but I didn't say anything to you, because I thought it was just harmless stupidity. But now I'm really worried she gave those tablets to my father, and maybe it's not such a harmless thing after all."

"One of the spells referred to a 'possession compound,'" said Celeste. "It said that the tablets would possess the heart of the person who consumed them, making them fall in love."

"Like an aphrodisiac?"

"Not exactly. I saw a spell which said it was for taking control of a person's thoughts and feelings, controlling their decisions and being able to make them do what the person casting the spell, and giving the tablets, wanted."

Levent's mind seemed to wander and while she spoke Celeste noticed his eyes fixed on a point across the room. He suddenly stared at her as if he were about to choke.

"What is it?" she asked him. He shook his head. "Are you OK?" she asked again.

"I've suddenly thought that, maybe, when you were ill.... I just suddenly wondered if she gave *you* something. I mean, put something in your food. Something from that *cadı* that was supposed to do magic on you. Nilüfer's parents couldn't work out what the illness was. They said the symptoms weren't like any illness they knew. But I doubt they would have considered if you were poisoned..."

Celeste felt numb at this idea. She thought of the horrible night she had felt so ill and of the strange dreams she had had while she was delirious with fever. Could Leman really have been behind her illness? It was too much to think about at the moment. She looked at her watch and realised it was just two minutes to midnight.

"Time for the countdown," she said to Levent, standing up from the table and picking up her champagne glass. "Let's look at the city."

She walked over to the window and Levent followed her, standing beside her as they looked out over the sea and the illuminated city on the Asian shore and waited to count down the seconds to midnight. Celeste gripped her glass of champagne, looked at the tower blocks in the distance and the car headlights moving down below, and thought about little Tekin somewhere out there, alone and cold and afraid. She looked at the black water of the Bosphorus and for a split second considered that his body could be down in its icy depths, but then she refused to allow herself to consider this a possibility. Levent's face was reflected in the glass, looking pale and worried and as if he had suddenly aged ten years in a matter of hours. He had just failed an important exam, his father was seriously ill in hospital, and he had reason to suspect that his mother may have poisoned his father. Between them, they had very little to celebrate.

"Time to count down," he said, softly. He pushed back his cuff and lifted his Rolex watch in front of their faces so they could count down the seconds together. When the New Year came in Celeste was ready to raise her champagne glass and drink a toast, but Levent turned to face her, leaning down to look into her eyes with his face so close that she felt his warm breath on her cheek, and then suddenly he was kissing her and the surprise made her drop her glass of champagne. The glass tinkled as it shattered on the floor and she felt tiny droplets of the cold liquid splash against her leg. He slipped his arms around her waist and pulled her closer to him, and she realised that what she had been needing more than anything in the world was a comforting embrace and some real affection. And the more Levent kissed her, the better she felt.

FIFTEEN

Maryam's House

When Celeste woke up early on the first of January, two thoughts came into her head at more or less the same moment. The first, as always, was of Tekin. The second came with a jolt as she remembered kissing Levent last night. What an embarrassing mistake! How could she have been so foolish as to kiss the boy she lived with? Leman's son and prize possession! He had become such a good friend and she had ruined it. Her stomach tensed up into a knot, an even tighter knot than usual.

She had been feeling homesick and thoroughly miserable about Tekin last night, not to mention Leman's attempts to cast magic spells on her. Levent, she pondered, had been in a similarly wretched mood, probably worse. No wonder they had wanted a bit of comfort. He was likely to be thinking the same as she was right now, wondering how he could tell her that it had been nice for one evening, but that was all. What should she do when she saw him this morning? Act as if nothing had happened? That approach usually only worked on English boys. No, she would have to be a mature adult and talk to him.

Maryam had the day off today, so Celeste made breakfast by herself in the kitchen and sat at the table leafing through a magazine while she waited for Levent to come downstairs: she could hear the boiler running, which probably meant that he was in the shower. The magazine's advertising content interested her more than the articles as, like the ubiquitous billboards and immense advertising banners covering entire walls of apartment blocks in the city, these advertisements were dominated by photographs of blonde women. Most of them were dark-skinned with heavy eyebrows, and their hair had noticeable black roots. Why were the advertisers obsessed with blonde hair when black hair was so beautiful, she wondered.

"Good morning!" called Levent from the doorway, shaking her from her thoughts so unexpectedly that she jogged her cup and spilled some tea onto the magazine page. She was surprised to see him looking so lively at this early hour, especially considering the events of the previous evening at the hospital.

"Oh, hello," said Celeste, immediately feeling shy. She studied the way his shirt moved across his chest and biceps as he raised his hands to turn the collar down and push back a shock of wet, black hair. She had been surprised at how lean and muscular Levent was when he had embraced her the night before. Because of his pampered looking face and baby hands, she had expected him to be flabby. He seemed to exude an aura of vitality this morning despite the worry that showed on his face. He took two cartons of Ayran from the fridge and sat at the table opposite Celeste, passing one carton to her and opening one for himself.

"About last night," began Celeste, unexpectedly feeling a lack of breath with which to push the words out of her throat.

"Yes," said Levent cautiously as he sensed Celeste's mood.

"It was very nice, but, I just wanted to check, well..." Levent looked at her expectantly, waiting for her to continue. "I mean, we can still be friends like before, can't we?"

"We can always be friends," said Levent, breaking into his usual dazzling smile. "It was very nice for one evening, but it doesn't have to change anything. Don't worry." He seemed to have read her mind and his reaction confirmed, for Celeste, that he had already been planning to have the same type of conversation with her. Strangely, she didn't feel the surge of relief and satisfaction she had anticipated.

After breakfast Celeste went into the living room, wanting to be alone for a while. She found Leman, whom she had assumed to be still asleep, sorting fretfully through some of her stacks of newspapers. She was wearing her pink dressing gown with her hair bundled up in a towel around her head. Her cigarette gave off a wisp of smoke in the ashtray on the round coffee table near her. At first Celeste thought she was throwing some of the papers away, but then she saw that she was sorting them by date order. She would snatch up a handful from the top of a heap, apparently selected at random, and rummage through them with ever increasing frenzy, scrabbling at the paper like a gerbil building a nest. She was gradually reducing the semblance of order that Maryam constantly strove to maintain into a crazed whirlwind of loose paper.

"Many of these newspapers is missing," she complained resentfully as she took a drag on her cigarette. "Maryam, she always throw some out when I am not here. She think I don't know she throw them away. She's a lot bitch."

"Are you sure she does?" asked Celeste, a little hesitantly. "Maybe they're all here. There are so many piles, it could be easy for them to be at the bottom of another heap."

"Not, not at another bottom. They gone," insisted Leman, huffing and puffing in frustration as she deposited crumpled newspapers in an ever increasing circle of separate, messy stacks in her efforts to track down the missing editions. She picked up a small shot glass from the coffee table, which Celeste had not noticed, and drained it in one tense gulp. Celeste wondered if this was what the beginning of a nervous breakdown looked

Evil Eye

like. She tried to lend Leman a hand by checking the date on a few newspapers and adding them to the appropriate piles. Leman re-checked each paper that Celeste moved, fretting grumpily in case one of them were out of place and mumbling to herself ramblingly in Turkish. The towel on her head slipped sideways as she bent down to pick up some other newspapers that had slipped half under the sofa, so she pulled it away impatiently. Some locks of her wet hair clung to her pale, sagging face. The grey roots looked far longer than they did when her hair was dry and the loose skin under her chin seemed more wrinkled and somehow sadder. She looked softer and much older and somehow acutely, intensely, excruciatingly vulnerable. Celeste felt a surge of pity and was surprised at how upset she felt to see Leman reduced to this condition.

"Why don't you leave these papers and get ready to go back to the hospital?" she suggested tentatively. "I'm sure Ferhat can't wait for you to get back to him."

"I have to find it first," said Leman in Turkish, looking as if she might cry. "I didn't go to sleep when I got in early this morning, because I immediately came in here to look. I can't give up until I find it."

"What is it you're looking for?" asked Celeste.

"That newspaper with the article about Tekin when he was rescued from the earthquake," answered Leman, on her knees on the floor rustling her way through a new pile of papers as if nothing else in the world existed for her. "When I know the date and page of the newspaper edition his photograph was in, I can call the newspaper to obtain a copy. Then they can print it in that newspaper with the appeal to look for him." Celeste said nothing, but renewed her efforts to help Leman put her newspapers in order.

The household fell into a routine over the next fortnight. Leman and Levent would stay at the hospital all day and take turns to come home for showers and brief rests. Celeste had the impression that Leman slept very little even when she went to lie down, as she developed ever darker bags under her eyes and seemed more and more absent-minded and generally slower at doing things as time wore on. Her nail varnish became chipped and the grey roots of her hair grew longer than Celeste had ever seen them. Levent would come home after midnight and get up early, have his showers with a speed unprecedented on his part and eat a packed breakfast of plum jam sandwiches prepared by Maryam in the car on his way back to the hospital. Celeste tried to offer as much practical help as she could and went to the hospital a couple of times when she was off work to see Ferhat, who seemed to be recovering steadily, albeit extremely slowly. Levent would give her updates on his father's condition when his mother was not around. The doctors said Ferhat's recovery had had a couple of 'setbacks' and, although Levent was not sure what that meant, he knew they could expect a long stay in hospital before Ferhat would be well enough to come home. Levent confided in Celeste that he often wondered whether the potion his mother had been giving to Ferhat all this time had contributed to his difficult recovery.

"Haven't you asked her about it yet?" asked Celeste, shocked. "You have to confront her! You can't just pretend it didn't happen."

"I can't deal, and more importantly my Dad can't deal, right now, with what her reaction will be. Basically, however I choose to phrase it, I'll be accusing her of poisoning him and I have to wait until all of us can handle that. Dad needs to get stronger first."

As usual Celeste looked forward to the times she could spend at the orphanage. She spent her lessons with the classes she disliked at the school dreaming of the little boys and, of course, thinking of Tekin all the time. Two newspaper articles were printed about Tekin, both featuring the photograph of him being lifted out of a heap of rubble after the earthquake which Leman had so desperately searched for. All the while Celeste counted the days until Heather was due to return to Istanbul. They had agreed before Heather departed for England that they would meet at Heather's flat as soon as she arrived from the airport. Zeliha would be away seeing her daughters so they would be able to talk freely and Heather had made it clear before leaving that she would want a full update on the situation between Zeliha and Ferhat.

Sitting at the kitchen table in Cihangir with a pot of tea between them, Celeste was now retelling events of the night of Ferhat's heart attack instead; news far more dramatic than Heather had anticipated.

"Poor Ferhat!" exclaimed Heather. "Do you think he found it too stressful splitting up with Zeliha? Could that be what caused it?"

"No, there's worse," said Celeste. "It turns out that Ferhat's so-called called cholesterol tablets, which Leman guards with her life, were actually nothing of the sort. She's been putting some other tablets in the jar. So she might have been poisoning him."

"No!" was all Heather could reply, placing a hand over her mouth and staring at Celeste with her crystal blue eyes.

"Levent thinks she definitely did," said Celeste. "He was devastated when he found out. On top of all the shock, finding that out...." Celeste was tempted to tell Heather about the kiss, but she knew Heather's reaction would be an explosion of laughter and teasing about the prospect of Leman as her future mother-in-law, and she was not in the mood for joking; not about Levent and not about anything else either, for that matter. Her feelings about Levent were not clear and she preferred to avoid thinking about the subject while she still felt unable to come to any conclusion.

"How did Leman act when she saw Ferhat in hospital? Do you think she actually wanted to bump him off?" asked Heather.

"Suffering heroically is how I would describe her that evening. She's been there by his side all the time. I don't know if she intended to kill him, but I don't think so. She's a total wreck now."

"Do you think she knows he's dumped Zeliha?" asked Heather.

"Definitely," said Celeste. "She was confident and looked triumphant afterwards. She looked like the cat that got the cream. She's also got rid of that oil lamp in the writing bureau, and nothing else of a creepy nature has popped up around the house, so she evidently thinks the witchcraft is no longer needed. But she's changed now. She seemed to be cracking up the morning after Ferhat's heart attack." Celeste described how deranged Leman had seemed searching for the newspaper containing the photograph of Tekin.

"Did she find it?" asked Heather.

"Yes, she did. She called the paper in the morning to ask for the photograph. I offered to take care of it so she could head off to the hospital, but she wanted to do it herself. Delegation isn't her thing." Celeste drained her cup of tea and poured another one. "I never know if I respect her or despise her. She makes me feel confused and uncomfortable even just thinking about her. Anyway, how was your trip home?"

"It was a bit of an ordeal to be honest," said Heather. "Everyone was nice but I still can't deal with them yet. You know, after what happened. I ended up taking refuge in my parents' house for the last week and pretending I'd already come back here. Which brings me to a proposal I have for you. What would you think about sharing a flat with me? Do you know how much longer you want to stay in Istanbul?"

"I haven't thought about it," admitted Celeste. "I'll bear it in mind. If I decide I'm going to stay here for a while longer, I'd definitely like to rent a place with you. Meanwhile, how's poor old Zelly Belly? Have you seen her since you got back?"

"No," answered Heather. "She was devastated those last few days I was here after Ferhat came to the flat. It broke my heart to see how she suffered. I feel awkward that I can't offer her the comfort I'd like to, because I'm having to pretend I don't know anything's changed."

"Poor Zelly," sympathised Celeste.

"After a few days she started trying to pull her socks up a bit," said Heather. "It must have given her such a shock. Look at this." Heather stood up and opened one of the cupboards, where Zeliha usually stored her vast supplies of biscuits. It was empty apart from a solitary can of chickpeas. "She threw everything away," said Heather, opening another cupboard and showing Celeste that it was also completely cleared out apart from two boxes of herbal teabags. She even threw open the fridge and pointed out that all the sweets, Turkish delight, *halva*, jam, honey and butter had now been eliminated.

"She started a drastic diet the week after Ferhat dumped her. Unfortunately," added Heather, regaining her usual, cynical attitude, "she's decided to do the Beverly Hills Diet."

"What's that?" asked Celeste, nonplussed.

"It's that old one from the eighties, where you only eat one type of food all day. So you can have unlimited oranges on Monday, then nothing but pineapples on Tuesday, and then a heap of potatoes on Wednesday, and so no. She was accumulating a compost heap of lettuce leaves in her colon in quantities I just couldn't believe. Then she went and had a cabbage day just before I left. The gas was asphyxiating."

"Maybe you should buy her a decent diet book to get her onto a more sensible diet," suggested Celeste.

"Yes, or else buy myself a good gas mask to wear around the house," agreed Heather, earnestly.

"Poor Zeliha," sighed Celeste. "Has she still been doing her aerobics in front of the telly?"

"Oh yes," said Heather. "She puts on a horrific cerise velour tracksuit to show she means business. She still can't bend and I honestly don't think she realises she's not actually doing the same movements as that Lycra-clad hairball on the telly. Though now that she's developed a flatulence problem, it's probably a damn good thing she can't do those deep bends." Celeste had to laugh but she noticed that even Heather looked a little guilty about making jokes at Zeliha's expense. "She had her hair done before she left," Heather added, suddenly. "She had it cut shorter and dyed dark brown. It was a great improvement. She immediately looked about ten years younger. And she bought a new coat and got her nails done too."

"I just hope some of this will boost her morale a bit," said Celeste.

"I'm sure spending time with her daughters will be doing her good," said Heather. "That's the best therapy for her." Celeste studied one of the photographs of Zeliha's daughters which was held on the fridge door with a magnet shaped like a fish. She found her mind wandering to Tekin and wondering whether she would ever see him again. "Don't go getting melancholy on me," said Heather. "I can see I'm losing you. You're drifting off into your own head again. Listen, let's have a quick, early dinner and go to the cinema. There's a film on that supposed to be very good."

"That sounds like a good idea," agreed Celeste. "I haven't been to the cinema in Turkey before." She hoped the film would distract her from her obsessive thoughts of Tekin. While Heather started preparing some food,

Evil Eye

Celeste looked around the kitchen for something to clean. In Zeliha's house, there were always plenty of opportunities to roll her sleeves up. She started with the work surfaces, first spraying ammonia to dissolve the droplets of fat Zeliha always splashed about when cooking, and then scrubbing them with a cloth. Next she set to work on the sink, which had a streak of rock-hard melted cheese running from one corner right up to the plug hole. As she worked away at it, scratching and peeling it until she had removed every trace, she felt herself begin to relax slightly and let out some of her stress.

"How long has that melted cheese been in the sink?" she commented finally to Heather. "It was so hard and well stuck on. I see why you get fed up with Zelly sometimes."

"What melted cheese?" asked Heather sounding baffled. She walked across the kitchen and glanced into the sink. "Oh dear," she said, the smile freezing on her face. "That was silicone. The sink's cracked. It leaks underneath."

"Oh no!" gasped Celeste.

"Zelly got a man round to do that repair because she's too hard up at the moment to buy a new one. I think you've done enough cleaning now. Sit down and eat. Grub's ready." Heather placed both hands on Celeste's shoulders and physically steered her away from the sink.

They ate quickly and set out on foot in the already dark evening. It was very cold and humid, so they decided not to wait for a bus as they preferred to keep moving. The cinema was only fifteen minutes' walk from Heather's house but Celeste's toes were completely numb by the time they arrived. She was greatly relieved to see the brightly illuminated cinema entrance in a small side street and dart into the warm lobby, feeling her fingers burn as she fumbled to unbutton her coat. Looking around the interior of the cinema made Celeste feel as if she had travelled back in time. There were no sweets, popcorn or drinks on sale, just an open ticket booth near the entrance to the lobby and a large, red velvet curtain behind which was the only screen. The interior of the cinema seemed still to have the original décor from decades ago, which looked as if it had once been fairly elegant but was now mainly crumbling plaster and peeling paint. Most of the other people at the cinema were couples or young men, all smoking frantically in the lobby right up to the last moment when a bell rang to indicate that the film was about to start.

The cinema only had a single projector, apparently, as each time the reel finished the last few inches of the spool of film would flap for a few moments, and the audience would have to wait until the next reel was loaded before the film continued. Celeste was unable to pay any attention to the film, which was not the one Heather had anticipated. Instead, the cinema was showing a film involving a family in Anatolia who encountered endless tragedies and constant crying, interspersed with village celebrations at which everyone, men, women and children belly-danced around camp fires through the night and ate strange foods which Celeste did not recognise. The sound quality was poor and the actors spoke so fast that Celeste failed to understand lengthy portions of the conversation. Her mind wandered constantly to Tekin, searching her memory as she had done a thousand times for anything he may have said that could give her another clue about where to search for him, and racking her brain for any other idea that might help her find him. Her mind jumped to and fro between Tekin and fretting guiltily over the silicone repair she had scraped away from Zeliha's kitchen sink. She was so tense that she found it a challenge to sit still in her seat. After about an hour, the reel of film flapped for longer than usual and the lights came on.

"Has something gone wrong?" she asked Celeste. "I mean, more wrong than usual each time the reel needs changing?"

"No, it's the fag break," answered Heather. "Turks can't last the length of a feature film without their nicotine, and they can't let them smoke during the film because the place gets so full of smoke that you can't see the screen. So they have about half an hour as an interval to puff away like chimneys."

As they reached the lobby Celeste started to laugh at the sight of the entire cinema audience lighting cigarettes. She saw one man with two lit cigarettes in his hand, smoking both at once. The grey clouds of smoke wafted up to the high ceiling and filled the hall until she could hardly breathe and her eyes stung and, as Heather had said, she could not see from one side of the lobby to the other.

"Are you enjoying this film?" asked Heather, tentatively.

"Erm, well... I can't understand much, to be honest," admitted Celeste, breaking into a cough.

"Neither can I," said Heather. "It all sounds muffled. To be honest, it's deathly dull, isn't it? And I'm so tired. I couldn't sleep last night because I get nervous about flying and then I had to get up at five-thirty for the flight this morning. I slept about three hours at most. "

"I can't face another hour or so of this," agreed Celeste. "It's dire. Shall we go and get some hot chocolate in a café instead?"

"Good idea, said Heather, heading for the door immediately.

After the asphyxiating cinema lobby, the chilly night air felt refreshing and clean despite the usual traffic fumes. They trudged side by side along the narrow street under the yellow light of the lamp posts, falling silent for a few minutes. Vaguely aware of a man walking several yards behind them, Celeste's mind raced again and again over the same obsessive thoughts as usual. Her fretful musings were interrupted by the sound of metal heel caps clicking rapidly on the pavement behind her. The man had caught up in just a few seconds and was now far too close, as if trying to push his way between her and Heather. Then she realised his hands were on her bag. Her shoulder was yanked down towards the pavement so hard that her right knee gave way. The mugger continued tugging at her bag with both hands. With the strap, still hooked around her shoulder, he was jerking her down further until she fell painfully onto hands and knees. Trying to snap the shoulder strap, he repeatedly dragged her to and fro, left and right. They seemed to last forever, these few, terrifying seconds.

She sprawled on the dirty wet tarmac, scrabbling to find her feet. Her heart pounded against her ribs and, in her terror, the breath stuck in her throat. She was unable to scream, unable to gasp, unable to whisper or even let out a breath. She saw nothing but her assailant's feet beside her hands on the dark pavement. She smelt his leather jacket and felt the smooth, chilly surface of one sleeve sweep her cheek. She barely saved herself from falling onto her face. Suddenly a handful of hair at the nape of her neck was tugged sharply upwards. Heather was turning back, and letting out a cry of shock at the very moment the handle of Celeste's bag finally, thankfully snapped and she was freed at last.

When at last her voice worked again she shocked herself with the fury in the scream she let out after the fleeing thief. Before she knew it she was chasing him, flying through the dark street ignoring the objects he threw from her bag as he ran. All the time she was howling with rage; she screamed at him to stop, screeched like a banshee so bystanders would know he was a thief, but he ran so fast that nobody had the time to react or, maybe, the courage to try to stop him. Hardly aware of where she was running, or whether Heather was behind her, she sped on as if her feet did not touch the road, down several narrow streets and a tiny alleyway so small she could have touched the walls each side as she ran. Still sprinting at full speed she came to a dual carriageway across which she followed the man without pausing to look left or right, and sped on into a labyrinth of twisting side streets, turning left and then right as he led her deeper and deeper into a tangle of slums until finally she noticed Heather's voice screaming far behind her;

"Stop, Celeste! Are you mad? Stop!" and she slowed and came to a panting halt, watching the thief disappear around a distant corner with her bag tucked under his arm.

"What ever were you thinking?" cried Heather, petrified, when she finally caught up. She bent over, gasping to regain her breath. "Someone like that would stick a knife in you if you ever caught up with him."

"I'm sorry," said Celeste, feeling electrified by the chase she had put on and somehow exhilarated after the release of pent up energy. "I didn't think."

"I've got as stitch," gasped Heather as she clutched the hem of her coat, drawing in a few deep gulps of air. "You must be very fit. That chase nearly killed me."

"Sorry," said Celeste again.

"Have you any idea where we are?" Heather asked eventually, standing upright.

"No," admitted Celeste, looking around her. She started to take in her surroundings in the gloom; the houses without windows, the plastic bags taped across some of the openings, what looked like a bonfire inside an open garage. There was a group of three children, none of them over the age of five, sitting in a gutter, but no sign of an adult.

"Neither have I," said Heather, "But I can tell you now, it's not a place people like us should be in."

Celeste turned her head to search for any sign of another adult. These children's mother must surely be nearby. As if from nowhere a man in a tweed jacket appeared wielding a bottle of Eau de Cologne, which he splashed liberally over a handkerchief and held under Celeste's nose.

"You've had a terrible shock," she realised he was saying. "This should help you to compose yourself. What exactly happened?"

Heather was in better control of herself than Celeste and more able to summon up the Turkish necessary to recount the experience. The man told them that there was a police station nearby and that he would walk there with them if they wished. It turned out to be very close by indeed, and Celeste was immensely relieved to enter its warm, neon lit interior and find herself surrounded by uniformed policemen. She and Heather were offered chairs while the man who had accompanied them to the station remained with them. After a brief wait an officer approached and the man asked Celeste and Heather if they wanted him to wait with them, or if they would be all right alone. Celeste thanked him profusely for his kindness and told him they were fine.

As they continued to wait, a little boy who looked about seven years old started chatting to them. Celeste, still agitated after her struggle and wild chase, was happy to talk to him and recount the experience, thinking hard to recall as many details as possible. He asked relevant questions and seemed genuinely interested in every detail of her anecdote. Something about his relaxed manner and cheerful smile reminded her of Levent, with his easy going attitude that was always able to make her feel as if nothing were too great a problem. The sight of his tousled black hair and dimpled cheeks made her want to smile back every time she looked at his cheeky face. A few of the policemen patted him on the head and ruffled his hair as they walked past the desk, and one offered him a boiled sweet, which he accepted enthusiastically. While telling the boy every detail she remembered, she realised that she had not seen the man's face even for a second, but Heather said that she had had the chance to get a look at him and might recognise him if she saw him again. When a policeman came to take down their details, he slammed a very large, black book onto the desk in front of them.

"Have a look at these, and let me know if you think you recognise the man in here," he said. Heather opened the book gingerly, and pored over the first page. Pasted onto it were at least twenty photo-booth sized pictures of dark-skinned men with unkempt black hair and large, droopy black moustaches. She turned the page and saw another array of mug shots, each seeming identical to the last. Page after page of the book was filled in the same way.

"There are hundreds of them," Heather said in awe.

"What a horrible book," said Celeste, turning away.

"It's grim, isn't it?" agreed Heather. "They're all gruesome. There's not a good looking one among the lot of them."

"It's not supposed to be a dating agency, for heavens' sake!" exclaimed Celeste. "Don't any of them look like him?"

"They're all the flipping same!" protested Heather shrilly. And indeed they were. After a few more minutes of idly leafing through the book simply to decide which she thought was the ugliest of the lot, Heather apologised to Celeste. "I'm so sorry. I've just got no idea if he's in here."

"Never mind," said Celeste. "If this lot are all on the loose, they weren't exactly likely to catch him anyway, were they?"

"Have you found the one who did it?" cut in the little boy, who had been listening intently and looking intrigued as they spoke together in English.

"Sadly not," said Celeste in Turkish. "There's not a chance of recognising him among these ugly mugs." The boy laughed so cheerfully that Celeste actually felt herself cheer up too. She was glad this little boy was here, whoever he was. "Anyway, why are you here?" she asked him. "Is your dad one of these policemen?"

The boy laughed heartily. "No! I got arrested," he answered, smiling cheekily.

"What for?" cut in Heather, her eyes narrowing.

"Picking someone's pocket," he replied, still smiling.

Celeste was shocked that he was so blasé about stealing from innocent people, apparently insensible to the distress it caused them. For a split second, she felt like hitting him over the head with the book of mug shots.

He showed no sign of guilt or even awareness that picking pockets was wrong. She stood up and walked towards the policeman who had brought the book of photographs, telling him regretfully that neither she nor Heather could identify the man from the pictures.

"I'm really sorry," he said. "We hardly ever manage to catch these people. If anyone brings in your bag or any of your documents, we'll contact you. But I must warn you, that's highly unlikely. Round here, nothing worth taking lies on the pavement for long. The children here have nothing. They'll even put up a fight over a piece of silver foil or a polythene bag with a hole in it."

"Is that why you're so kind to the little pick pocket?" asked Celeste, nodding her head towards the little boy.

"Partly," confessed the policeman. "He's in here all the time, this one. He's a lovely kid, little Ahmet. He certainly doesn't steal from greed. He comes from such a poor family I don't know how his mother feeds all his brothers. In fact, to be honest, I don't think she manages. She's on her way now. Anyway, we'll take you home when a squad car becomes available in the area."

"That's kind of you, but I'm sure we can get to a bus stop if you'll give us directions," said Celeste.

"Out of the question," replied the policeman calmly. "This neighbourhood is far too dangerous for you to walk around in. You'd be right back in here in two minutes and you'd certainly not be as lucky as you've been this time, believe me."

"If you say so," agreed Celeste. "Can I ask you another question?"

"Of course," answered the policeman.

"How many missing children are there in Istanbul? And how many of them get found alive eventually?"

"We have hundreds of children registered missing," the man answered. "This is a city of over ten million people so that's normal and, like anywhere else in the world, we hardly ever find any of them. Unless they reappear within two or three days, one has to assume they probably won't be found alive. Why do you ask?"

Celeste told him about Tekin. She stumbled over her words and in her nervousness went off at a tangent, first talking at length about what a unique adorable child Tekin was and then bitterly criticising Leman for her initial attitude to his disappearance.

"I think the lady who runs the orphanage must deal with children's suffering all the time," commented the police officer, "and I'm sure she knows the statistical likelihood of this little boy being found. She may seem hard-hearted but frankly I think she's just being realistic. I know that's hard for you to accept and I sincerely hope the little boy will be found. But it may be necessary to brace yourself for the worst."

Celeste felt as if all her insides had been removed and she was a walking shell. Her head spun as she turned to head back to the desk where Heather was waiting for her, playing a clapping game with the little pick pocket. Suddenly Celeste stopped in her tracks. She heard a woman's voice, a voice she knew so well. She looked at the doorway and there in front of her, like a divine apparition, stood Maryam festooned with children. Baby Yakup was perched on her hip, gripped by one strong arm. With the other hand she held a dainty little girl who looked about three years old, with dark, mesmerising eyes identical to Maryam's and the same glossy black hair, falling about her shoulders in thick unruly locks. Clinging to Maryam's flowery skirt, the one with a hole in the side, was a little boy slightly smaller than the girl, and beside them was another boy, who looked older than the girl.

At the sight of Maryam, Celeste's emotions were suddenly too much to hold inside any more and she burst into tears. Maryam, amazed to see Celeste in the police station in that part of town, patted her shoulder while Heather put an arm round her and led her to the nearest chair. Once Celeste had started crying she was not sure exactly what she was crying for the most; whether it was over the frightening experience she had just had, or for the confirmation of what she most feared, that she would probably never see Tekin again. Maybe she was also crying over the sinister things Leman had tried to do to her, for Mr. Demirsar's dead little boy and of course, as always, for her mother as well. Now she had started crying she realised how many things she had to cry for and she was afraid she would not be able to stop. She took deep gasps of air and her shoulders shuddered. She deliberately let her hair slip over her face as she hunched over her own lap, trying to block out the world.

Heather produced a clean handkerchief while she explained to Maryam how they had ended up in her part of town. Ahmet the little pickpocket sidled up to them and listened to the whole story. He started to rummage deep in his trouser pocket and when Celeste looked up at him for a moment he triumphantly produced the small boiled sweet from the policeman, which he placed in her hand.

"Eat something sweet to make you feel happier," he said. This innocent gesture brought a smile to Celeste's face even though the tears were still streaming down her cheeks. "How come you know my Mummy?" he then asked Celeste, glancing up at Maryam.

Before Celeste could answer, Maryam looked down at him furiously and launched into an angry diatribe about the evils of theft. She shouted so fast and used so much vocabulary Celeste did not know that Celeste could scarcely follow her sermon. Celeste watched the smile on Ahmet's dimpled little face gradually fade until his crestfallen and subdued expression made her feel as if the sun had just gone behind a cloud. Her own feelings subsided as they were overtaken by her pity for little Ahmet. Maryam very rarely lost her temper and the other children cowered at her furious words even though they were directed at their older brother.

"What did I tell you about making me come out here again, Ahmet?" demanded Maryam at the end of her tirade. "I've told you a thousand times not to go out stealing from people. I'll call the circumciser first thing in the morning!" Ahmet's eyes grew wider at these words and one of the policemen came and told him not to be afraid, and that he wasn't really in too much trouble. Maryam's wrath turned on the policemen. "You're no better," she told him. "How can I teach him it's wrong to steal if a policeman in uniform says it's all right?" The policeman had no answer for her. "Can I take him home now?" she asked, finally.

Another man approached holding a form on a clipboard, and told her that it had to be completed and she had to sign at the bottom. He started asking her if she knew how to write, but the man who was now patting her son's head very quietly told him not to bother with a form. He clearly knew already that she could neither read nor write, and was willing to waive all the formalities. Maryam, hardly taking any notice, handed Yakup to Celeste so she could reach out and give Ahmet a sharp cuff around the head, at which he scarcely batted an eyelid.

"Would you two like to wait at my house rather than here?" invited Maryam. "It's very close." Celeste felt very vulnerable and thought she may cry again, and was consequently keen to leave the police station as soon as possible.

"Yes please," she answered hastily.

"Do you want me to come with you?" asked Heather in English. Celeste could see that Heather felt exhausted. Her eyelids were half closed and dark shadows had formed under her eyes.

"You look half dead," Celeste commented.

"I don't want to just abandon you in this state, but I'm so tired I'd rather wait here and doze in a chair till I can go straight home," said Heather. "Would you mind? I will come along too if you want me with you, though."

"Don't worry about me," reassured Celeste. "I'm all right now. I'll be fine with Maryam. I just hope they can take you home as soon as possible." She shifted Yakup onto her other arm and started gently humming a tune to try to calm him, as he had started fretting. "I'll come by myself, as Heather's going to stay here till they can take her home," Celeste told Maryam in Turkish.

Evil Eye

"Yes, come to our house and we can play," added Ahmet, brightly. He squeezed between Heather and Celeste, grabbed a handful of Celeste's coat the way all Maryam's children habitually hung onto her skirt, and turned to leave.

"You're not playing with anyone," said Maryam, sharply. "You're in big trouble." She bent down to deliver a remarkably hard smack to his bottom which sent him springing forward and clapping his hands to his buttocks. Celeste saw him wince for a second and then harden his face and force a smile.

"That didn't hurt," he declared, resolutely.

"My home's not like Leman's house, I must warn you," said Maryam, ignoring Ahmet as she led Celeste, with baby Yakup in her arms, out of the police station. "Come on, then. Come on, children."

"I'll send a car to your house when there's one ready to take the English lady home," offered the policeman as they left, looking thoroughly baffled as to how the English tourist and Maryam, the regular at his station, seemed to know each other so well. Celeste called goodbye to Heather as she was towed into the street by Ahmet, who was already telling her all about his home. He seemed oblivious of the cold wind and the rain which had now started pouring down heavily. Celeste tucked Yakup inside her coat to protect him from the rain and tried to drape her scarf around his head. She thought of Tekin and wondered where he was going to sleep on this dark, freezing night.

When they reached Maryam's house, it looked very much as Leman had described it; a kind of shack that appeared largely to have been improvised out of scraps found lying around a building site. Inside, it was not as bad as she had expected. In fact it felt welcoming and cosy and, at first sight, it seemed better than Leman's description of it. Yet when Celeste had time to study the interior more carefully, she realised that Leman had been very accurate in her description of the place.

From the unsurfaced street outside, which was really more of a muddy wasteland, she stepped directly into the kitchen, which had a small sink in the corner and a table in the centre. There were no fitted kitchen units. Instead, a very old wooden dresser with several of its doors missing held most of Maryam's possessions. For additional storage there was a row of nails hammered into the wall with various plastic bags hung on them. A small selection of pots and jugs hung on nails on the opposite wall, above a two-ring stove balanced on a wooden stool, beside which stood an *Aygaz* canister.

As Leman had said, there were no windows, or at least, no windows made from glass. Instead Maryam had carefully secured transparent polythene across the frames, which ruffled in the wind and made a constant background noise as they spoke. Celeste could see through a doorway at the back that there was just one other room, partly screened off by a torn curtain. It was carpeted with sleeping bags and mattresses where, presumably, the entire family slept. Maryam shooed all the children into this back room and told them to play there without disturbing her and 'the visitor.' Meanwhile Celeste sat at the table, still holding Yakup in her arms. He seemed tired as his eyes repeatedly drooped almost shut before lazily opening again each time she or Maryam spoke.

"He should be asleep soon," commented Maryam. "He's just had a feed, so he should have nothing to complain about. Anyway, how are you now? Would you like some tea? I know you always want tea when you feel upset."

Celeste said she felt like drinking a cup of very strong coffee instead, so Maryam unhooked a long-handled jug from the wall above the stove and spooned in the coffee and sugar, holding the jug under the tap to add the water. Celeste tensed when she saw this. She had never drunk tap water in Turkey. Everyone she knew kept large glass bottles of purified drinking water in the kitchen and only used the tap water for washing. It smelled so heavily of chlorine that Celeste was sure it would be bad for the stomach even if all the germs were killed. But she had told Maryam she would like some coffee. How could she change her mind now?

"Leman told me you don't have running water in your house," said Celeste.

"We do," cut in Ahmet, reappearing in the doorway between the two rooms. "It gets cut off very often, but it usually comes in the evening for at least an hour," he explained authoritatively.

"It's not as predictable as that," contradicted Maryam, patiently. "I keep these buckets full of water for when we need it. Go and play with your brothers, Ahmet." Celeste noticed the two buckets, one below the sink and one beside it.

"Leman said you don't have electricity either," added Celeste.

"We didn't at one time. But she hasn't been here for a very long time. She probably doesn't know we have it now."

Celeste looked more carefully around the kitchen while she rocked Yakup gently to sleep. Despite the shabby condition of the walls and everything in the house, Maryam clearly kept the place spotlessly clean and she had pinned all kinds of decorations on the walls to brighten the place up. There were some picture postcards, a large *nazar boncuğu* and various other trinkets which Celeste suspected may have been items Leman had given Maryam when she no longer wanted them. There was no sign of any toys but the children seemed happy all the same.

"Where shall I put Yakup?" asked Celeste, once he was soundly asleep and very quietly snoring. Maryam took him gently from Celeste's arms and laid him in a large oval basket on the floor, lined with a folded blanket. She lifted a corner of the blanket over him and tucked it around his body tightly. Celeste watched the coffee and took it off the stove as it started to froth up and rise to the top of the jug. She poured it into two tiny cups, placed them on the table and sat down with Maryam. Before taking a sip of coffee, Maryam pushed up the sleeves of her jumper and Celeste saw that her right arm was horribly bruised, with large purple and blue swellings from the elbow almost reaching the wrist. Celeste almost jumped with shock.

"How did you do that?" she gasped.

"My husband," replied Maryam casually.

"He hit you?"

"Yes," said Maryam.

"Does he often do it?" asked Celeste, confused and baffled by Maryam's apparent indifference.

"Whose husband doesn't hit them sometimes?" was Maryam's reply, as she pulled her sleeves back down to her wrists again and took a sip of coffee.

"But doesn't it make you angry?" asked Celeste eventually.

"Of course, but what can I do?" shrugged Maryam.

"Why don't you leave him?" asked Celeste.

Maryam laughed. "Where would I go? And what would happen to the children? He'd just hit them instead." Maryam realised that Celeste was utterly baffled. "He's not all that bad really. I know plenty of women with far worse husbands. He keeps out of my hair a lot of the time, and he does bring home money when he can. He's good to the children, most of the time. I'm definitely better off as I am."

Celeste was already feeling the stimulating effect of the caffeine making her more alert and awake. She finished her coffee and wondered what Maryam's life might be like without her husband. In what way might it be worse?

"My real worry is my oldest son, Ahmet," Maryam went on. "He spends all day wandering the streets and I can't keep an eye on him. I can't take him to Leman's house every day with Yakup."

"I thought you usually left the kids with your sister when you come to work," said Celeste.

"Yes, but she's got four of her own. She can't manage all of them. Ahmet goes off on his own and she says she doesn't manage to stop him."

"Do you know where he goes?" asked Celeste.

"He goes scavenging for things left on the street that could be useful, and he talks to the street children who teach him how to steal," replied Maryam. "He says he wants to help me. He sometimes brings home sheets of plastic, mugs, all kinds of things that are quite handy."

"What are you saying about me?" asked Ahmet, appearing in the doorway again.

"Ahmet," Celeste asked him, suddenly having an idea, "if you wanted to find a certain little boy living on the street, how would you look for him?"

"Go to where the children sleep at night," shrugged Ahmet, as if baffled to be asked such an obvious question. "To the places where they hide."

"Do you know these places?" asked Celeste.

"Of course," said Ahmet. "Why? Are you looking for someone?"

"Yes. His name's Tekin. Do you know any little boys called Tekin?"

"No," replied Ahmet. "But I could ask around."

"I hadn't thought of asking my children if they'd know how to find the lost orphan," said Maryam, taking the coffee cups from the table and starting to wash them at the sink.

"He's very small," said Celeste, holding her hand horizontally to indicate Tekin's height. "He's got light brown hair and blue eyes, about the same colour as mine, maybe a bit greener."

"There's a very little boy with blue eyes who turned up recently," said Ahmet. "He sleeps with two other boys quite near here." Celeste's heart skipped a beat and the breath caught in her throat. "But his name's not Tekin," Ahmet continued. Celeste's shoulders sank as she realised how willing she had been to deceive herself with false hope. "His name's Pazar."

"Don't be stupid," said Maryam, turning to look at Ahmet as she dried a cup with a frayed cloth. "Pazar isn't a name. It's a day of the week."

"Well that's what he says his name is," protested Ahmet, chuckling.

Celeste had taken a moment to remember that Maryam would not recognise the significance of the name Pazar, but now she was on her feet and the effect of the caffeine was nothing compared to the effect of realising that Tekin was nearby, was within her reach.

"It's him! It's him! Oh, take me to him right away! Please!" she was shrieking, unable to control herself. "Maryam, please, we have to go and get him right away."

"Calm down, calm down," said Maryam, trying to sound soothing.

"I'll bring him here," said Ahmet, already heading for the door.

"On your own?" said Maryam. "What are you thinking? It's night time. Get in here immediately!"

"If we go in the daytime he won't be there," explained Ahmet, exasperated. "The children only hide there at night."

"Well I'll come with you," said Maryam.

"You can't come with me. If they see adults, the children will all run away, or go into other hiding places where they can't be found. I have to get him on my own."

Maryam glanced at Celeste, and hesitated.

"I'll only be fifteen minutes, Mum," said Ahmet. He was hopping from foot to foot as he awaited permission from his mother to sprint out of the door on his mission to find the homeless boy, Pazar, and bring him to the English lady who wanted to see him. His innocent enthusiasm at the chance to help Celeste was the first sign of behaviour that seemed as young as his age. In every other respect he seemed far more canny and shrewd than such a young child.

When he darted off into the night, Celeste began to sit through the longest wait of her life; and it only took fifteen minutes, as Ahmet had promised, before he reappeared in the doorway. He strode proudly into the kitchen, his hair glistening with raindrops. Behind him he towed a filthy, ragged and soaking wet Tekin who somehow looked smaller than ever before.

"I looked after your teddy," Tekin announced to Celeste as he produced Bruno the bear from inside his jumper.

Celeste lunged at Tekin, swept him into her arms and gripped him so tightly he could hardly breathe. For the second time that evening she found herself weeping.

SIXTEEN

The Storyteller

Two Sides of a River
Nasreddin was sitting on a river bank when someone shouted to him from the opposite side:
"Hey! How do I get across?"
"You are across!" Nasreddin shouted back.

Tekin sat on Celeste's lap and clutched a lock of her hair in one of his tiny fists, holding Bruno the bear nestled in the crook of his arm, while Celeste hugged him tightly. He released his grip on Celeste only to accept the slice of buttered bread and cup of milk that Maryam offered him. When Celeste asked Tekin about how he had lived on the street he just shook his head silently at first, the way he had done the first time they had met and Bűlent had told Celeste the story of the earthquake which buried them alive. While Tekin drank his milk, Ahmet described the place where Tekin had been sleeping, the entrance of a derelict building which the other children had filled with cardboard boxes and a large plastic rubbish bin tipped on its side. After Tekin had finished eating, he added in a quiet voice that he had been all alone for days - he had no idea how many - but then he had found the group of children living rough who had invited him to sleep with them in their shelter. They had taken him begging with them, too, telling him they could get more money than usual with him around because he was so young and little. Adults often gave them coins and they would share everything they had, but there were many days when he had had nothing to eat at all.

"You smell like a wet dog," commented Ahmet, smiling as his infectious laugh filled Maryam's kitchen with optimism. Tekin laughed too.

"I slept with that dog every night," Tekin answered. "He kept me nice and warm." He looked up at Celeste to explain. "We found a dog and adopted him. I tied him up when I came here but I want to go and get him, to take him to the orphanage so we can keep him there. I can't abandon him."

"He's a very nice dog," added Ahmet. "He's dark brown like chocolate."

Celeste took Tekin home to Bebek when the police car came to collect her. Leman, who had spent all day with Ferhat's in the hospital, was already in bed when they arrived so, rather than wake her up that evening, Celeste decided to get up early to speak to her before she left home for the hospital the next morning. Levent was still awake and was utterly overjoyed that Tekin was safe. While Celeste filled the bath with water and some of her perfumed bubble bath for Tekin, Levent played a game with him by hiding a sweet in one hand behind his back and making Tekin guess which hand it was in; if he guessed correctly, he could eat the sweet. Celeste noticed that Levent didn't say anything about the fact that Tekin had run away or ask what had happened to him; he simply played with him as if Tekin had just dropped in for a visit. As a result Tekin seemed his normal self, contented and cheerful.

In the bath, Celeste scrubbed Tekin's hair three times and supervised his washing to make sure he removed all traces of grime. She cleaned under his fingernails with a brush and examined him for signs of lice. She scrubbed him with a flannel and probed his ears with cotton wool buds until he objected loudly. With some of baby Yakup's toy boats in the bath they created terrible storms by splashing water until they capsized and then, finally, Tekin announced that the water was freezing and he would like to get out.

"My mummy used to play with me in the bath," Tekin told Celeste as she handed him a towel. "In the orphanage nobody has time to play with us." Celeste felt guilty that she had let him half freeze and kissed him on the forehead by way of apology. "I think we should give your bear a bath like that now," Tekin added thoughtfully. "I tried to keep him clean but he got wet, and the dog sometimes licked him."

"Don't worry, I'll wash him later," Celeste reassured him, glancing at Bruno on the bathroom stool. He looked decidedly threadbare and in need of a good, long drubbing in the washing machine.

"He's happy to be with you again," said Tekin. "Almost as happy as me."

Tekin's hair had grown so long he almost looked like a girl and Celeste took some time drying it with her hair dryer. In place of pyjamas, all she had to dress him in was a replica Turkish national football shirt and shorts donated by Levent, which were slightly too large for him.

"I wore that kit when I was three," said Levent. "I could never bring myself to let Mum throw it away."

"It's all right as pyjamas," Celeste sighed, "but he'll freeze tomorrow."

"I've got a cowboy costume stashed away somewhere," offered Levent. "In the morning we can see if that'll fit."

Tekin and Celeste managed to squeeze into Celeste's narrow single bed together for the night. Celeste sat Bruno the very dirty bear on her desk and told Tekin he would keep watch over them for the night. Tekin was so

Veronica Di Grigoli

small and moved so little while he slept that Celeste almost felt as if she were sharing the bed with a soft toy. She herself slept better than she had done in weeks, maybe months. She woke up before Tekin, but the sun was already high in the sky. She lay beside him for about twenty minutes listening to his regular breathing and looking at his tiny mouth lying slightly open as he slept peacefully on the pillow. There was no sign of all the shocking experiences this little child had lived through on his smooth and serene little face.

When they went downstairs, Maryam was in the kitchen busily mopping the floor with ammonia. The windows were all open despite the chilly wind but there was no need to ask why; the room smelled so strongly of cigarette smoke it was obvious Maryam was letting some more breathable air into the room.

"Good morning," she said, first to Tekin and then to Celeste. "How did you sleep?"

"I felt so warm last night," Tekin commented. "It was like the times I shared the bed with my aunt when she visited us in the old house."

"Leman and Levent have gone to the hospital," Maryam told Celeste immediately. "Levent told his mother that you'd found Tekin and she was very pleased. She asked that you take him to the orphanage yourself, as she's going to be at the hospital all day. Levent has left some clothes for Tekin on that chair." She indicated with her head. "He said he hopes they're not too big."

Celeste gave the clothes to Tekin to put on immediately as his bare arms and legs were already covered in goose bumps. He cut quite a dash in Levent's old cowboy costume, despite the fact that the trousers needed double turn-ups and the shirt and jacket sleeves had to be rolled into thick wads of material around his forearms. Celeste let out a wry smile as she wondered for a second whether Leman had also worn her cowboy costume today. She was gradually feeling more light hearted as the reality of the fact that Tekin was safe and sound sank in. She had imagined she would feel a surge of excitement and joy but instead it was a gradual process of relaxation as the stress that had become a part of her began slowly to melt away.

Celeste invited Maryam to join her and Tekin for breakfast.

"I dare not do that any more," said Maryam. "You know how Leman is."

"Yes, but she's at the hospital and there's no way she'll find out," said Celeste. "Come on."

Celeste carried a tray laden with *beyaz peynir*, white cheese like feta, and slices of crusty white bread, a bowl of black olives, a plate of boiled eggs, butter and a pot of honey into the breakfast room. Maryam followed with a plate of honeydew melon sliced into chunks, a jug of fresh orange juice and a pot of Celeste's 'health tea' from the Egyptian Bazaar. Tekin's eyes looked as if they would pop out of his head.

"Am I allowed to eat as much as I like?" he asked, repositioning himself centrally on the thickly cushioned chair and swinging his legs contentedly under the table.

"Of course," answered Celeste.

"Oh goody," exclaimed Tekin, who then proceeded to astonish Celeste and Maryam with how much he managed to consume. He finished off two eggs and two slices of bread with feta cheese, eight olives, another slice of bread dripping with honey, a large plate of melon and two glasses of orange juice. Maryam said she had already eaten breakfast at home but she still decided to eat some bread and honey and Celeste, who lately had become used to finding she struggled to eat anything, was also surprised at how much her appetite had returned.

"Have I got to go back to the orphanage today?" asked Tekin just before popping a large chunk of melon into his mouth. His blue-green eyes gazed up at Celeste as he chewed with gusto.

"Yes," she replied, wishing she could say 'no.'

"Do I have to go this morning?" he asked when he had gulped the melon down.

"Why don't you take him out somewhere nice first?" suggested Maryam. "Even though he was very naughty," she added, giving him and glance which let him know she was a mother who knew how to deliver a sharp punishment when it was needed.

"I suppose I could," said Celeste, glancing at Tekin who was now so absorbed in pouring honey from the serving spoon onto a piece of bread already loaded with white cheese that he seemed not to have heard her. Celeste was pouring tea for herself and Maryam when an announcement came on the radio, playing quietly in the corner, urging people to look for Tekin.

"That's funny, they're talking about another little boy called Tekin on the radio!" exclaimed Tekin, delighted. "And he's the same age as me, too!"

"They were talking about you," said Maryam, smiling.

"Which reminds me I need to make a phone call," said Celeste. "Did you know you're famous now?" she added, winking at Tekin.

"Do the other boys at the orphanage know I'm famous?" Tekin asked.

"Yes, they do," confirmed Celeste.

"Do lots of people know I'm famous?" asked Tekin.

"Everybody," said Celeste.

Tekin looked astonished and delighted.

"Can I have a cup of 'health tea' like you ladies?" he asked.

Celeste poured him a cup, and he had to look at the flowers in the pot several times to check that they were the same as the ones he had seen before, when he and Celeste had had 'health tea' together at Heather's flat. In the end Celeste put two spoonfuls of flowers from the pot into Tekin's cup so that he could see them as he drank. Once he was happy with his colourful blossoming garden in a cup, Celeste left the table and telephoned Attila to tell him the good news and ask him to let his journalist friend know that, thankfully, the radio announcements could stop.

"Oh, that's such wonderful news!" said Attila's wife Berna, who answered the phone. Celeste heard her immediately telling Attila in the background. "Can we meet the little boy?" she asked.

"Of course," said Celeste. He's at home with me at the moment. I'm taking him to the orphanage later."

"I've had an idea," said Berna. "Would you like to take him for a trip on the yacht before leaving him at the orphanage? It seems a shame to find the poor child and just take him straight back there after all he's been through. Let's give him some fun first. The yacht's moored right where you live in Bebek at the moment. We were planning to invite you today anyway, as we were going for a day out. "

"Well, I don't see why not. I think that sounds like a lovely idea," agreed Celeste. "Thank you."

We'll come and collect you in the car," said Berna. "Don't go anywhere! We're on the way."

When Berna and Attila arrived at the house in Bebek they were both laden with carrier bags of children's clothes; warm trousers, jumpers and anoraks, pairs of shoes in various sizes and underpants, socks and vests. Celeste was amazed at their thoughtfulness and delighted that Tekin would not have to go out dressed as a cowboy and feel cold for the day. She beamed with smiles as she looked through the clothes and showed them to Tekin.

"We thought he might need some clothes but we didn't know the size," explained Attila. "We just bought some different sizes because we thought there are bound to be boys at the orphanage who can use all the things that don't fit Tekin."

"Now tell me, young man, who was it that found you?" Berna asked Tekin when they were ready to set out, crouching down to his level and straightening out his red jumper and blue corduroy trousers.

"Her son," said Tekin, raising his arm and pointing at Maryam. "He found me and the dog. He knew how to take me to Celeste. And they gave me milk and biscuits."

"Well, in that case, we'd love to meet your son," said Attila, smiling at Maryam.

Berna joined him in trying to convince Maryam to let them collect her children and take the entire family with them on the yacht trip. Maryam protested, quite rightly, that Leman would definitely be justified in sacking her if she came home and found her out of the house. Celeste also sensed, perhaps more importantly, that Maryam felt like a fish out of water with these people, not because they were unfriendly but because they came from a different class of society, they were educated, and they had different ways. Being a foreigner, Celeste could easily glide from one level of society to another and, in her own way, fit in at any level; whereas Maryam would never even have had a chance to converse with Berna or Attila if Celeste and Tekin had not brought them together. Yet Celeste was very keen for Maryam to come, and even more convinced that her children deserved the chance to go on the yacht. They might never get another invitation like this in their lives. And Celeste hoped that Maryam's natural spontaneity and instinctive curiosity would sooner or later overcome her shyness.

"I could call Leman at the hospital and ask if she'll give you a day off, under the circumstances," offered Celeste.

Maryam looked terrified.

"She'll never say yes," she muttered.

"I'll call her," said Attila. He left the room and returned after less than a minute. "The woman's a push-over," he announced. "She said yes immediately."

Attila and Berna set off with Maryam in the car to collect her children from her sister's house and bring them back to Bebek, where the yacht was moored, while Celeste waited with Tekin in Leman's gaudy living room. When they all arrived, Maryam's children were in such a state of excitement that the adults could not be heard above their cries. Only baby Yakup had been left behind as he was too small to go on a boat. Attila had evidently enjoyed being in a car surrounded by over-excited children and chatted with them cheerfully as they strolled along the sea front, ignoring the fact that Maryam repeatedly tried to calm them down and told them to stop disturbing the lady and gentleman.

"Where is it? Where is it? Is it that one?" they shouted, pointing at every vessel in the water from a Russian military ship to a leaky old wooden fishing boat dragging a torn old net behind it.

"Here we are. Everybody halt!" exclaimed Attila, revelling in the whoops of delight surrounding him.

"We're going sailing," Maryam's tiny daughter Ebru informed Celeste breathlessly as she stood on the pavement and critically scrutinised a fish stall.

Attila's speedboat was waiting to take them out to the yacht, which was too large to come up to the water's edge. Berna stepped in first and Attila passed the children to her and the uniformed skipper one by one.

"We're in a yacht!" the boys shouted as soon as they were on the water.

"No, this isn't a yacht," corrected Celeste, pointing out to sea. "There's the yacht."

Maryam said nothing and looked nervously at the rocking boat for a few moments before stepping in.

"Sit down or you'll drown!" she hissed anxiously as she hastily grabbed Ebru, who had stood up in the boat and was trying to look for fishes by leaning out over the side.

"Who's been putting all that spinach in the water?" Ebru asked, pointing at some clumps of seaweed bobbing in the wake of a passing fishing boat.

"It's not spinach," said Tekin, checking carefully. "That's broccoli."

Ahmet took Ebru by the hand and pulled her towards him to make her sit near the centre of the boat. The skipper was ready to help them on board when they reached the yacht and three other men came by briefly but then dashed off to prepare to set sail. The yacht had two sails which impressed the boys immensely, and an array of rooms inside which impressed everyone. The cook came out to greet his employer and guests and then disappeared back inside the kitchen to gut some fish which he had already caught for their lunch that morning.

"This is vast!" exclaimed Celeste, looking around her.

"Sixty feet," answered Attila.

Attila offered to give them a full tour of the yacht as soon as they were aboard. Celeste was surprised to learn that the yacht had a dining room and various bedrooms with a heating system like central heating, and was also equipped with a washing machine as well as a kitchen and centralised stereo system to play music. She could not help mentally comparing the yacht, with its immaculate wooden fitted furniture, to Maryam's home. To her relief, Maryam seemed far more at her ease once they were aboard the yacht although she told the children to stay inside, not only because there was a chilly wind but more importantly because she was worried they would fall in the water. Attila and Berna both agreed that this was a very sensible idea.

"And where are we going?" asked Celeste.

"We'll head down southwards as far as Dolmabahçe Palace," said Attila, "which is opposite Üsküdar, and then turn around and sail back here and on to Rümeli Hisarı. That way we'll get two chances to see the Kız Kűlesi – the Maiden Tower – and then Dolmabahce Palace, Cıragan Palace, Ortaköy with the lovely mosque, Beylerbeyi Palace, the military school and Arnavutköy before getting back here to Bebek and seeing my favourite place, the European fortress Rümeli Hisarı. After that we'll see if the weather's suitable to go out towards the Black sea. I always let the skipper decide what he thinks best."

The yacht was starting to move and the children pressed their noses to the window eagerly to make sure they didn't miss a thing. Once they had started to proceed southwards, Attila pointed out the various landmarks that could be seen from the shore. Maryam sat with her hands tucked neatly in her lap looking as if she hoped to avoid committing any social gaffe or disturbing her hosts by speaking, yet Celeste noticed her bright eyes darting about enthusiastically to drink in every detail. The yacht's cook, meanwhile, brought coffee for the adults and orange juice for the children, along with a large plate laden with Turkish delight, *halva*, dried figs and dates, baklava and various nuts.

"This is nice for the children, but we must stop him keeping all this stuff on board," said Berna quietly to Attila. "My husband has high cholesterol and he's trying to give up eating things like this," she explained to Celeste and Maryam. "But the cook's working against him!"

"Let's all sit around the table together," invited Berna, looking at Maryam and drawing out a chair for her. The boat rocked gently when larger vessels passed and Celeste was pleased to feel more stable once she was comfortably on a chair.

"Will you tell us a story?" Tekin asked Celeste when they were all seated.

"Would you like to hear the story of how the Bosphorus got its name?" offered Attila, happily. "We call it Boğazı, but this name is derived from the name they use in Yunanıstan, in Greece."

"Yes, tell us the story," said the children enthusiastically.

"The ancient Greeks didn't know about Allah the one true God," began Attila, the children's eyes all gazing at him intently, "so they worshipped all kinds of different gods who looked like humans, only taller and more handsome. One day Hera, who was the Queen of the gods, looked down on earth from heaven and noticed a suspiciously big, thick cloud blocking her view. She was angry because she thought her husband Zeus was doing something naughty, so she blew the cloud away and, guess what?"

" She was right?" asked Tekin.

"Yes! There was Zeus sitting talking softly to a cow. It wasn't an ordinary cow. It had golden horns and soft white fluffy fur and beautiful big eyes with long eyelashes. It had flowers behind its ears and smelled of perfume. Zeus was stroking it. Hera realised this was very, very odd, even though she wasn't sure exactly what her husband was up to, so she asked him to give her the cow as a present. That way she could keep an eye on it."

The children gazed at Attila, enthralled.

"Zeus couldn't think of an excuse to say no, so he gave his wife the cow and she tied it up to a tree with a very short rope, so it couldn't lie down very comfortably. Hera decided that, instead of keeping just one eye on the cow, a hundred would be better. Now, it just so happened that she had a friend named Argus who had a hundred eyes! Can you imagine how ugly he must have been? With eyes all around his head?"

Tekin and the other children exchanged glances and started to laugh.

"Were they all at the front, or some at he back of his head as well?" asked Ahmet.

"They were all around his head. Everywhere," answered Attila, smiling happily at the children's enjoyment of his tale. "But the advantage was that he could see everything in every direction. Only two eyes had to go to sleep at any one time. He sat watching Io all day and all night and gave her grass to eat. Zeus was very upset to see the cow tied up like this because, really, she was his secret girlfriend! Yes, her name was Io. He had quickly used magic, you see, to turn her into a cow to stop his wife Hera finding out about her. But now she was stuck as a cow, so Zeus had to find a way to get her back from his wife. That way it would be safe to turn her back into a lady.

"Poor Io's family went searching for her everywhere. They were desperate, wandering the fields and the villages, calling her name. Io! Io! They stopped when they saw the beautiful cow tied to the tree and admired her lovely horns and fluffy hide. She tried to tell them who she was, but when she tried to say 'Hello Daddy,' do you know what came out of her mouth?"

The children shook their heads.

"'Moo! Moo!' she bellowed. Moo!" Attila raised his voice and the children joined in mooing with him. "She was more terrified than they were. The next day they came back and she realised she would have to try writing, so she used her front hoof to write her name, Io, in the dust. Then they realised who she was, and they cried! Boo hoo! Poor Io! Meanwhile Zeus had asked Hermes, another god, to help him save Io. Mercury could travel very fast because he had special shoes with wings on, so his feet flew when he ran. He could even run up in the air. But he wanted Argus to think he was just a shepherd so he took his special shoes off and hid them, and went to see Argus holding just his Pan pipes. That's a musical instrument made from reeds of different lengths, which play music a bit like a flute. He started playing lovely, relaxing music to try to make Argus fall asleep. And do you think it worked?"

"Yes!" Shouted Tekin.

"No!" Shouted Ahmet.

"No! Quite a few of his eyes fell asleep, but not all of them," said Attila. "Some stayed open the whole time."

"How many stayed open, exactly?" asked Tekin.

"About twenty-two, I'd say," answered Attila. "So Hermes tried something different. He sat down on the grass, being careful to leave a nice bit of grass for Io to graze on, and started to tell Argus stories. He told him lots of tales and went on and on. Finally he started telling him the story of how his beautiful musical instrument, the Pan pipes, were invented. By this time it was really late, and Hermes made the story go on and on and on, so eventually Argus started nodding off. Some eyes closed, and then a few more, until eventually there were only two left open. Then, eventually, they gradually sank and closed as well and he started snoring loudly. Hermes jumped up, grabbed a sword, and chopped his head off.

"When Hera found out that they had killed her friend, she was furious! She sent a gadfly to sting Io's rump. Gadflies are great big insects that have a terribly painful sting, and it pestered her so much that she went dashing all over Europe and Asia to try to get away from it. First she swam through the Ionian Sea, which is the sea near Greece, but it followed her. Buzz buzz buzz! Then she dashed around Yugoslavia, still mooing all the time and kicking her hooves in the air because the gadfly was biting her buttocks non-stop. Then she ran all the way up a mountain and then back down again, and built up such speed that she jumped across the Bosphorus on one single leap, still mooing. In Greek, *bous* means cow and *poros* means crossing-place, so Bosphorus means 'crossing-place of the cow.' And that's why our sea is called Bosphorus."

"But the story hasn't finished yet, has it?" asked Tekin, looking a little disappointed. "What about the lady?"

"Oh no, it hasn't finished," Attila reassured him. "After that poor Io ended up on the banks of the Nile in Egypt, where her lover Zeus eventually caught up with her and with his wife Hera. Zeus asked his wife Hera if Io could please be turned back into a person now. Please, please! And Hera said yes, so long as Zeus never went to visit her ever again. So gradually her hooves turned into hands, her big hairy cow ears shrunk down into human ears, her nose got smaller and all her fluffy white fur fell out. In the end the only thing left of the beautiful cow was her lovely big eyes with fluttering great long eyelashes."

"And what happened to Argus with all the eyes?" asked Ahmet. "Did they bring him back to life?"

"Unfortunately they couldn't. Even the gods couldn't bring dead people back to life. But Hera put his hundred eyes on the tail of her pet peacock. And that's the reason why peacocks have all those big, staring eyes on their beautiful tails."

"Really?" asked Ebru.

"Yes, really," said Attila.

As soon as Attila had finished his story he popped a piece of *halva* into his mouth and swallowed it quickly before his wife could intervene.

"Look, there's the *Kız Kűlesi*, the Maiden Tower," he exclaimed, pointing out of the window as it started to drizzle. The water looked dark grey rather than blue under the overcast sky now, and the currents of water that rocked the boat seemed to be stronger than before. Celeste looked at the shoreline, fading into a monotone grey silhouette and seeming further away the heavier the rain fell. The Maiden Tower, in the sea nearer to them, seemed clearer.

"Is it true that's named after the story of Hero and Leander?" asked Celeste.

"Well, strictly speaking it's just a lighthouse to help ships navigate," said Attila, "and the story of Hero and Leander took place in the Hellespont, the other strait between Europe and Asia that's south of here. It's called the Dardanelles now."

"What's the story of Hero and Leander?" asked Tekin, looking excited about the prospect of hearing another fairy tale."

"It's a bit rude," answered Celeste. "It's a grown-up's story."

Tekin's green eyes opened wide, while Ahmet laughed.

"I want to hear a rude grown-up's story!" he insisted. Maryam told him to be quiet and behave himself.

Celeste glanced at Attila, who was smiling broadly. In the overcast gloom that was descending over the water his teeth somehow looked even whiter than normal.

"Please tell us a story," begged Tekin.

"Yes, please," asked Ebru.

"All right, then," began Celeste. "Once upon a time there was a young lady called Hero, who lived in a tower in the middle of the sea, just like that one."

"Was she a prisoner?" asked Maryams's daughter Ebru, who had been listening intently.

"No," answered Celeste, "she was a priestess of Aphrodite, the goddess of beauty and love. Aphrodite had lovely long hair and was very tall and wore soft, silky clothes every day and put on lots of perfume, and flowers in her hair," added Celeste. "And Hero used to dress the same. Hero's tower was close to one shore of the Hellespont, which is a narrow piece of sea like the Bosphorus, where we are now. A young man called Leander, who lived over on the other side, fell in love with her because she was beautiful. She would light a lamp at the top of the tower and he used to swim across the sea every night to be with her and cuddle her and kiss her," added Celeste, wondering whether she had made a mistake to start this story. The children listened intently, expectant looks on their little faces.

"Where did he kiss her?" asked Ahmet with a cheeky grin.

"In the tower, silly," said Ebru impatiently.

"But one day the weather was terrible," Celeste continued. "There was a storm and the waves were huge, and the current sucked Leander under the water time and again. The wind blew Hero's light out so poor Leander couldn't even see where the tower was. He drowned in the sea. When Hero realised what had happened she jumped from her tower into the sea and killed herself, too."

When Celeste finished the story she found herself being stared at by five disappointed little children. They not only looked short-changed on the story front, they were aghast that the beautiful lady and her friend had both died.

"That story was rubbish," pronounced Ahmet definitively.

"Yes, it was," agreed Tekin. "I think you should draw pictures and forget about telling stories, Celeste *Abla*. We like his stories," he added, holding his arm out straight and pointing a finger directly into Attila's face. Celeste couldn't help laughing and Attila and Berna chuckled as well.

"I'll tell you another story then," said Attila. "This one's about war and fighting. It's the story of when Istanbul was captured by the Turks of the Ottoman Empire. It used to be called Constantinople in the olden days."

"When did that happen?" asked Celeste.

"Tuesday the twenty-ninth of May, fourteen fifty-three," answered Attila smiling. "The date is regarded by many historians as the end of the Middle Ages as a historical period, and the start of the Renaissance. The fall of Constantinople caused a kind of exodus of Byzantine Greek scholars into Europe. The flood of Classical Greek literature they took with them partly triggered the European Renaissance."

"Is this a grown-up story?" interrupted Ebru anxiously.

"Sorry. I'll make it as childish as possible," Attila reassured her. "Once upon a time, there was a sultan called Sultan Mehmet the Second. In those days, people had wooden ships with sails and wore metal armour and rode on horses to go into battle. The people all thought that Mehmet was a bit of a twit and that he had no idea how to fight or capture cities or rescue maidens or anything like that. Poor Mehmet! Nobody thought he was a hero.

Veronica Di Grigoli

"Now, everyone wanted to capture Istanbul at that time. You see, in those days it was more beautiful than it is now and there were no traffic fumes. Mehmet secretly decided he wanted to capture Istanbul just to prove to everyone how brave he could be. His grandfather had already built a fortress in Anatolia called *Anadolu Hısarı*, the Asian rock, and Mehmet built another one, called *Rumeli Hisarı*, the European rock, because it was in Rumelia, the European side of Istanbul. Oh look, I've timed this so well! There it is. Look, children."

Everyone looked out of the window to where Attila pointed and there was the medieval fortress, spreading up the hillside from the waterline. Two massive, multi-tiered stone towers high on a ridge of land and a third one closer to the sea were linked by a network of crenellated walls. Stone steps and walls ran up and down the hill, punctuated by a series of additional smaller towers. It was magnificent and Celeste, who had already visited it several times, stared spellbound by the splendour of the sight now that she could view it from the water. She had marched up the countless steps to the top one sunny afternoon and revelled in the spectacular view across the navy blue Bosphorus under the cloudless, royal blue sky. The crenellated tops of the heavy walls and towers conjured up images of medieval knights and maidens engaged in noble and heroic struggles. Celeste imagined herself wearing a wimple and hanging her impossibly long hair over the side of one of the towers as a noble knight rode his trusty black steed at a gallop along the narrow top of the steeply sloping perimeter wall to her rescue.

"Look very carefully, children," said Attila. Celeste was dragged from her little daydream back to the twenty-first century. "You see those giant towers? Well, they had great big cannons up there that they could fire at any ships or people trying to come near them. Bang! Bang! Bang! They made a terrible noise that echoed all across the sea and back again from the buildings on the other side. It would have been louder than anything you've ever heard."

"Louder than an earthquake?" asked Tekin.

"Maybe as loud as an earthquake," said Attila. "Now look again. Can you see the walls around those towers? Can you see odd pieces of stone and bits and bobs that don't match, embedded in the walls?" Celeste screwed her eyes up but could not see what Attila referred to. "When Mehmet's army was putting up this castle, they were in a terrible hurry. They did it very quickly. They didn't have time to get new stones for all of it, so some of it was made from leftovers and scraps of other buildings" said Attila. "Now, the ruler of Istanbul at that time was called Constantine and he asked the people in Europe for help when he realised Mehmet wanted to invade. Hardly anybody wanted to help him because all the

Europeans kept arguing with each other in those days. Lots of people in the city were scared and they decided to escape in ships. We Turks had more ships and more people, you see, so they already thought they were going to lose."

"Is this ship we're on going to sink?" asked Ebru. "It's rocking a lot."

"No, all boats do that," reassured Attila. "Especially in bad weather." He glanced out at the rain, which was now falling very heavily. "I suspect the skipper will come down in a minute to suggest we stop near Bebek and don't go out to sea."

Sure enough the skipper did come down and make that very suggestion.

"We could go out if you really want to," he added. "But the weather could get worse and the visibility would be poor so I'm not sure there's really much point. We could stop off near Bebek for lunch and then go ashore."

"Let's do that'" agreed Attila. "You're the boss."

"So how did Mehmet capture the city?" asked Tekin. "Did he fire lots of cannons?"

"Well, in the beginning he didn't have very good cannons. Then a mysterious man called Orban turned up. Some said he was from Hungary and others said he was from Germany. Do you know where those places are?"

The children shook their heads.

"They're in that direction," said Attila, pointing to the west, "a very long way away. Well, Orban said he could make cannons so powerful they would smash down any wall that existed. So they gave him everything he asked for, and he made the biggest cannon in the world. It was a cannon so big that it was nearly five times as long as I am tall. And it was so thick that a man could crawl inside it, even a real fatso. It could fire a cannonball one mile, which was a very long way, about from here to where that fortress is right there. But unfortunately there was a problem. Can you guess what it was?"

"No!" chorused Tekin and Ahmet with the younger boys.

"Well, the cannonballs they had to use were so big and so heavy that nobody could lift them! Everyone had to huff and puff together until they could heave a ball up into the giant cannon, and that took three hours. And they didn't have many of these jumbo sized balls, either. And they needed sixty oxen and over four hundred men to drag the cannon along. They dragged it up to that fortress and fired it at the city walls for weeks. But guess what happened? It took all morning to reload it with another ball each time they fired it, so the Byzantines – those were the people in Istanbul - had time to rebuild each bit of wall it knocked down before it was ready to fire another shot!"

The children all laughed at this and Maryam, Berna and Celeste joined in.

"They did everything they could to invade the city. There was a giant chain stretched across the sea at the Golden Horn to stop ships getting in, and there were tunnels dug all over the place. But nothing seemed to work. Mehmet called his advisers and they told him to give up trying to capture the city. Nobody thought he would ever manage it. Poor Mehmet! He was really fed up. Nobody took him seriously. Then suddenly one night, there was an eclipse of the moon. Do you know what an eclipse is?"

"Of course they don't, Attila," said Berna.

"Yes, of course we don't," repeated Tekin.

"It's when there's a shadow on the moon," answered Attila. "The moon used to be the symbol of Istanbul, so people thought it meant bad luck for the city. Then four days later there was a terrible fog, which as you know never happens in May. Have you ever seen fog in May?"

"No," said Ahmet. "But I'm only seven."

"Well I haven't either, and I'm fifty-five," said Attila. "Everyone found it really spooky. When the fog cleared in the evening, people saw a strange light flickering around the dome of the Ayasofya, which was a very important church for the Christians in those days. People said that the light was the Holy Spirit leaving the Cathedral, and they were terrified. The Ottomans decided to attack the next day. There was a terrible battle. People fired cannons all over the place. They waved swords around and chopped heads off. There was a terrible amount of noise and dirt everywhere, as there always is in battles. Eventually the Turks managed to get into the city, grab everything and take over.

"On the third day after the Turks had taken control of the city, the Sultan Mehmet celebrated his victory with a great and wonderful procession in the streets. He told everyone that he wanted peace, and he wanted everyone to be friends now. He felt very proud that he had invaded and captured the city. He had shown he wasn't a wimp after all. The people called him 'The Conqueror.'"

"You see, That was a good story," said Ahmet to Celeste when he was sure Attila had finished.

They moored near Bebek to eat a huge lunch of fresh fish and delicious vegetables followed by cakes and sweets, which Berna barred Attila from eating. From where Celeste sat she could see Leman and Ferhat's blue and white house on the shore, sitting between the neighbours' creamy yellow villa on one side and the rose pink house on the other. All the houses along that stretch of shore were painted in delicate pastel colours and the street suddenly came to life like a row of jewels as the rain stopped and a shaft of sunlight broke through the dispersing clouds. Above the multicoloured houses a rainbow appeared in the sky, standing out all the more brilliantly against the sky which still looked menacingly dark.

It was gone three o'clock when they took the speedboat to shore. Attila and Berna insisted on loading Maryam and her children into the car to drop them off, and they offered to drop Tekin at the orphanage afterwards as well, so Celeste waited at home with him until they returned.

"We have to save the dog," he insisted when they were in the car. "I promised him I would take him to the orphanage. And I told my friends about the orphanage as well. I'm sure Leman would let them live there too. What do you think, Celeste?"

"If there's isn't space at your orphanage, I'm sure Leman will arrange for them to live in another one," said Celeste.

Eventually Tekin made a triumphant return to the orphanage with a beautiful chocolate coloured mongrel and his three new friends. Bülent was so pleased to see him he almost strangled him and refused to let go of him for at least half an hour. A temporary administrator who had been trying to hold the fort until Leman's return said he would do all he could to make space for the boys in that orphanage. He explained apologetically that everything would have to be checked and confirmed upon Leman's return, however. Meanwhile the cook heard the news of Tekin's arrival and ran into the entrance hall to greet him, tears streaming down her chubby cheeks. She smothered him in her ample bosom until he could hardly breathe and Mr. Demirsar was so moved that he suddenly had to rush off and do an urgent job in his store room.

Celeste was loath to leave Tekin despite the fact that he seemed overjoyed to be back home again, but she reassured herself that she could come back to see him in the morning. She tried to make herself leave, going back inside several the building times before eventually deciding to telephone Nilüfer from Leman's office. Nilüfer almost deafened her with her delighted reaction at the news Tekin had been found.

"I'm leaving him at the orphanage now and I'll need your cheerful company tonight," Celeste warned her.

"If anyone can cheer you up, I can!" laughed Nilüfer, braying in delight.

Nilüfer arrived at the house in Bebek that evening wearing a tight pair of brown trousers tucked into knee-length boots with impossibly high, spiky heels and a wide belt sitting on her hips. Her hair seemed far longer than it had done last time Celeste had seen her, and Celeste was intrigued to calculate how rapidly it must have grown. It was a mass of big, bubbly curls now and dyed a deep honey blonde, highlighted with silver streaks. Celeste tried to run her fingers through her own hair, still matted and knotted by the wind and salt air that morning on Attila's yacht, and found her hand trapped in a mass of tangles. As Nilüfer sat down on Leman's white and gold couch and withdrew a cigarette with her French-polished nails, tapping it end-wise against the box before lighting it, she somehow looked at home in this overly elaborate room.

"You need tighter trousers," said Nilüfer. "Your old ones are getting much too lose. They look like pyjamas!" She burst into her usual raucous laugh. "I'll take you shopping next week and we'll get you some nice new clothes."

"That would be nice," said Celeste.

"Do you think Levent is all right?" Nilüfer suddenly asked in a low voice, speaking in English as she usually did with Celeste. "I'm worried about him. His Dad being in hospital is making him too stressed."

Since Levent was already at home, Celeste moved from the armchair to the sofa, sitting beside Nilüfer so they could hear each other while talking at a whisper. She debated whether to tell her about the fact that Leman may have poisoned Ferhat. She decided that, since Nilüfer was a close friend of Levent's, it was up to him to decide whether he wanted her to know. But she decided to tell her about the kiss. Surprisingly, Nilüfer did not say anything while Celeste told her what had happened on the night of New Year's Eve and how she had resolved the situation the next morning. Celeste was surprised at her reaction. There was not a trace of her usual guffawing laugh and not even a smile. She looked worried.

"Poor Levent," Nilüfer said finally.

"What's so terrible?" asked Celeste, baffled.

"Well, I think he's in love with you. I think he's been failing all his exams because he can't stop thinking about you."

Hearing Celeste laugh at this, Nilüfer chorused in with her customary donkey bray.

"I don't think so!" protested Celeste.

"Why do you think he invited you to the New Year's Ball?" Nilüfer continued bluntly, taking a quick drag on her cigarette and then holding it down at her side, as far away from Celeste as possible since she knew Celeste did not like the smoke. She turned her head to blow the smoke out of her mouth sideways. "He must be really keen on you if he invited you."

"Oh, that was just because Leman was hassling him to find a girl to invite," protested Celeste, "and he asked me go as a favour so she would leave him alone. I know that for certain, because they were talking about it over breakfast. She was nagging him like mad. I'd only just arrived here, so he probably intended it as a kind gesture to me as well," she added.

"Guys don't invite girls to that ball as a kind gesture!" spluttered Nilüfer, smoke puffing out of her mouth as she spoke. "All the girls at the university are mad about him, but he doesn't take any notice of any of them."

Celeste looked sceptical.

"Look," persisted Nilüfer, "we all thought he was going to go to the ball with another girl at the university called Nur. Several people told me they heard *her* invite *him*! That's why I was really surprised when you told me he had invited you. Don't you remember that day we went to the Topkapı palace? You realised I was surprised he'd invited you, but I couldn't say anything about Nur in case you were offended and decided not to go with him. He must have told her he wasn't going with her any more when he invited you, because she was really upset and she hasn't spoken to him since."

"So why do you think was he so cool when I said that I just wanted to be friends, the day after we kissed?" asked Celeste. "He seemed to know what I was going to say. He basically said it for me. It was pretty obvious he was already planning to say the same thing to me."

"Well I think that's because," said Nilüfer, pausing mid sentence to stub her cigarette out in Leman's Wedgwood ashtray and turning on the sofa to look Celeste directly in the eye, "that's because he's a really nice guy. He's sensitive to other people's feelings. He's always considerate. He's not like most guys. You can't have a platonic friendship with other Turkish boys the way you can with Levent, not even if you've been friends with them since you were tiny kids, like me and Levent. Turkish men don't know how to be just friends with a girl. Levent's not like any other Turkish guy. I'm surprised you haven't realised that."

Celeste thought about the conversations she had had with Levent. She remembered making him tell her about his circumcision, talking about his father's affair, about his mother; chatting about everything under the sun and never feeling awkward.

"If I'm honest, I don't think I've ever actually had a friendship this good with an English guy, either," she said, looking pensive as she twisted her hair into a bunch at the nape of her neck and pulled it forward over her shoulder.

After Nilüfer and Celeste had drunk some tea in the kitchen, Levent arrived. Nilüfer sprang to her feet when he entered and greeted him with a hug. Celeste had never seen her demonstrating so much affection towards him. He certainly looked in need of a hug. His eyes lacked their normal sparkle and looked grey rather than blue, and somehow his skin looked sallow. In fact Celeste had never seen him look so miserable. She wanted to hug him herself but felt awkward and embarrassed, and instead patted his arm and felt stupid.

"They got back the lab results," he announced, still standing in the hallway and taking off his coat. He hung it carefully on the coat stand rather than flinging it vaguely at the banisters as he usually did. "She did poison him." Nilűfer said nothing, but turned to look at Celeste as if checking whether she had heard correctly. "Mum poisoned Dad," Levent explained as briefly as possible. "She put some tablets from that fortune teller woman - you remember the one she used to go to - in his bottle of tablets for lowering his cholesterol. Well, the doctor said the tablets weren't actually poisonous, they were just useless herbs, but they contained a lot of liquorice, which made his blood pressure very high."

"Is that was made him have the heart attack?" asked Celeste. "Liquorice?"

"Combined with his high cholesterol, yes," said Levent. "He wasn't getting any medication to lower his cholesterol, since Mum was throwing away the real tablets."

"But why would she do that?" asked Nilűfer.

"A possession compound," answered Celeste. "The tablets were intended to capture the heart of the person they were given to. Leman was trying to make her husband fall in love with her."

"Worse than that. Control him," said Levent, bitterly.

"Oh my God," said Nilűfer. "Does your father know? And how is he today?"

"He seemed a bit better," said Levent. "When my mother wasn't there, he told me about his mistress and said he kept thinking about her all the time he was ill. He said he can't see the point of living the rest of his life unhappily. He asked if I would forgive him if he left Mum and went to live with this other woman."

"What did you tell him?" asked Celeste and Nilűfer simultaneously.

"If he leaves, I'll be alone with Mum and she'll be unbearable. My life will be hell. But how could I ask him to stay? With a woman who almost killed him?"

Celeste did not know what to say. She exchanged glances with Nilűfer.

"I want to throw away that egg in my room and those bottles in the fridge," Levent announced suddenly. "Except I don't feel like touching that horrible egg."

"I'll do it," said Celeste.

"And we'll do the bottles," said Nilűfer, beckoning Levent towards the kitchen. "Come on."

Levent's room seemed slightly tidier than usual. While bracing herself to pick up the bowl of water with the horrible rotten egg in it, Celeste was distracted by some sketches Levent had drawn, lying among the jumble of papers on his desk. Half hidden under several economics textbooks and open folders of notes, which mostly contained photocopies of pages of Nilüfer's handwriting interspersed with graphs, were several still life drawings in oil pastels, some pencil sketches of the city and studies of random objects. Levent's drawing style was very different from Celeste's and she examined the way he used the pencil to shade and outline the contours as she leafed through them.

Suddenly she almost dropped the whole sheaf of papers when she came across a picture of herself, wearing the red dress Levent had given her to wear to the Freemasons' dinner. He had drawn her face and hair with a lead pencil, colouring just the dress and her lips in red. Then she noticed below his signature that he had written the date; he had drawn the picture during the week he had sat in her room night after night, and day after day, while she was delirious with fever. The likeness was perfect, her face turning to look over one shoulder with a slight smile half formed on her lips. He must have drawn the image from memory, though, because at the time he drew it, she had been lying on her bed in the gloom, drenched with sweat and turning constantly on her pillow amid a tangled mass of sweaty curls. In the bottom corner of the page, opposite his signature, he had written firmly '*Seni seviyorum*,' 'I love you. ' Below this, more faintly, he had written a second line; '*Sensiz yaşayamam*,' 'Without you, I am not alive.'

SEVENTEEN

The White Opal Pendant

Ferhat came home from hospital after a stay of over a month. He was brought home by Mehmet who looked relieved and very pleased to see his employer back on his feet, albeit still fairly unstable ones. Ferhat said he would like to have a bed set up in the living room for a while, not only to avoid having to climb up three storeys to his own bedroom but also because he would be sure of company in the day time if he stayed in the living room. Celeste wondered if it were also an excuse to avoid sharing his bed with Leman while he built up enough strength to tell her he was leaving her for his mistress.

Leman revelled in having her man back at home with her in her own domain. She spent hours arranging the entire living room in a way she felt would be most comfortable for her husband, opening the sofa bed and repositioning it so that Ferhat would have the best view of the television as well as the panorama out of the window, despite the fact that he could see far more sky than city from his low position in bed. She made Maryam clean like a maniac but banned her from using any products that would produce an unpleasant smell which may disturb the patient. She also made Levent help her drag a low chest of drawers across the room so Ferhat could use it as a bedside table upon which to place his necessities. On the other side of the sofa bed she placed a console table laid out with the medical equipment she needed to ensure the highest quality of care for her patient: a thermometer, pain killers and disinfecting wipes, perfumed tissues, plain tissues and a small basket with the various bottles of tablets they had brought home from the hospital arranged in it like a fruit display. She abstained from smoking in his presence and formidably reproached anyone who dared to open a window in the house, as this would create a draught that could make the invalid catch a chill which, in his weakened condition, could potentially be life-threatening. She also turned the heating up to its highest setting day and night, with the result that Levent took to walking around the house in T-shirts and Maryam frequently developed underarm sweat patches or body odour after particularly vigorous sessions of scrubbing and disinfecting the house to safeguard Ferhat's delicate immune system against microbes.

After Ferhat had been home for three days Celeste decided to take him some of her art books to flick through.

"I don't know why I didn't think of showing them to you before," she told him. "I'm sure these will help pass the time when you get bored of the television."

Ferhat immediately reached for the remote control and turned off the variety show which had been boring him into a stupor, disdainfully chucking the remote control onto the bedspread. He thanked Celeste charmingly for her thoughtfulness and invited her to sit on his guest chair beside the bed and chat to him, if she had the time, while he flicked through the first book.

"I feel so hot I'm beginning to perspire," he confessed. "My wife has taken her anxiety to avoid letting me catch a chill to extreme lengths, I fear!"

"I hope you're not actually developing a temperature," said Celeste. "Would you like the thermometer?"

"I'm sure I don't have a fever. Leman would never allow that. I'm sure every germ that used to live in this house became afraid of her and fled," said Ferhat with a wry smile.

Celeste wondered how she could help him. They both knew it would me more than their lives were worth to risk turning the heating down or opening a window.

"I could bring you some cool water and flannel," she offered finally.

"That would be very kind of you," Ferhat thanked her. "If I dampen my forehead and temples it should be quite refreshing."

Celeste found a clean flannel in the bathroom cupboard and brought the large bowl from the kitchen that Levent had filled with water for her when she was sick with the fever. She dipped the flannel into the water, wrung it out and passed it to Ferhat, who wiped it across his forehead and then over his whole face.

"Yes, that *was* very refreshing. Thank you," he said, passing it back to Celeste.

She dipped it in the water again and just as she was handing it back to Ferhat a second time, Leman entered. She had returned home from her hasty foray to procure fresh fruit and vegetables for the convalescent.

"What you doing?" she asked urgently as she snatched the flannel from Celeste's hand and dumped it into the bowl with a splash. "This isn't how to do refresh the forehead."

She strutted into the bathroom as fast as her short, stocky legs would carry her. The acetate lining of her skirt made a loud rustling sound against her glossy tights in a way which showed she meant business. When she returned she was holding a different cloth, made from white linen with flowers embroidered at the corners, and the same bowl. This time the water contained a generous dash of Eau de Cologne. Placing this on her medical table she pushed Celeste gently but firmly aside to clear herself more space in which to work and proceeded to dip the cloth into the perfumed water and dab her husband's brow in just the same way that he had been dabbing it for himself a few moments ago.

"My dear husband, are you feeling better now?" she asked him, caressing his shoulder.

He said he was absolutely fine. Leman fixed Celeste with a stare to make sure she understood, now, that only *she* knew how to take proper care of her ailing husband, and only under *her* devoted care would he recover. Celeste wondered whether Ferhat had yet decided when to tell his wife he would be leaving her for his mistress as soon as he felt well enough.

Several weeks went by and everything remained the same in the beeswaxy and smoky-smelling house in Bebek. The days began to lengthen and some of the first signs of spring warmed the humid walls and steamed up windows. Some days were so sunny and mild that Celeste could go for a walk along the sea front wearing only a light sweater, revelling in the fresh, salty sea breeze that caressed her cheeks and neck and blew so much obsolete tension out of her knitted brow and twisted hair. Ferhat became more active around the house although he seemed in no rush to return to work. As time went on, Celeste began to wonder if he had had second thoughts about leaving Leman for Zeliha. Leman gradually resumed some of her former activities, going back to the orphanage part time and visiting the beauty salon once a week. She returned home one day with honey-blonde hair, layered and highlighted in copper, and with metallic gold nail varnish to match. She looked so much softer and gentler with the lighter hair colour that Celeste was tempted to believe she had really changed, that she might have become a milder and more placid person. Meanwhile Celeste's friendship with Levent continued as it had before, relaxed and open and apparently unchanged by the kiss they had exchanged at New Year, although Celeste continued to think of it fairly often and wondered if Levent did, too. Levent himself was changed noticeably by the events of the New Year. He spoke to his mother differently, more like a fellow adult who simply did not expect to have his decisions made or problems solved by her. Maryam told Celeste that he kept his room tidy these days and even put all his dirty clothes in the laundry basket rather than on the floor. She also told Celeste he had stopped asking for his favourite brands of ice-cream and other foods and that she no longer even paid attention to what was in the fridge or the freezer. Then one day he asked his father if he could have driving lessons.

"I can't keep using Mehmet as my personal chauffeur," he said. "Would you lend me your car sometimes if I learn to drive?"

Celeste was even more struck by how he had subtly changed one day at breakfast when Leman noticed the jar of plum jam was almost empty, and officiously summoned Maryam.

"It doesn't matter," Levent insisted. "There's plenty of honey and cheese and other things to eat. It's probably healthier for me to have something less sugary, anyway."

"My darling son," cooed Leman, reaching for his cheek, "you always were so unselfish."

Levent said nothing, but rubbed his red cheek a few times where she had pinched it.

One day Leman telephoned the house at lunchtime when Celeste had just returned from teaching at the school.

"Celeste, you can come orphanage now?" she asked, skipping the usual formalities.

"Yes," answered Celeste, wondering why she was being summoned in this way. What could Leman have in store now? What further tragedy could have struck the boys?

"There come to orphanage this morning one lady, that say she want to take Tekin. She say she been looking and she his family. We must see her papers and everything. You want to come for this meeting? I know this very important for you. I think you like to be here for this. Yes?"

"Oh yes, definitely," said Celeste. "It's thoughtful of you to ask me. Thank you. I'll get in a taxi right away. But what does Tekin say about this woman?"

"He not seen her yet. He still at school," answered Leman.

Celeste felt numb in the taxi on the way to the orphanage and she concentrated on observing everything she could see from the window rather than try to think about the meeting she was about to join. She walked towards the orphanage entrance with trepidation. This could be the day she had tried to imagine a thousand times, the day Tekin's dream would come true; yet she felt mainly trepidation and anxiety. She pushed open the large wooden front door, which seemed heavier than usual, and went directly to Leman's office. Knocking gently on the door she went straight in and found herself staring at a young woman who looked startlingly like herself. Her eyes had a searching, optimistic look and their shape was precisely that of Celeste's, even though they were greener. Her mouth smiled back just as Celeste's did from the bathroom mirror when she finished brushing her teeth every morning. Her chin and her cheeks were the same shape and, over her similarly broad brow, thick unruly curls cascaded untidily to her shoulders. The only differences were that this girl's eyebrows were slightly heavier and her nose was just a little larger than Celeste's, and her hair was cut shorter. This was Tekin's aunt, precisely as he had described her in every way.

Celeste found the experience of standing face to face with her strangely comforting. She felt as if she knew this girl already, as if she had already seen her a million times. And since Tekin loved her so dearly, Celeste knew she was a good person.

"I'm Celeste," she said. "I work at the orphanage teaching English. You must be Tekin's aunt."

"My name's Meltem," she said in English, smiling broadly. She looked at Celeste with an intrigued, fascinated expression and Celeste suspected she wanted to comment on how similar they looked but was unsure what, exactly, to say.

"This lady has come for Tekin and so we need to check all the documents," said Leman from behind her desk. She spoke Turkish, which was strange for Celeste, who so rarely heard Leman speaking her mother tongue.

"Hello Leman," Celeste said. "Thank you for calling me. It was considerate of you to think of me."

"How could I not think of you when this lady walked in the door?" laughed Leman. "Celeste does a lot of work at the orphanage and has looked after Tekin a lot," Leman explained to Meltem. "She knows him very well, so I felt it would be appropriate for her to be involved in this meeting."

She gestured for both of them to sit down at the desk.

"I can't wait to see Tekin," said Meltem. "What time does he usually get back from school?" She pushed her hair back over her shoulders in a way which reminded Celeste of herself.

"Quite soon," Leman answered. "I'd like to get the main part of this meeting over before he arrives, if possible."

"That's fine," said Meltem happily. "Tell me what you need from me. I've brought all the documents I have."

Celeste had time to study her while she spoke to Leman. Meltem was so excited at the prospect of seeing her nephew again that she could hardly contain herself. She was overjoyed and it showed on every muscle of her face. Celeste wondered what her own face was showing.

"I need to see your identity card to start with," began Leman. "Essentially I need enough documentation to prove you really are Tekin's aunt."

"Ah," said Meltem. "I'm not, technically speaking, his aunt."

"What?" asked Leman, frowning. "Did you just say you're not his aunt? How did you think I could let you take him away? We can only give children to a blood relative, and we have to jump through hoops even if they are an aunt of uncle. If you're not actually related then I can't let you take him, even if he knows you and wants to live with you. Your only hope would be to apply to initiate an adoption process."

Meltem listened calmly and, much to Celeste's surprise, continued smiling while Leman spoke.

"I'm sorry, I didn't make myself clear," she explained calmly when Leman had finished speaking. "I'm Tekin's mother."

"What?" asked Leman for the second time. She gave Celeste a meaningful glance, indicating that she now believed she was in the presence of a time-waster. "We have on file the death certificate of both Tekin's parents," she stated firmly and decisively, reaching for her pack of cigarettes and lighter near the ashtray. She offered one to Meltem, who refused. Meltem waited for her to release the first blast of smoke before explaining.

"I got pregnant by accident when I was only nineteen years old," she began. Leman very slightly and almost imperceptibly raised her eyebrows at this. "I was a university student in the United States. I was planning to marry Tekin's father when I finished my degree but he was killed in a car crash when I was just two months pregnant. I was in such a state emotionally that I was in no condition to take care of a baby. I couldn't return home and let everyone see I was having a child when I'd never been married. Also, my parents didn't want me to lose the opportunity to finish my degree. So my sister and brother-in-law fostered him and told everyone he was theirs."

"So you're saying that his parents were really his aunt and uncle?" asked Leman.

"Yes," confirmed Meltem. "They'd already been married eight years and my sister was desperate to have a child. She came to stay with me in America for six months so that nobody at home would know I was actually the one who'd been pregnant rather than her. She told people she was having pregnancy complications and wanted to be in America where the medical care is the best. But anyway, since I'd just lost my finance nobody questioned her decision to go. The truth is, I couldn't have survived that period without her. I was failing all my exams and I'm surprised I didn't lose Tekin as I hardly managed to eat a thing some days."

"So Tekin lived all his life with your sister, until the earthquake?" asked Leman, frowning again.

"Yes. I visited twice a year, as often as I could. We decided to tell Tekin I was his aunt, and to let him know the truth when he got older. We thought otherwise he would let the secret out. We thought if people came to know he was really my child, the person who'd suffer the most would be him."

Celeste realised she had held her breath for the entire length of Meltem's speech and suddenly let out a sigh. Leman closed her eyes and took a long drag on her cigarette as if hoping to draw inspiration from the nicotine.

"Have you got a way to prove this story?" she asked finally.

"I've got his birth certificate," began Meltem. "He was born in the United States. I've got the hospital dismissal documents and a few of his other medical records. He's also on my old passport. I got him added as my child so I could bring him over here after he was born." She opened her bag and took out a rigid folder from which she produced the papers she had mentioned. Leman held her hand out to look at the documents, producing her reading glasses from her handbag behind the desk and perching them on the end of her nose.

"Tell me," asked Leman, "why did you take over a year to come for Tekin? It's been a long time since the earthquake."

"I was hoping you could explain that to me," replied Meltem. "I was told he'd been sent to this orphanage." She looked in her folder and produced a piece of paper with the name and address of an orphanage in Ankara written on it, which she slipped across the desk to Leman. "They told me he only stayed there for a few weeks and was then transferred to another orphanage, as that one was full. I stayed in Ankara for months while I tried to track him down. He seemed completely untraceable. You can't imagine how much money I had to pay out in bribes to get people to help me. Nobody suggested he'd been sent as far away as Istanbul for over nine months and then, after wasting all that time, suddenly an address was produced from a folder someone had had lying around their office the whole time."

Her voice cracked as she described her desperate search. Celeste remembered all her own sleepless nights, the nightmares that had played on her worst fears, waking up drenched in sweat and tormenting herself with dreadful imaginings of Tekin's fate. Yet her torment must pale beside this woman's - his mother's – struggle to find her son.

"Do you know this orphanage?" Meltem asked. "They assured me he was supposed to be sent there, but when I went, they insisted they'd never had him and that at the last minute he'd been transferred to another orphanage. But nobody could tell me which one." Meltem broke down in tears. "Some people in one of the offices there insisted he'd died in the earthquake, and that there was a misleading paper trail as a result of an administrative error. They actually succeeded in convincing me for a while."

Celeste moved closer to Meltem and put her arm around her shoulders. Meltem immediately reached for her hand and looked her in the eye as if appealing for protection. It was as if she had decided to trust Celeste to save her from her own emotions, just the way Tekin had done when they had first met.

"Yes, I know this orphanage," said Leman in her soothing voice. "It's a good job they didn't send him there. It's very large and badly run, not only from an administrative point of view but also in terms of the care they provide the children. We pay a lot of attention to cleanliness and good nutrition here. I personally spend a lot of time procuring clothes and other resources for my boys, in addition to what the state provides. But anyway, I'm going off the subject. How did you find him in the end?"

"I'd given up hope and started to accept that he was dead," said Meltem. She held Celeste's hand tightly and her face still glistened with tears but she looked calmer now. "I returned to the United States to be with my husband for Christmas and to have an operation which I'd been postponing for a long time."

"So you got married?" interrupted Celeste. "Congratulations."

"Yes," said Meltem, smiling at last. "Thank you. I met David a bit after Tekin was born. It was very hard to part with him after the birth, and David helped me a lot through that difficult time. Our wedding was just two days after the earthquake took place, so it wasn't a very happy occasion, unfortunately. We went ahead because it was too late to postpone it. But, anyway, the marriage is more important than the wedding."

"You were saying how you found this orphanage," interrupted Leman.

"Three days ago," said Meltem, "a friend called me saying she'd just come across an old newspaper from December with a picture of Tekin in it." Meltem took a newspaper page out of her folder. It was not the edition with the old photograph of Tekin when he was rescued from the earthquake, but the earlier one, with the pencil portrait Celeste had drawn. She spread it out on the desk and looked at the picture for a moment before speaking again. "She and I both last saw Tekin when he was three, but this picture looked so much like him we were sure it was the same Tekin. Then she found this other paper, and we were sure." Meltem produced the later edition, with the photograph Leman had worked so hard to find.

Leman looked contented when she realised her efforts had not been wasted. She stubbed out her cigarette and ran her fingers through her newly blonde hair to fluff it up, glancing towards the window when she heard the chugging engine of the school bus pulling up outside the front gate. Tekin had arrived.

"Shall I go outside and meet the boys while you carry on here?" offered Celeste. Meltem wiped away her tears and nodded.

"Thank you," said Leman, peering over her glasses to scrutinise Meltem's passport.

The boys were all very excited to see Celeste and she did not have much difficulty leading them into the art room and occupying them there while Leman talked to Meltem in the office. She decided to tell them a Nasreddin Hoca story she had read in Levent's book.

"Do you know this one?" she asked them before beginning. "It's called 'Spare Some Change?'"

"I'm not sure," said Bűlent. "Tell us the story and we'll see."

"She tells awful stories," Tekin told the other boys authoritatively. "But let's see what this one's like."

With a wry smile, Celeste began:

"Nasreddin Hoca's old house had a leaking roof and eventually the Hoca decided to fix it, so he borrowed a ladder and, with great difficulty, climbed up to the roof. Just as he was setting to work, he heard a knock on the front door down below. He looked over the edge of the roof and saw a stranger standing there.

"'I'm up here,' Hoca shouted. When the man looked up, Hoca asked him 'What do you want?'

"'Please come down,' replied the man, 'I've got something to say to you.' So poor old Hoca climbed down the old ladder, wobbling all the way. Once on the ground he asked the man again what he wanted.

"'Change,' said the man. 'Could you spare me some change?' Hoca thought for a second and then told the man to come up to the roof with him. Hoca in front, the beggar behind him, both panting for breath, climbed up the ladder. Once on the roof top, Hoca turned to the man and said: 'I don't have any.'"

The boys thought about the punch line for a moment then began to laugh. Celeste taught them the English phrase to 'be done by as you did' and they laughed more and more. They liked this idea.

"That was a good story," said Bűlent. "She doesn't tell rubbish stories, Tekin."

"Yes, that one was good, but Nasreddin Hoca stories are always good," insisted Tekin.

They were about to take Celeste outside to the yard and show her the tricks they had taught the new chocolate-coloured dog when Leman came in to the art room and asked Tekin and Celeste to accompany her to her office.

"Has he been naughty?" asked several of the boys.

"No," answered Leman. "We've got some very good news for him."

Celeste led Tekin by the hand to Leman's office but when they reached the door Leman stopped her.

"Send him in alone," she said quietly in Turkish. "They deserve this moment to themselves."

As she closed the door behind him Celeste heard a shriek of delight and saw Tekin launch himself through the air at Meltem. Through the closed door she and Leman heard Meltem let out a sob. Celeste was taken aback to see Leman's eyes brimming over with tears.

"I never thought this day would come," said Leman. I never dared to hope for it."

And she turned and walked briskly away on her own.

Meltem opened the door after a long time, Tekin still in her arms and gripping her tightly. She seemed pleased to see Celeste still waiting patiently outside.

"Tekin's been telling me how much he loves you," she said. When Tekin turned to look at Celeste, the resemblance between mother and son struck Celeste like a thunderbolt. No wonder so many people had mistaken her for Tekin's mother. Now that she saw him beside Meltem she realised the colour of their eyes was identical. And that was when all the last twinges of anxiety left her. She saw how at home he looked on Meltem's lap. Tekin was going to spend the rest of his life with the right person.

Completing the necessary administrative procedures for Meltem to take Tekin away with her took several weeks. Celeste was pleased, as it gave her time to get used to the prospect of not seeing Tekin again before he actually had to leave. Meltem spent as much time as she could with Tekin and wanted Celeste to join them whenever she could. She discussed with Celeste the effect that being taken to another country and leaving his friends behind could have on Tekin. They also debated whether it was a good idea to tell Tekin immediately that Meltem was his mother, not his aunt.

"Perhaps he needs to digest one surprise at a time," said Celeste. "He's had so many changes in the last year or so. I think you'll know when the time is right."

Meltem thanked Celeste countless times for everything Celeste had done for Tekin and implored her to stay in touch.

"Tekin has told me he has another aunt now, so you're part of the family," she said. "You must come and visit us in America if you can. We're bound to come to Turkey again, too, and we'll certainly want to see you here."

Tekin took Celeste's hand when his mother said this and held it tightly.

Celeste wondered at this moment whether to take the gold foil pendant from her chain bracelet and give it back to Tekin, for him to give to his mother. It had been his 'treasure,' practically his only possession and he had chosen to give it to her. For a moment she imagined putting the little 'treasure' into Tekin's hand and wrapping his fragile fingers around it, telling him it was for him to give to Meltem as she was a pretty lady. Still holding hands with Tekin, she crouched down to kiss his cheek and looked into his innocent, crystal eyes; Meltem would watch them grow a little older and wiser every day, would see the innocence fade into maturity and perhaps even observe them develop a few wrinkles at the corners many years from now. Meltem would see him grow taller and stronger and become a young man. Meltem would shape the person that Tekin would grow into. Celeste decided to keep the pendant for herself. It had been a gift from the innocent, vulnerable little Tekin she would always carry around in her heart and for her it would always be a symbol of generosity, and of pure, unadulterated selflessness.

Celeste and Maryam had far fewer of their secret breakfasts together, as the family now made far more effort to breakfast together every day and Celeste was naturally expected to join them. She found breakfasts with the family more relaxed than before, not only because Ferhat was no longer in a hurry to rush to work and Levent was present from the start rather then appearing still dripping from the shower when the rest of them had almost finished eating; but also because they no longer had periods of sulky silences, nor strained attempts to make civil conversation with each other merely for the sake of practising their English with the subsidised lodger. Maryam took to cleaning obscure corners of the house, emptying out and dusting long forgotten cupboards and storage rooms out of earshot of the family, knowing that Celeste would seek her out and there they could catch up on their private chats and gossiping.

"My children keep asking to see you again," Maryam told Celeste from the loft hatch one sunny afternoon. A flurry of dust mice fluttered slowly to the floor as she leaned over the hole in the ceiling. "Not baby Yakup, because he still can't talk, but the others ask about you nearly every day."

"Even though my stories are rubbish?" joked Celeste.

Maryam laughed.

"They enjoyed that day on the yacht so much. I think it was good for them to meet someone intellectual like you." Celeste was not used to being called an intellectual and now it was her turn to laugh. "I've learnt so much from you," Maryam explained, "because you've taught me about another culture, which is basically another way to see the world. And you know so many things from reading all your books."

Maryam passed a few grimy bags down to Celeste and then swung her legs over the edge of the loft hatch and started to descend the ladder. She came tripping down with a dainty grace and festoons of black, sooty dust following her. When she reached the floor she straightened her head scarf and shook out her shirt, filling the air with dust.

"I've learnt a lot from you, too, you know," said Celeste. "I really admire you." Maryam looked at Celeste in disbelief. "You don't have an easy life but you're always so positive. You never seem to get discouraged. Your determination is an inspiration to me."

"I'm nobody special," retorted Maryam, bending over to examine the contents of the grubby bags she had found in the loft. "When life gets hard you have to keep on trying, otherwise you get trampled all over." Maryam pulled a pair of copper candlesticks, one of them slightly dented, and an ornately framed mirror out of one of the old bags. They were tarnished and dirty but would once have been very pretty. "I might ask Leman if I can have these," thought Maryam out loud.

"I bet she didn't even know they were there," said Celeste. "I'll polish those up for you. I know how to get them really nice and shiny."

Maryam smiled.

"Not until I've asked her for them, though," said Maryam, turning one of the candlesticks around in her hands to admire it and covering it with grimy black fingerprints. When it was thoroughly dirty, she picked up the other one and, giving Celeste a sly look, touched it in several places with her grubby fingers.

"There, I'm sure she'll say I can have them," she concluded, satisfied.

"I want to ask you something, Maryam" said Celeste. "I know you didn't want to tell me at the time, but I'm going to ask you again anyway. When Leman threatened you, after you told her you knew all about Ferhat's secret lover, what did she say? How did she scare you so much?"

"I pretended it was a threat, but it wasn't," said Maryam. "She told me she had always known who his lover was, and that she'd met her once. She said she was a fat ugly Turkish woman and she couldn't see anything about this woman that was better than her. She said that was what hurt her so much, that despite all her efforts to be as attractive and successful as possible and to do all she could for her husband and her son, Ferhat preferred this woman."

"But you seemed so shaken after you came out of Ferhat's office that day," said Celeste. "You were white as a sheet."

"Leman told me she'd always kept it secret from everyone because the humiliation would be so great, not only for her but for Levent too, and even for Ferhat. Then she broke down into tears. I felt so much pity for her. I know most people would have taken advantage of seeing her in that state and would have used it against her, but I didn't want to do that. For me it was so unusual to feel pity for another person I didn't want to spoil it. She'd spent so much time feeling pity for me. I liked feeling it the other way round. I learned from you to know what real compassion is, and I showed it to her. I promised her I wouldn't tell her secret to anyone else. But now I've trusted you with the secret."

"I won't tell anyone," promised Celeste.

"I know," said Maryam. "You know how to respect other people's secrets. That's another thing I've learned from you."

"I'd love to see your children again," said Celeste. "Let's take them for a day out somewhere next time you have a day off."

"We'd all like that," smiled Maryam, her big dark eyes catching the light of the afternoon sunshine slanting in through the top floor window.

When Ferhat seemed to have recovered fully from his heart attack he declared one day at breakfast that he was ready to return to work part-time. Celeste asked Levent later that morning if this meant he was ready to break the news to his father that the 'old type' of tablets to reduce his cholesterol that he took before his heart attack, the brown ones, were not actually tablets for cholesterol at all and had not been prescribed by any doctor. Levent looked back at Celeste and pouted.

"I suppose I have to," he sighed.

"Would you rather not tell him?" asked Celeste, surprised.

"To be honest, yes," confirmed Levent. "Things are nice like this. They don't have sulky silences, he seems happy and relaxed and Mum is being nice, too. I wish things could just stay like this."

"Well," said Celeste. "Don't tell him if you don't want to."

That afternoon, however, while Celeste was sorting through the textbooks in her large shoulder bag in the hallway, she heard Levent talking in his father's study. She wanted to find a specific exercise for her afternoon class but could not remember which book she had seen it in, so she placed all the books on the table near the study door and started scanning the contents pages.

"I didn't want to tell you," she heard Levent saying, "because the last few weeks have been so much better than usual, and I'd have liked things to go on as they were. But in the end I had to let you know, because there have always been too many secrets kept in this family and I don't want to do the same. And anyway, you already told me you were planning to leave Mum so I knew things wouldn't last like this."

"Son, I'm impressed and proud of you," said Ferhat. "I'm also ashamed that, as your father, I'm the one who should learn from your good example when it should be the other way round. It's time to end the secrets. For a start, I've already decided not to leave your mother. She's taken such devoted care of me since I had that heart attack it's clear she had no intention to do the harm she did."

"You know, she also poisoned Celeste," added Levent, sounding anguished.

There was a long pause in which Celeste heard the rapid beating of her pulse throbbing in her ears, her heart beating furiously against the inside of her ribcage until she felt her chest might burst open. She stared blankly at the page of contents swimming in front of her eyes. The sound of her breath as it wheezed in and out of her tightened throat seemed to deafen her.

"You remember when Celeste was so ill that Nilüfer's Mum and Dad said she was dying?" said Levent. "Celeste doesn't know yet, but I found a bottle of liquid from that *Cadı* with a piece of paper saying it was supposed to withdraw the essence of beauty out of Celeste and transfer it to Mum. I'm still trying to figure out how to break that news to her."

Celeste stood stock still, her hand poised in mid air above the stack of books as she strained to hear every word.

"I can't justify what your mother did to that poor girl," said Ferhat, "and it's not my right to forgive it either, but I can at least take some of the blame."

Celeste fixed her gaze on the huge, blue glass *nazar boncuğu* that hung just inside the front door to protect the household from the evil eye, from the curses that jealous eyes could unwittingly cast. She remembered Maryam's words of warning months ago: 'Envious people can invoke the evil eye. Their jealous glances summon it, and it casts illness and death.' Leman's envy really had brought illness and almost death as well.

"Jealousy," Celeste heard Ferhat continue to his son, "is surely the most dangerous and destructive emotion. Envy of people who have what we desire, and fear of the harm jealous people can do, created a cult in ancient times which the Islamic faith has never been able to rationalise away. I've had a lot of time to think lately – something I tend not to do when I'm working – and I realise I've been very unfair to your mother. I think she resorted to desperate measures as I made her feel desperate. I should have realised when I married her she would resort to anything to get what she wanted. It's the thing that made me fall in love with her in the first place."

"Granny said you never fell in love with Mum," said Levent, sounding surprised.

"There were a lot of things your grandmother, magnificent woman that she was, didn't understand. I always found it ironic that she failed to understand your mother, as they were cast from the same mould. Yes, my beloved son, I was very, very much in love with your mother. I deeply admired her tenacity and the fact that she never let herself be led by others; the fact that she would never give up. Anyway, it's time I started concentrating on trying to be a good husband and father. So I'm going to stay with Leman and you, forget that other woman, and I promise you that you'll see more of me than you have done before. I want to begin helping you with your studies, for a start."

Celeste heard Leman climbing the steps to the front door so she hastily slipped her books back into her bag and hung it back on the coat stand.

"Hello, Leman," Celeste greeted her, the woman who had nearly killed her. "I was just sorting out some books for the students at school."

"Don't forgetting boys in orphanage and their English lessons too," responded Leman as she slipped her magenta satin jacket off and draped it carefully over the coat stand. "Tekin's friends in orphanage, ones that stay behind, think how it is feel for them that Tekin go. They needs you more in this period, more than before."

At the mention of Tekin's name Celeste, from sheer force of habit, touched the little gold foil pendant he had given her, which she wore attached to her chain bracelet. Should she confront Leman? Was there any point? What was done, was done. There was no way to go back now. What could she hope to achieve by arguing with a woman capable of such jealousy she came within a hair's breadth of murder? It was better to walk away. Touching Tekin's pendant again, Celeste thought of the boys at the orphanage and knew Leman had spoken wise words; the other boys would be needing her more now that Tekin was going. And she would need them more, too. She resolved to spend the next day at the orphanage.

The rest of today, though, would be for herself. She telephoned Heather and asked if she could meet her for dinner.

"I'll cook some decent grub at home," offered Heather. "I don't fancy any of this tripe soap or paper kebabs. Come over to my hovel whenever you're ready."

"I've just overheard a pretty hair-raising revelation," Celeste promised.

"I'll have a cup of nest coffee waiting for you," promised Heather enthusiastically.

"I'll be there in a couple of hours," said Celeste.

First, she was going to take a walk along the sea front alone. Before leaving the house she ran up the two flights of stairs to her room and took the white opal pendant Leman had given her, the one she had put aside and stopped wearing several months ago. She held it in her hand and stepped out of the house, gazing across the road at the deep blue sea and the slightly lighter blue sky flecked with snow white clouds. When she reached the other side of the road a group of three boys playing chase along the pavement pushed past her and one of them, the same height as Tekin, shouted sorry as he ran on breathlessly after his friends. She ambled along at a leisurely pace among the groups of people out for a walk in their smart clothes, the fisherman selling grilled fish on toast and the old men wearing flat caps concentrating intently on the sea as they held their fishing rods out over the water and waited hopefully.

She wondered how much longer she would live here in Istanbul. She would definitely move out of the house in Bebek. It would be fun to take Heather up on her invitation to rent a flat together. Then she could see how things developed with Levent. It was definitely time to tell him how she felt about him. She was ready for a new relationship at last.

A fisherman standing by a stall ahead of her picked up a bucket and tipped out its contents on the pavement; seawater stained red with fishes' blood and bobbing with guts, heads and tails. Immediately a group of at least fifty seagulls circling overhead gathered and flew down in a tightly packed flock, like a missile. They landed on the wet pavement and began to feed on the glistening maroon viscera, pecking viciously and flapping their wings at each other as they jostled to pick at the nutritious morsels. Their frenzied movement and the fighting determination of every one to eat more than his companions held Celeste enthralled for several minutes and she stood still, watching them, until they gradually realised they had eaten everything and one by one hopped and fluttered away. The boys who had rushed past her as she crossed the road came running back the other way and she realised the older two were about the age of her two youngest brothers, whom she had not seen for the best part of a year.

She walked along the pavement until she came to the same fish stall she had stood by when she first came to Bebek. She stood right where the old woman in a blue headscarf had read her palm and given her a *nazar boncuğu*, which she had briefly considered throwing into the sea. The woman had told her she was here to find a lost person, and she had been right. She had told her she might die, and she almost had. What else had she said? That this year would prepare Celeste to become a mother. She thought of the mothers she had met in Turkey: controlling Leman; negligent Maryam; Zeliha the absent mother, the follower; Roxelana the lioness of a mother; and Meltem, the secret mother. Which one was she like? Then it suddenly struck her. She was like her own mother. For the first time since she had died, thinking of her mother made Celeste feel happy, not melancholy.

The spring sunshine played gently on the rippling water of the Bosphorus and Celeste stood for a moment, feeling it warm her face as the breeze blew gently in her hair. She walked right up to the water's edge, raised her hand high above her head and threw the white opal pendant as far out into the sea as she could. It made a relatively small splash and then the waters of the Bosphorus settled back over it, leaving no sign of ever having been disturbed.

Veronica Di Grigoli